Praises for
Love, the Tie that Binds

"Sheila Eismann, author of both fiction and non-fiction books, has done a masterful job in creating a fictional three book series about a ranching empire in a high desert mountain region. The intriguing storylines include masterful deception, heartache, arson, embezzlement, seduction, manipulation and control together with romance, weddings, and new life with the birth of new babies. With her creative talents and ability to write, she pulls you into the lives of the colorful characters as they come alive off the pages of this series. They work through tragedies to bring hope, healing, reconciliation, and love to this fictional community."

∞∞ Lesta Chadez, Spiritual Song Writer, Author of Treasures Hidden in Plain Sight, a collection of poems and short stories.

"The third story in The Sabblonti Series is full of joy and humor, yet wolves are lurking, too. This is a fast paced and enjoyable visit to the Ridgemonte Ranching Community."

∞∞ Cathie Richardson, Illustrator, Author of books Lila's Garden and Viola's Friends.

"The happenings on the Sabblonti Ranch are captivating. Author Sheila Eismann makes it easy to fall in love with every fascinating character in the surrounding community. Follow these beloved characters as the plot twists and turns carry them on their journey to healing, reconciliation, and new beginnings."

∞∞ JoEllen Claypool, Editor, Author of A Realist's Guide to Being A Pastor's Wife, The Secrets Behind the Eyes, The Battle for Christmas, Are You on the Verge of a Spiritual Heart Attack?, and Truth in Troy Valley. Claypool is also a contributing author to the Creative Authors' Workbook Journal and The Eclectic Collage Series, Volumes 2, 3, and 4.

Sheila Eismann

Sheila Eismann

The Sabblonti Series

Jantzi's Jokers

A Stormy Year

Love, the Tie that Binds

BOOKS BY SHEILA EISMANN

A STORMY YEAR

A WOMAN OF SUBSTANCE

HEART TO HEART FROM GOD'S WORD

LOVE, THE TIE THAT BINDS

JANTZI'S JOKERS

POETRY TIME – VOLUME ONE

RECOGNIZE YOUR CIRCLES

STIRRINGS OF THE SPIRIT

STRAIGHT FROM THE HORSE'S TROUGH

THE CHRISTMAS TIN

Sheila Eismann

Book Three of The Sabblonti Series

S

Sheila Eismann

Desert Sage Press

www.desertsagepress.com

Sheila Eismann

Published by Desert Sage Press. All rights reserved.
www.desertsagepress.com

Printed and bound in the United States of America.

Cover: Indie Cover Design, Lynnette Bonner, Designer.

Illustrated by Cathie Richardson. All rights reserved.
www.countrygardenstitchery.com

Interior graphics purchased from Shutterstock & Istock with license.
Interior graphic used by permission from Becca Howell.
Interior graphic used by permission from Desert Sage Press LLC.

ISBN: 978-0-9897133-2-0
Library of Congress Control Number: 2019901129

DEDICATION

Book Three of the Sabblonti Series is dedicated to couples, families, and communities who bind together in good times and bad to help one another in whatever way possible.

All things grow with love, the basic need of everyone.

"Love Is"

Love is like a flower
    that never fades away.
It blooms forth ever so brightly
    and does not close at the end of day.

Love is like a fragrant aroma
    that lingers in the air.
Its scent grows even stronger
    when matched up with a pair.

Love is like a delicious dessert
    piled high with whipping cream.
It covers over a multitude of sins
    and helps you live your dream.

Love is that touch of a tender hand
    that signals you are special.
It's quite often extended
    just when your need is crucial.

Love is the song that plays
    upon the tender strings of your heart.
Its melody is the shield
    that will protect you from the fiery dart.
So reach out and
    See
    Smell
    Taste
    Touch
    And listen to love today!

You'll be glad you did,
    and it will keep you from fading away.

Sheila Eismann

ACKNOWLEDGEMENTS

I want to express my heartfelt thanks and appreciation to Cathie Richardson, Fhonda Turpin, JoEllen Claypool, and Lesta Chadez for their combined professional assistance and guidance during the time in which I penned *Love, the Tie that Binds.*

In addition, I want to thank my Lord Jesus for helping me every day in every way. With Him, all things are possible. I'm grateful for The Holy Spirit and His gifts of creativity which are inherent within each of us in various forms.

Sheila Eismann

INTRODUCTION

As the author of this three-book series, I would like to extend a hearty welcome to you as you enter into a fictional world of a high desert mountain region comprised of six counties in the northwest.

The majority of the cattle ranches were homesteaded in the 1800's after the land was cleared of sagebrush and rocks. Some of the meadows containing native grasses have been in place since then, but new pastures and feeding areas were seeded in the decades after the turn of the century.

The cattle were driven into the high country during the summer months and brought back down to the lower elevations late in the fall. The ranchers sometimes sold and shipped cows to other parts of the country. Breeding bulls were a crucial aspect to the ongoing development of herds. There were bull pastures on some of the ranches. Beavers built their dams on the streams that flowed through these pastures which created ponds.

Bobcats, cougars, coyotes, and wolves were always lurking in the high country seeking to devour the cattle, horses, and cow dogs. There's an emergence of wolves in Book Three.

More than ample snowfall in the mountains most years kept the rivers, streams and reservoirs full. Prior to the homesteaders arriving, there was a flood one spring which changed the course of the river as it cascaded down the mountain sides. When all this water came rushing down, it brought trees, brush, and debris with it. This made a new channel in the river in the northeastern portion of Chrebine County which flowed into the lower, southeastern part of Shadow Butte County.

With water being so vital, there's been only one major dispute in this regard when one of the characters forged a land deed to pirate the coveted Alder Creek and reservoir which is owned by the Merrill Ranch. This matter finally gets rectified in this book, *Love, the Tie that Binds.*

The Sabblonti Cattle Ranch is by far the largest spread. *Jantzi's Jokers,* Book One of the series, includes the details of the passing of the second generation of the family, Ace Sabblonti, and his wife, Jantzi Belle Siddonz Sabblonti. Pursuant to the specifications contained in Jantzi Belle's will, Stormy Castins, the oldest daughter, inherits everything. Sarita Sabblonti, her younger sister, is cut out of the will.

As the reader will discover in the second book titled *A Stormy Year,* it doesn't take long before Stormy lets the vast domain fall into shambles. As anyone in real life can attest, there's a drastic difference in working for an honest living versus inheriting a large fortune. She's created to be an enigmatic character. If you can figure her out, you'd be well on your way to becoming a psychologist or psychiatrist.

Just in case you might think that a somewhat sparsely populated region is void of any mystery, drama, intrigue or excitement, read on! The census of an area has no bearing upon whether or not there are characters who stay on the straight and narrow path or those who traverse the wide, dangerous, swaths of land. Mirroring real life, there are triumphs and tragedies along with victories and defeats.

Before starting to read this book, I would encourage you

to take a few minutes to familiarize yourself with the family tree, map, and legend in the front of the book. Also, there's a cast of characters in the back.

After penning the first book, I received emails, telephone calls, and written letters with reader's sentiments. They had definite opinions as to whether or not one character should marry another one; who should be punished for his or her actions; who they trusted and did not; and what made them happy or sad. I commented to someone, "Oh my goodness, some readers think these are real people!"

Obviously, none of the characters mentioned on any of the pages are real. Perhaps there are those with whom you can identify or relate.

Thanks for reading, and enjoy!

℥ *Siddonz* &

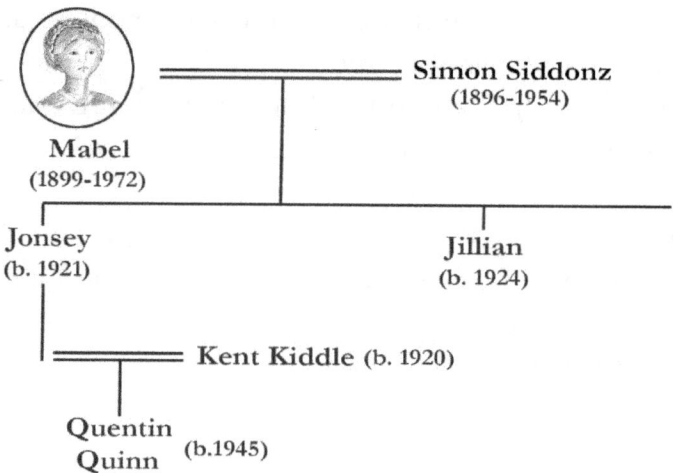

Mabel
(1899-1972)

Simon Siddonz
(1896-1954)

Jonsey
(b. 1921)

Jillian
(b. 1924)

Kent Kiddle (b. 1920)

Quentin Quinn (b.1945)

S *Sabblonti Family Trees*

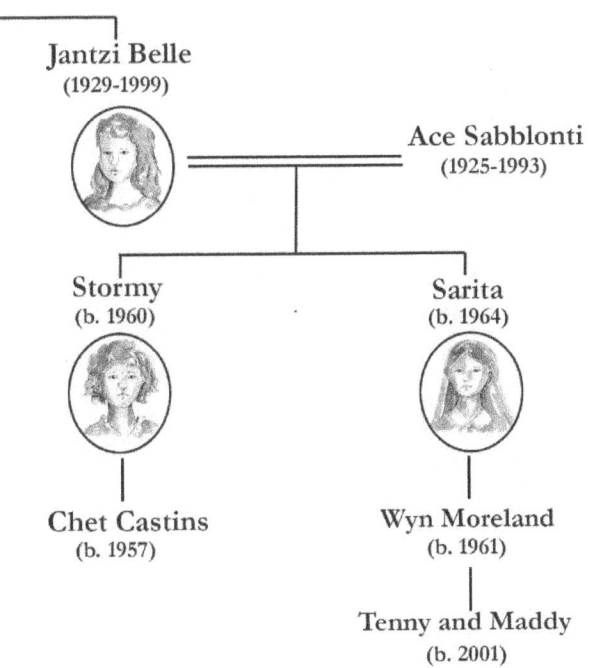

Jantzi Belle
(1929-1999)

Ace Sabblonti
(1925-1993)

Stormy
(b. 1960)

Sarita
(b. 1964)

Chet Castins
(b. 1957)

Wyn Moreland
(b. 1961)

Tenny and Maddy
(b. 2001)

Sheila Eismann

Legend

 Ace Sabblonti Ranch

 Nelson Merrill Ranch

 Tom Toppens Ranch

 Rees Broomfield Ranch

 Wilbur Drebner Ranch

 Main Highway

Ranch Road

Meadows/Pastures

 Creek/River

 Reservoir

County	* County Seat
Blunte County	Blademere
Chrebine County	Limnosa
Clarey County	Horsewood
Ignee County	Cinder Valley
Shadow Butte County	Ridgemonte
Tranquility Falls County	Fantone

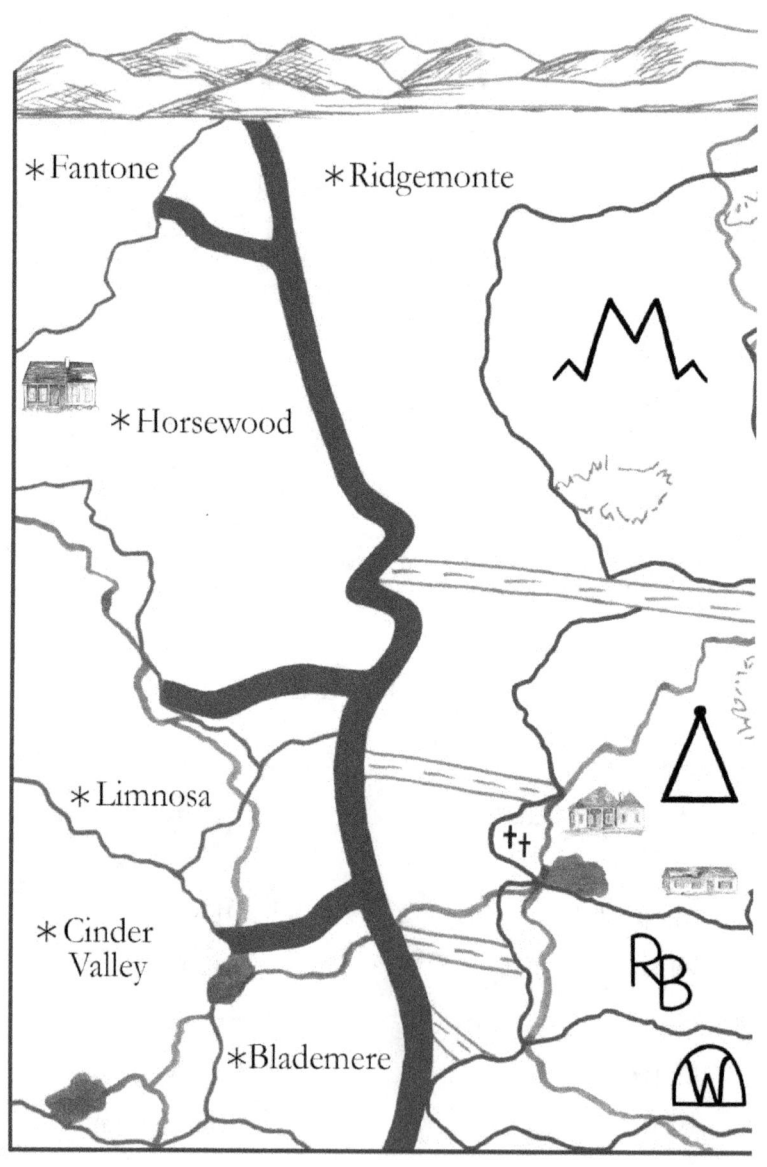

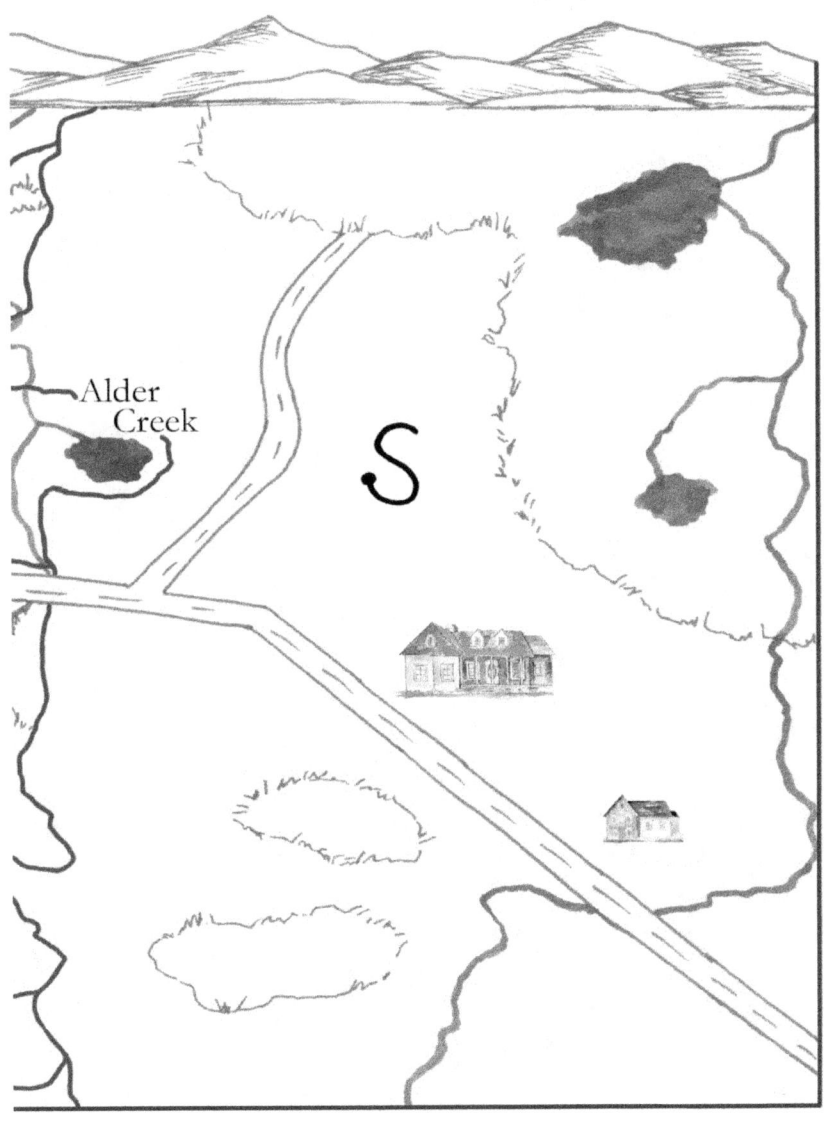

Alder
Creek

S

Sheila Eismann

CHAPTER ONE

A polar vortex blasted all six surrounding counties in the high desert mountain region mid-Monday morning, January 8th, 2001. Dense, wet snowflakes fell at a forty-five-degree angle. Only the geese flying overhead didn't seem to be bothered by the inconvenience.

Stormy Castins, troubled heiress to the vast Sabblonti cattle empire, searched for several days before locating the following ad in her local telephone directory:

A CONFIDENTIAL, TRANQIL SETTING IN FANTONE, TRANQUILITY FALLS COUNTY, TO ASSIST INDIVIDUALS, GROUPS, COUPLES AND FAMILIES OVERCOME STRESS, EMOTIONAL AND/OR RELATIONSHIP PROBLEMS OR TROUBLESOME HABITS. LET US HELP YOU ONTO THE PATH TO RECOVERY & VICTORY!

DRS. FILAN, MARKEETH & ZENER
933-062-1124

Having driven 43.75 miles on hazardous roads, Stormy entered the medical office complex and pressed the elevator button to take her to the 4th floor. The harried clerk ushered her into the doctor's office with instructions to select a seat.

Stormy's enlarged pupils couldn't focus upon the black and white zigzag lines, continuous scrolls, and geometric patterns showcasing her surroundings. The ceramic, zebra-print lamps along with the cheetah-fabric pillows stacked on the Hibbard flowered, botanical print couch only magnified the problem. So much for a typically calm or plain interior office design or designers.

Dr. Martin Markeeth's pen shook as he frantically drew squares on the paper, one inside the other, until the ink overflowed from the green polka dot paper onto his desk. He'd not yet uttered one word or professionally introduced himself to Stormy.

She sat still as a concrete statue in the matching zebra-print, upholstered chair. *Do men actually use purple pens? Since when did that trend begin? Perhaps Marty, as one of the ads had referred to him, or Dr. Martin Markeeth as he was better known in this Northern Medical Community, should make an appointment with one of his colleagues. Is there any truth in advertising?* Stormy nervously chewed on her fingernails.

Dr. Markeeth asked, "Did you bring your paperwork with you?"

She flung the eight-page, incomplete, *Confidential Patient Questionnaire* across the psychotherapist's untidy desk which landed smack dab in front of him. She probably couldn't do that again if her life depended upon it nor could she bring herself to answer any of his questions, whether in written or verbal form.

He turned each of the pages as he continued to make bizarre facial expressions. Dr. Markeeth opened his desk drawer and shoved the paperwork inside.

"Stormy, what are you afraid of? There seems to be no one who's fearless. Anxiety caused by fear exists in many forms." Inside his office, there was deafening silence for the next twelve minutes as Dr. Markeeth watched the hands on the tiger-shaped clock on the wall. He didn't seem to be in any white-hot hurry. Neither did she.

Dr. Markeeth instructed, "Your finger wouldn't be quite as red if you hadn't wound it so tightly with your ivory, monogrammed, tatted-edge handkerchief. Please remove it, and flex your forefinger several times to get the blood flowing again.

"Would you like to make an appointment sometime in the future? These arctic blasts blow completely through our mountain regions. Some of my patients have more patience when the calendar turns to July."

She stood to her feet, pursed her lips, and replied, "No thank you, Dr. Markeeth. There's probably not a doctor alive today who can help me with what I really need. Send me your bill."

"My initial consultation is always free. I'm not going anywhere anytime soon, so if you change your mind, please call and make another appointment. I'd be more than happy to help you get to the root of your anger and on the road to happiness. You'll never find it looking through the prism of your past. Anger can take us places we never knew existed."

Dismissing every word he said, Stormy stomped out of the dark slate gray, stucco medical office complex.

Dr. Markeeth walked to the back room of the clinic and carefully opened the door to his large bird cage housing a bevy of Mourning Doves.

Softly pecking the wooden bottom of the cage as she consumed the *Mountain Specialty Dove & Quail Mix*, one of the hens gently hopped onto Marty's left hand. He carefully stroked her slender tail as he spoke ever so softly, "I think it's time to set you free in honor of my most recent patient who refused my help. Here's to hoping she finds freedom sooner rather than later."

The bobbing of the small-headed dove reminded Marty that it would not be too awfully long until fishing season opened when he could try his new pole with some white, red, and blue-striped bobbers. His third wife had gifted him the new fishing gear for Christmas just fourteen days ago. Speaking of trying to find the route to happiness . . .

Wheeuuuuu! Wheeuuuuu signaled the hen's departure from the northeast window on the fourth floor of 7192 Oaknest Street, Fantone, in Tranquility Falls County. She flew over the bare landscape searching for a safe place to land her delicate feet. The red-tail hawk population had increased 50% over the past five years, so the doves were more skittish than ever.

Dr. Markeeth quickly closed the remaining windows and doors to avoid hearing the soft, drawn-out laments from the remaining birds. After locking his office door from the inside, he whispered his daily sorrows as he paced back and forth in his black and white, circular-striped stocking feet on the orange, paisley carpeted floor. *Would a new location give me a fresh start? How do I overcome my failures?*

Stormy left Fantone in a fury as she ranted, "Why did I waste my time on this yard-bird Markeeth anyway? His office is about as tranquil as a scorpion fighting a psycho schrew. Speaking of psycho, I think this psychotherapist needs to make an appointment with his fellow psychiatrist. No wonder normal people such as myself never go see these types of whacko-birds. There's got to be someone who can help me keep the ranch and my handsome husband!"

Love, the Tie that Binds

The rear end of Jantzi Belle's old pickup fish-tailed a few times along the highway as Stormy's tormenting inner voice returned. *What will happen when Chet finds out the truth?*

CHAPTER TWO

Small chunks of oatmeal, toast, and scrambled eggs in the bottom of the master blue bathroom sink greeted ranch foreman Wyn Moreland when he started to wash his hands after doing his early morning chores. Sarita Sabblonti Moreland, his dearly beloved wife of twenty-three weeks, was resting comfortably in their bedroom inside their manufactured home situated on the Tom Toppens Ranch.

As he knelt down by her side of the bed, Wyn stroked her pale white cheek and kissed her ever so gently.

"I'm sorry to have left the sink in such a state. I barely had enough strength to get back into bed."

"Don't worry your pretty little head over something like that. I clean up after cattle all day long. If you don't start feeling better by the end of the week, I think I should take you to Evergreene Medical Clinic in Ridgemonte and let Dr. Den Merenspinn take a gander at you. I know how to doctor cows and horses, but I sure don't want to take any chances with my most prized possession."

Pulling Grammy Mabel Siddonz's double wedding ring pattern quilt to her chin, Sarita mustered her best smile as she limply squeezed Wyn's left hand. "There's a bowl of split pea and ham soup for you in the fridge when you come back to the house for dinner."

Wyn drove to the Toppens Bunk House to confer with Spence Woodson, Toppens Ranch Assistant Foreman, and hired hand, Fenn Bridgemore. Neither one of them were there, so he left a note on the kitchen table reminding them to continue with the perimeter fence checks and horse tack repairs.

Returning home, Wyn opened the back door to the mud room of their house and inhaled the aroma of freshly baking dill bread. He spread the current cattle ranching magazine in front of him as he enjoyed the culinary spread on their drop-leaf kitchen table. Green colored broth sloshed over the brim of the soup bowl after Wyn dropped his spoon inside and exclaimed, "You'd think the price of those yearling Hereford bulls would quit sky-rocketing one of these days!"

Three loud raps on the front door startled him even further. "Who's here this time of day in this frigid weather?" Before answering, Wyn tip-toed to the master bedroom door and quietly closed it.

"Well, I'll be double-dipped if it isn't my good o'l bro-in-law, Chet Castins! Where's your physical therapist, Evan Briarley? Have you sent him packing yet?"

After exchanging mutual slaps on the back, Wyn & Chet waited momentarily for Evan to come in from the cold. Chet suggested, "Let's huddle around the wood burning stove in the living room. That outside weather isn't fit for man nor beast."

"Forget the living room routine," Evan said. "I vote we lift that table leaf and round up some vittles. Wyn, surely you have enough to share with your relative and his assistant, don't you?"

Scanning the row of canned goods inside the kitchen

pantry, Wyn selected soup, red kidney beans, and corned beef hash. Opening the tops with his utility knife, he dumped the contents into a cast iron skillet. Four back-to-back beeps emitted from the bread- baking machine signaled the loaf was fully baked.

Evan offered to remove it and place it on top of the cooling rack. His self-imposed diet wasn't working very well which he attributed to his body going into self-preservation, famine mode especially in the dead of winter. When he eye-balled the baked loaf, he guesstimated 12 slices, one inch thick. Since Wyn had already eaten dinner, perhaps he'd be kind enough to give some of his share to his guests.

Glancing across the kitchen counters, Evan didn't see any butter. It was an insult to any manner of dining to skimp on this with freshly baked bread of any variety. He was beyond confident that if he could find a lady friend, he could decrease his belt size as he would have something else to fixate upon besides groceries.

Chet reached inside his left shirt pocket and retrieved the purpose for today's unplanned visit. He placed it where Wyn would be sitting, taking great care to lay it as flat as possible.

Not standing on formalities, Evan polished off one bowl of the soup combination and two slices of bread before Chet could sit down.

Wyn approached his seat and saw the frayed, singed, scrap of knitted yarn. He asked, "Did you bring this with you, Chet? Where on earth did you get it? Wait just a dog-gone minute here! This looks like part of Spence Woodson's hand-knit muffler that Priscilla Fletcher made for him a year ago. The one that Shane, former Toppens cowhand, stole and hung on the rabbit brush on the main highway. We know it wasn't cowpoke Luger that did it because he writhed and screamed in pain while Spence twisted his arm behind his back until he swore he wasn't guilty. The edges look like they've been through a fire."

Holding the scrap close to his nostrils, Wyn inhaled deeply and wrinkled up his nose. "Funny thing. When I spotted the remainder of that scarf on the rabbit brush last year, it didn't look like this. Have you showed this to Spence yet?"

Chet waved both arms back and forth in front of him. "Whoa! Slow down there, pardner! One question at a time is all I can handle. I meant to bring it with me when Evan and I came over for Christmas dinner. I plum forgot it which is probably just as well since I didn't want to ruin the best and most important holiday of the whole bloomin' year.

"Two of the Sabblonti Ranch hands, Yatey and Ruston, found the yarn scraps when they rode the Sabblonti upper summer range late last fall looking for strays. This wasn't the only thing they found."

Serving piping hot coffee in pint jars with handles, Wyn said, "Continue, Chet. Don't leave me hanging."

"Several cow and calf pairs were casualties as well. Still can't figure out how the fire got started in the first place."

Evan couldn't tolerate it a minute longer. "I'm a far cry from a county sheriff or a police detective, but sure looks to me like it was that weasel Shane who probably started the fire. How else would the remnants of that scarf have gotten up there? The whole knitted muffler couldn't have been that large to start with. Lord only knows where Shane is right now. He's probably still on the run."

Wyn and Sarita's wedding clock chimed twice. Patting his stomach with satisfaction, Chet reared back and shifted his body weight to his left side.

Wyn continued, "How's your leg coming along, Chet? It's been just over a year since you wrecked your rig, hasn't it?"

Chet stood up, leaned against the weight-bearing wall in the kitchen, and stretched his right leg and foot back as far as he could. "It's better now than this time last year, that's for sure. Evan and I go see the doc next week, so I should know more then."

Out of sheer force of habit, Evan had cleared the table and washed the few dirty dishes in the kitchen sink while Wyn and Chet batted the breeze.

"The Mrs. will sure appreciate the clean-up job," Wyn said.

Rinsing out the double sink with the small spray hose, Evan whirled around and inadvertently sprayed his left side. "Speaking of whom, where is she? I completely forgot to ask."

"My bride, Sarita? Oh, she's resting quite comfortably at the moment." Wyn asked, "Regarding the subject of wives, how are things with your better half, Chet?"

"Improving. Odd thing though. She asked Evan to drive me to the Main Sabblonti Ranch house this morning, so we could get a few things settled and launch our new year. When we arrived, she was gone. Maybe she's back there now. When it comes to Stormy, one never really knows when the next storm will blow in."

CHAPTER THREE

*L*ingerie? *Lounge wear? Split-riding skirt? Western best? Something tells me less is better, but how will I keep warm?* Stormy calculated her options as she stood in front of the oak-framed, oval mirror in her bedroom on the third floor of the Main Sabblonti Ranch house.

Chet directed, "Drive right up to the front door, Evan, but don't accelerate straight through it! Looks like Stormy's home, so I need to strike while the iron's hot. You might as well head for the Lower Sabblonti Ranch house. If I'm not there by supper time, come back and get me. Don't forget to feed and water the hounds and the equines. Adios."

"Here's your cane, Chet. I hope you score on many fronts."

"Score? Who's keeping score, Evan?"

Not bothering to rap with the horseshoe knocker, Chet opened the front door, removed his outerwear, and tiptoed into the living room.

The sweet scent of Gardenias evoked pleasant memories from years gone by. Glorious flashbacks of their wedding night seared Chet's overactive mind. Lost in the moment, he leaned his head back in the brown leather, overstuffed recliner and closed his eyes. *Oh, what I wouldn't give for a redo of the past ten years beginning on day two after I married*

33

Stormy!

As her red-slippered feet arrived at the bottom of the steep staircase, Stormy suddenly halted. If Chet sensed her presence, he was not letting her know. Checking to make sure her knee-length, beaver fur coat was securely fastened by the lone clasp in the front, she glided across the floor, stopping six inches in front of him. "I sincerely apologize that I wasn't here this morning when I told you I would be. I had an emergency to take care of in Fantone."

With one of his robin egg colored blue eyes wide open, Chet asked, "Emergency? You drove all the way over yonder to Fantone on these roads? You look mighty fine to me. What gives with the fancy coat this afternoon? Seems sorta silly to be wearing it with those froofy slippers."

Stormy burst out laughing as she looked at her feet. "I guess they don't go with my fifth wedding anniversary gift, do they?"

"Everyone has their own comfort level. How about I build a fire?"

"That would be heavenly. Would you like a nice cup of hot, flavorful coffee with real cream?"

"Sure. Might as well make a full pot as I might be here for a spell."

The ashes from their Tuesday evening, January 2nd, 2001 rendezvous were still resting in the grate inside the fireplace. Chet grinned from ear to ear as he carefully scooped those out and placed them inside the old aluminum bucket shaped like an overly large oil lamp.

Salina Bevvins, one of the clerks at The Shadowy Merc in Ridgemonte, would be fried if she knew her love notes and cards addressed to Chet during 2000 had been torched in the fireplace. "Good riddance to bad rubbish!"

"Chet Carleton Castins, I sincerely hope you were not speaking to me just then." Stormy nearly dropped the piping hot peacock themed coffee mug on top of Chet's head before setting it on a coaster.

"Simmer down there, Stormy. I was just addressing the unopened communications I received last year. No worries."

"Just when I thought we could have a meaningful conversation, you have to dredge up a topic from the sewer. Keep the lid on that toxic waste dump, will you please?"

Aromatic pitch sizzled from the juniper logs in the fireplace. Chet patted the cushion on the love seat. "My beautiful, lovely wife, would you please sit here by me as I have something very important to show you?"

Stormy folded both arms, turned the corners of her lips downward, and turned to face the fire.

Should have kept your thoughts to yourself, Chet. He walked up behind her, wrapped his arms around her waist, and drew her closer to him. She did not resist. "Aren't you burning up in that heavy coat standing next to the hot fire?"

"I feel a draft coming up my legs which keeps me on the chilly side."

Chet cocked his head to one side. "Well then, take your coat off."

"Uh, I'd rather keep it on right now until I feel warm all over." Eventually Stormy sat down in the love seat.

Unsnapping the white pearl snap of his pocket on his long-sleeved western shirt, Chet pulled out the singed scrap of brown and burgundy yarns. Stormy bobbed her head from side to side as he swung it back and forth like a pendulum several times.

"Stop, Chet! That's making me dizzy." He held out his right hand in front of her. She looked down, then into his eyes, and placed her hand inside his. With the yarns laying on his thigh, Chet reiterated what he knew thus far regarding the fire last fall on the Sabblonti Cattle Ranch. He also informed her that a portion of the herd had perished due to a respiratory disease.

Desperation hit her body like a lightning bolt. Stormy withdrew her hand from his and started rocking the top half of her body back and forth.

"Stormy, are you going into a trance? Stay with me now. I need you to be strong for us and our ranch." She dropped her head into her lap.

Chet stood to his feet and gently helped Stormy to stand. "Dance with me, please."

"Dance? Surely you jest! You've never liked to dance much at all. What has gotten into you anyway?"

Drawing her close enough to where her cheek touched his, he whispered, "I've always liked to slow dance, but only with you. It's that triple two step I don't much care for."

Firmly planting both feet on the floor and not budging, Stormy burst into tears. Chet gingerly dried them with his lapis blue wild rag as he reassured her, "The only thing that kept me sane after I received the disastrous news regarding the huge loss of the cow and calf pairs was knowing we still had that cold, hard cash in all of those bank accounts at Cattlemen's Central. Whew, what a relief that was! It should be a comfort to you, too. At least we don't have to worry about money after our roller coaster ride last year."

Screaming at the top of her lungs, Stormy ran up three flights of steep stairs, and locked herself in Jantzi Belle's old bedroom. She hurriedly removed her beaver fur coat revealing her light lime green, chiffon, fairy princess costume. Stepping closer to the mirror, she realized the effects of consuming so many late-night snacks over the past few months. Food was the salve she'd liberally applied to her self-inflicted wounds.

"Oh mirror, my mother's mirror, is my fairy tale life coming to an end? My husband didn't even notice that I'd straightened my hair! "

There was no way Chet's right leg injury would allow him to walk up those stairs. He went into the kitchen, lifted the telephone receiver, and started dialing the number for the Lower Sabblonti Ranch house.

Evan answered on the eighth ring. "Chet, is that you calling?"

"Taxi service, please, el pronto!"

"Sure thing. Has Stormy locked you out of the house?"

"No, she's locked up elsewhere."

CHAPTER FOUR

"122/82. Dr. Merenspinn will be pleased to see that your blood pressure is back to normal, Chet. You've also put on a few pounds. Holiday habits do that to some of us," commented Nurse Nancy Pritchurt. She smiled broadly at Evan as she patted the extra-large, frosted lemon cupcake design on the front of her uniform. "Now you know why my family calls me *Cupcake*." Gauging from his peripheral vision vantage point, it did not appear to Chet that Evan grinned back.

"Let's see, it's been one year and three weeks since your horrific accident. Since I just started at the clinic the first week of this month, I'm trying to get caught up to speed regarding the patients, their medical histories, and so forth. The doctor will see you soon."

Chet rolled his eyes, stared at the beige colored ceiling momentarily, and kept his comments to himself. Evan rolled a black pen between his thumb and finger as he worked the crossword puzzle in the local newspaper. Thirty minutes elapsed.

"Doc needs to hire some more docs, wouldn't you say so, Chet?"

"Well, at least he doesn't charge by the hour, or does he?"

Suddenly, a very harried Dr. Merenspinn entered Exam Room 4 of his Evergreene Medical Clinic in Ridgemonte. His short, cropped, grey hair was slicked straight back and his overgrown, dark, curly, black eyebrows moved up and down as he spoke. "How are things, Chet? Let's take a look at your chart here. It's been a couple of months since your last visit. How did you manage through the holidays?"

"I'm doing lots better, Doc, which is a huge praise. It's mostly due to Evan and all of his physical therapy workouts. Not to mention his meal preparation and the other umpteen things he's done for me. I wouldn't have made it without him. That's for sure."

Dr. Merenspinn examined Chet's right leg, his range of motion, muscle strength and balance. He continued with some basic stress tests and related medical techniques.

"Are you having any pain anywhere, Chet, or still taking any pain meds?"

"Very little pain at all, Doc. And no, I've not taken any pain meds since about last September. It seems like all of a sudden within the last couple of weeks, my leg healed up. I've been able to start walking a lot better. Most of the time I don't even use my cane. I've tried to be extra careful with the icy surfaces and don't venture out much if that's the case. Also, I'm in the process of getting things fired up at the ranch again which is my lifeblood. So, I'd say the horizon is finally starting to look much brighter."

It was hard to miss Evan's increasing smile. Nurse Nancy misinterpreted his Cheshire cat grin resulting from Chet's victory over his prior year's physical challenges, so she smiled broadly. When doing so, the small gap at the top of her front teeth formed a perfect heart shape.

I sincerely hope Evan isn't that much older than I am. I wonder how I could find out for sure. He's not wearing a wedding band. Since he's not, maybe there's hope for us in the future. I desperately want to marry someone who's in the medical profession just like me. It would be the medical marriage made in Heaven! Evan might not mind someone who's a titch large since he's built like a fridge himself. But with men, one can never be too sure. Most of them probably have their list of priorities just like women. One other small item. I would like to introduce him to a new hairstyle. Perhaps something a little snazzier. Maybe not a full on quiff hair job as that may not match his personality once we get beyond the preliminary aspects of our relationship. I could blow dry his hair for him before we left for work in the mornings.

"I can release you to start driving some Chet, but use moderation," Dr. Merenspinn warned. "I don't want you getting back on a horse for a couple more months. That will put it about mid-March, so let your leg continue to heal some more until then. It'll really give you something to look forward to. I recall speaking with you about perseverance on one of your prior visits. Some of these fiery trials like you went through can really test a man's mettle. Make an appointment at the front desk. Take care."

Chet and Evan shook hands with Dr. Merenspinn and thanked him profusely. Nurse Nancy seemed to linger a little longer inside the examination room making sure she'd entered all of the doctor's instructions onto Chet's chart as Evan pretended to be reading the current issue of a medical journal. As soon as she exited, Evan declared, "Chet, we're outta here this very minute."

Gliding his fingers through his overgrown black hair, Chet chuckled before donning his cowboy hat. "You're all shook up again, aren't you, Evan? Did you like the look of those cupcakes on that uniform? Which do you prefer, lemon or strawberry? Frosted with sprinkles or just plain?"

"Knock it off, Chet! Definitely not in the mood for your ribbing."

Just as they were leaving the clinic, Chet spotted a green pickup in the parking lot. Squinting his eyes to take a closer look into the bright sunlight, he asked, "Say Evan, isn't that Wyn and Sarita getting out of that rig over there? I wonder why they're here. Hope everything's alright."

"I didn't see either of them. Might have been. Speaking of rigs, have you thought about getting your replacement pickup? Better get that insurance company dialed up, Chet. It'll be interesting to see where my next physical therapy job lands me. This one's been a wild ride!"

"Are you wanting to stay in Shadow Butte County or get on down the dusty trail?" asked Chet as they got inside Evan's brown van.

"I haven't given it much thought lately. All trails lead somewhere, don't they? I'm more concerned about you than I am myself. The real question is whether or not Stormy's willing to be the wife she needs to be."

Chet fingered his brown leather checkbook cover before counting the number of blank checks inside. The Sabblonti Cattle brand wasn't as crisp and clear as it was when his mother-in-law, Jantzi Belle Sabblonti, had gifted it to him nine years ago. His checkbook cover wasn't the only thing that had faded over the years.

Evan strummed his pudgy fingers on the steering wheel. "What say you, boss?"

"I'm sporting black duck tales, Evan, so let's head to the

barber shop for a trim. I noticed a few grey streaks the other day. Gotta get rid of those."

"We blonde dudes don't have to concern ourselves with stuff like that. It takes longer for the grey hair to show up on us. That's what you get for being dark headed."

"Just drive, dude!"

CHAPTER FIVE

Bzzzzzzzzzzzzzzzz! Bzzzzzzzzzzzzzzzz! Blackberry juice oozed over the sides of the eight-inch square aluminum baking pan onto the bottom of the oven. Shortly thereafter, greyish black smoke started to fill the kitchen area.

Just in the nick of time, Spence Woodson opened the front door of the Toppens bunkhouse and left it that way. Hurriedly removing the charred remains, carrying it outside and dumping it on a pile of snow, he ordered his Bernese Mountain Dog, "Leave it, Miggy."

Fellow ranch hand, Fenn Bridgemore, could see the discolored air flowing from the bunkhouse as he emerged from the tack shed where he'd been repairing saddles and bridles ahead of the spring ranching season. He wasn't about to let this one slide. Quickening his pace, Fenn stepped across the threshold, "Need some cooking lessons? Better get that petite, strawberry blondie friend of yours out here right away. Or is she still under her mother's left thumb?"

"Zip it, Fenn!" snarled Spence.

"Well, at least it's not MY dinner you cremated!"

Miggy dutifully followed his master as they walked toward the Toppens Ranch house.

Fenn checked the temperature dial on the stovetop

which registered 450 degrees. Glancing at the side of the box which originally contained the blackberry cobbler mix, he noted that the directions stated, "Bake at 350 degrees for 20 minutes." He flipped all the dials straight up to where they read *OFF*. Fenn noticed Spence did seem to be off his game the past few days. Had he bit off more than he could chew with the Fletcher lash-up?

Miggy barked loudly as she paced back and forth on Tom and Merna Toppens' front porch. Just as Spence turned to walk away, Tom opened the door. "Howdy, come on in. We're just gettin' goin' for the day." He bent down to rub Miggy's face and patted her on the back several times. Spence removed his hat, coat, and gloves and moved closer to the wood-burning stove in the living room.

Merna, Tom's wife of fifty-three years, sat in her rocking chair covered with a denim, Nine-Patch Pattern quilt tied with red yarn. Fortunately, when she'd taken a bad fall on the ice Thursday morning, January 25th, she'd ended up with a stable fracture as opposed to a comminuted one. After examining her at Mintner Medical Center in Ridgemonte, Dr. Linke decided to place Merna's right wrist in a cast to err on the side of caution. Her age, coupled with osteoporosis, despite drinking gallons of whole milk, were some of the determining factors.

Spence sat cross-legged on the floor in front of Merna. Miggy was intrigued with a small pile of various fabrics lapped over the side of Merna's sewing basket. Just before her fall, she'd started on a new set of spring kitchen curtains featuring a red gingham, checkered border with red and yellow wildflowers on a white background. Spence crawled across the floor and carefully folded the fabrics to where they would fit inside the blue striped sewing box and closed the lid. Miggy plopped down in front of Merna placing her right front paw over her left one, stretching out the full length.

Laying on the floor while leaning back on both arms and stretching his legs forward, Spence asked, "Does it hurt to move your fingers, Merna?"

Continuing with the gentle circular motion of her right hand, Merna replied, "It's a little hard to tell at this point. Before I left the hospital, Dr. Linke told me it was important to keep my fingers moving to prevent them from getting stiff. I ended up being allergic to the initial pain medication that he prescribed for me, so he's phoned another one into the Ridgemonte Rx. To tell you the truth, I'm more concerned with Tom and how he'll manage trying to be a nurse-maid to me than I am about my right arm. He's seemed overly tired lately and his back is giving him fits this morning. He's not really wanting to drive into town to get my medicine."

The elderly health situation tugged at Spence's heart strings. Tom and Merna had become like a second set of parents to him. With his mother still living in West Virginia and his father along with his step-father being completely out of his life, surrogate family ties were precious. "I'd be more than happy to drive into Ridgemonte and get what you need. What time does the drug store close?"

Tom's booming reply could be heard from the back of the house, "6:00 on winter nights." He walked into the living room, "As long as you're headed that way, let me give you a list of stuff to pick up at The Shadowy Merc. Canned groceries are better than no groceries."

"I guess every cloud does have a silver lining," Spence commented as he recounted his feeble attempt to bake something sweet to lift Merna's spirits for the day. She got such a kick out of his story. Laughter truly is the best medicine. Had he not botched his culinary endeavors, he'd not be so keenly aware of assistance needed on the home range.

Tom's proverbial list had grown from two items fifteen minutes ago to about twenty-five. Spence had trouble deciphering some of the handwriting, so he read aloud just to make sure he would be purchasing exactly what the Toppens desired.

"Shall I sign a couple of checks and send them with you, Spence?" Tom asked.

"It would make me nervous to be carrying two signed checks without the amounts being filled in. But thanks for letting me know you have that much trust in me. It really means a lot."

Patting Spence enthusiastically on his back, Tom reassured him, "You wouldn't still be my assistant foreman if that wasn't the case. I'll call the Ridgemonte Rx and tell them you'll be picking up Merna's prescription. Are you getting Fenn whipped into shape yet?"

Donning his new hand-knitted muffler from his fiancée, Priscilla Fletcher, Spence replied, "Fenn's a bit more of a project than I would have anticipated, but it's all good. We'll make it work. Toppens' teamwork makes it happen!"

Merna sneezed several times into her handkerchief. "Oh, I sure hope I'm not coming down with a cold on top of everything else that's gone haywire lately. My sleep has been interrupted as I've had this troublesome feeling that I can't shake off."

After Tom left the room, she whispered to Spence, "Speaking of projects, how are things with Francie and Priscilla Fletcher following your Christmas day gathering?"

Clenching his teeth together, then relaxing his jaw muscles somewhat, Spence whispered back, "Francie's still frozen. I don't know what it will take to thaw her out."

Merna smiled confidently. "Heat usually takes care of that."

CHAPTER SIX

Colorful cardinal couples posed on a light sage green background as they perched on brightly colored pink and white floral boughs. The repeated design showcasing the male leaning oh, so closely to the female, needed to be stenciled the full length on the top edge of the kitchen walls. *Where was my mind when I embarked upon this hair-brained scheme?* Since it was the weekend, and having slept in until 11:00, Priscilla Fletcher desperately hoped she could finish the project by Sunday night before starting her work-a-day world at the Shadow Butte County Recorder's Office in Ridgemonte.

As she stood on the eight-foot step ladder, she thought she caught a glimpse of a black, white, and brown object jumping up and down in mid-air. Sure enough, it was her! Priscilla squealed loudly and nearly missed the bottom two steps on the ladder when climbing down. Running to open the front door, she almost tripped over the gallon bucket containing the extra paint and brushes. A spill would have been disastrous on the hardwood floors of her newly rented duplex. "Miggy, my Miggy! Come see Mommy!"

A bit taken aback that his canine received a heartier welcome than he did, Spence slowly closed the door behind

48

him. *Will my day improve soon and very soon?*

Waving a light orange colored sponge in the air, Priscilla asked, "Would you like to lend me a helping hand, my handsome fiancé? I could give you the one, easy lesson on stenciling. Boy howdy, I sure didn't expect to see you today. What's up?"

Miggy butted the paint bucket supplies with her nose several times. Priscilla and Spence were both momentarily distracted and did not notice the can of red touch up paint spilling onto the floor until it was too late. Priscilla took Miggy to the guest bedroom so the clean-up could begin. She just took it all in stride when commenting, "It's no big deal. Can you please grab the trash can from under the sink for me and the paper towels on the counter? Just think, it could be worse than this when we start having our kids. Actually, Miggy's great training ground for parenting."

Spence folded his arms, spread his feet apart, looked all around the kitchen, then bent down on all fours and started wiping the floor as Priscilla removed the grey, latex gloves she'd been wearing. He wasn't in nearly as cheery of a mood as she seemed to be since he'd allotted only a few minutes to stop by and apprise her of Merna's injury and the latest news at the Toppens Ranch. He explained her plight as he tore the paper towels from the roll, one by one.

With Spence on all fours, Priscilla got down on her hands and knees to clean the floor a second time. As she came right up beside him, she playfully leaned heavily into his left side which caused him to lose his balance. He rolled over onto his back and started to belly laugh. He removed his hat and rubbed his temples and eyes. Priscilla moved closer to him and bent down toward his face. Spence

49

reached up, held her face between his hands, and gently pulled her close to him for a nice, long kiss.

Suddenly, the kitchen door flew wide open with much force and banged into the wall nearly breaking the twelve-inch-long by four-inch-high glass insert at the top.

"Priscilla Pauline Fletcher!" screamed her mother, Francie. "Stand up right now! What do you think you're doing? You look like some animal on the kitchen floor. I knew I couldn't trust you two to be alone for more than five minutes. Spence, if you know what's good for you, you'd best be on your way while I have a word with my one and only daughter."

Spence and Priscilla sat up, crossed their knees, folded their hands, and placed them in their laps. Since it was her mother standing inside Priscilla's rented duplex, Spence deemed the next chess move belonged to Priscilla who looked back at him and started laughing uproariously.

Francie lunged at Priscilla and lifted her leg to kick her, but Priscilla managed to get out of the way just in time. Spence jumped to his feet and stretched out both arms to keep Francie separated from her daughter. "Hold on, now ladies. Let's not get carried away here. Francie, you have no clue what's transpired within the last ten minutes and have no right to judge us.

"Have you so quickly forgotten that we are officially engaged to be married? And for your information, the only animal here is our beloved Miggy who's corralled in the guest bedroom during cleanup. Come to think of it, we're all animals here today. Or are you a plant? Generally, scientists describe most living things as either a plant or an animal."

Scowling, narrowing her eyes, and leaning against the

refrigerator, Francie replied, "Don't be impudent with me, Spence Woodson. A word to the wise: I would be trying to get on my good side if I were you."

Spence walked to the kitchen sink, squirted some hand soap onto both hands, and leisurely washed. Turning to face Priscilla, he inquired, "Doth thou have a towel I could use, my dearly beloved, or would you like to dry my hands for me?"

Francie continued to fume. She raised her hand and started to shake her left forefinger in the air.

Miggy came barreling out of the bedroom and ran right into Francie, knocking her onto the floor. Spence walked a few steps forward and offered his hand to help her to her feet. She glared at him as she refused his hand.

"Priscilla, I'd best be on my way and get Merna's new prescription to her. Carry on. I really like your cardinal theme. Doesn't the male look stately, sorta like me?" He winked with his right eye as he donned his hat and coat. She winked back with her left eye.

Her mother's ill-timed, ranting tirades were nothing new following Priscilla's dad's death. Something new was Priscilla's learning to tune them out for the sake of her own sanity and freedom. One-half hour later, there was finally silence inside the duplex.

Francie rose from the couch in the living room and stood in the doorway to the kitchen, carefully scrutinizing every square inch of it. "That last stencil you put up there looks like it's about one-eighth of an inch too high. You might want to redo it. The male's red hood makes it look like it's too tall of a covering over the female."

Stepping back about ten feet and eyeballing her artistic

endeavors for the day, Priscilla replied, "It doesn't bother me that the male towers over the female and is her protective covering. It's another expression of profound love. As for that last stencil along with all of the others, they look perfect to me. Just like Spence."

Francie narrowed her gaze, looked down at her ringless hands, and turned them from side to side. "On the subject of love, where's that fancy, pink, topaz and diamond engagement ring of yours? Lost it already? I still wonder if it's the real McCoy or just some lab generated replica. I mean, after all, where would Spence get that kind of money on a cowhand's wages?" She patted all four of her blue jean pockets and the front pouch of her faded, navy blue, hooded sweatshirt. "Where are my car keys? Oh my, where's my purse? I hope someone hasn't stolen them. Did I lock my keys in my car?"

Once again, the kitchen door flew wide open and banged into the outside of the duplex unit, this time cracking the twelve-inch-long by four-inch-high, leaded glass insert at the top.

CHAPTER SEVEN

Belligerent bill collectors from far and wide had been calling for a solid month. Stormy knew beyond the shadow of a doubt that if her parents, Ace and Jantzi Belle Sabblonti, were still alive, they would be horrified. The Sabblonti Cattle Empire had lacked for nothing since the day the vast land mass had been claimed, cleared, and homesteaded by Ace's father in the 1800's. She didn't need to ask herself how it got to be in such shambles.

The sun's rays on the western kitchen window of the Main Sabblonti Ranch house formed the perfect reflective pool in the kitchen sink as Stormy stared into it. For some reason, her face looked drastically different than normal. The light rays had not distorted it. Something else must have done that. Granted, she was not the same person after her mother died in December of 1999. Could a dynasty be depleted in fourteen months?

Searching the archives of her mind produced virtually no answers or insight. There was no use going to the gravesite to ask Jantzi Belle any more questions since she'd not answered any on the previous visits. There'd been only stone, cold silence from the frigid headstones. *None of my ancestors let any sagebrush grow under their feet. Neither must I. All of them were action-oriented western wonders. I must become*

53

one myself.

Chet and Evan had spent all day Friday, February 2nd, driving around Cinder Valley for a change of scenery. Evan had suggested they take the day to collect some sunshine for both of them. His hopes were drastically dashed upon entering *Country Cate's Western Wear* when he learned that Shasta, the former head clerk and merchandise buyer, was no longer gainfully employed. It would be most difficult to drive to Bryan in search of her, especially considering the fact that his aged, brown van might not be roadworthy enough to drive across the border to the neighboring state, much less the Lone Star one which was over 2,900 miles away.

With Stormy not answering the telephone day or night and parking Jantzi Belle's old pickup inside the hay barn and locking it every night, Chet assumed that she was out of town visiting one of her maternal aunts, Jonsey or Jillian. While it would be quite out of the ordinary for Stormy to even entertain the thought of doing something like this, one could never predict what she would do on any given day. She would most probably give the bookies in Vegas a run for their money.

The peacock-themed kitchen clock ticked eleven minutes past 6:00. Stormy lifted the receiver on the kitchen wall phone and dialed the number for the Lower Sabblonti Ranch house. No one answered after forty-two rings. *Chet never goes anywhere except to the doctor. No doctor's offices are open past 5:00 on a Friday afternoon. I wonder if something bad has happened.*

Running up three steep flights of stairs and down the hallway to Jantzi Belle's bedroom, Stormy entered the master walk-in closet. She selected one of her mother's western wear, business ensembles, touched up her makeup, chose matching silver and ruby accessories and raced back down the stairs.

Stormy was half way down the lane after having left the ranch house when she remembered she needed to get the key to the Lower Sabblonti Ranch house from the wooden key rack inside the kitchen. Looking at the branches on the quaking aspen trees in the front yard, she observed there was not a one of them moving in the slightest; however, Stormy felt a fresh rush of confidence blowing through her. *Time to ride this wind!*

Never having driven as fast as she now was toward the ranch house where she'd previously lived for nine and one-half years with her husband, Chet, Stormy slammed on the brakes as she entered the front driveway when she spotted the old, brown, four-wheel drive pickup. Evan's van was nowhere in the vicinity. She jumped out, and ran toward the house. Turning the handle, she discovered it was locked up tighter than a drum.

Blue barked incessantly from the living room as she pounded her fist on the front door. She'd forgotten the key which was still inside the cab with the ignition idling. Finally locating it after digging around in the bottom of her hand-tooled, red, leather purse, Stormy dashed to unlock the door.

Out of the blue, she heard a menacing voice behind her, "Where are you headed with your pants on fire, girl?"

Whirling around, Stormy stood her ground. "What are you doing here, Salina Bevvins? You have no right to step foot onto our private property trying to stake a claim to my private property, Chet Carleton Castins."

Salina doubled over in laughter and accelerated her torment. "Stormy, you're pathetic. If only you could see yourself like everyone else does. You might have been one, hot fox some years ago, but not now, baby cakes. No wonder Chet is no longer attracted to you. Most men want a real woman who knows how to take care of a man. Not someone who ignores him for over a year!"

Stormy charged forward and raised her hand to slap Salina who managed to duck and jump off the front porch. As she sauntered back to her Aunt June Slader's pickup, Stormy grabbed the slow cooker sitting on the front porch, ran behind Salina, and hurled the contents on top of her.

"Oooooooooooooouch, that's hot!"

The bean broth scalded Salina's scalp. Stormy whooped and hollered, "You might need to shampoo your long, sleek, witchy locks twice to get rid of that concoction you brewed and attempted to deliver to MY husband. You'll NEVER have him, so don't even try. Women like you are hiding everywhere, just like cockroaches that need to be exterminated once they're discovered. You might think you're beautiful and talented, but beauty lies in the eye of the beholder. Better look elsewhere for yours. Maybe there's some sorry, unsuspecting sap you can lasso who'll come into The Shadowy Merc. Get off our ranch now, or I'll call my buddy, Jeff Jensen, Shadow Butte County Sheriff, and have him haul you off in his paddy wagon!"

Evan was right in the middle of telling Chet one of his college fraternity stories when they neared the Lower Sabblonti Ranch house. "Don't look now, Chet, but it would appear as though we've got company. Did you issue some invitations you didn't tell me about? I think I'll park down by the barn, and you can hoof it to the house. What say you?"

With bulging eyes, Chet couldn't quite believe his eyes. His first glimpse was that of Salina's jet-black hair, to which she'd added a bleached white stripe down the center, now covered with baked beans and diced bacon chunks dangling from the bottom edges. "Uh, Evan, I think since I'm the less upwardly mobile of the two of us, I'll sit this one out and let you run the interference. Besides that, you're physically stronger than I am. My muscles have really gotten weak since my accident."

Turning the van's steering wheel sharply to the right, Evan flipped the headlights to high beams which shone ever so brightly and directly into Salina's eyes. She hunched down and ran toward the driver's door of her aunt's pickup, jerked the door open, revved the engine, and took off. Loose pea gravel flipped everywhere as Salina forced the gas pedal to the floor metal. Evan laughed so hard tears ran down both chubby cheeks.

"Chet, movies can't even compete with real-life enter-tainment like this!"

Calming and collecting herself following her surprising show of force, Stormy stood confidently on the front porch as she waited for Chet and Evan to get out of the van and walk toward her. Enthusiasm surged straight through her arteries and veins.

"Good evening, my wonderful husband! Evan, it's nice to see you as well. Have you had a good day? I most certainly have. It's not very often that I get to run a skunk off our property."

Spellbound, Evan looked at Stormy, then at Chet, then at Stormy once again. Chet appeared totally nonplussed.

Evan smiled at Stormy, inserted the key into the lock, walked in, and headed straight to the kitchen to fill Blue and Beebee's dog dishes with food and water.

Stormy leaned against the western side of the Lower Sabblonti Ranch house and motioned with her hand for Chet to come near her. He could move a lot faster these days since he'd pretty much retired his walking cane. Unsure as to exactly what Stormy wanted or what her next move would be, he most certainly wasn't prepared for it.

She reached inside his unzipped, black, fleece-lined vest and placed both of her hands on his waist. Using as much strength as she could muster, she pulled him very close to her. Standing on her tip-toes, she delivered the best kiss of all during the entirety of their wedded days. Chet didn't muster an ounce of resistance, but fully leaned into Stormy. All became quiet on the western front.

Emerging from the bathroom down the hallway, Evan opened the refrigerator to select the ingredients for supper. He chose three large, baking potatoes which needed to be scrubbed under cold, running water. Automatically going through the motions of the nightly ritual for the past year, he whistled softly to himself. After placing the potatoes in the oven, he walked into the living room to start a fire in the fireplace. He nearly keeled over when looking out the front window, whirled around and headed back into the kitchen. Evan chuckled. *You'd think they're two people courting, and I'm the chaperone.*

Sabblonti Ranch tri-tip steak, sautéed mushrooms, fully loaded baked potatoes complete with twelve full slices of crumbled bacon, and baked eggplant drowned in dill Havarti cheese was on tonight's menu along with key lime pie and whipped cream from a giant-sized pressurized can. Evan wondered if he should let Chet and Stormy know that dinner was ready. Overcooked steak wasn't fit to eat as far as he was concerned. Thankfully, he heard the front door open followed by loud laughter.

Stormy's growling stomach could be heard high above the sizzling of the thick steaks inside the cast iron skillet. "Something smells so good!" she exclaimed.

Evan stuck his head around the kitchen corner into the front entryway. "Mrs. Castins, we would be honored if you would join us for supper this evening."

"It would be my distinct pleasure, Mr. Briarley."

The dinner conversation was light and pleasant to accompany the ample, scrumptious spread. Since he'd never experienced Stormy's attempt at pouring on her charm, Evan wondered if he'd been transported to another planet in the midst of it.

The sun had long since slipped over the high, western, snow-capped mountain peaks as Evan finished washing the dishes. Before seasoning the large cast iron skillet used to cook the entrée for supper, he was dying to know how this night would end. His favorite TV soap-opera wasn't nearly as good as the last couple of hours had been on the Sabblonti landscape.

"There's something extremely urgent that I need to show you at the Main Sabblonti Ranch house first thing in the morning, Chet. Evan, you're welcome to join us for breakfast if you'd like, say around nine-ish? That would give you a chance to help your patient with his physical therapy routine. Any takers?"

Chet started clapping. Evan didn't really know what that signaled, so he followed suit. "Nine on the nose it is, darlin'! You don't have to ask me twice."

"Me either," Evan said.

Bidding the two western gents good evening, Stormy drove ten miles per hour from the Lower Sabblonti Ranch house to the Main Sabblonti Ranch house. She desperately wished there was a way to bypass the next twenty-four hours, but she'd made a gigantic mess over the past twelve months, so she most certainly needed to start cleaning it up. There were times during her forty years that she'd been able to amaze even herself. Tomorrow had better be another one.

CHAPTER EIGHT

Racing footsteps made several trips up and down the hallway on the third floor of the Main Sabblonti Ranch house between the hours of 2:00 and 4:00 a.m. Windows on the southeast side of the house opened and closed. Despite having shoved small orange plugs as far into her ear canals as she could and pulling several layers of blankets over the side of her head, sleep eluded Stormy. The mysterious, invisible intruders returned for more rounds of harassment.

During the years in which Stormy and her sister, Sarita, had slept on the second floor of the enormous ranch house, neither of them experienced anything of the kind. Janzti Belle never mentioned it either, especially after Ace died in 1993.

Had Dr. Markeeth not appeared to be weirder than a wooden watch during her initial appointment with him on January 8th, this was one of the things on Stormy's list she was prepared to speak with him about. If there was ever a time when she needed a good night's sleep, this was one of them. Staying up quite late to rehearse her smooth Saturday morning lines to Chet wasn't very wise either. Time to cut her losses and move on.

What will I serve for breakfast? The only thing I've ever made is oatmeal which turned out too runny most of the time. I can barely cook toast in the toaster without burning it! I overcooked the scrambled eggs, so they tasted like sawdust. I should have gotten out of bed earlier to watch how Chet cooked his breakfasts all those years. So what if Salina Bevvins can probably cook better than I can? Not for long. Today's a new ranching day at the Sabblonti Ranch.

According to the homesteading advice written by hardy, pioneer women which Stormy had read the past couple of months, a dip in the closest creek was the way to launch a victorious day. In addition, it was of the utmost importance to rinse one's hair with cold, running water after massaging a tablespoon of cider vinegar throughout, even to the very ends. She decided she might as well give it a whirl!

It took twenty minutes for her teeth to quit chattering before she could brush them. Another sudden ray of insight flashed through her mind.

Why not get all dolled up in the same get-up I wore to the Ignee County Rodeo board meeting on Friday night, March 3, 2000, minus the red hat, of course? That may be a titch over the top for breakfast. After all, this is going to be a combination business and breakfast get together. One must be careful not to wear too much red for certain kinds of meetings since it signals power, dominance, and control. However, Redhaven colored red lipstick should be fine. That's one of Chet's favorites.

Donning her semi-sheer, long-sleeved, black blouse with glittery accents; red and black, ankle-length tartan, 100% pure virgin wool skirt; and fancy, black, dress boots bolstered Stormy's growing confidence. *Not so fast. Better shed these dress boots with the one-inch heel this early in the morning. They will probably decrease my speed to get everything ready in time.* Tardiness wasn't one of her trump cards this time around.

"Biscuits! That's it! Where's Grammy Mabel Siddonz's recipe box? That old, wooden chipped one with the Siddonz Cattle brand on the front that Poppy Siddonz made for her?" Stormy asked as she rummaged through the closets in all of the bedrooms on the second and third floors of the Main Sabblonti Ranch house. As a last resort, she checked inside Jantzi Belle's office. Sure enough, it was at the far end of the top shelf. Had it not been for the Siddonz family cattle brand burned into the wood, she'd probably wouldn't have seen it.

§

In her haste to find the recipe, the box slipped from her hand, dropped onto the floor, scattering the recipe cards and yellowed ones previously clipped from ranching magazines. The downstairs mantel clock bonged eight times.

The family recipes starting with the letter "B" landed underneath the desk in the cluttered office. Finally locating the one titled *Buttermilk Biscuits* erased another fifteen minutes from the clock. Clenching the recipe between her top and bottom teeth, Stormy slid down the long, wooden bannister. Jantzi Belle certainly wouldn't have approved of that last maneuver! Stormy felt Chet was sure to be pleased when she answered the door with her red colorful apron showcasing the Sabblonti Cattle brand in the middle of her torso.

"Mix or sift together dry ingredients," Stormy read out loud.

"Since I don't have a sifter, I guess I'll just mix. What's a sifter, anyway?

"3 cups flour

"1 ½ Tbsp. baking powder

"¾ tsp. salt

"¼ tsp. baking soda

"There are big *T's* and little *t's*, but what's the difference?

"Must mean you use a big measuring spoon for the big *T* and a little measuring spoon for the little *t*. Seems logical to me.

"½ cup shortening

"1 ¼ cups buttermilk.

"BUTTERMILK????

"All I have is good ol' regular cow's milk.

"Can't I just cut up some chunks of butter and plop it into the milk?

"No wonder I don't like to cook. Who has time time to frap around with these sorts of things?

"Surely this *Winning Western Recipes Cookbook* will instruct me what to do if I don't have the real deal."

Stormy hurriedly flipped to the back of the 8.5 x 11-inch, buttercup yellow cookbook secured by grey duct tape on the outside, locating *Buttermilk Recipes*. Fortunately, there was an asterisk beside those words taking her to page 52 providing the *Emergency Substitutions*.

Her finger traced the words as she read, "For each cup of buttermilk needed add 1 Tbsp. of vinegar or lemon juice. Let mixture stand for five minutes. There's that big *T* again, so I assume I just use the big one. Vinegar? No problemo. Just used that on my pretty locks. Ugh, gotta run back up those blasted stairs and get it again!"

The telephone started ringing at 8:15. Stormy cautiously considered answering it, but opted not to, just in case it was another collection agency. *Better take the phone off the hook and shove it inside the bottom desk drawer upstairs before Chet and Evan arrive.*

"Back to this biscuit project," she murmured. "Cut in the shortening until mixture resembles coarse crumbs." She brushed her apron with the palms of her hands.

"Cut, like with a pair of scissors?"

Whack, whack, whack.

Throwing the kitchen shears into the sink, Stormy recoiled at the thought of placing her hands inside the large green and white striped mixing bowl containing the dry ingredients and shortening, but she knew of no other way to make it look like coarse crumbs.

"Make a well in the bottom of your mixing bowl, pour in buttermilk; stir quickly with fork."

Stormy threw her hands up in the air. "What's a well in the bottom of a bowl? I'll just dump this mock buttermilk in here and stir with this meat fork.

"Knead gently to combine mixture, pat dough to about 1/4-inch thick, cut into biscuits. Place on ungreased cookie sheet. Bake at 450 degrees for approximately 15 minutes.

Makes about an even dozen.

"Knead? How do you knead? I'll just punch it back and forth for a few minutes. Oughta do the trick." Plopping the dough onto the kitchen counter, Stormy furiously patted it down. She reached into the kitchen junk drawer and located a twelve-inch ruler. Leaning down to where her eyes were parallel to the countertop, she eyeballed the dough and determined that it was sufficient for the ¼ inch instructions.

"Now what am I supposed to do? I can't bake this whole slab of dough! I have no idea if Mother has a biscuit maker in this kitchen." Nervously glancing at the clock, Stormy chanted, "Round, round, round, round, what's something that's round in this kitchen or this house?"

She grabbed one of the turquoise, peacock-themed coffee mugs, inverted it, and cut the biscuits from the dough. It was 8:50 a.m. After placing them in the oven, she opened four pouches of *Western Sidekick Country Sausage Gravy Mix* to which she added four cups of whole milk instead of water. Stirring with the over-sized fork, she questioned why there were still clumps of the dried mix floating on top.

Her slippered feet were light as feathers as she seemed to fly around the first floor of the Main Sabblonti Ranch house for the next ten minutes while the biscuits baked and the gravy simmered. Now, here was one area in which she had a boatload of experience. Jantzi Belle insisted that the dining table in the living room be kept formal at all times, especially after she'd driven to Blunte County three decades ago and purchased all that high dollah western furniture and furnishings.

While she was growing up, it was Stormy's daily duty to make sure the formal dining area remain neat and tidy. She couldn't figure out why this mattered since there was rarely a visitor, family or otherwise, inside that domain.

With the sagebrush scented candles burning ever so brightly, the large, mahogany table formally adorned, and strong, fresh coffee brewing in the coffee maker, Stormy's look of sheer satisfaction said it all. She'd even remembered to open a fresh jar of Chet's favorite choke-cherry jelly that he ate by the heaping spoonfuls. She was just removing the biscuits from the oven and placing them inside the basket lined with the blue-and-white checkered dishcloth when Chet slipped behind her. Rubbing his right hand across her back caused her to drop one of the biscuits onto the floor. He caught her as she jumped backwards into his arms. Spinning her around, he spotted the Sabblonti cattle brand on the front of her apron which he traced with his forefinger. Stormy giggled. "Nice apron, sweetheart."

Evan came through the door just in time to see the big embrace. He quietly removed his outerwear and hung them on the coat tree in the slate entryway. Looking for the first opportunity so he wouldn't feel awkward, he entered the kitchen and asked, "Need some help, Stormy?"

"Oh, good morning, Evan! Sure, I'd love some. Would you mind placing the gravy inside the gravy boat for me and setting it on the table? Coffee this morning, anyone?"

"You bet!" Chet and Evan boomed in unison.

Breakfast was ready at exactly 9:00. Stormy thought, *Now if the rest of my day goes this well, I'll be ecstatic!*

"Please take a seat around the table, and I'll join you in just a flash." Stormy hung her apron on the hook inside the pantry, closed the door, straightened her blouse, smoothed her skirt and entered the living room. Chet sat at the head of the table since Ace, her father, was no longer with them. Evan was seated to his right. He'd lifted the cloth to scope out the biscuits and gently laid it back down. Just then he looked up and raised both eyebrows as Stormy sat down on the left side of Chet. She'd placed her right hand on his thigh under the table. "Go ahead, dive in before everything gets cold," she directed.

Evan selected four of the biscuits, laid them on his large dinner plate, and passed the basket to Chet. He surveyed the table for butter, but couldn't see any. "Stormy, if you can direct me to the butter, I'd be happy to get it for us. I kinda like a little biscuit with my butter and gravy."

When Evan walked into the kitchen, Chet leaned to his left and whispered, "For breakfast? You're dressed like this for breakfast? How am I supposed to stay concentrated on my meal?"

Squeezing Chet's thigh, Stormy smiled and whispered, "Breakfast will be over soon enough."

Evan returned with butter in hand. Having done a considerable amount of cooking in his adult lifetime already, he praised Stormy to the hilt for her culinary endeavors. After polishing off the four biscuits smothered in ladles of gravy, he took a fifth biscuit and meticulously laid it on his plate. Taking his fork, he carefully separated each layer.

"I don't know when I've eaten better biscuits. My hat's off to the cook! Even this fruit compote isn't half bad. I'm not a big fruit fan, but this is the perfect accent for this tasty breakfast. Well done, Stormy." She was too nervous to eat much of anything until she saw how everything had turned out, then consumed only one biscuit with just jam. No butter or gravy for her as she deemed it too many calories.

Small talk coupled with several cups of coffee burned another hour and a half off the clock. "I'd be happy to clean up the kitchen and wash the dishes, Stormy," offered Evan. "I've had a lot of practice doing that the past year at the Lower Sabblonti Ranch house. Somehow, though, I didn't end up with dishpan hands!"

Stormy declined Evan's offer and didn't snap back regarding her failure to complete her wifely duties for the past twelve months.

Evan could tell he needed to beat feet and make himself scarce. "Well, if you'll excuse me, folks, I need to head into town to get some supplies. Anything in particular that you need or want from The Shadowy Merc, Chet?" Stormy flinched when she heard the name of the mercantile in Ridgemonte. It was six of one, half a dozen of another as to whether or not she drove into Ridgemonte or Cinder Valley in the future to get her own supplies.

First, she would need to paint the fragile, financial picture using as many bold colors as possible. The pale ones just wouldn't cut the mustard this late in the morning.

"Not that I can think of, Evan. Just the usual stuff. Watch out for that Black Raven when you're at The Merc. Or was it a skunk that Stormy shooed off our property? Either way, stay on your toes, and don't get waylaid or sprayed."

CHAPTER NINE

Zeros. Lots of zeros preceded by several sets of dollar signs. $00.00, $00.00, $00.00, $00.00, $00.00, $00.00, and $00.00. Taking one, long look at the bottom lines on the last pages, Stormy secured the bank statements between her right thumb and fingers, walked slowly down the three steep flights of stairs, and placed them behind her back before entering the living room.

Chet had poured yet another cup of strong coffee to which he'd added several spoons of real cream. He'd offered to help Stormy clean up the kitchen after Evan left, but she told him that could wait. There was something else far more important to take care of at the moment.

Since she'd disappeared to the third floor of the Main Sabblonti Ranch house and had been gone for close to a half hour, Chet's imagination ran wild with what Stormy just might be doing in the upstairs bedroom. He sat in the love seat with his right leg stretched across the camel-colored hassock. His hopes were severely double dashed when she reappeared wearing the same clothing ensemble she'd worn for breakfast.

"Would you like to sit at the kitchen table, Chet?"

"Why would I want to do that? We spent half of the

morning in there." Patting the cushion on the love seat, he whispered, "I want you to sit right here. Very close to me. We've got a lot of lost time to make up."

The fresh application of Redhaven lipstick served to accentuate the color drained from Stormy's face. She fanned her face with the stack of papers which helped to open the eyes of her heart. *Chet had grown even more handsome within the last year if that was even possible. His dark hair and mustache accentuated his blue eyes and square shoulders. Small wonder Salina Bevvins had tried to stake her claim several times to no avail. Had there been other women who'd tried to steal his heart?*

Stormy announced, "Well, I guess there's no time like the present to inform you of the stark truth. After you take a look at these statements, I have a long, sobering story to tell you." She laid the first set in front of him. He sat up straighter, placed a small, green corduroy pillow on his lap, narrowed his eyes, and began to study the figures.

She rose from the hassock and hurriedly made her way down the hallway to the bathroom. Turning the faucet on full blast, she threw cold water on her face. *I can't faint now!* She clutched the sides of the sink with both hands waiting for the sinking sensation to flee. Peeking around the corner before entering the living room, Stormy's heart sank as she viewed the torn chunks of papers littering the living room floor. Many torn pieces. *That's exactly how my heart feels right now. Many torn pieces. What will it take to make it whole? How do I mend it again?*

Chet jumped to his feet and grimaced when forgetting that his right leg was not yet 100% healed. "You'd better have an exact explanation for all of those zeroes, Stormy Suzanne Sabblonti Castins! I'm half tempted to drive to

Cinder Valley first thing Monday morning to see Duncan Dunne to have Castins permanently removed from your name. How could you have blown over a half of a million dollars cash within the last year? My medical bills could not have drained that much from our bank accounts, especially since our medical and auto insurances would have covered most of it. I've not even had a chance to buy my replacement pickup yet."

Quickly regaining her strength, Stormy sprung in front of Chet. Landing inches from his chest since he was a foot taller than she was, Stormy's hand flew in the air to slap Chet's cheek. He grabbed her wrist just in the nick of time. "You're totally in the wrong here, and your first reaction is to attempt to hit me?" She let her head drop into his chest as she sobbed uncontrollably.

It took a few minutes for Chet to simmer down. He gently lifted her head as Stormy stepped backwards. "Let's discuss this like two rational adults, shall we?"

She ran down the hallway to the bathroom, removed her soaked, semi-sheer black tunic, wrapped herself in a bath towel, and reappeared in the living room.

"I'll put another log on the fire," Chet offered.

"Would you, please? That's so kind of you. Okay, I'll start first. Somehow, I think you might have something to add along the way as well."

"Don't take all day. Just hit the high points."

Scooting the hassock directly across from Chet as he sat on the love seat, Stormy fully launched into her explanation as she hunched forward, inches from Chet's face, "Since I falsely assumed that you'd been carrying on with that skunk Salina Bevvins, I devoted the first half of the year 2000 to reinventing myself because I thought you no longer loved me. Also, I desperately needed help with the ranch since you were so seriously injured."

Chet interrupted, "Let me stop you right there. I've never carried on with Salina Bevvins in any way, shape or form. Purge that rotten notion completely from your mind. You could have asked me for my expertise regarding the Sabblonti spread at any time, but you chose not to. Don't even attempt to lay any of this at my feet or saddle me with it, because I'm not responsible. Choices have consequences. Actions have aftershocks. You created this earthquake, or so it would appear on paper."

Stormy slowly raised her head, stared at the ceiling, batted her eyelashes, and sat up straight. "Based upon the suggestion of Blake Benson, Southwest District Brand Inspector, I hired Less Alotto to manage the ranch and his wife, Meg, to mind the money. Little did I know until the damage had been done that Meg embezzled over half of the money in our bank accounts."

Chet stood to his feet and started pacing the living room floor, watching the figures fly through the air as he kicked the torn pieces of paper. "How do you know she embezzled the money? Can you prove it? Have you contacted the authorities to start the investigation to get her slapped in the clink? Remember, you're on the hook here. Don't try to dangle Blake Benson on the same one you're hanging from. Even though he might have suggested something, you made the final decision."

With the towel securely wrapped around her torso, it was impossible for Stormy to flail her arms. She walked around the corner to the entryway, removed Chet's vest, slipped it on and zipped it up to her chin. She continued to explain before re-entering the living room. "Part of what you tore up were the bank statements from the Bank of Blunte showing the bank account Meg established there in the name of *Double A Enterprises.* She mailed the deposits to the Bank of Blunte, wrote trailer loads of checks to fake businesses for large sums of money, then cleaned it out right before she and Less flew the coop with our cash."

Chet inched closer to the fireplace to keep warm as he studied the flames dancing in front of him. "How did Meg get past the bank manager to fleece most of our dough? Those kinds of things usually only happen in the movies or western paperbacks."

Sitting calmly on the love seat and wrapping a polar fleece lap quilt around her shoulders, Stormy replied, "It was a comedy of errors. Or should I say, a horror of errors? The Bank of Blunte was very short-handed the day Meg blew in and gave some sob story about her dying mother, so the twit clerk counted out our money and gave it to her."

Glaring at Stormy, Chet continued, "And no one is looking for those thieves to recover it? What have you been doing since that happened? That's been about two-and-a-half months ago! Lotsa luck trying to find them now. It would be like tryin' to find last year's snow. Why didn't you tell me earlier? What happened to the rest of the money? You've only accounted for about half of it this far into your sob story."

Stormy held out both hands, turned them over to look at her palms, and turned them back over again, stroking her 3 carat, horse-shoe shaped diamond wedding ring set Chet had given her when they married in 1990 in one of the

74

gorgeous meadows on the huge Sabblonti Cattle Ranch.

"Part of my reinventing project included the purchase of a five carat, princess cut, white gold wedding ring set. Since I thought you no longer loved me and had set your sights on Salina, I wanted something that did not remind me of you knowing full well that she would never own anything as extravagant as that. I also purchased a brand spanking new, cherry red pickup that had the Sabblonti cattle brand painted on the door panels."

Chet boomed, "Ha! So, Evan was right all along."

Startled, Stormy asked, "What do you mean, Evan was right all along?"

"He spotted your red pickup one time when we were in Cinder Valley after seeing the ophthalmologist. Also, he saw it parked down the lane when Wyn and Sarita got married. I sure didn't see you at their wedding that night."

Shifting in the love seat and wrapping the polar fleece blanket even tighter around herself, Stormy whispered, "I was there. Since I'd gone to the 75th Annual Ignee County Rodeo & Roundup first, I missed the wedding. I was there in time to see Salina Bevvins make a supreme play for you when she leaned into your chest flaunting her femininity in front of your face. When you didn't take the bait, I thought perhaps you still loved me. Speaking of the rodeo, I also donated $150,000 to the board to help sponsor the event."

Chet threw his hands in the air and bellowed at the top of his lungs, "You did whaaaaaaaaaaaaaaaaaaaat?"

"I didn't stutter, Chet. I was blinded by jealousy and naivety. There's more, unfortunately."

Standing slowly to her feet, Stormy walked closer to the fireplace mantel sincerely hoping that the chill in the room hadn't also settled inside Chet's heart.

"I purchased thousands of dollars of women's clothing and accessories from Country Cate's Western Wear in Cinder Valley. I tried to return them at the end of December, but since it'd been over 90 days since I purchased them, I couldn't do it. I wore one of the clothing ensembles this morning for breakfast. Judging from your gaze, I could tell you liked the way I looked in it. So did Evan. Do you prefer my hair better now that I have started straightening it? Perhaps you were not fond of my dark, curly locks.

"I was able to return the pickup, but I didn't recoup much of my original expenditure. Then, to top it off, Less Alotto told me right before he disappeared with Meg that some of the cow and calf pairs had died as a result of a respiratory virus or some such. I wasn't too worried about that since we have so many cattle on the ranch."

Stepping four steps forward, Chet placed his forearms across the mantel and bowed his head. Fresh pitch oozed from the logs that crackled inside the fireplace. Remembering that he still had the singed scrap of yarns in his coat pocket, he walked into the entry way and located it. By the time he got back into the living room, Stormy was leaning against the opposite end of the mantel. He walked closer to her, stopping inches from her face and dangled the pieces of yarn in front of her. Her bloodshot eyes darted back and forth as she followed the swaying motions.

He opened the pearl snap on the pocket of his light blue, country western shirt, stuffed the remnant securely inside, and closed the snap. "Hopefully reality will set in pretty darn quick. Like I told you before, I have no idea how many cow and calf pairs died in the range fire or from the respiratory virus on another part of the spread.

"Since Doc Merenspinn just released me to start doing some things, one of my first orders of business is to number the herd, if I can find any to count. One other thing: money can protect people from the consequences of their conduct, but they still have to be held accountable. That includes you."

"What are we going to do now, Chet?" wailed Stormy. He approached her, unzipped the front of his vest she was wearing, removed it from her, and put it on. Walking into the kitchen, he grabbed the keys to Jantzi Belle's old pickup from the wooden key holder mounted to the wall and headed for the entry way.

After donning his cowboy boots, coat, hat, and gloves, he turned the doorknob as Stormy screamed, "Chet, I need you. Don't walk out on me now!"

CHAPTER TEN

Bags of shredded coconut, bittersweet chocolate bars, white chocolate chips, sliced almonds, whole pecans, pistachio pudding mixes, a small bottle of maraschino cherries, toasted marshmallows, three one-pound cans of butter-flavored shortening, two twenty-five pounds sacks of white flour, twenty-five pounds of granulated sugar, four boxes of powdered sugar, three sacks of brown sugar, a bottle of almond flavoring, a box of baking soda, a large can of baking powder, five dozen eggs, one-half gallon canola oil, dark chocolate chips, a jug of molasses, five fresh lemons, & sprinkles and decorations of various kinds formed the dome shaped pile.

Only during the days of the annual Briarley family reunions had Evan seen so many items from the baking aisle of a grocery store crammed inside an oversized cart. He'd let his imagination run wild with the possibilities of what might be transpiring back at the ranch after leaving Chet with Stormy for the day. His soul had become knit to Chet's soul the past year while he'd taken care of him 24/7 following his horrific auto accident. Maybe this was the downside to being a merciful caregiver when it was all said and done. Oh well, another assignment was sure to turn up somewhere. It always had in the past. However, none of his prior ones had been spiked with as much drama or intrigue as this one had been. Being a prolific reader, he'd yet to find any novels at the Ridgemonte Public Library which could rival real life during the year 2000 in the high desert mountains where the deer and the antelope played and the skies were cloudy certain days.

Hurriedly pulling his grocery cart backward to avoid even having to say *Hello* to Nurse Nancy Pritchurt who was definitely lost in her own world, all Evan heard was, "Better learn how to drive there, cowboy!"

Leo Jeelon, Shadow Butte County Deputy Sheriff, continued, "Sorry, I didn't know you were going to slap it into reverse so quickly. I was just trying to find some marshmallow crème to go with my coffee."

Evan reached behind his right hip and gently pushed Leo's cart back a couple of feet. Turning around, he hesitated before he spoke knowing full well that once he did, he would be trapped. Lowering the volume of his voice, he replied, "No biggie. The Shadowy Merc needs to widen their aisles as far as I'm concerned. Judging from your attire, you must be one of the county mounties. By the way, I'm Evan Briarley."

Extending his right hand, Leo said, "Nice to meet you. Yes, I'm one of the deputies. Are you new in these parts?"

"Not exactly. I'm a physical therapist and have been here for a number of years."

"Live in Ridgemonte with your wife and kids?"

"Don't have a wife or kids."

Returning from her sweet fantasy world, Nurse Nancy definitely heard that reply. Whirling around, she dropped her clipboard securing her lengthy grocery shopping list and gel pen onto the floor. Turquoise ink splattered in front of her feet. Leo hesitated to see if Evan would be the gentleman, bend down, and pick it up. Since Evan opted to hunch forward and lean over the front portion of his cart, Leo walked around him, retrieved the pen from the floor and handed it back to Nurse Nancy.

"Here's this, Miss. I saw where your clipboard landed underneath the shelf below the jars of corn syrup. Just a second, and I'll get that for you."

Nurse Nancy dug around in the bottom of her purse in search of the small piece of paper. "Thank you, sir."

Closing her fingers over her left palm, she walked up to Evan and tapped him on his right shoulder. "Oh, this is too good to be true! Look, Evan, I was destined to encounter you today. Let me read this to you. It was the message inside one of my fortune cookies from last night's late dessert. Are you ready?"

Deputy Jeelon belly laughed. Evan refused to lift his head.

"You're just so cute, Evan! Playing possum with me, aren't you? It's okay if you're a little bashful to start with. You know what they say. Those quiet guys always score the plum wives. Oh, I almost forgot to read you my message. 'You will meet the man of your dreams in the most unusual place.' "

While still not making eye contact with Nurse Nancy, Evan replied, "Looks like you're going to be baking for an army."

"No, just me; however, I'm not technically single as I live with Sir Shelton, my Siamese cat. He's one of the classic, seal point types, and is very smart and affectionate. I had a solid silver bell made for him to wear around his neck. The jingling sound throughout the house makes me so happy!

"My baking marathon will take place this weekend, so I can have all sorts of treats waiting for you when you come over for coffee and dessert."

Evan exhaled slowly. "There's no spare space in my schedule since I need to get back to the Sabblonti Ranch to take care of my physical therapy patient."

Wagging her forefinger in front of Evan, Nurse Nancy chuckled, "Well, you're not going to be able to use that excuse much longer, are you? Have you so quickly forgotten who charts the doctor's orders? Busted, Evan!"

This time it was Deputy Jeelon's turn to scoot his shopping cart backwards. "It feels about 450 degrees in this baking aisle even though it's a frosty 33 outside. I'll leave you two flirty birds to your futures and dessert. Best of luck, Evan. I think you're going to need it." Deputy Jeelon could be heard laughing out loud two aisles away.

Spinning the empty cart around quickly, Evan headed for the front check-out stand and pushed it into the long line of similar ones. Shaking his head as he ran toward his brown van in the parking lot, he said, "Ah, forget about it! I can drive to Fantone for milk. Better yet, find a milk cow in a barn somewhere. Life has got to be a lot more tranquil in Tranquility Falls County. Strange women are coming out of the sagebrush!"

CHAPTER ELEVEN

Nurse Macey Meadows had sweet talked Nurse Dawn Rowann into taking her Saturday shift at the Mintner Medical Center in Ridgemonte so she could help Dr. Ben Shaw stock shelves in his vet clinic. Standing on a piece of plywood supported by two heavy ladders, Macey almost lost her balance and fell off when she saw Chet walking as fast as he could without his cane toward the back door. "Benny, come quickly, we have company!" Only Macey was allowed to call the good animal doctor by that first name. Chet pounded on the door several times before Macey could get down from the ladder or Dr. Shaw could open it.

"Come right on in, stranger! What brings you here on a frigid morning like this one?"

"Need to talk immediately, Doc. No time to waste."

"Would you like me to leave and return later?" offered Macey.

Chet started pacing back and forth between the front office of the vet clinic, throughout the exam rooms and the surgical room, all the way to the back door as he muttered fragmented sentences. Alarmed, Dr. Shaw shrugged his shoulders and the corners of his mouth turned downward.

He looked at Macey, "I'm so sorry this surfaced just when we were trying to get together for the first time since Christmas. I know it's been a long seven weeks since we've seen each other. Here are the keys to my pickup. Let the engine warm up for about five minutes before you turn the heater on full blast. Can you give us at least an hour or so? Chet's been dealt a bitter hand for way too long. Time to get some favorable cards or a new dealer."

"Most certainly. I know how to make myself scarce when I need to. A friend in need always takes priority." Bundling up in her variegated sapphire and antique white winter scarf, matching gloves and stocking cap along with her lapis blue winter coat, Macey's pearly white teeth showcased inside her pomegrante tinted lips made it difficult for Dr. Shaw to concentrate on the next task at hand. Her green eyes beamed brightly underneath the illuminated incandescent lights mounted in the ceiling of his storage room.

Could women shift their emotional gears faster than men? Blowing her a kiss, he mouthed the words, "Thank you. You're the best!"

She blew a kiss back to him. "So are you! Back in a flash, Benny."

Taking the liberty of opening one of the refrigeration units in the back of The Shaw Vet Clinic, Chet bent down and narrowed his focus to read the fine print on the bottle labels. "Got anything in here you can inject me with?" Taken aback somewhat, Dr. Shaw opted to squelch his humorous reply with a serious one. "Ah, come on, Chet. It can't be that bad, can it? Pull up a chair, and I'll round up some stout coffee."

Settling into a recliner and adjusting the foot rest to alleviate the pressure from his right leg, Chet glanced around the room. "I'm all coffeed out, Doc. Appreciate the offer. Comfy set up you've got here. Sorry to barge in on you like this, especially when you were with Macey. Has she been hangin' out here a lot lately?"

Dr. Shaw handed Chet a glass of lime mineral water. "Here, this will help soothe your nerves. I've got some ginger root herbal pills if you'd like something to help your digestion. Getting all riled up is hard on the digestive system. You should know that from raising cattle and horses all these years. Believe it or not, this is the first time I've seen Macey since Christmas Day."

Chet gulped down the entire glass of mineral water. "Sounds like you two need to tweak your scheduling or get new lives."

"Slowly working on it, Chet. I'm somewhat frustrated because there needs to be about three of me at my clinic and four of her at the hospital, but it's not about Macey or me at the moment. It's all about you. Speak on."

Chet tightened his grip on the empty twelve ounce glass and pulled his fist back to his shoulder. "I feel like throwing this right through that window over there!"

"Here, I'll take it, Chet. That won't accomplish anything. Chards of glass are not easy to clean up."

"Neither is the giant mess I've discovered. While Stormy and I were apart for a full year, the Sabblonti cattle herd ended up in disarray. The heiress to the family fortune has no fortune."

The telephone inside the vet clinic started ringing repeatedly. "Those calls can go to voice mail for the next short while. I'll keep one ear open to see if there are any dire emergencies. Talk fast, Chet, in case there are, and I need to bolt out of here."

Dr. Shaw listened intently as Chet poured out his his heavy heart to him and recounted what Stormy had told him earlier that morning. With each wave of bad news, Dr. Shaw sunk deeper into the chair in which he was sitting. When he got to the part about the Alottos stealing the Sabblonti's money, Chet stared at the ceiling as tears gushed down both cheeks.

Yes, grown men do cry at times. Even young ones do. At forty-three, he was ready to saddle his gelding, Blitz, and ride off into the next sunset, even in the dead of winter. He'd landed in Shadow Butte County a little more than a decade ago and couldn't quite believe his good fortune at the time. Never dreaming he'd score the largest cattle spread in the entire state by way of his marriage to Stormy, that dream had turned into the biggest nightmare of his life. He could always go back to the horse racing world which he'd loved so much. There was never a dull moment there either. Guaranteed.

Call number four announced a whole new boldness to both men. "Hi, there, Dr. Shaw. You must be hiding my knight in shining armor inside your clinic right now. I know Jantzi Belle Sabblonti's old pickup when I see it. I've also memorized those license plates. I'll be there in just a jiffy. Can't wait to see the most handsome cowboy on the planet. Wow, what a hunk! You're not exactly homely, but Chet Carleton Castins beats you in spades as far as looks and physique any ol' day of the week. When I read my horoscope in *The Ridgemonte Rider* yesterday it said that I would be embarking upon a brave new world if I chose to be brave. Ooooooo-la-lah!" Fortunately, the preselected time frame in which to record voice mail messages on the machine had expired.

Dr. Shaw headed to the front of his clinic as Chet followed. "Let me do the talking, Chet. Matter of fact, don't you need to use the can right now? I'm sure you do!"

All decked out in her signature raven black clothing ensemble, both innerwear and outerwear, Salina Bevvins reached down to turn the door knob of the vet clinic front door just as Dr. Shaw opened it and stepped outside.

"Wow, this is first rate customer service! It's not you or your skills that I'm inquiring about this afternoon, Dr. Shaw. I'm here to see MY one and only, Chet Castins."

"He's not here. Furthermore, Chet is a married man who's not one iota interested in you. I have some sage advice for you: quit chasing him and leave him alone, once and for all. Find someone to help you rid yourself of your evil, seductive ways. Then plan to pursue a single man in this area since there are plenty of them."

Dr. Shaw pulled his Double Mackinaw hat tighter over his ears, crossed his arms over his chest, spread his feet apart, and continued, "Please leave now."

Salina crossed her arms, dangled her oversized black purse in front of her, spread her feet apart, and replied, "What are you going to do about it if I choose to stay? You can't force me off your property. Somehow, you just don't seem like the type. I don't think you've got it in you." She sneered causing her thick application of black lipstick to smear across her extra-long, pointed, canine tooth.

"I will call the authorities, report a disturbance, and

have you removed from my property."

"Disturbance? I haven't caused any kind of disturbance. Yet. Remember, Chet won't always be able to hide on your property. I'll snare him sometime when you're not looking. Hide and watch. I'll teach you a thing or two along with that wretched ex-wife he's soon to have!"

Salina stomped back to her Aunt June Slader's old brown pickup, gunned the engine, and left the parking lot, leaving a large, fresh oil spot on the concrete. An elongated black plume of smoke from the broken exhaust pipe streamed after her.

Dr. Shaw secured the front door behind him including the dead-bolt lock. Checking to make sure the burglar alarm mounted to the wall read *Stay*, he walked to the back of the clinic to find Chet who was resting his eyes while reclining in the comfy chair. "What'd you end up telling her, Doc?"

"I told her you weren't here and to leave you alone once and for all."

"But I am here."

"Technically speaking, it depends upon the definition of *here* which means *in this place or in this spot*. Since I was standing outside my office door, you were not in that exact place or spot at that exact moment, so you were not *here*."

Chet laughed out loud. "Are you sure you shouldn't have pursued a career as a lawyer instead of a vet? Glad you ran her off. I wonder if she's off her rocker."

Dr. Shaw located a large pad of paper he'd received as a promo from *Total Stockmen Supply House*. "Rocker, no clue. The only rocker I know of is the one I need to purchase sometime in the near future, so Mrs. Ben Shaw can rock my little boys to sleep."

Cocking his head to the left, Chet asked, "Are you holding out on me, Doc? You've got a lot of ground to cover before you get a kid in a rocking chair! First you've got to get the woman, court her, propose to her, get married up, then comes the *rock-a-bye baby*. Just make sure you keep him out of the tree tops, so the cradle doesn't fall! What are you going to do if you end up having all girls and no boys to carry on your family name?"

Clicking the *Total Stockmen Supply House* pen several times, Dr. Shaw said, "I'll take whatever I can get, whether it's boys or girls. First things things first. I'm working on getting my woman. Everything will fall nicely into place after that. With the brevity of your situation and the hour, I can't believe we're talking about my future when it's yours that's in such jeopardy. If you want to save the Sabblonti Ranch, you've got to plan your work and work your plan."

A fresh wind of wisdom seemed to suddenly blow right through Chet's mind onto the pages of the promo pad as Dr. Shaw wrote as fast as he could. Simultaneously, Salina Bevvins was penning her seductive lines on the reverse side of the aquamarine cardboard she'd forgotten to throw away after receiving her latest mail-order lingerie combo. She had to shorten her sentences somewhat to fit them inside the female-silhouette pattern.

Brushing her palms together with much satisfaction, Salina walked two blocks and came to the passenger side of Jantzi Belle Sabblonti's old pickup to see if it was unlocked.

Score! Yes, Brave New World, here I come! She turned the cardboard face down, kissed it, and placed it under a faded, navy blue sweatshirt with a lariat sitting on top of it.

"Let's play Checkers, Chet! Most every cowboy knows

how to play that game. The next move is yours. I plan to capture all of your pieces, so you'll have no available moves. I will definitely win this game."

CHAPTER TWELVE

"In the stillness,
In the serenity,
I never dreamed I'd be here with you.

Loving you more than life itself
In the vast, wild, wild west.
Listening for each breath you take
Making my heart thump inside my chest.

Young love, first love
Is the richest kind of love.
Each word you speak to me
Is like the sound of a gentle dove.

Enraptured by the gentle stroke of your hand
Only you know how to make me soar,
Higher than the highest golden eagle
Above the mighty desert river shores.
Desiring days without end
And nights right next to you,
Can time please stand still

While you're still within my view?

In the stillness,
In the shadows,
Please don't leave me now!"

Merna Toppens gripped Tom's hand as she voiced her private thoughts.

"It had started out as one of the best days, so how could it have turned out to be one of the worst days? Life can be less than predictable anywhere at any time, but it sure wasn't meant to be scripted like this. How is one ever supposed to know what will be the last smile, word, or glimpse before the sun finally sets? Desires left unfulfilled are the worst kind on earth. Everyone surely has them. Some are expressed whereas others are never to be revealed.

"Man has been created so differently than woman, but they are definitely meant to be together. And the longer they are together, the better. Two hearts, beating together, are much stronger than one. The more entwined, the more cherished, forges an unbreakable bond. True love isn't just a fantasy. There are no words to describe it. One has to live and experience it to know it first-hand.

"Big and strong, that's how I like my man. I wonder what you're thinking this very moment. May you know how much I truly love you, world without end. In the stillness. In the shadows. Love knows no end. We never meet anyone by chance. You're my man."

Suddenly, the door flew open and she had visitors, even though she wasn't expecting any. After saturating her third, floral, cotton handkerchief, but before she could get it stuffed inside her brown, hand-tooled leather purse, someone hugged her from behind. Sarita knelt down by Merna's side, but soon had to sit in the chair next to her since she'd felt so weak lately. Her baby bump was starting to show a bit under her blue striped maternity top.

Wyn wiped a tear from his eye with the cuff of his red-plaid flannel shirt. He scooted a chair very close to Merna's, held out his hand, and she placed her left one inside his since her arm was still in a cast. In the stillness, in the shadows, the only sound that could be heard was Tom's labored breathing through the ventilator.

"Merna, that's one of the most eloquent, heart-felt tributes I've ever heard. I wasn't trying to eavesdrop when you were pouring out your heart to Tom," Sarita explained. "Do you think he heard you?"

"Yes, I'm confident that his spirit heard me."

"I'm sorry I wasn't right there with you to take Tom to the hospital," offered Wyn. "Thank God for Shadow Butte County Emergency Services. Spence, Fenn, and I've been tracking a cougar that's coming down way too close for comfort. Two nights ago, we took shifts around the clock. We built a fire on that one ridge and lit up the sky with some rifle rounds, so hopefully that will scare him away for a while. I needed to ride as high as I could in the same area this afternoon to see if I could spot any new tracks. Couldn't find any, so maybe we've bought some time."

Sarita tried to speak, but her words were caught at the base of her throat, and she couldn't release them. After swallowing hard a few times, she asked, "Merna, can I get you something from the cafeteria? Oh dear, I completely forgot. They're closed until morning. I have a few packages of saltine crackers with me that I'd be happy to share with you."

Shaking her head back and forth, Merna replied, "It's okay, honey. I'm not hungry. Just scared. Dr. Linke didn't paint a very pretty picture when he made his rounds a short while ago. He indicated this particular type of pneumonia is a rare bacterial strain which can onset quickly. Tom's left lung has completely collapsed. It's all happened so quickly."

What little color Sarita had in her face vanished. "I'm sorry I've not been to see you and Tom much lately. I'm having quite a challenge with my health. During my last appointment, Dr. Merenspinn hinted that he might need to place me on bed rest. That would really put a monkey-wrench in things if that were to happen since my due date is August 1st or thereabouts."

Only Merna could pull from her reserves to comfort others when she needed comforting herself. She gently patted Sarita's tummy. "It's vital you take care of yourself and do exactly what the doctor tells you to do when he tells you to do it."

Wyn's offer to head to the *Meat & Greet Drive Inn* to get some supper was definitely appreciated by the women.

During his absence, Merna spoke in hushed tones. "Those pesky foxes had been getting into my chicken house, so Tom was bound and determined to trap them. He'd caught several and was really on a roll. Four days ago, he slipped and fell into the creek on Rees Broomfield's Ranch. I don't know how long he'd been in that frigid water before Rees discovered him and brought him home. Since Tom's back has been acting up, he's definitely not as strong as he used to be. Often times our active minds cannot keep up with our aging bodies. I didn't discourage him from trapping since he was enjoying himself and wanted to show his love for me by protecting my hens and rooster. Tom was always my protector."

Nurse Dawn Rowann came in to check on Tom's vitals, increased his oxygen, and noted his decreased blood pressure. He struggled to breathe and cough. Nurse Rowann hugged both Sarita and Merna and slipped quietly out of the room.

Sarita walked closer to Tom's bedside to get a few extra tissues for Merna, so she could dry her tears as she continued, "After Rees brought him home, he stayed with me until I could get Tom settled. I kept the fire stoked as hot as I could around the clock, but he just couldn't seem to get warm. His appetite was still pretty good for the next day, and he didn't start to run a fever until yesterday. Then things went downhill quickly. I didn't realize the younger men were on a hunt for the cougar. I'd gone to the bunkhouse a couple of times, but no one was there. I was so worried about Tom, it didn't occur to me to leave them a note or to call down there. Well, he's in the best place he can be right now."

Merna's stomach growled just as Wyn walked through the door. "Mama Merna, I had them wrap our sandwiches in tin foil to try to keep them warm. I hope you like them. Even though it's below freezing outside right now, I had them make you a strawberry milkshake because I know that's your favorite."

There was no way Merna wasn't going to drink every drop of that milkshake, no matter what the temperatures might be. The grilled cheese and ham sandwiches were a big hit. Wyn had ordered two for himself, of course. He ended up eating half of Sarita's since she seemed to have little appetite these days. She did ask for everyone's sliced pickles, however, since she'd been craving those along with banana splits. Wyn didn't mind fixing as many of those as she'd wanted to try to help her gain a little weight.

An hour later, Nurse Rowann came to check on Tom again and encouraged Wyn, Sarita, and Merna to go home for the evening and get some rest. Merna resisted, saying she wanted to spend the night at the hospital, so a bed was brought in for her. Beyond exhausted, she managed to sleep through the normal nighttime sounds of Mintner Medical Center, even with her right arm in a cast and laying in a strange bed.

CHAPTER THIRTEEN

Bolting upright in bed as he gasped for breath, Wyn felt clammy all over. The digital clock on his side of the bed read 3:11 a.m. *Something's wrong. I sense it. I know it.* Gently tapping Sarita on her back, he whispered, "Are you awake?"

"Yes, I've been laying here for about an hour wide awake because my spirit has been restless. I don't know what to make of it." She rolled onto her back as Wyn leaned on his left elbow. "I'm going to drive to the hospital. I won't have a moment's peace until I do. Can you call Spence at 5:00 and ask him to take charge of things today at the ranch? He'll be up by then or at least he's supposed to be. Get some rest. I'll be back later."

Kissing her softly on her cheek, Wyn hurriedly got dressed and drove from their manufactured home on the Toppens' Cattle Ranch to Mintner Medical Center. He entered through the Emergency Department Door and ran to Tom's room. When he opened the door, no one was there.

After inquiring at the nurse's station, Wyn finally located Merna sitting in a chair in a private waiting room. Sobbing as her diaphragm heaved up and down, she didn't hear him enter. He sat cross-legged on the floor in front of her and held her hand. Through a steady stream of tears, she eked out the words, "He's gone. Forever. The love of my life. I never had the chance to say good-bye. Death is so cruel. My heart is broken. My life is shattered."

Wyn pulled up a chair to sit as close to Merna as he possibly could. He shed tears he didn't even know he had stored up for Tom, the only father figure he'd ever known, even if it was for such a short period of time. Smothering silence engulfed the room.

Since he'd been raised in the Boy's Home, Wyn had zero experience in awkward situations, whether they be social, personal, familial or whatever type. He just sensed he needed to stay right by Mama Merna's side and let everything else unfold. He'd given a fleeting thought around Christmas time about what would happen to Merna when Tom eventually passed away, but in Wyn's mind, that was supposed to be at least two decades from now. Definitely not today, February 10th.

There was scarcely enough room for the fur trapper visitor to stand inside the doorway of the private waiting room. Sporting a broad-brimmed white hat with a turquoise band, rusty-colored cow hide vest with large white spots, bear-claw necklace with turquoise insert, small brown pouch tied to his hand-tooled leather belt, denim jeans, and dark, brandy leather, midnight rider cowboy boots, he rested his extra-large hands on his hips. Wyn halfway expected him to pull back his vest and produce a six-shooter.

Merna jumped up from her chair, ran toward him, and fell into his gentle embrace. He let her cry some more tears as he'd been through these types of sad circumstances countless times in the past. She eventually took his right hand and led him in front of Wyn. "I'd like you to meet

Preacher Len Longbowe. He and his wife, Lizzelle, have been in these mountains for years. Preacher Len is sometimes referred to as *Steady Len*." With very unsteady hands, Wyn shook the preacher's hand.

Lizzelle, wrapped in a wool, vintage, kimono fabric cape, extended both hands. The cream and caramel colors matched her skin tones perfectly. Grey curls bounced on her shoulders as she walked. Her eyes emitted tender sentences without her mouth moving.

"How'd you find out so fast, Preacher Len?" Merna asked.

Sporting a physical frame so large, Wyn expected a reverberating response, but was pleasantly surprised with such a quiet one. "Word travels like lightning around here, especially when it's someone as highly regarded as Tom Toppens was. I'm not trying to horn in at the wrong time or uninvited, but felt stirred in my spirit to stop in. I've been here most of the night anyway as one of our flock is in the hospital." Preacher Len felt Wyn's searing stare burn right through him. Especially the small pouch tied to his belt.

Merna choked on her few words, "I'm a firm believer that whoever and whatever we need shows up just when we need it. No need to apologize. I'd be honored if you'd help with Tom's Memorial . . ." Her weak voice diminished in the distance.

Loosening the strings of the pouch, Preacher Len adjusted what was in the bottom of it. "If you'd like, Merna, why don't I plan to drive to your ranch in the next day or so and pay you a visit? We can talk more then as to how you'd like to handle things."

"I would appreciate it so much. My legs feel like overcooked noodles and my stomach's doing summer saults. Oh, no, how will I ever be able to lay in my bed without Tom there? He's never been away from me one single night for over fifty-three years. Help me!"

Unscrewing the cap of a small bottle filled with a golden looking substance, Preacher Len offered, "Would you like me to anoint you with my oil and speak a word of comfort over you?"

Wyn gently squeezed Merna's hand as if to signal it would be safe. He hoped it would be. He'd never even heard of such a thing, but this was inside of a hospital, so it should be okay. Placing his right forefinger over the top of the small bottle and inverting it twice, Preacher Len stood to his feet. He made one small vertical line on Merna's forehead and then one horizontal one. Looked like a "T" to Wyn.

Preacher Len screwed the cap back onto the bottle, rubbed the excess onto his wrist, and said, "May you be filled with strength, peace, hope, and love." Those words seemed to comfort Wyn as well.

Since Merna didn't pass out right there on the hospital floor, Wyn surmised everything was safe. He waited. So did Preacher Len. Merna's small frame trembled. Wyn asked, "Are you cold, Mama Merna? Looks like you're shivering."

"No, son, not shivering. Just felt a surge of heat travel completely through me. Nothing like that has ever happened before. Now I'm warm. I'm not as fearful as I was a few minutes ago, thankfully."

Beads of perspiration had formed along Preacher Len's forehead. He pulled a blue bandana from his cowhide vest pocket and patted his face. "I never knew you and Tom had a grown son, Merna. Wyn, it's great you can be here to help your mom, especially right now."

Cupping her mouth, Merna laughed, "Oh, Preacher Len, Wyn's like our adopted son. The way Tom and I bonded instantly with him, he surely could have been our biological boy. Our little Toby's been gone for well over fifty years now." Another dam of tears broke as Wyn cradled Merna in his arms.

A few minutes later, Preacher Len looked at him and whispered, "Lizzelle and I'll drive out to the ranch later. We're here for you. Whatever you need, please let us know. We mourn with those who mourn."

Wyn studied Preacher Len's back as he walked out of the room. *Had he killed that bear with his own hands or shot it with a rifle before extracting its claws for his neck adornment?*

CHAPTER FOURTEEN

A warm chinook wind rocked the tree branches as it whistled throughout the six counties of the northeastern high desert mountain region on the morning of February 13th, 2001. Lambent's Funeral Home had been in charge of the private internment services on the Toppens Ranch at 11:00. Owner Larry Lambent possessed the perfect combination of solace and wisdom for most any country family. He'd suggested having the private family gathering followed by a Memorial Service to include the community commencing at three in the afternoon at the Ridgemonte High School Auditorium. Tom had been laid to rest on the southwest corner of the ranch, right next to little Toby. With Wyn on Merna's right side and Spence on her left, she'd made it through this part of the ordeal.

Marita Merrill had corralled her neighbors from far and wide to prepare a funeral meal. The savory aroma of beef with all the fixin's greeted every person who walked through the auditorium door. Merna was confident that's what Tom would have preferred. Unlike Jantzi Belle Sabblonti's funeral conducted in the exact same place on December 29, 1999 wherein there were seven people in attendance, including two of Lambent's employees who conducted the funeral, all 1,500 chairs were full with standing room only to pay their respects to Tom.

Preacher Len Longbowe inhaled deeply then exhaled as he approached the podium. Gazing across the room filled to capacity, he knew few words were needed, but every one of them needed to count. He removed his cowboy hat and laid it on top of one of the bales of hay placed next to the base of the podium. Tom's well-worn trail saddle, horse blanket with the Toppens cattle brand, lariat, spurs, red and white wild rag Merna had sewn for him, and two of his favorite cowboy hats adorned two other bales.

Sympathy cards overflowed from the inverted hats onto the hay and ultimately the hardwood floor. Preacher Len emphasized what an outstanding husband, father, rancher, neighbor, friend, and mentor Tom had been to so many people. A kinder man had never been born. He never knew a stranger, and countless ranching families had eaten many a meal inside the Toppens kitchen which afforded Tom the opportunity to dispense his wit and wisdom. Preacher Len concluded with, "Life is but a vanishing vapor. Death can come calling for any one of us at any moment. We must be ready."

Honorary pallbearers were Wyn Moreland, Spence Woodson, Dr. Ben Shaw, Rees Broomfield, Nelson Merrill, and Wilbur Drebner. Fenn Bridgemore stayed back at the Toppens Ranch to keep an eye on everything.

Following the brief eulogy, the portable tables and chairs were set up for the community meal. As sad as she was, Merna smiled inwardly as she sat and greeted so many neighbors. What a tribute to her beloved husband!

Sarita overheard her telling Rees Broomfield's wife that

for some odd reason, and for the one and only time in their married life, Tom had said to Merna the night before he died, "Goodbye, my love" instead of his usual, "Good night, my love." She'd heard him as clear as a bell. It was as if he knew beforehand.

In the sheer sea of humanity inside the auditorium, perhaps no one had paid particular attention to the fact that Stormy had indeed accompanied Chet to the funeral. Since he was now driving Janzti Belle's old pickup until he could get a replacement one, this left Stormy without any wheels. It was a titch chilly outside to ride a horse from the Sabblonti Ranch clear into Ridgemonte, so she'd called Chet at the Lower Ranch house last evening and asked him for a ride. He'd hesitated at first, then consented. Evan had warned him that even snakes could be seen periodically in the dead of winter in the high mountain desert region, so he'd best be careful. Chet had nodded affirmatively.

Sparks flew immediately when Stormy discovered Salina's love note buried beneath the old sweatshirt and lariat on the front seat when she moved them, so she could sit in the passenger seat. Chet disavowed any knowledge of how it could have gotten inside the pickup as she rolled down the window to throw it out. Since that was considered "littering," which came with a hefty financial fine, Stormy reconsidered.

Before tucking it inside her large purse she queried, "What's the matter? Don't you want people to see your dirty laundry? This cardboard lingerie silhouette obviously showcases someone else's wear other than mine. Just when I thought we could start to patch things up, this surfaces."

Her ranting continued unabated until Chet slammed on

the brakes, turned sharply to his right, and asked, "Do you want to walk to Tom's services? If so, keep it up. If not, put a lid on it."

Half-way through the chow line, Marita discovered they were short of butter. This would never do since ranchers liked lotsa butter with their freshly baked crescent rolls, so she dispatched Wilbur Drebner's wife to The Shadowy Merc in pursuit of some. Store clerk Cannaleah's check-out line was closed, so she was forced to go through Salina Bevvins's who was her normal chatty, snoopy self.

"Good grief, your family must like butter! Ten pounds at a clip is a lot," Salina commented.

"Oh, it's not just for my family," explained Debbie Drebner. "We're running short at the Toppens Memorial Meal."

"That's right! I completely forgot that was this afternoon. Are there many ranchers there since Tom was one?"

"There are so many people there you can't believe it! Of course, everyone thought the world of Tom Toppens, Wilbur and me included."

"Your total is $21.35. You did want salted butter, didn't you? Unsalted butter is better for baking."

"I'm sure the hungry ranchers and their family members won't mind if it's salted or unsalted," replied Debbie as she laid the exact amount of change on the counter.

"I'll double wrap this for you since it's sorta heavy. I don't want the grocery bag to blow out on you. No one wants to keep a rancher waiting, least of all me."

Salina walked hurriedly to the back of the store in search of the manager who was nowhere to be found. One of the employees thought he'd taken a bank deposit to Cattlemen's Central and would return in a few minutes. Stepping inside his office, locating a piece of paper and green marker, Salina scribbled a note and left it on his desk:

Family Emergency. Need to leave immediately. Will be back shortly. Did not have time to clean out my till. Will do that when I return. Thanks for understanding on such short notice,

Salina

Unlocking her personal locker, she grabbed her purse and ran to the employee bathroom, brushed and fluffed her long, black, sleek locks, applied a fresh coat of dark purple lipstick she'd purloined from the personal care aisle at the store earlier that month and exited through the back door. Desperately hoping her Aunt June Slader's old brown pickup would start on the first try, she exhaled deeply as she gunned the engine and headed for the high school.

After going through the food line, Stormy had set her plate next to Chet's and gone in search of a glass of water or fruit punch. Encountering her sister, Sarita, at the beverage table, Stormy was surprised to learn that she was going to be an aunt this coming August. How august!

Bulldoggish and brazen as ever, Salina entered the auditorium and went straight to the head of the line, cutting in front of people with not even as much as a *pardon me, please,* all the while filling two plates as she juggled them in each hand. She'd spotted Chet sitting in the back corner of the room.

He appeared to be by himself and was looking to his right, deeply engrossed in a conversation with Evan and Delbert Dawson. Delbert was in the midst of a long, drawn-out story about a race car driver going off the side of a cliff. Chet was completely unaware Salina had slid Stormy's plate to her left as Stormy had gone in search of something to drink. Salina wanted to visit the dessert table a second time before sitting down, so three plates of uneaten food sat on the table to the left of Chet.

When Stormy returned, she had no clue whose two plates of uneaten food had been placed in her spot, so she slid them to her left at the foot of the table. Due to the sheer volume of human voices inside the auditorium, Delbert was nearly shouting as he attempted to finish his story. All of the men were clueless as to their present surroundings. Seriously speaking, there was no avid storyteller quite like Delbert Dawson. Small wonder that his dealership sold more vehicles on an annual basis than any other in the entire state, bar none.

After taking her third bite of food, Stormy looked up, then stood up. "What are you doing here? Who invited you?"

"Since when does anyone need an engraved invitation to a community wide funeral?" snapped Salina. "When did you crawl out of your snake hole to see the light of day anyway? Hiss, hiss, Stormy Sabblonti. Ready to shed that Castins from your name when the regular snakes shed their skins this spring? Or is it during the dog days of summer that it happens? You, of all people, should certainly know the answer to that one!"

Stormy unzipped her purse, removed the cardboard

lingerie silhouette, and threw it, attempting to hit Salina right square in her face. "Here, I believe this belongs to you. It sure isn't mine." Landing on the hardwood floor, it was immediately picked up by a curious young boy returning to his chair at the next table. He wrinkled his little freckled nose as he smelled it and ran toward his mother. "Mommy, mommy, look what I found! This picture looks like your underwear, 'cept it's a different color. It's got pretty letters all over it. Can you read it to me like you read my bed time story?"

Salina stomped toward the next table, "Give me that right now!"

"Not before I read it. Chet Castins most certainly is not your husband, but is he your . . .?" Letting out a loud gasp, the young mother quickly cupped her right hand over her mouth. "You Marriage Wrecker! You should be ashamed of yourself. Scandalous. Have you no shame? If you know what's good for you, leave this minute and take this garbage with you! Or are you the trash?"

Delbert had just ended his dramatic race car tale, so all Evan heard was the word "garbage." He assumed someone was asking for help to clean up the tables. It was time to clean up alright, but not the tables just quite yet. "Looks like you better referee this match, Chet!"

"Sorry, Evan. Never did learn the official female game regulations."

Chet walked toward the rear hallway leading to the men's bathroom. Evan assumed he was using the facilities which assumption proved to be false when Chet never did return. He'd headed straight out the back door, fired up Jantzi Belle's pickup, and headed for the Lower Sabblonti

Ranch house post haste.

Francie Fletcher helped Marita Merrill clean up the kitchen as Rees Broomfield and Wilbur Drebner stored the portable tables in their secure spot. When Merna made the rounds to profusely thank everyone for their love, comfort, and assistance, Francie offered to lend her a helping hand inside the Toppens ranch house, if necessary, in the future. Merna said she would give it some thought.

Hiding in one of the bathroom stalls for a considerable amount of time, Stormy finally re-entered the auditorium to find only Preacher Len and his wife, Lizzelle, left inside who were putting away the portable podium and PA system.

"Do you have a ride home, Stormy?" asked Lizzelle. "If not, Len and I could give you a lift."

"I'll double check. I think Chet's still outside in the parking lot talking to some other ranchers."

Preacher Len spoke up, "The parking lot's empty. I just took my satchel out to my rig, and there's not a soul around. Everyone's gone home after a long, emotional day."

In Lizzelle's mind, trying to give Stormy a hug was like trying to embrace a steel wall.

"Chet's probably just gone to pick up a few supplies. He should be back in a few minutes to get me."

"Are you sure about that?" asked Preacher Len. "Just to be on the safe side, we can drive you home."

"It's getting pretty late in the day, so that's probably the best idea," acquiesced Stormy.

Despite repeated attempts, neither Preacher Len nor his wife, Lizzelle, could engage Stormy in any type of conversation en route to the Main Sabblonti Ranch house. As they were entering the driveway, Preacher Len said, "I was trying to remember, Stormy. How many years ago did I perform the wedding ceremony for you and Chet in the picturesque meadow on your giant cattle ranch? Has it been about a dozen?"

"We're coming up on eleven this year."

"Life can get really hard sometimes," Preacher Len lamented. "You've lost both of your parents, and Chet was in that really bad accident last year. We're not promised that every day is going to be peaches and cream or a bed of roses. Thorns seem to pop up every now and then. Lizzelle and I help couples iron out their wrinkles if they have any. Please keep that in mind. We're here if you need us."

Before closing the passenger door, Stormy stated, "I never did learn how to iron. In fact, I don't even own one. Thanks for the lift."

CHAPTER FIFTEEN

Sailing through the air, across the counter top, and onto the floor behind her, the receptionist bent down to pick up the light blue colored *Desert Rancher's Insurance Company* official check No. 349287, complete with its genuine, embossed sticker discouraging forgery and other such related activities. Chet's intense eyes followed the check as the woman said, "This must be yours."

"It is, and I didn't intend for it to land over there. I told Delbert I'd be in today. Sure hope he's still here."

"I'll find out for you. Keeping up with him is a full-time job. He covers more ground in one day than about five other men put together. Be right back."

Delbert's boisterous laugh could be heard from fifty feet away which was welcome news to Chet's ears. "Come into my office, Mr. Castins. Are we ready to do business?"

"Cut the Mr. Castins comedy routine. I'm here on official business, but not that official. Since I finally wrung the money out of that insurance outfit for my replacement rig, I'm just going to endorse the check and hand it over. Will that work for you?"

"You betcha! I take pretty much everything except Monopoly Money these days. Hold on a second. Let me take a gander at that. Who's it made out to anywho?"

Flipping the check back over, Chet squinted to read the fine print, "Looks like Chet OR Stormy Castins."

Rocking back in his office chair, Delbert almost rocked too far. "Whew, good thing it did not read "Chet AND Stormy Castins. Even though this is a community property state, that would have required both of your signatures which would be no problemo, I'm sure. Yes, go ahead and endorse it using my official Dawson Dealership blue pen. How much do you plan on adding to this amount for the full purchase of your new pickup?"

Motioning for Delbert to hand him the blue pen once again, Chet took it from him, tore a small piece of paper from the Dawson Dealership memo pad, and wrote:

$$0$$

Delbert pursed his thin lips twice, then grinned from ear to ear. "Got it," he said. "Sit tight. I'll be right back." In his absence, Chet surveyed the walls of Delbert's office displaying all of the various awards he'd been given over the decades. If he continued to be so charitable, Delbert just might have to build a bigger office. Some of the photo frames featured Delbert with the proud owner of the Shadow Butte County Fair Grand Champion 4-H steer for umpteen years. Dawsons had contributed a considerable amount to their community.

It was kind of a quirky thing, but Chet had never really understood one aspect of Delbert's personality. He rarely wore a cowboy hat. For someone, especially a business owner in the thick of cattle and horse country, how could that be? He always wore a baseball cap instead. A black one with white lettering. Delbert said that wearing a cowboy hat interfered with his ability to make quick mental calculations. Or was it actually because Mrs. Delbert Dawson didn't particularly care for cowboy hats?

Sliding a set of keys onto a new Dawson Dealership key ring, he handed them to Chet. "Must be your lucky day. Late yesterday afternoon, I took in a real cream puff. Hardly ever get those in these parts. Most ranchers run their rigs 'til the wheels fall off. The only reason I ended up with this one was because, unfortunately, a young couple decided to split the sheets with neither one of them wanting the pickup."

"Cream puff, Dawson? You running a bakery in the back or something?" Chet swirled the keys around and around on the key ring.

"Not yet, but who knows what the future holds? I just might parlay that into my expanding business ventures someday. Let's go through the back door so you can see if you want this one. I think the detail crew just finished working on it."

Chet nearly slipped on the icy surface of the northern exposure when exiting the building. He'd been so sidetracked that he'd forgotten to put his cane inside Jantzi Belle's old pickup before driving to the dealership. Dr. Merenspinn had not yet given him the total green light following his auto accident over a year ago.

Instant skepticism graced Chet's face. Putting his hands inside his back pockets, he walked around the pickup three times, opened the doors, looked under the hood, inspected the interior and looked at the tires.

"Want to take it for a spin, Chet?" offered Delbert. "Cream puffs always come with low mileage, are in excellent condition, and are a steal of a deal. Believe it or not, this is sort of a posthumous favor I'm doing for your mother-in-law, Jantzi Belle. She forked over a ton of cash for my business over the decades, so I don't mind cutting you some slack just this once. No high pressure, you understand. Is there something about it that doesn't strike your fancy?"

Chet lifted his cowboy hat with his left hand, ran his fingers through his hair a couple of times with his right hand, and situated his hat perfectly on his head once again. "The color. I'm not keen on bright yellow. Everything else is great!"

"I totally understand. That's why I don't roll many yellow ones in every year. Matter of fact, it was the ex-husband of the young couple that ordered that specific color for his bride. He wasn't real keen on it either. She was sort of one of those types of women that it was hard to say 'No' to. I've got other used rigs on the lot. I can have my son, Brent, drive a few of them over here, and you can take them for a test run as well. I'll be here the rest of the day. No hurry."

Looking at his pocket watch and realizing it was going on 4:00, Chet said, "Okay. I'll take this one for a drive. Got any gas in it?"

"Double check the gauge when you get inside. If not, pull up over there, and tell the guys to top it off for you.

Those gallons are on me this time."

Chet drove around Ridgemonte for the next forty-five minutes. At one point, he came to a four way stop and noticed a vehicle parked up the street about thirty feet away with its hazard lights blinking brightly. With the western sun in his eyes, it was a little hard to determine what was going on. He slowed down and contemplated stopping with an offer to help. As soon as he recognized Salina's profile as she stood next to the closed driver's door, he turned his face sharply to his left, stepped on the accelerator, and headed for the outskirts of town, back to Dawson's Dealership, and into Delbert's office.

"Runs like a top. I'll take it, Delbert. Anything else I need to do?"

"Just sign the paperwork here which is like signing your life away, but every man does that at least once in his life, right? How long you and Stormy been married?"

"Too long. I mean seems like it's been about a decade or so. You know how it is. A guy forgets after the years go racing by."

Delbert folded Chet's set of papers and placed them inside an envelope. "Oh, I almost forgot! What do you want to do with Jantzi Belle's old rig? We didn't even talk about a trade in or anything for that."

"That'll be up to Stormy to decide. But could you do me a small favor? Would you mind parking it inside one of your garages, so it's completely out of sight until Stormy comes to get it?"

Suddenly Delbert remembered the scene at Tom Toppens' Memorial dinner. "Sure can, Chet. Anything for a sale. Is there anything else I can do for you?"

"Not right now. At least my critters will be able to spot me coming a mile off in this thing. I'd better get my flak jacket on 'cause I know I'm going to take a ribbing from my fellow ranchers. Oh well, it beats hoofin' it everywhere. Thanks, Delbert."

"Don't mention it. Best of luck." Delbert watched as Chet walked with a slight limp toward his new rig. *Just what was that cardboard silhouette during Tom Toppens' Memorial Service dinner all about anyway?* He dared not mention it to his wife who camped on the phone for hours most days in between watching her favorite soap operas while the housekeeper washed the Dawson family duds with her favorite brand. Was there a Shadow Butte County soap opera of which Delbert was currently unaware?

CHAPTER SIXTEEN

Supply cabinet No. 14 located on the southeast side of the first floor of the Mintner Medical Center in Ridgemonte had ALWAYS been under secure lock and key. It contained primarily hydrocodone, methadone, oxycodone, and OxyContin. Since the day Nurse Macey Meadows had been officially hired, general surgeon Dr. Linke's mantra had been, "Our hospital needs to make sure our patients are being adequately treated for pain." In part, Macey could definitely understand this as who likes to be in pain, whether post-surgery, chronic or otherwise?

When Macey arrived for her 7:00 a.m. – 3:00 p.m. shift on Thursday, February 22nd, Jed Brennon's wife had just been wheeled from the Recovery Room into Room #119 following her shoulder surgery. Jed and his family owned and operated *Jed's Appliance Center* in Ridgemonte. Most of their banner business corresponded with the annual sales of the first and second calf heifers along with the steers on the local ranches. In the absence of one of Brennon's sons to help load a washer and dryer set being sold to a customer in town, Mrs. Brennon was assisting her husband when the washer fell off the loading ramp onto her left shoulder.

Mrs. Brennon indicated her pain was currently a "10" on

a scale of one to ten. Dr. Linke ordered Oxycontin. After unlocking the cabinet, Macey dutifully removed one tablet, placed it inside a small, white paper cup, and logged the information on the pre-printed sheet secured by the clipboard hanging inside the cabinet. She securely locked it and walked down the hallway toward Room #119.

Oops! Forgot to fill in the rest of the information on the form. Sorry, Mrs. Brennon. I know you're in horrific pain, but this will just take a minute.

After removing the clipboard hanging on the inside wall of the storage cabinet once again, Macey logged the appropriate information filling in the date, time, patient's name, dosage, lot number on the outside of the cardboard box containing the medication, and meticulously counted the total number of bottles of each drug. She'd previously alphabetized each one which expedited the inventory process.

The remainder of the day flew by as Macey darted from room to room taking care of patients. The hospital seemed near capacity with surgery patients, newborns, a strange outbreak of digestive issues connected to a contaminated water source in town, and the elderly battling the usual winter respiratory issues.

Never seeing eye to eye with Dr. Linke, Macey avoided looking him in the eye when she passed him in the hospital corridor at half past two. He stopped abruptly, "How's our patient, Meadows?"

"Which one?"

"What do you mean, which one? The most important one, of course."

"Dr. Linke, we have oodles of patients today. We're

near capacity, and you ask me *which one*?"

"Listen, Meadows, I don't need any of your guff. Not today. Not ever. The patient to which I am referring is Mrs. Jed Brennon."

"How was I supposed to know you were referring to her exactly?"

"Make it your job to know, Meadows. Or maybe you need to look for a new job elsewhere. You've been right square in my sights for quite some time now. Watch your step."

"Is that a threat?"

"Consider it a warning."

"It's harassment."

"'Tis nothing of the sort. You need to toughen up or you'll never make it anywhere in the real world."

"Isn't Mintner Medical Center considered the real world?"

Suddenly, Dr. Linke's teeth started visibly chattering. He rubbed his hands up and down his arms as if trying to stay warm. He bolted to his left, and fell against the door when trying to enter the *Employee Only Bathroom.*

Following her demanding shift at the hospital, Macey drove home, drank a cup of hot tea, and enjoyed a nice, long nap. Later that evening, she spoke with Dr. Ben Shaw on the phone regarding her encounter with Dr. Linke.

"I wonder if there's something physically wrong with him," said Dr. Shaw.

"I would have no idea. He's always been ultra-difficult. The nurses avoid him like a sidewinder. The hospital board would probably never get rid of him since his relatives lived here in the past. For some unexplainable reason, he seems much edgier lately. He snaps at most everyone for little or no reason. I overheard him telling Nurse Dawn Rowann the other day that he suffers greatly from insomnia."

"Does he take much time off or an extended vacation to get rested up? I know the demands of being a county vet in these vast mountain regions, but there are also other docs at Mintner."

"Come to think of it, I can't remember when he's not been at the hospital. I mean, it's not like he takes a month or so off at a time. It can't be the case of not having the financial means to do so. He doesn't even have a wife or family. He just lives with his elderly mother in town."

Macey walked to the coffee table in her living room. She rubbed the velvet petals between her fingers. "Before I say goodnight, I want to thank you for my lovely bouquet of yellow roses for Valentine's Day. At least you didn't gift me another one of those boxes of gaggy chocolates like you did last year."

"Speaking of chocolates," Dr. Shaw said, "We need to have another evening where we make our own hand-dipped ones like we did last year. I can still taste those. Yum! And, you're more than welcome for the roses. What weekends are you free next month?"

"Uh, oh! I completely forgot to tell you that I offered to work two of the weekends so that a couple of the other nurses could go on spring break with their school age kids. Sorry about that! I'll be glad when summer settles in. This getting dark at 5:00 p.m. business is for the birds!"

Dr. Shaw flipped the pages of his desk calendar back and forth. "Maybe since you're working the weekends in March you can ask those gals to take a couple of your weekend shifts during the Merry Month of May."

"What's so special about May other than my birthday?"

"You. I just might have to 'nursenap' you."

"Nursenap me?"

"Yes, you know. Instead of kidnapping you, I'll plan to nursenap you."

"Good night, Benny. I love you the world full."

"I love you too. More than you will ever know."

Macey could hear Mrs. Brennon's loud moaning coming from Room #119 at 7:10 the next morning.

"Hold on, let me get your vitals. How's your pain level right now?"

"It's still over the top at a ten. Did the doctor prescribe more pain meds for me?"

"Let me check your chart to make sure. The OxyContin you received yesterday during my shift is a brand of time-released oxycodone that's supposed to work up to twelve hours. You had another one at 7:30 last night, so the doctor has indicated you can have one at 7:30. That's just a few minutes from now. Have you been able to eat anything?"

"I've not had much of an appetite. I'm just trying some soft foods this morning. I hope they stay down."

"Me too. I'm sorry you're having so much pain. That was a really nasty shoulder injury you suffered."

"I know. I shouldn't have even entertained the thought of trying to help Jed load that washer and dryer. What was I thinking of anyway? My medical bill will negate any profit we could have hoped to make on that sale."

"I'll be right back with your medication, Mrs. Brennon."

Macey opened the storage cabinet and searched for the already opened bottle of OxyContin which was nowhere to be found. Tracing her right forefinger across the chart, she saw where Nurse Caroline Crutchens had listed one tablet as being dispensed to Mrs. Brennon at 7:30 p.m. on February 22nd. She counted the total number of bottles remaining in the cabinet. There were eleven. Concentrating on the inventory chart one more time, Macey made a mental note that her co-worker, Caroline, had listed thirteen bottles. This was the exact same number Macey had counted yesterday morning.

Thankfully some of the patients were being discharged from Mintner Medical Center early in the day. When she could finally catch her breath, Macey stopped in front of Charge Nurse Joyce Stone's station with the clipboard in hand. They compared notes regarding the dates various medications had been ordered and delivered. Joyce's figures matched those entered on the inventory sheets inside Storage Cabinet No. 14.

Major concern suddenly settled upon the nurse's station. Seated in her ergonomic office chair while resting her arms on the desk top, Joyce said, "Nurse Meadows, it would appear as though we have a major problem."

"Yes, Nurse Stone, it would appear so."

Dr. Linke had an uncanny knack of instantly appearing out of nowhere. In fact, neither Joyce nor Macey had seen him all morning long.

"Nurses, plural, are you still the problem?"

"No, doctor, we're not the problem here," said Nurse Stone. "There's a discrepancy as to the inventory of the drugs kept under lock and key in Storage Cabinet No. 14."

"What kind of discrepancy?" demanded Dr. Linke.

"According to both my inventory records and those just

produced by Macey, we are two bottles short."

Dr. Linke jerked the stapled chart from Macey's left hand. "Nurse Stone, could you please hand me your paperwork as well?" He seemed to take an inordinate amount of time to study both sets. Perhaps he was memorizing them.

Five minutes or so later, he threw them in front of Nurse Stone. "You figure it out. That's part of your job description in case you'd forgotten. I'll bet the error lies with Meadows. She's been a suspect for quite some time now. This drug disappearance will most likely confirm it."

"Are you accusing me of stealing narcotics from Mintner Medical Center, Dr. Linke? I've done nothing of the sort since the day I signed on here. That's a fact."

Drawing his thin, boney, forefinger next to his lips, he whispered, "Shhhhh. Don't raise your voice Meadows. Might disturb our patients or wake them. I'll apprize the hospital board of this supposed difference in the number of drugs ordered and our present inventory. Back to work, serfs."

"What would you suggest we do now, Joyce?"

"Just keep doing what you've been doing all along, Macey. Fill in the inventory charts accordingly. Also, bring your compact camera to work so that you can start taking pictures of the inventory inside the storage cabinets. Make sure you keep it under wraps. Dr. Linke does seem somewhat rattled. Don't allow him to rattle you."

Nurse Meadows massaged the top of her head, rubbed her eyes, and pinched her cheeks a few times when completing her charting for her shift. Placing her initials on the last line, she suddenly overheard, "Hello, Ridgemonte

Rx, this is Dr. Linke. I'm phoning in the refill prescription for my elderly mother, Mrs. Cecilia Linke. Same as you've had on file for quite some time now. The Oxycodone, 30 mg, thirty-day supply. I'll be down to pick it up before you close. Mother's in terrible pain these days and is unable to drive. Thanks."

Macey stood still as a statue after the clipboard fell to the floor which sounded like a moose's long call. *I'll be dead meat if Dr. Linke turns right and not left. He never uses the phone in this area. What's with him anyway?*

To soothe her nerves on a highly, nerve-wracking day, Macey stopped by The Shadowy Merc on her way home and headed straight for the frozen foods section. Opening the door to the ice cream section, she selected the cherry chocolate sundae variety.

"I'm going whole hog tonight. Whipping cream, salted peanuts, and extra chocolate sauce. Who cares if it's only a cloudy twenty-nine degrees outside right now?"

Locating the milk and honey bath salts on Aisle #11, she grabbed three bags and tossed them into the cart, breaking up a few of the nuts inside the sealed bag.

Cannaleah was the only checker at the counter. An elderly lady was reaching inside her overflowing cart and placing the items on the conveyor belt.

"May I help you?" offered Macey.

"No thanks, sweetie. I've not had time to do my bar-bell exercises today or lift my weights, so this whole grocery store work out is in lieu of that. You're so kind to offer, however."

Macey leaned over the front of her cart. What she wouldn't give for a massage right about now. Her mind drifted back to the events and heated conversation earlier in the day.

"That will be $204.82. Do you need some help getting that out to your car? Our box boy would be more than happy to assist."

"No, Cannaleah. Like I tell you young darlings every time I come in here, I can fend for myself. I'm not that old yet. Just turned seventy-nine. Spry as a young chicken, or so I like to tell myself. Haven't been sick a day in the past twenty years. Passed my last driving test with flying colors. Even the authorities couldn't believe I did as well as I did for as old as I am."

"Okay, Mrs. Linke. Just remember we're here if you need us."

Slowly setting her supplies on the counter, Macey looked straight at Cannaleah and inquired, "Who is that lady again? Did you say Mrs. Linke?"

"Yes, she's Mrs. Linke. The sweetest, elderly lady you would ever want to meet. I can't believe she's that old. She's in great health, still drives, and can totally fend for herself. I hope I can do all that she does when I reach that age. Most days I feel seventy-nine even though I'm only thirty-three!"

"So, is she Dr. Linke's mother?"

"She sure is! You know, he's one of the doctors at the hospital. Of course, Mrs. Linke usually doesn't say much about him. I'm sure it's because those high-profile medical people have to keep their private lives to themselves. Do you happen to know Dr. Linke? I guess he's not married yet which really surprises me. Being a rich doctor and all."

"Cannaleah, would you mind putting those bath salts in

separate bags since they're kind of heavy?"

"I'd be happy to. Looking at all of these sweet treats, one would think you've had a rough day."

Macey secured her purse over her shoulder. "I have, but something sweet usually ends up helping to answer some of my questions and solve my most pressing problems."

"Never heard of that before. Maybe I should try it sometime."

"Yes, I would highly recommend it. You'd be amazed at the results."

CHAPTER SEVENTEEN

"**V**anishing twin syndrome. I'll bet that's what we have going on here. Let's look at these ultrasounds one more time," instructed Dr. Merenspinn. "It was taken at eleven weeks and showed two sacs but only one heartbeat. The second ultrasound taken two weeks later showed two heartbeats and one sac. There are limitations to ultrasounds. Sarita, since you've been bleeding a little, I'm going to place you on bed rest and prescribe extra iron for you until your twins arrive."

"Bed rest?" echoed Wyn. "Yes, bed rest," confirmed Dr. Merenspinn. "Sarita, you're thirty-six and this is your first baby, so there's some inherent risk, especially with twins. We can order some additional tests to see if they reveal any other genetic abnormalities if you'd like."

"You don't need to order anything extra," Wyn replied firmly. "We're fully trusting you, Dr. Merenspinn, and totally trusting the outcome." Sarita labored to flash her smile of agreement to Wyn.

"There's also been a nasty strain of flu going around," said Dr. Merenspinn. "With you getting lots of rest, good nutrition, and extra iron along with your pre-natal vitamins, you should be fine. I do need to confirm one thing with you, however. Do you have someone who can help at home with all of the household chores, cooking, and so forth? If not, you will need to get some assistance right away. It's imperative that you stay off your feet, especially in your last trimester."

"We have Mama Merna, uh, I almost forgot," said Wyn. "Her arm is still in a cast, and then she transitions into a sling. On our way home today, we'll stop by and get some ideas from her. She's never without a solution."

"Take care, Morelands. Please stop at the front desk and make your next appointment."

Sarita muffled her crying inside her powder blue, snowflake-patterned, winter scarf as Wyn drove from Ridgemonte to the Toppens Ranch house. In some respects, she wished she'd not cut her hair so short until the start of summer. Her long hair had added some additional warmth. "I just hate to bother Merna with anything so soon after she's lost Tom. What will we ever do, Wyn?"

The aroma of simmering chicken noodle soup escaped into the cold winter air as soon as Merna opened her front door. "Land sakes, you two, what are you doing out on a day like this? Both of you look like you've just seen a horror movie!"

Wyn, appearing to be strong and outwardly brave, had little appetite despite the flavorful soup, pea and carrot salad, freshly baked bread and gingerbread complete with real whipped cream garnished with ground ginger. He talked about their visit with the doctor for twenty straight minutes. Sarita enjoyed a second helping of everything including the dessert while Wyn remarked, "I can't believe you prepared all of this using just one arm."

Quickly standing up, Merna proclaimed victoriously, "I've got the perfect idea. In fact, why don't I call her right now?"

"Call her?" Wyn asked.

"Why, yes. I'll contact Francie Fletcher to see if she can come stay with you during the week and then go home on the weekends. What a splendid idea!"

Never having crossed Mama Merna in all the time he'd worked for the Toppens, Wyn squirmed back and forth as he sat at the head of the kitchen table. "Do you really think that's the best idea? She seems like she lives in an underground cave most of the time and never bothers to warm up when she's around people. She treats her soon-to-be son-in-law, Spence, like cattle dung. There's got to be someone else who can help us until you're on the mend, Mama Merna."

Looking down at her arm, Merna strummed her fingers across the gray cast. "I'm so sorry to be laid up when you need me the most. It's vital that my bones heal correctly, so I can hold those bundles of joy when they get here."

"What about my sister Stormy?" suggested Sarita. "She's not doing much of anything and this might be just what the doctor ordered to repair the breach in our relationship."

Wyn burst out laughing.

"What's so funny?"

He reached across the table and gently wiped the ginger powder from Sarita's upper lip. "It looks like you have a new shade of lipstick. You're just glowing!"

Sarita continued, "Plus, if Stormy could help us, we wouldn't have to pay her as she and Chet inherited the ranch and family fortune after Mother passed away."

Wyn cleared the dishes from the table and proceeded to wash them. He laid them on the table for Sarita to dry with a clean purple-ribbed, cotton cloth. He stated, "Good thinking. It would certainly be worth a try."

A large plate nearly slipped from Sarita's hands onto the floor. "I'm a firm believer in at least attempting to extend the olive branch or whatever branch it's supposed to be," Sarita said. "I guess we could call it the *Sabblonti Branch* now that we're branching out."

Merna returned from the bedroom down the hallway. "Now, I don't want you kids worrying about money as far as your twins are concerned. Wyn, you've got the Toppens Ranch to ride herd on. There'll be loads of assistance to help you corral those twin cowboys of yours."

"What if they're cowgirls?" asked Wyn.

Merna beamed. "We'll take whatever we can get. I'm so hungry for a baby to hold in my arms."

Sarita slept from 1:30 in the afternoon until five minutes past five. Mama Merna had graciously sent home two quarts of homemade soup along with an extra loaf of homemade bread and the rest of the gingerbread. She'd also included the remainder of the freshly whipped cream and placed the ginger powder inside a small, plastic baggie to help calm Sarita's stomach.

Stormy had spent the last few days calling virtually everyone she could think of to get a ride into Ridgemonte to pick up Jantzi Belle's pickup. She couldn't connect with a single soul. Highly annoyed that Chet hadn't seen to have it delivered to the front driveway of the Main Sabblonti Ranch house after purchasing his used, yellow pickup from Dawson's Dealership, she was growing as irritable as a young kid having hatched chicken pox on a blistering summer day in the desert.

When the phone rang thirty minutes later, Stormy clinched her teeth together, opened her lips, and exhaled. *Control yourself. You need help, remember? Don't revert to your old ways. Keep throwing away those rotten leaves and turn over the new ones.*

"Hi, Chet! How's my hunk of a hubby? I've just been waiting for your call. You must be terribly busy despite the fog and frigid temps."

Sipping on her warm, lemon-ginger, decaf tea, Sarita replied, "Hi Stormy, sorry to disappoint you. You sound happy and well. Do you have a few minutes to visit right now or are you super busy?"

With her first instinct being to abruptly hang the phone receiver up, but realizing she must reconsider, Stormy continued to pour on the charm, "It's so nice to hear your voice, Sarita. No, not too awfully busy right now. I was just thinking about what Chet would like for supper. You know how that goes. How do you keep so many menu ideas for Wyn? Do you use a cookbook?"

"I use one every now and then. So, has Chet moved back into the Main Ranch house and Evan Briarley returned to work at the Shadow Butte Physical Therapy Clinic in Ridgemonte?"

Parsing her words carefully, Stormy continued, "Oh, sister, you know how busy these ranchers are no matter what the season is. As far as Evan is concerned, I'm not totally sure if he decided to go back to that same clinic or not. I'll have to confirm that with Chet. What's new in your quiet, boring world these days?"

Patting her stomach with much satisfaction and smiling contently, Sarita transitioned, "At the end of my doctor appointment today, Dr. Merenspinn placed me on bed rest until the twins arrive. I wasn't quite expecting anything that drastic, or at least not yet, so I'm calling to see if you would be willing to come down to our place and help me during the weekdays?"

Stormy choked. All Sarita could hear for the next few minutes was coughing and gulping water from what she assumed was a glass or cup. The next thing she heard was a dial tone.

Tossing the receiver into the air, Stormy screamed, "Who does she think she is? What a joke! She expects me to go down to that wretched manufactured home of hers and wait on her hand and foot. Not on your life! Did she say TWINS?"

When the phone rang again a few minutes later and hoping it was Chet, Stormy answered cautiously, "Hello."

"Are you okay?" asked Sarita. "It sounded like you were having a coughing fit or something. At any rate, what are your thoughts about lending Wyn and me a helping hand when we really need one?"

"As much as I'd truly love to help you, it just wouldn't work out as I have such a busy spring planned. I'm riding the range with Chet and assisting him with general ranch work."

Sarita wrapped the afghan tightly around her legs as she felt a chill. "You're going to be riding the range? Isn't that a first for you? I didn't think you particularly liked doing those sorts of things. Since you were bequeathed the Sabblonti spread and all its holdings, why don't you just plan to hire some more ranch hands? That's what I would do if I were you."

Stormy hurled her coffee cup against the kitchen counter. The stoneware chips tumbled to the floor, adding a new colored dimension.

"What's that sound? Did something break? Maybe it's just the phone connection. The wires get frosty in the winter time, so perhaps that's what's making that awful crackling, transmitting noise."

"Never mind what you thought you heard. And you'll never be me, so don't even try to be."

Sarita had established firm boundaries in her life prior to her mother's death which helped to absorb the shocks and insults which followed. She dialed the number for the Toppens Ranch House. Intuitively Merna completely forgot to answer with her normal cordial greeting. "She declined, didn't she, Sarita?"

"Yes, Mama Merna, she sure did. Shall we proceed with Plan B?"

"Without a doubt."

CHAPTER EIGHTEEN

Car insurance - $81.78

Gas for car - $30.00
Utilities - $259.00
Home insurance - $68.96
Medical Insurance - $271.37
Telephone - $72.43
Food/General Supplies/Toiletries – $200.00
Misc - $27.00
Emergency Fund/Repairs – $58.00
TOTAL ------------ $1,068.54

Francie Fletcher had just about worn out her fingers working and re-working the figures for her decreasing monthly budget. *Thankfully, I have no medical expenses and am blessed with good health.* She laid her cheek on top of her crossed forearms resting on the table top.

Also, she had learned to discern when a debilitating migraine headache lurked in her presence. *Best be careful and not lapse over into that pain. My dearly, departed husband's small social security check of $1,068.00 per month isn't affording much security these days. How's a displaced homemaker supposed to continue to make her home, much less hang onto it?*

Since it was the lunch hour when the phone rang, Francie leaped to answer it, hoping in vain it was her precious daughter, Priscilla Pauline. She'd not heard from her since the scene with the dog Miggy and all that ensued which occurred inside her rented duplex. Francie supposed she should have offered to have the front door repaired, but she surely couldn't use her Emergency Fund for such trivial things as that.

Earlier in the day, she'd addressed the spider plant in her living room since that seemed to be the only audience she had these days. "Priscilla's a full-time employee of the Shadow Butte County Recorder's Office, so she could just pony up the money herself for repairs. And, she even has benefits that come with her job! Furthermore, let that hot shot, Spence, jack of no trades, much less master of none, attempt to fix the door. That ought to be worth the price of admission to watch that feeble effort."

The pleasant voice on the other end was not what she was expecting.

"Francie, is that you?"

"Hi, Merna. I've been meaning to call you since Tom's funeral to see how you're doing. Please forgive me for not checking in. How are things?"

"I'm maintaining. I'm actually calling on behalf of Wyn and Sarita who are expecting doubles in August."

"Doubles, as in twins?"

"You heard me correctly. Unfortunately, with my arm still in a cast, I'm not able to help out as much as I'd like. Dr. Merenspinn has just placed Sarita on bed rest, so they desperately need someone to help them. Any chance you'd be available or interested?"

Francie fixated on the column of figures in front of her. "I could render some assistance, but I wouldn't be able to drive back and forth every day, especially in this winter weather. I can't afford snow tires for my car either."

Rocking back and forth in her recliner rocker just anticipating what it was going to be like to rock twins to sleep, Merna suggested, "I've already given some long-range thought to all of this. Let's see. Tomorrow is March 1st, so that's the perfect time to start a new job! Would you be willing to live with the Moreland's during the week and do the cooking, housekeeping, take Sarita to her medical appointments, and basically whatever else they need? Oh, I might mention that since Sarita has been bleeding some, she's scheduled to see Dr. Merenspinn every two weeks, so he can keep a close eye on her. I think he's just the best country doctor! How about you? What's your opinion of the doctor?"

The vice grip was tightening between Francie's ears, so she gently moved her head from side to side stretching her neck muscles slightly as she leaned across the threshold from the kitchen into the living room. "Truthfully, as far as Dr. Merenspinn goes, I've never been to see him. If there's a high point in the midst of my life right now, it's that I'm as healthy as healthy can be.

"I was a bit put off by the doctor's comments last summer when Wyn and Sarita got married, however. He just assumed that because Priscilla caught Sarita's bridal bouquet, she would marry Spence straight away. Also, he just seems rather aloof to me. You know, one of those highly educated types who's very impressed with his own importance. About as cold, attractive, and interesting as a cadaver, not to mention his eyebrows have their own language."

Merna glanced out the window as the sun broke through the gray inversion sky. "Is the fog lifting in town, Francie, or is it still socked in? Looks like it's starting to fade out here in the countryside. I love watching my backyard birds in winter. That's what I like to call them anyway. I find comfort in the smallest of things these days. The way to love anything and everyone is to realize that you might not have either someday. All things grow with love."

Francie didn't bother to look outside to see what was going on. Her brain forecast was cloudy with a 100% chance of precipitation. "What does the job pay, Merna? That'll be quite a bit to do every day for Wyn and Sarita. Are they high maintenance, difficult people or how well do you personally know them?"

A soft answer could lessen the temperature of most scalding inquiries. "I feel I've gotten to know both of them quite well, especially since Tom promoted Wyn to Toppens Ranch foreman before he died. I helped Sarita plan her wedding which was a pure joy and delight.

"The job pays $50.00 per day. That's a little more than the current minimum wage. Plus, you can stop by the ranch house here and fill the gas tank for your car whenever it's getting low. We've got that big 500-gallon tank behind the barn. You'd still be able to go home on the weekends to check on your own house to make sure the pipes aren't freezing and all of those worrisome items. Wyn's gone most days, so it would be just you and Sarita inside the house. Her disposition is as pleasant as a bluebird singing on top of a tall mahogany tree. Not to mention the fact that she sleeps quite a bit as she needs to rest."

Sitting down at the table and continuing with her calculations while listening to Merna, Francie responded. "I realize it's not back-breaking type of work, but I just feel so awkward going into a stranger's house, much less sleeping there. How about Sarita's sister? What's her name again? Is she available? I mean, when someone's own kinfolk can't help out, that's saying something!"

Hoping the conversation wouldn't take this turn, Merna spoke carefully, "Stormy's her name. Sarita has already asked her, but apparently she's quite busy running the Sabblonti Empire these days."

Dollar signs registered in Francie's sleepy eyes. *Empire. What I wouldn't give to be married to someone with some money for a change, but I know there's not a man who will ever replace my dearly beloved. I wouldn't dream of dishonoring him by getting remarried. The entire time hubby and I were married, he was a self-employed finish carpenter and handy-man. Guess I should have learned some kind of craft or trade myself.*

"When do you need your answer, Merna? I'd like to think on it a little bit, and then I'll let you know."

Regret seized Merna's heart for even calling Francie in the first place. "That would be fine. I need to know by tomorrow morning, so if you don't want the work, I can start calling some of our other ranching friends who are very neighborly."

The figures across the top of the calculator read, $50.00 per day x 22 days per month, average, = $1,100.00. Francie wadded up the list of her monthly bills and threw it into the kitchen garbage can. Begrudgingly she replied, "Okay, Merna, but it's really only because of you that I'm willing to do this. I feel like you've just laid a six-month guilt trip on me. At $1,100 per month, that totals a $6,600 transgression trip."

Merna tilted her tired head back on the rocking chair headrest. "Honestly, Francie, don't let it trip you up. That was never my intent in the first place. Negative people make healthy people sick. Perhaps I should just withdraw my offer and spend the evening calling those residing in our ranching community.

"The day of Tom's funeral, you offered to help me at my ranch house if I needed it, so I didn't think you'd mind me asking you to extend that offer to Wyn and Sarita. When it's all said and done, this doesn't have anything to do with the fact that your future son-in-law, Spence, works for the Toppens Ranch, does it?"

"Bear in mind that future son-in-law and actual son-in-law are two entirely different things, Merna. What time do I report for work tomorrow morning?"

"It's a new beginning, so 8:00."

CHAPTER NINETEEN

Dressed in her faux, all white, knee-length, hooded coat mirroring the fur of the Addax Antelope, Stormy stood on the side of the road near the Main Sabblonti Ranch house. She'd still been lounging in her nightwear the last three mornings when she'd noticed two sets of bright headlights driving from the Lower Sabblonti Ranch house toward the main highway leading to either Ridgemonte or one of the nearby counties. It had taken her that long to hatch her latest scheme to catch a ride into town. March blew in like a lion driving the stinging ice crystals like a furious charioteer which forced Stormy to face west. *How will Chet or Evan ever see me in this blasted weather?*

With her stocking cap and hood over her head, it was difficult, if not almost impossible, to listen for the sound of an engine over the roar of the wind. She stepped into the center of the road and started doing jumping-jacks. Stormy landed on her behind three times but was bound and determined not to miss her slim chance. She'd been housebound with no wheels for fifteen days since Len and Lizzelle Longbowe had delivered her to the front porch of the Main Ranch house following Tom Toppens' funeral.

Coupled with the intermittent power outages, Stormy had spent a great deal of time lying in bed with as many covers piled on her as she could find. Her lack of foresight to garner a supply of winter wood for her fireplace hadn't helped her lack of survival skills. During 2000, Sabblontis had lacked for nothing, but 2001 dawned with an entirely different story including several challenging chapters. And it was only March. What would the remainder of the year produce?

Prior to leaving the Lower Sabblonti Ranch house, Chet had suggested to Evan that he head out first. If he experienced any difficulties on the road, Chet would be following closely behind in his 4-wheel drive rig.

Evan braked suddenly, nearly sliding off the road. Stormy's repetitive arm and leg movements were what he'd spotted first which was nearly too late. His van lurched to a halt, forcibly thrusting him into the steering wheel.

Stormy ran around to the passenger side, but not before falling one more time. She pounded on the locked door. Not realizing that the self-locking mechanism kicked in every time he started to drive, Evan fumbled around with his fingers pressing various buttons to try to get the door opened. Stormy didn't let up. When the black knob mounted on the inside of the door flew up, she jerked the door open and fell into the seat.

Chet had initially started out with his border collie, Beebee, sitting in the front seat until he saw how miserable the weather was. He opted to turn around and take him back home for the day. That delay had ultimately prevented him from rear-ending Evan.

Squinting to discern what was going on, Chet stroked his chin a couple of times. "There's no telling what Stormy's up to now. One thing about it, she's learning what it's like to be inside a real storm nowadays. Do you agree, Beebee?" Looking to the side, he continued, "Oh, right, you're back home, outta sight."

"Good morning, Evan. It's so nice to see you," Stormy said. "Thanks for showing up when I need you to show up. Did they teach you that in your physical therapy classes? Drive me to Dawson's Dealership. Now."

"I'm not shifting from *park* into *drive* until you change your tune. Gratitude is an attitude. Try asking again. If you weren't Mrs. Chet Castins, I would bodily remove you from my vehicle with my bare hands."

"So sorry. The cold does this to me. Would you please drive me to Dawson's Dealership, so I can get Mother's old pickup? You'd think my husband would've had it delivered to the Main Sabblonti Ranch house for me. I don't know what's gotten into him over the past fifteen months."

Opening the driver's door, and leaving it open, Evan walked back to Chet's pickup and motioned for him to roll the window down. "Your wife needs a ride into town. Do you want to take her or do you want me to do the honors?"

Shaking his head back and forth in sheer disgust, Chet answered, "If you could, that'd be great. I'm supposed to meet a rancher from Tranquility Falls County at 8:00 this morning at the diner in Fantone. From the looks of these roads, I might be a little late. Since he's wanting something from me, I know he'll wait."

Evan hunched forward in pain silently hoping he wasn't going to need a physical therapist of his own later today. "Since Dawson's probably doesn't open for another hour or so, and you're the one with the most reliable rig, why don't you drive around me and take off?"

Chet's pickup crept along the main highway heading northwest to Fantone. He looked down at his speedometer which registered 25 miles per hour. A green pickup closely resembling that of Wyn Moreland's approached him in the oncoming lane. Chet overcorrected after realizing his passenger wasn't Sarita. *Who's riding with my bro-in-law this early in the morning coming back from Ridgemonte? Do tell, Wyn!*

Dawson's Dealership was locked up tighter than Fort Knox when Evan delivered Stormy in front of the main door. "Sorry, I have an early morning appointment, and I can't be late. Stay warm." She walked around in the front parking lot playing a game that she and her sister, Sarita, had enjoyed when growing up on the Sabblonti Ranch. "Scatter, geese, scatter!" She pretended one set of foot prints were hers and the other her sister's.

This was the last thing Delbert Dawson, owner of Dawson's Dealership for the past forty-four years, expected to find in his main parking lot on a turbulent Thursday morning. "Looks like some homeless person trying to stay warm and looking for a handout. Good thing I stopped for doughnuts for the crew at The Shadowy Merc."

Priding himself on being able to learn the names of and recognize the faces of the majority of Shadow Butte County's residents, he was hard pressed to remember this particular one who ran straight to his pickup. Delbert veered sharply to his left to avoid hitting her.

"It's about time you showed up for work! Who opens up this joint anyway?"

Carefully balancing the box of thirteen doughnuts in the crook of his left arm, Delbert punched the numbers on the keypad to unlock the front door and disengage the security alarms. He reached for a box of tissues on the front counter and handed them to Stormy. Twin thick mucus strips had frozen below her nose. Delbert lost his appetite for his extra-frosted maple bar. Make that two he'd selected for himself from the bakery. "Can I help you, Miss?"

Swiftly removing her hood and stocking cap, Stormy glared at Delbert. "Don't *Miss* me. The only thing that's missing is my mother's pickup. I didn't see it on the lot. You'd better not have sold it or you will pay double or triple!"

"You must be Stormy Castins. Yes, I have your mother's vehicle here. I've kept it locked up at night per special request. I'll get you the keys, so you can be on your way."

Stormy picked the frozen chunks of mucous from above her lips and stuck them onto the tissue. "Per request? Per whose request? Why would it need to be locked up? Are you withholding pertinent information from me?"

"Your deceased mother would probably have preferred to have it kept privately secured until you came to get it, don't you think?"

Blowing her nose into double thickness tissues which seeped completely through, Stormy searched for a trash can. Finding none, she laid them on the Customer Service counter. "While you're getting Mother's rig, I'll just help myself to some of your doughnuts. They look so good. I'm starving. Got any coffee to go with it? Oh, that's right. I zoned out there for a moment. You just got to work for your shift for the day, didn't you, or is your dealership *A-rated* so the coffee brews overnight just waiting for early morning customers like me?"

From the corner of his right eye, Delbert could see Stormy lift the box lid, reach inside, and finger several of the doughnuts before selecting one of his maple bars. The scrambled eggs he'd cooked himself before leaving for work floated to the base of his throat trying to escape. "I'll open the rear overhead door, so you can back out." He laid the keys on the counter.

As Stormy exited the large parking lot of Dawson's Dealership, still not having turned the pickup's headlights on, Delbert threw the box of doughnuts into the outside dumpster.

S

Before stopping at the Emergency Room of Mintner Medical Center, Evan listened to a gaggle of geese flying overhead. After registering at the desk, Nurse Caroline Crutchens helped him into an exam room. The x-ray technician had not yet reported to work due to marginal road conditions, so Caroline was pulling double duty. Dr. Linke had ordered a set based upon Evan's complaint of chest pain.

Prior to writing the order, Evan had surmised that something seemed terribly amiss with Dr. Linke. His walk wasn't fluid or natural. It was almost robotic. The same with his speech which was incoherent at times. Maybe he'd been on shift more than twenty-four hours. But still, a medical practitioner should be more proficient. Evan's intuition kicked into high gear. Dr. Linke's coloring was whiter than the palest shade of pale. Checking his wrist watch, Evan noted it was now 9:10 a.m. He didn't wait for the results from Mintner.

Light snow continued to fall making road conditions worse. Evan's feet nearly flew out from under him when he tried walking on the sidewalk. The young girl working at the front counter of Evergreene Medical Clinic was a fill-in for the day from the Temp Agency. "Good morning, sir. Your name and date of birth please, and what time was your appointment?"

"My name's Evan Briarley. I don't have an actual appointment. I was hoping to see Dr. Merenspinn this morning. It's very important."

Scanning the Thursday schedule, the receptionist saw no empty slots. It was blocked in solid with a steady string of names. "Dr. Merenspinn has no wiggle room today. If it's something urgent, perhaps you should stop by the hospital. It's not that far away."

Holding onto the front counter and stretching backward to alleviate some of the pressure, Evan replied, "I've already been over there."

"Weren't they able to help you?"

"Sort of. Things seemed a bit disjointed, I guess you could say."

Just then, Nurse Nancy Pritchurt exited one of the exam rooms and carried a folder to the front counter. She spotted Evan and lit up like The Rockefeller Center at Christmas time.

"Oh, hellooooo, Evan! Chet isn't on the schedule for today. I've checked it every evening when I leave work because I knew March 14th would be here soon enough for his last appointment."

Evan coached himself. *You have a decision to make. What'll it be? Pride or pain?*

Lacing his fingers together on both hands, he stretched his arms the full length behind the counter. "It's not Chet that needs the doctor this morning. It's me."

Nurse Pritchurt opened the door leading into the hallway for the exam rooms. "Sunshine has smiled on you, even if it doesn't look like it's gotten fully dressed for the day. Must still be in its pajamas and hiding somewhere. We had a no-show this morning which is probably due to the treacherous conditions. I do have one empty exam room. Let's have you go right in here before the next wave of patients arrive for their appointments. Do you feel cold? I'll get your vitals really quick."

Evan flushed as red as a sliced, ripe beet ready to eat. Nurse Nancy seemed to be taking the utmost care in checking his temperature, pulse, oxygen level, and all of the preliminary requirements. Her gentle, merciful touches glided across his heart like a dragonfly skimming the top of the water in search of its dinner. "No alarm bells on your basics. I'll round up Dr. Merenspinn for you." She stood right in front of Evan as he sat on the green exam table, savoring every sight, smell, and sound of him.

Ten excruciating minutes turned into forty. Dr. Merenspinn greeted Evan with his signature slap on the back. Evan winced in pain. "Nurse Pritchurt says you weren't on our regular schedule. In fact, you're a first-time patient with a brand-new chart. What's going on?"

"I had a slight mishap when driving into town this morning. I had to slam on my brakes to avoid hitting a pedestrian head on. My chest hit the dashboard with a bit of force, so I'm hoping I've not broken any ribs."

As Dr. Merenspinn applied slight pressure to Evan's chest, he asked, "Was your seat belt securely fastened?"

"Seat belt? I don't pull it across my chest and fasten it until I get to the main highway. Since I wasn't in a full-on crash, my air bag on the driver's side of my van didn't deploy."

A few notes were made to his chart after which Dr. Merenspinn directed Evan to follow Nurse Nancy to get his x-rays taken. In between taking the four x-rays ordered by the doctor, Evan noticed that she'd lost some weight. Or was she wearing a larger size uniform? "Let's head back to the exam room," she directed. "The results should be back in no time."

Evan laid on his side on the table in Exam Room No. 5 while he waited for Dr. Merenspinn which intensified the pain level. *Perhaps Shasta, head clerk of Country Cate's Western Wear in Cinder Valley, had made the best chess move. Was it high time for him to head to the state where everything is BIG, BOLD, and brimming with BRAVADO?*

Twin knocks on the exam door startled Evan who'd almost dozed off, despite his discomfort. Dr. Merenspinn inserted the x-rays into the machine mounted on the wall and flipped the light switch on. "We've got some good news here. I wouldn't have put you through the radiation process, but since you expressed your pain level as a nine, I decided to anyway. None of your ribs are broken. They're quite bruised and should heal in about four to six weeks. I'm going to prescribe some pain medication to help you breathe and cough properly. Make sure you take them as directed. Severe pain can lead to shallow breathing wherein you don't cough, so you might develop a bronchial infection. You don't smoke do you?"

"Not any more. I did for a short time when I was in college. You know the fraternity-sorority routine, I'm sure."

The doctor nodded affirmatively regarding the college remark. "One other thing on the meds. Stay ahead of the pain curve. Don't wait until it becomes really intense. As your ribs begin to heal, you can cut down on the dosage. Any history of stomach ulcers or stomach bleeding?"

"Negative. I've got the cast iron gut."

Dr. Merenspinn reared back with a hearty laugh. "Don't abandon your humor. It'll definitely help. You'll need to be careful at work that you don't try lifting anything too heavy. Just about forgot! Are you still working for Chet Castins?"

Evan bent forward and placed his arms across his chest. "Yes, we're on the tail end of my employment there."

"Talk to him about switching roles for a few weeks until you get on the mend. It'll be somewhat the same drill for you that it was for him following his auto accident. Take your medication in moderation. Rest as much as you can. Icing and some immobilization are recommended so that your ribs can heal naturally, especially in this frigid, late winter weather.

"You can also support your ribs with a pillow while coughing. Most of these instructions are common knowledge to you already since you're a PT. You can be your own best, cooperative patient."

Getting ready to walk out of the exam room and as was his normal habit, Dr. Merenspinn drew back his right hand to deliver his signature double pat on the back, but finally remembered that was not such a good idea at the moment. "Make an appointment at the front desk. Heal quickly."

Nurse Nancy dropped her head as a lone tear drop fell to the floor. Lifting her chin, she explained, "I sincerely wish you lived and worked in Ridgemonte so that I could make your meals and hand deliver them to you daily. I could even bring you some homemade goodies. You like desserts, don't you?

"I completed my bake-a-thon after I saw you in the grocery store, but I put everything in the freezer. I'm not partaking now that I'm in refresh and makeover mode. This is still one of my favorite sayings, however, 'Sweets for the sweet.' "

Visions of sugar plums were not dancing in Evan's throbbing head.

CHAPTER TWENTY

"Shadow Butte Sheriff's Office Dispatch, what's your emergency?"

Stormy's head whipped back and forth as she watched the beehive of activity on a frantic morning.

The dispatcher continued, "We'll get someone out there as soon as we can. How many of your cows did you say had been shot?" She nodded her head up and down as she listened to the caller on the other end of the line.

"Yes, I definitely understand. We've called in deputies from other counties to help handle the traffic accidents and everything else that's erupted today."

Sheriff Jeff Jensen and all of his deputies scrambled around the countryside covering one emergency right after the other. Stormy laid down on the wooden bench in the hallway outside the sheriff's office, and covered herself with her faux, all white, knee-length, hooded coat. It wasn't quite as pristine now that it was flecked with maple sugar frosting stains. When the chatter became too much for her, she covered her head with the hood leaving just enough space for her to breathe. She awakened suddenly when she thought she heard the word *squatter*.

"Yes, thank you, I'll take a drink of water. That's so

150

professional of you to offer." The dispatcher ushered her into Sheriff Jensen's office. Stormy slammed the door.

Operating on empty as he leaned back in his chair, Sheriff Jensen began his inquiry. "What can I do for you?"

"I fully expect you and your staff to cancel everything you're doing right now, and from this moment forward, concentrate on catching those scoundrels who stole my Sabblonti wealth."

"Wealth? Sorry, it's been a very long day already, and it's only 3:00 in the afternoon. I'm unaware of what you're talking about."

The heat vent behind her belched a full hot blast. Stormy jumped in the air and removed her white coat, red polar fleece, sleeveless vest, and sweatshirt. Unsure of when she was going to stop, Sheriff Jensen ran to open the door.

"Did I make you nervous? I'm only planning to bare my full story, nothing else."

Handing her a yellow standardized complaint form, he directed, "Please fill this out. I'll be back in a couple of minutes."

One of the dispatchers was just clocking out for the day when he met her in the hallway. "I desperately need your help for a bit. Got a livewire in there. Need backup assistance. She's the type that might fabricate. None of us need that, least of all me. I'm facing re-election next year."

When writing out the pertinent information, Stormy used two lines on the pre-printed form for every line of text. Shoving it in front of the sheriff's face she said, "You don't need your glasses or contacts to read that. I made sure of it."

None of his facial muscles moved. Only his eyes blinked a few times. "I'll contact the Blunte County Sheriff since that's where the Bank of Blunte is located. Do you know where these Alottos are now by chance? You've waited almost three months to report this embezzlement. Criminals can cover a lot of ground in that length of time. It'll also be necessary to bring in federal authorities since we're dealing with two separate banks and possibly additional states in this situation."

"Wah, wah, wah, wah. That's what you sound like to me. You're getting paid by the residents of this county to do your job, so just do it. I don't expect you to explain every single, solitary step to me. My cattle empire consumes my every waking moment. Find those Alottos." Stormy stormed out of the Shadow Butte County Courthouse.

The dispatcher couldn't help herself. "Did she say Alotto? Like when someone buys lottery tickets or is playing the lottery?"

Sheriff Jensen quipped, "It gets even better than that. Guess what their first names were?"

"I have no idea after a gnarly shift like the one I've just survived."

"Less Alotto and Meg Alotto. Over 260 Grand was their lotto. Technically speaking, it wasn't really a lottery. That's how much Meg embezzled from the Sabblontis when she worked as their bookkeeper. That's a lot of moolah!"

$$S$$

Chet Castins entered the Feather Nest Diner in Fantone two hours later than he'd planned to meet Tranquility Falls County rancher, Vaughn McJune, who'd consumed nearly two pots of coffee while not so patiently waiting. "Sorry, the weather's a fright. Following my bad wreck last year, I don't light up the road like some cowboys do."

"How you farin' these days? I didn't know you'd had a tough time of it."

Ravenous, Chet skimmed the menu. "Much better. It was touch and go for several months. The worst is behind me now though. What's good at this greasy spoon?"

Vaughn stacked the mustard, catsup, hot sauce, packets of grape jelly and salt and pepper shakers between them as he pushed his coffee cup against the partition in the booth. "Most everything. I've never eaten anything here that wasn't fit to eat. I'm still working on roundin' up a cook, if ya know what I mean, so I dump a lump of dough here most months. How 'bout you? Are you married up?"

Chet closed the laminated menu which slipped off the table onto the floor. "Yes, a legally married man I am. Let's get down to ranching business. How many breeding bulls do you have now?"

"None, but I'm looking to get some. Do you know a guy by the name of Blake Benson by any chance? He's the Southwest District Brand Inspector. I got your name from him. He thought you might be interested in selling some of yours."

"Blake? Matter of fact, I've known him for several years. Busy guy, that one. I haven't seen him in about the last year and a half. He must still be in these parts if you talked with him recently."

A svelte, blue-eyed, blonde waitress clicked her red pen as she flipped the page of her order book. She laid it on the table so she could adjust her straw cowboy hat. "Hi, gents, what can I get for you? Our dinner special is an open-faced beef brisket sandwich with mashed potatoes and country gravy, niblet corn with pimentos, and a couple of dinner rolls for $5.95. You can add a slice of pie for a buck."

Chet grinned. "I'll take that. What kind of pie?"

She turned the order booklet over and started to read, "Pecan, cherry, apple, peach, mince-meat, or banana cream."

"Pecan. Would you mind heating that for me? I'd like it after my sandwich, please."

Her blue eyes zeroed in on his blue ones. She'd never seen any quite that hue showcased inside such a handsome frame. Flustered, she asked, "I lost my place. What did you want again?"

He stared at the catsup dispenser. "The dinner special and heated pecan pie. Can you add a tall milk, too?"

She turned to face Vaughn. "How about you, sonny? What'll it be?"

He turned his fork over and over again on the tabletop. "Exact same thing."

"Nice. You two are easy to please. That's what I like." Desiring to linger longer at their table, the clanging of the bell and repeated sounds of, "Order Up!" fried the waitress's nerves.

During their dining, Vaughn launched into his rodeo background which winning purses and titles had provided enough to purchase a small spread in Tranquility Falls County and rent some more grazing land across the line into Clarey County. An unexpected inheritance from his paternal grandmother afforded him the opportunity to purchase some purebred commercial heifers which were scheduled to be delivered next month. Two more hours flew by as he and Chet haggled back and forth regarding prices and managed to exchange a few lines of frontier folklore.

The stiffness in Chet's right leg signaled it was time to close the deal. "I can peddle you at least four bulls as soon as the weather clears up a bit. More if you'd like. That'll work just great for me as I hope to have them located and rounded up by then. You can come to the ranch and pick out the ones you want. Write your number on this napkin. I'll call you in the next couple of weeks."

Vaughn dug a round toothpick from his shirt pocket to dislodge a piece of pecan nut caught in between his back molars. "I'm so stoked to build a herd of deep-bodied cattle that are heavily muscled with good conformation. If you've got a bull that's been throwin' those kind of calves, that'd be my first choice. I like my cattle on the calmer, gentler side. I'm also lookin' for a woman like that too. Seems most of them don't much go for a short, ruddy, cowboy with a pigeon-toed walk. They don't even hang around long enough to look at my silver buckle collection."

"Can't offer much advice in the female department. Slinky, my favorite bull, sired those kinds of calves you're talking about when he was much younger. He's way too old now for a herd builder. I'm sure I've got some others that'll fit the bill."

Vaughn held his right hand in the air to signal the waitress they were ready for the check. She leaned into the table, slipping Chet a piece of paper.

Call me any day after 6:00.
933-062-0666.

Waving the order slip back and forth between Vaughn and Chet, she teased, "Who's buying today?"

Vaughn grabbed it from her hand, trying to grasp her fingers at the same time. She darted back to the cash register.

Chet handed the piece of paper with the red writing on it to Vaughn.

"What's this?"

"Her number. Call it sometime. See what happens next."

"She gave it to you, not me."

"Number one: I'm married. Number two: I don't call numbers that end in 666. I'll buy next time."

S

Francie's first day on the job had flown by even though she wasn't traveling at 33,000 feet. She'd managed to get the laundry caught up, fix a large dutch oven of swiss steak stew, serve Sarita a healthy, warm lunch in bed, vacuum and mop all the floors, and scrub the bathrooms. If every day went as smoothly as this one, she definitely wouldn't mind living way out in the sticks with the hicks, at least during the weekdays. *Why can't Priscilla find a professional man and marry him instead of one of these cowpokes? I wouldn't care if he took her out of state.*

Laughter streamed from the mud room in the back of the house. She scampered into the kitchen since she'd not seen Wyn after he dropped her off at their house earlier that day. Best to act extra busy on Day One.

Wyn explained to Spence Woodson, "Here's that bees wax waterproofing stuff I was telling you about. It works great for an all season leather protection. Kinda funny, though. They call it *Three Seasons.* I guess you don't need it for the fourth one."

The beef broth splattered on the clean kitchen floor as Francie dropped the large slotted spoon. She grabbed for the paper towels, got down on her hands and knees, and proceeded to wipe up the spill which bled under one of the baseboards.

Wyn continued, "As I started to say, Spence, I forgot to tell you what's cookin' in our house. Francie's staying with us 'til the kids get here. Doctor's orders. Would you like to join us for supper?"

"No, thanks," Spence said. "It's my turn to cook at the bunkhouse tonight, so I'd best head on over there. Fenn and Miggy will be waiting for me. The menu might not be as tasty since I've been gone all day, but at least it won't be seasoned with strife."

Wyn waited. Invisible glue sealed Francie's lips shut. Spence had a flashback of himself and Priscilla on the kitchen floor of her rented duplex cleaning up after their dog, Miggy, when she spilled the red paint. *Look who's on the floor now! Francie will have to clean up her own mess.*

CHAPTER TWENTY-ONE

Focusing his eyes straight ahead on the road with a secure grip on the steering wheel, Dr. Shaw rubbed Macey's left ring finger between his thumb and middle finger. A succession of sabotages had managed to disrupt every weekend rendezvous they'd planned for one-fourth of the year.

His index and middle fingers of his right hand moved across the seat of his veterinarian pickup in a mock repetitive spider motion gripping her thigh as she squealed, then asked, "How am I supposed to enjoy the scenery while you're distracted from driving?"

Macey didn't fully intend for her playful pinch to make him squirm. She added, "I don't see any green on this official holiday, so I'm perfectly legal when I did that to you. With my emerald eyes, I'm in the clear every St. Paddy's day."

Dr. Shaw turned off the main highway onto the side road, drove where there was no road, and parked behind Chet's yellow rig. "Tonight, under the lamp light, how about we spice it up with some adventure instead of the standard Irish holiday fare?"

Macey turned the temperature dial down, unbuckled

her seat belt, and bent down to securely tie her snow-pack boots. "Anything you want to build is fine with me."

"Build? Never read that one before in the culinary dictionary."

"It's from my daddy's one liners. I hope you can meet him someday. I think you'd really like both of my parents."

Dr. Shaw and Macey were the last to arrive. He added, "How's this for a tease ahead of tonight's offering ~~~ chorizo, potato, onion, garlic, cilantro, and red bell pepper empanadas? Maybe we can add a few drops of green to our milk."

"Sure. I'll raid my spice cabinet and bring the color."

Chet walked with purpose to the driver's side of Dr. Shaw's truck. He addressed both passengers, "I don't know how your day's going so far, but we've got some different action going on here. Thanks for always letting the residents interrupt your lives. A doctor and a nurse. Sounds like a match made in the west to me, even if one's an animal MD. Speaking of animals, we need your expertise."

Macey stepped inside Dr. Shaw's tracks who did the same behind Chet as they walked to join rancher Nelson Merrill, his wife, Marita, and others from the community. Just inside the boundary line of their property, Nelson had discovered a ghastly sight. Normally he didn't venture that far until the end of March, but he needed to measure the land area to reseed a pasture to take full advantage of the spring run-offs. The blood-soaked clumps of hair from a herd of White-tailed deer were scattered in between the ravaged carcasses.

"This is a relatively recent kill," opined Dr. Shaw. "With the prolonged drought we had last summer and fall coupled with an early snow fall, that would have driven the predators to a lower elevation than normal. They run on top of the snow whereas the deer and elk break through it."

Turning his right hand in a circular motion, Nelson signaled for the others to follow him up the hill and behind a rock outcropping. He gestured to the cow skulls which were separated from their legs, rib cages, and other body parts. "Looks like those killers got drunk on the blood of some of my herd and drug the remains from here to there. These cows must have gotten separated from the herd when we were doing the fall round-up last year."

Macey's compassion wasn't strong enough to hold the contents of her stomach. She walked back a few yards and wretched onto some rabbit brush. *Such good camouflage.*

Spence Woodson asked, "Nelson, are you sure these aren't coyote kills? This area's crawling alive with those sly critters."

"Let's keep going," Nelson directed as he continued to walk through a narrow area leading to the water as the others followed single file. They bunched up like a herd of cattle next to the creek. Rees Broomfield almost destroyed the critical evidence, but Nelson grabbed the back of his coat and pulled him aside. "Look! They're back. We've not had to deal with this for years."

Chet bellowed, "That's a wolf track. Dead to rights it is! Wish I could bend down and take a closer gander at it."

The water flowed around the rocks and boulders in the creek bed as it slapped against the banks. If it could talk, certainly there would be award-winning stories.

Nelson wiped his face with his black and white bandana and shoved it inside his coat pocket. He got down on his hands and knees and traced his fingers all around the large pawprint. Using four fingers of his right hand, he firmly pressed upon the indentations. "This pack must have been extra hungry as they normally attack the pregnant cows only, to extract the unborn fetus while the mama is still alive, leaving her behind. Obviously, that's not what happened here. Hunger combined with a killer instinct is a deadly duo."

Dr. Shaw pulled the hat flaps over his ears as the temperatures started to drop. "A wolf will return to its kill as many times as necessary to consume it. That's why the remains are spread all around here. The real concern is for any cattle which are pastured close to wolves as they can experience lower pregnancy rates, weight loss, and overall reduction in gain for their calves."

Marita caught a glimpse of Macey rocking her feet back and forth. "Are you getting chilled?"

"Somewhat."

"These guys could stand out here all night long and chaw about these wolves. If we head back to our rigs, they will follow."

Nelson posed one final question, "So would you say this is a straight wolf kill based upon the deer residue back there, Doc? I was concerned about some sort of disease along with it."

Nodding his head up and down, Dr. Shaw agreed. "I would surmise the pack won this one."

Playful as ever, Marita shouted, "Last one to the Merrill truck has to forfeit a homemade Carmel Pecan sweet roll!"

Just as Marita turned to flash her pearly whites to Macey, Nelson ran behind his bride, scooped her off her feet, and whirled her around. Macey was beginning to enjoy this group of ranchers more by the hour.

Three large thermoses of piping hot coffee served in Styrofoam cups trumped the icing on the rolls. Nelson devoured his in four bites. Marita gently wiped the excess from his mustache.

"Thanks, everybody," Nelson said. "Marita and I don't know what we'd do without all of you. With Tom suddenly being put out to pasture, our friendship is priceless. The land will always be here, but we won't. Let's plan to gather at our ranch in a few weeks to hash this out and get a game plan together to take to the powers that be."

Frowns of doubt creased Wilbur Drebner's face. "Lots of luck on that plan, Nelson."

"I'm with Nelson on this one," stated Rees Broomfield. "We've got to join our ranching forces together. Otherwise, we'll all be wiped out in short order."

Dr. Shaw's diplomacy rose to the occasion." It would definitely be worth a try. Unfortunately, it's one of those hot-potato situations where it's tough to keep politics out of it."

"Time for this rancher to head home," Nelson said.

Macey got inside the cab of Dr. Shaw's pickup as he lingered to speak with the Merrills for a few more minutes.

"Sorry to keep you waiting, Macey. I should've started the engine to warm it up. These ranchers are like family to me. When one hurts, we all do."

"I can see that. No wonder you love what you do so much."

Looking out the passenger window at different scenery than when she'd entered the upper mountain region, Macey shrieked, "Wait! Stop right here. I didn't know that line shack was over there. I'd love to get a picture of it with the setting sun. Then I could send it to my daddy who's always asking me to send him some photos of the area."

"Your parents have not yet visited you?"

Macey retrieved her small camera from her backpack. "No. Every time they've planned a trip, either Grandpa or Grandma Meadows gets sick, has to go through surgery, or something else. This will only take a couple of minutes.

Thanks for waiting."

"I'm in no hurry. Take your time. Good photography is like a lot of other things in life which cannot be rushed."

Every time she grinned, his heart opened up just a little bit more.

Dr. Shaw turned the ignition off, got out of his pickup, and checked to make sure all of the compartments in the back were closed and locked since the road coming in was bumpy in some places. He watched as Macey trudged through the sagebrush and tall grass to snap a few photos. The lighting and angle were perfect in the early evening.

Small pockets of snow adorned the eastern side of the smaller of the two mountain peaks. Man's paintbrush couldn't hold a candle to nature's in this setting. Soft, slate gray rock sat above the dark charcoal below on the taller mountain. A fully adorned snow cap covered the shorter one which gave the illusion of the mountain bearing large teeth.

The sun's yellow rays were enveloped in bright orange mingled with bluish-purple hues. Reddish-orange, wild currant bushes lined the banks next to the water accentuating the large rock outcroppings. One needed to remember where he was so as not to confuse them with hump-back whales. Some scenes stand forever.

Truth be known, Dr. Shaw had never been in this area of the Merrill Ranch. He walked toward Macey, wrapped his arms around her, and kissed her like he meant it. *That's when the real picture should have been snapped!* She felt the camera starting to slide down her side, but she was able to grab the black fabric loop with her finger before it fell to the ground.

"Thank you for stopping for me, so I could take that picture. I want to gift it to Daddy for Father's Day. I'm going to frame it in some barn wood. What do you think of that idea?"

"I'm sure he'll love it, just like he does you."

CHAPTER TWENTY-TWO

Dr. Shaw turned the pickup key inside the ignition to the right. After several attempts, his rig would not start. He lifted the receiver of his SAT phone, but there was no dial tone. Removing it from the dashboard mount, he walked in different directions trying to pick up a signal to no avail. "We're dead in the water right now, Macey."

"We're not dead, and we're not in water."

"Okay. I'll let you win the semantics round on this one, but we'd better get a plan together quickly as the sun's going down. Let's walk over to that line shack and see what gives."

Pictures of Macey's parents, Doug and Sherry Meadows, flashed through her mind. She could never recall a time when either of them was at a loss for a remedy. *What would they do if they were in a jam like this one?*

Arriving at the shack before Macey who'd stayed back at the pickup for a few minutes, Dr. Shaw realized he needed a hammer to loosen the board nailed across the one and only door. She was too far back for him to yell and ask her to fetch one, so he hoofed it back.

"What's up, Doc?"

Macey would be good for him in the long run as she could maintain a sense of humor. His was running quite low at the moment.

With hammer in hand, Dr. Shaw trudged back to the line shack, gently tapped the board loose, opened the door, and grabbed both sides of the jambs as he peered inside. Macey stuck her head under his arm. He pulled her close to him as the hammer fell to the floor.

"Let's start our thankful list, shall we?" asked Dr. Shaw as they started looking around and opened the cupboard. "There's a wood burning stove to cook with and to keep us warm, a lantern over there, and some wood to burn inside the stove."

Macey discovered a metal box with some freeze-dried food inside and blue enamel dishes along with a small plastic tub. She pumped the water handle up and down, but not a drop came forth.

"Another trip back to the rig," said Dr. Shaw. "I've got to get some water to prime the pump. You might as well walk back with me, so you can get your backpack and anything else that's in the pickup. We'll have to lodge here for the night."

He pointed to the one and only resemblance of a single bed with metal frame, thick wire springs, thin mattress, and dark brown wool blanket. "That'll be yours for the taking. I plan to sit by the stove and keep it full of wood. It's a toss-up as to which would be more uncomfortable, the wooden floor or the chair."

Her shoulders tightened as her eyes continued to drink in the bleak interior. *Passing my Registered Nurse Exam will be a walk in the park compared to the test of getting through this night.*

Lifting the tin canisters inside the metal box, Macey offered, "Here's our fine dining choices this evening at our new restaurant: chili, chicken something or other, more chili, and more chicken concoction. What'll it be for you, mon ami?"

He touched the tip of her nose. "Last time I checked my name was Benjamin Shaw, but of those offers, I prefer the chili. How much water do you need?"

She attempted to open the container, but the top wouldn't budge. "Do you have one of those gizmos that has about a dozen attachments to open this for me? As for H20, I will just have to experiment. Do you like yours thick or not so much?"

His laugh was the first one she'd heard in several hours. Dr. Shaw removed his multi-purpose tool from his belt and opened the tin. "Super thick, so hold the liquid on my account. That oxygen packet isn't added to the water in case you were wondering."

"I wasn't wondering. This is NOT my first day in the kitchen even if it's my first day in the boondocks."

With her petite appetite, Dr. Shaw ate what Macey left inside her bowl before they washed their eating containers and utensils. Her trip to the outhouse using his flashlight afforded just enough light as she looked up at the last quarter of the moon.

Unable to sleep due to the strong cup of caffeinated coffee she'd drunk so late in the afternoon, Macey tossed and turned during the night. The lumpy mattress combined with the squeaks from the metal springs just added to her misery. With eyes wide open after the chill settled inside the shack, she thought she heard the screeching sound of an inexperienced violin player in the distance.

Straining to hear, it suddenly dawned on her that it must

have been the call of the wild. She glanced toward the wood burning stove which produced no light. *How can men sleep through stuff like this? Reminds me of Daddy who wouldn't know if a tornado passed through.*

Daylight peered through the window above her head. The first priority was another trip to the outhouse. Macey rubbed her shoulders trying to warm up as she walked. She unlatched the door, spent a few minutes inside, emerged and secured the door. As she turned, fully-bared, inch-and-a-half long teeth were all Macey saw between where she was standing and the line shack door. "BENNY! HELP, BENNY! HELLLLPPPPP!"

Dr. Shaw jumped toward the window and saw the rear of the intruder. He grabbed his old Ruger Flattop which he'd converted to a .44 Special, opened the door, and emptied the cylinder.

Gray, black, white, and yellow streaked across the

horizon, up the hill, and completely out of sight.

Running straight to him and burying her head in his chest, Macey exclaimed, "My hero, you saved me!"

He wrapped his arms around her tightly and held her so close he could feel her heart pounding. "Not only from the four- legged wolves, but I'll save you from the two-legged ones."

It didn't take very long before the shack was toasty once again even if toast wasn't being served for breakfast. "Now that it's daylight, I'm going to walk over that next ridge to see if I can pick up a signal. Will you be okay while I'm gone?"

Her heart contradicted her mind's reply, "Yes."

Walking back and forth on top of the hill, Dr. Shaw finally located a signal. He placed a call to the Lower Sabblonti Ranch house. Since Chet was presently Evan's nursemaid and it was Sunday morning, he let the phone continue to ring. "Come on, Chet! Don't let me down."

"Chet here. What's goin' on?"

"Dr. Shaw. Chet, I'm shanghaied way up by the line shack on the Merrill Ranch. My pickup battery is kaput. Can you round one up and hustle out here?" The SAT phone blinked red for the last time and went silent.

Reconstituted, steel-cut oats and powdered eggs were a welcome sight when Dr. Shaw returned to the line shack. Macey's joy manifested as she held up the bottle of hot sauce she'd found in the cupboard. "One drop or two?"

"Make it three, please, and I've finally got some good news. I had just enough juice to speak to Chet and ask him to round up a battery for us."

She felt like dancing, but there was no room to dance.

"Wonderful. Who sells them on Sunday?"

He laid his fork on top of his uneaten eggs. "Hopefully The Shadowy Merc. If your stomach keeps growling, I'll share my breakfast with you."

Macey ate every last bite of her portion. They put the line shack back in order as best they could. Dr. Shaw walked outside, but there was still no sign of Chet. They'd saved two cups of coffee warming on the wood stove waiting for the fire to go out.

"Has your work at Mintner improved any since the last time we talked about it?" Dr. Shaw asked.

As she dried the last enamel plate with an old dish towel, Macey tightened her jaw muscles before replying. "Dr. Linke is becoming more difficult by the day. He's spinning completely out of control and acts like a mother bear robbed of her cubs. For some reason, he's not as vicious toward the other nurses as he is to me. According to him, I can't do anything correctly. It's starting to affect my health."

"In what way?"

She turned to place the hot sauce inside the cupboard. "I can't really go into that right now. Nurse Dawn Rowann traded weekends with me, so I could accompany you out here yesterday. Her friend is also a nurse who's embarked upon an intriguing career."

Dr. Shaw set his cup back on top of the stove and adjusted the multi-purpose tool more comfortably on his belt.

Macey leaned against the counter and faced Dr. Shaw. "Dawn's friend is a traveling nurse who only has to commit to one geographic place for six months at a time. The thing which really appeals to me about that system is not getting stuck with a cranky doctor. If there happens to be one, I can just move to another hospital or clinic."

"Are you sure that's the best career path to pursue? What do you really want out of life anyway, Macey?"

She shrugged her shoulders and placed her hands inside her pockets. "Maybe I just need to escape for a while and travel. Some days I think that's the way to go. Then other days my heart's desire is to settle down with someone I love more than life itself, be happy, and feel secure."

He emptied the contents of the old wooden apple box in the corner, placed it across from the chair by the stove, and sat on it. Patting the chair, he said, "Come here and sit by me." Extending both his hands, she hesitated before joining him and placing her hands inside his.

"I really hope you decide to stay because I love you, Macey. I've spent a lot of time thinking about this and our future together."

The front door opened without warning. "Where's the coffee?" asked Chet.

"We've consumed what little was here," explained Dr. Shaw. "We thought for sure you'd round some up and bring it with you."

Chet looked for a place to sit. Finding none, he stood against the counter. "Doc, the only thing you ordered was a battery. Must be your lucky day because you got the last one on the shelf in the back of the Merc."

"Grab your tools and let's get it installed. I owe you big time for this one." Thick frost on the road and a weak leg prevented Chet from keeping up with Dr. Shaw as they walked toward his pickup.

"You don't owe me a thing, Doc. It's high time I start

repaying you for all of the favors you've done for me the past year."

The frigid metal made it difficult to maneuver the tools to replace the battery as Macey paced the old wooden floor inside the shack.

"Fire it up, Doc, and let's see if our mobile mechanic efforts worked."

The pickup started on the first try, and Dr. Shaw turned the heater on full blast. The men sat inside the cab enveloped in comfortable silence as they stared at the frozen landscape. Chet's curiosity got the best of him.

"Did you snuggle up to stay warm last night, Doc?"

Narrowing his eyes, Dr. Shaw replied, "No, as a matter of fact we did not. I sat in the old wooden chair inside the shack, so I could tend the fire."

Chet winked, and said, "Such willpower."

"It's called respect."

CHAPTER TWENTY-THREE

Francie Fletcher placed the soft, white washcloth over the top half of her face allowing sufficient breathing room. She couldn't discern which was worse, her sudden, sharp back pain or the *THUD, THUD, THUD, THUD* jackhammer sensation underneath the table upon which she rested. The technician had given her ear plugs and offered her several choices of music while he conducted the procedure.

She dared not open her eyes, regretting the refusal of some pre-procedure sedation medication. During her office visit, Dr. Merenspinn had assured her there was nothing to be concerned about as a lot of people just slept through MRI's. *Make that two definite checks in the negative column for that country doctor, one from the Moreland wedding last summer, and now this which was no April Fool's joke!*

En route to driving home from Mintner Medical Center, which was no easy task, Francie stopped across the street from Priscilla's rented duplex. When she spotted the license plate **WOODSON**, she stepped on the accelerator, but not before refusing to wave at her future son-in-law who stood on the ladder repairing the glass insert in the top of the front door which she'd broken. He waved his red handkerchief in the air when he spotted Francie driving off. Priscilla warned, "That's a little dangerous until she accepts you."

"Red Rover, Red Rover, send Francie right over!"

"What if she never does thaw out? Will that delay our most important day?"

Spence reached inside his back pocket for the last nail to secure the wooden frame in place. "Your mother will never be able bury our wedding dreams or put the last nail in the imaginary coffin she's constructed in her mind. Let's hope she joins the Woodson herd." He placed the hammer inside his tool belt and climbed down from the ladder. "That will be $44.95 for the repair bill, Miss."

"Put it on my 2002-tab, Mister!" Priscilla giggled as she walked into the house and poured a fresh cup of hot cocoa for Spence. "Have you given some thought to where we'll live after we get married?"

He added three teaspoons of powdered sugar to his cup and stirred it slowly. "I keep asking around for possible places, but nothing's coming together just yet. Available homes aren't exactly popping up like ground squirrels all over the place."

"My lease on this duplex expires the day we plan to get married, so I could always renew it for another year if need be. That's a long way for you to drive to and from work every day though."

"Think positive. Something will come together for us even if the someone doesn't."

Priscilla grabbed her pink theme book on top of the fridge along with her pink pen. "Let's get back to this wedding planning business. I'm making two lists, one for the things you need to do and one for me."

He removed his cowboy hat and set it on the table as he tried to make his hair lay down on his forehead. "I only need one line on one piece of paper for my duties."

"And how would that read?"

"Show up for wedding."

Swatting his hand playfully, Priscilla asked, "How many weddings have you attended anyway?"

"One, which was Wyn and Sarita's last summer. I about had a nervous breakdown before that was over."

"What? All you had to do was appear at that one!"

Gulping the last of his cocoa, a few drops spilled onto the table.

Am I ready to get married?

"Lest you forget, Wyn completely forgot to get the marriage license ahead of time. If it wouldn't have been for Tom Toppens, God rest his kind soul, there would have been no official marriage license ahead of the ceremony," Spence said.

"You're making that up! I never knew that."

"No, I'm not. Ask Delbert Dawson. He can vouch for the story. There's only one thing I ask of you on our special day, please."

"Which is?" she asked.

"No surprises. I just want a nice, calm, enjoyable day with no funny business."

Priscilla clicked her pen, winked, and slowly closed the cover of the theme book. "I only have ONE BIG surprise. You'll have to show up on time to find out what it is."

S

The muscle relaxers Dr. Merenspinn had prescribed for Francie following her MRI weren't helping. Before leaving for her Monday morning appointment at the Evergreene Medical Clinic in Ridgemonte, she felt like kicking the cabbage-rose fabric living room couch which still protruded into the hallway.

During her annual, deep-clean spring routine of her house the fourth weekend of March, she'd lifted the end of it and tried to pull it away from the wall, so she could vacuum behind it. Her foot got caught underneath, and she fell backward. She laid on the floor for a considerable length of time before being able to get up and crawl to her chair. Francie spent quite a bit of time face down. Eventually, the pain subsided and the spasms lessened. *My health was perfect until this debacle!*

Nurse Nancy Pritchurt neglected to completely close the door to Exam Room No. 3 after checking Francie's vitals. Since it was too painful for her to sit on the exam table while she waited, she opted for the beige chair in the corner of the room closest to the door, and strained to keep her eyelids open. Her heart rate slowed as she fought sleep. Suddenly, she heard an unrecognizable voice asking Nurse Nancy, "Is it really true what women are saying about that Dr. Den Merenspinn?"

Definitely cautious when she needed to be and desiring

to maintain her current cushy employment, Nurse Nancy hesitated momentarily. "Since I just started at the clinic the first of the year, I'm not sure what you're asking."

"I've been told all shapes, sizes, and ages of gold-diggers are driving here from all sorts of places to stake their claim to him. I followed the advice of one of my neighbors. She couldn't make a strike, but I'm sure I can. Female prowess is beyond powerful. I've been practicing and calculating the past few months before I moved here lock, stock, and barrel. I know how to lasso Dr. Merenspinn and make his head swim, so I can become the new Mrs. Merenspinn."

Nurse Nancy opened the cupboard above the counter to get supplies to refill the containers. "What are you seeing the doctor for today, so I can make a notation in your chart?"

"General complaints."

"Nothing specific?"

"Not for your ears."

Leaving the page blank, Nurse Nancy picked up the New Patient folder, left the exam room, and placed it inside the wooden holder mounted to the outside of the door.

Not seeing a patient sitting on the table in Exam Room No. 3, Dr. Merenspinn called for Nurse Nancy. "I know she's in there. Follow me."

Both of them entered the room only to find Francie slumped to one side of the chair, sleeping soundly. The doctor mouthed, "Gently wake her."

Nurse Nancy wiggled Francie's arm a few times before she awakened. "Can we help you onto the table? It'll be easier for me to examine you while you're sitting there than in the chair."

"You don't need to help me, Doctor. I can fend for

myself." When she tried to step on the little black step-stool to facilitate her getting onto the table, pain radiated from her lower back.

A buzzing sound erupted from Room No. 4 as the red light started blinking. "Nurse Nancy, can you please see what's going on? I need you back in here as soon as possible, so I can continue with my exam."

Dr. Merenspinn leaned against the counter, pulled the Radiology Report from the folder, and read it thoroughly. "Francie, the good news is you don't have any ruptured discs or anything requiring surgery at the moment. These back injuries can be very painful. How are you doing?"

"I'm still in a lot of pain, but I'm thankful nothing's broken. It could be a lot worse."

Returning to the exam room, Nurse Nancy also read the MRI report as Dr. Merenspinn continued with his exam. He had Francie lay on her back, stomach and both sides as he applied pressure to different parts of her body in an attempt to determine pressure, pain, and tension points.

"Francie, just press that green button on the wall there after you're dressed, so Nurse Nancy and I can come back in and finish with your appointment."

Francie's ears perked up when she heard the last words from the female prospector in Room No. 4 as she left in a huff and a hurry, "What kind of a two-bit clinic are you running here? When I said I wanted to speak with the doctor privately, I meant just that. Who ever heard of a practitioner who insists his nurse be in the same room when he's examining a female patient? You need to come out of the stone age and get into the age of precious metals! Don't bother to send me a bill because I don't plan on paying it!

What a louse!"

Dr. Merenspinn was still laughing heartily when he re-entered Exam Room No. 3. "Oh, it takes all kinds to make the world go around, doesn't it? Okay, Francie. Continue with your muscle relaxing prescription which can be supplemented with an over-the-counter pain reliver if you like. Also, hold off driving for a couple of weeks. The angle you have to bend your right foot to press on the accelerator will aggravate those pulled muscles on your right side. Do you have any questions?"

Francie stared at the floor. "Can I use a heating pad or take a relaxing, hot bath?"

"It's best to use an ice pack. You can place it on your lower back, not to exceed twenty minutes every two to four hours. You'll just have to take it easy until your back muscles and nerves in your legs calm down quite a bit. You've really done a number on that back of yours. Didn't you ask for help to move your furniture? What about your daughter and new son-in-law? Couldn't they have helped you?"

"Spence is NOT my new son-in-law, yet. He doesn't even have a place for them to live after he and Priscilla get married. The worst of this is I just started my new job at the Morelands. Now I'll have to probably forfeit that as they need someone every day. I have no clue how I'll manage."

Glancing at her chart again as he made some notations, Dr. Merenspinn commented, "You've also lost weight, five pounds in less than a week. Are you able to fix meals, and are you getting sufficient protein which should constitute about ten to thirty-five percent of your total calories per day?

"In general, you should be eating about fifty grams

within a twenty-four-hour period. It's not hard to complete that, especially if you eat meat. A three-ounce serving has twenty-one grams of protein, give or take. A cup of beans yields about sixteen. And a cup of yogurt has around eleven or twelve. We're in the heart of cattle country, so protein is plentiful most everywhere."

He extended his right hand to help her down from the exam table as his coffee-colored eyes locked with her milk chocolate ones. Neither of them blinked. He slowly released her trembling hand from his. Nurse Nancy followed them, flipping the light switch off.

CHAPTER TWENTY-FOUR

"**B**lue 'n Beebee, get'n the rig! High time for you dogs to get with it." Evan raised the tailgate while staring at Jantzi Belle's old pickup parked right beside Chet's yellow one in the driveway of the Lower Sabblonti Ranch house.

Half of Chet's coffee spilled onto the front porch as he juggled two containers in between locking the front door and fastening the keys around his leather belt. He exclaimed, "Looks like this might be *Dude Day* at the Sabblonti Ranch!" He handed Evan his mug who stood against the side of Chet's pickup looking quite smug.

"What do you need, Stormy? We've got a very busy day ahead. Can't keep last year's cowhands, Yatey, Ruston, and their outfit waitin' any longer."

She reached down and tried to uncurl the small circles of leather around the eyelets of her mother's well-worn ranch boots. Stormy's lack of culinary skills combined with her depleted bank account necessitated loosening Jantzi Belle's western belt to the last notch. She'd been living on primarily canned carbohydrates stored in one of the back bedrooms which had been purchased prior to her mother's death. Jantzi Belle's cowgirl hat and chaps were too small, but that's all Stormy could find.

183

Chet shook his head in disgust. "Evan, I know you're not technically supposed to be driving yet, but can you follow us down to the corrals in Jantzi's jalopy? Looks like the Mrs. has something on her mind. Get in, Stormy. I don't have all day for your horsin' around."

She removed her gloves to adjust the heater. "You could try to be kind to me, Chet."

He sipped his coffee leisurely as he drove. "You came all the way down here dressed in that get up to suggest I be kind to you?"

Restraining her drama, Stormy folded her hands and placed them in her lap. "I'm fully offering my services to you for as long as you need them."

"Services? What kind of services? You make it sound like you're running a business or have something for sale."

"I could be of great assistance to you on our ranch if you'd let me. I can help with chores and ride the range."

As Chet choked on his coffee, he spit some onto the steering wheel and wiped it off with his left hand. Silence was golden for the remainder of the drive.

Several cow dogs sniffed his boots and pant legs as Chet got out of his pickup. Ruston had just finished replacing the broken poles on the far side of the corral. Yatey arrived on his horse at the bottom of the windbreak on the southeastern slope which afforded protection for the cows to give birth outside.

Stormy's attention was diverted to one of the other cowhands near a cow who had recently given birth and stood several feet from her calf. She walked toward him and watched in amazement. "Can I help you do that, please?"

"Sure. Just be gentle. Make sure ya dry it completely.

This one's mama didn't lick one of her babies after it was born, so I gotta dry it off. Grab one of those clean cloths from that wooden bin right over yonder. It helps to get its blood circulatin' right quick like. Guess this cow didn't much like twins."

Shoving her gloves in her rear pocket, Stormy started drying the baby calf. She looked down at her hands covered with afterbirth. *When Chet and I have our baby, someone else will dry him off and clean him up.*

The young cowhand dished out compliments as the sun streamed in and out of the white, puffy clouds. "You're a natural for this kinda work. We've been meetin' ourselves comin' and goin' because we've got to check the cattle every two hours from daylight 'til dark and once durin' the night. More often than that if it's stormin'. You ever been in a powerful storm? The more experienced hands take care of the taggin' and vaccinatin' which suits me just fine. I hate needles."

His words went in one ear and out the other. Stormy stroked the calf's face and hugged its neck.

"You musta had a lot of practice with your youngins'. How many you got?"

She gently rubbed the calf's ears. "None at the moment."

"You married up or lookin' for your cowboy?"

Stormy released the calf and leaned back on her elbows. "Do you always ask personal questions, especially of people you don't know?"

He brushed the dirt from his pant legs and kicked his right boot against his left one to loosen the caked-on mud. "The way I figure it, that's the only way ya find out what ya need to know. I'm lookin' to settle down with a pretty cowgirl someday. How old are ya anyhow?"

She walked to the cab of Jantzi Belle's old pickup and grabbed an old shirt laying on the seat and walked toward the creek close by. She bent too far forward, lost her balance, and slid into the water up to her knees. Her better instincts told her *don't turn around*. Keeping her head down, Stormy crawled out of the creek, removed her mother's boots, and dumped the water onto the bank. The young cowhand rushed to her aid, picked her up, and carried her to the lowest bale on the closest stack of hay.

Ruston and Evan laughed uproariously. Yatey, always a day late, a dollar short, and rarely in the know regarding social matters, ordered the two, "Get a fire built on the other side of that far corral, el pronto. Can't you see the damsel's in distress?"

Chet had his hands full grafting calves onto available cows, so he'd missed the mishap. His stomach signaled it was near dinner time. The flames from the fire shot straight up in the air courtesy of Evan's extra addition of logs. He tended a fire the same way he fixed a meal. Lots of add-ons.

Some extra-large clothing and a tattered coat were offered to Stormy by another one of the cowhands who'd been on night duty. She walked over the hill and found the privacy afforded by a thicket, so she could change her clothes. Ruston and Evan located two portable panels, placed them near the fire, and draped Jantzi's old ranch clothing over them to dry.

Stormy had not shed one single tear until now. She'd selected non-waterproof mascara when preparing for her outing. Now she wished she chosen otherwise as she wiped the black streaks from her cheeks onto the borrowed, long-sleeved shirt.

Yatey tied his gelding, Nickers, to the corral, opened his pocket knife and trimmed the extra-long hairs from his tail and forelock. Then he removed the sandwiches from his saddle bags along with the beef jerky, large bag of mixed nuts, and dried fruit chunks. He unrolled the tin foil and cut the sandwiches in half with his pocket knife.

Chet plucked the few hairs from the top of his sandwich and tossed them into the air. Stormy sat closer to the fire with some nuts and pieces of fruit cupped inside her palm. The young cowhand sat too close for comfort, so she paced back and forth in front of the flames.

"Working the cattle isn't going to take as long as I thought it would today," Ruston commented.

A slab of salami dropped from Yatey's bread. His collie snapped it up before he could bend down to get it. After taking a horn of water, he added, "There's no good time to lay this on you, Chet. As near as I can tell, you lost between half to two-thirds of your herd last year due to the fire and the bad algae in the pond. It's hard for me to quote you an exact number, but I'd say well over half. At least you still have most of your breeding bulls. Gotta have hope coming from somewhere."

Chet walked closer to Stormy. "You can take your mother's rig and head home now if you want to. Looks like you've had a miserable morning, and that's putting it mildly."

"You one of the new cowhands, Miss? I sure wouldn't mind ya stayin' on here for a spell with the rest of us least wise I could get to know ya better."

"Best get back over there by your boss, young man,

while I have a word with my wife."

He jumped to his feet and started to walk backward. "Wife! She never told me she was already hitched. I ain't that kind of a guy."

Chet raised his voice. "What are you up to now, Stormy? Were you encouraging that young man? You're almost old enough to be his mother!"

Keeping her volume in check, Stormy gritted her teeth and stood her ground. "You're trying to read something into a situation that was never there to be read. I merely offered to help him dry a calf which was rejected by its mother right after it was born. He paid me a nice compliment. At least he acted like he appreciated my efforts out here this morning. And speaking of being a mother, there's nothing in the world I want more than a child. Of all people, you should know that!"

She marched toward the portable panels, jerked Jantzi's clothing off the rails, and ran to her old pickup. Stormy drove five miles, turned the engine off in the middle of the dirt road, and cried until her eyes were swollen almost completely shut.

Stormy had no idea how much time had elapsed when she finally parked under the large Mahogany tree in the front yard of the Main Sabblonti Ranch house. An old white semi-truck hooked to an empty stock trailer drove in right behind her. The rancher's red, curly, overgrown hair stuck out the sides beneath his white hat. The tips of his cowboy boots scraped against one another as he walked toward Stormy. "Is this the Castins' Ranch by any chance? I sure hope so 'cause I'm gettin' low on gas."

Stormy laid the armful of semi-dry clothing on the hood

of Jantzi's pickup. "Are you looking for my husband, Chet?"

"Sure am! Sorry. I forgot to introduce myself. I'm Vaughn McJune. I've got a small ranch in Tranquility Falls County. Nothing compared to the Sabblonti spread, that's for sure. Looks like you've had another hard day's work. You guys calvin' somewhere on the ranch?"

She didn't extend her hand to shake his or answer his question, so he pulled his reddish-brown, leather wallet from his hip pocket and removed the creased check. "Can you give this to Chet? It's for some of his bulls that we struck a deal for a while back. He wanted his money up front, so here it is. Whereabouts would I find him this time of day?"

Stormy glanced down at the small box on the face of the check preceded by the $ sign. She'd not seen that amount of money in several months. "Yes, it's been a very busy calving season on the ranch. Just follow this road to the southwest, down past the lower ranch house and follow the creek northeast until you come to some corrals. You'll be able to see the cattle, corrals, and cowboys."

She unlocked the front door, walked across the threshold and locked it from the inside. Running up three flights of steep stairs, she showered and changed clothes as quickly as she could. Gliding down the bannister, she grabbed her purse and ran outside, jerking Jantzi's clothing off the hood onto the ground.

Stormy removed the orange blossom towel from her hair, turned the heater on full blast, and drove as fast as she could toward the main highway. Her dark hair flew in front of her eyes as she veered off the dirt road and back onto it several times. The ruby shade of lipstick she'd hurriedly applied while driving formed sawtooth peaks above her

189

upper lip. She entered the lobby of Cattlemen's Central in downtown Ridgemonte with seven minutes to spare.

Bank teller, Chara Tankton, surmised she'd seen just about everything there was to see during her fifteen years of steady employment at the bank. After Stormy brushed her hair back from her eyes, she finally recognized her. "Oh, my goodness, Stormy! That IS you. It didn't seem like the wind was blowing that hard when I took my afternoon break at 3:00. How may I help you today?"

"I've got a couple of deposits, Chara. We've been so busy calving on the big spread I've hardly had time to make it to town for our business errands. I'm sure that's a common complaint this time of year in cattle country."

Chara looked at the front of the check and turned it to the reverse side. "Yes, we do hear that a lot, but it's a good complaint as large calf crops mean lots of happy customers. This check is made payable to Chet Castins, but he's not endorsed it. Also, you said you had a couple of deposits? Do you have another check?"

Stormy dug around in the bottom of her purse looking for a pen. "He's running so late today and was so far out on the ranch when I finished helping that I completely forgot to have him do that. Since we've been married so long and the accounts are joint ones in both of our names, can you just go ahead and deposit it for us, so I won't have to make another trip into town? Silly me. I only have one deposit. What I meant to say is that I want to deposit some of this check into our operating account and open a brand-new account."

"Our manager, Stewart Sanders, left just a few minutes ago," explained Chara. "I think our assistant manager, Lonnie Browne, is still here. You remember Lonnie, don't you? It looks like he's just now locking the front door from the inside since it's a couple of minutes past six." Chara signaled to Lonnie that she needed him at the front counter.

Lonnie walked around the side and stopped to Chara's left. "Need some assistance?"

"I've got a non-endorsed check that she wants to deposit. Stewart's gone for the day." Before looking up, Lonnie scanned, *Payable to* CHET CASTINS. He strummed his fingers on the counter and turned the check over twice. Looking at Stormy he said, "I deem we can make an exception this one time since the family's had numerous accounts with us for decades."

"Thank you, Lonnie. I really appreciate it." He walked back into his office and closed the door.

Chara asked, "How much do you want to deposit into your operating account, Stormy?"

She added some figures on the back of a blank deposit slip, crossed them out, and continued to write some more numbers. "How about I deposit $39,000 into our operating account and $10,000 into the new account?"

"Lonnie's the only one still at work who can help you with that. Please come with me, so we can get that taken care of." She tapped on Lonnie's door who was playing hard of hearing, so she knocked louder as she waved the partially completed deposit slip. He opened the door. "I neglected to tell you that Stormy needs to open a new account."

He motioned for her to sit in the chair across from his desk. Stormy launched, "It's great to see you, Lonnie. Have you been busy at the bank? You've been the assistant manager for quite some time now, haven't you? Do you like what you do? I think it's important for people to enjoy their jobs, don't you?"

After Lonnie had selected the account number from the packets of *New Accounts* in his office drawer, he completed the general information he'd gleaned from Stormy's prior accounts. He directed, "Please sign on the bottom line where the black "x" mark is located. I'll make a copy. You can take this home, have Chet sign it, and mail it back to me in this pre-stamped envelope."

Stormy smiled with much satisfaction. "Oh, that won't be necessary, Lonnie. I'm going to be the only one signing the paper since this is my nursery account."

"Are you planting a fruit orchard on your property this spring?"

"No, Lonnie. It's not that kind of a nursery."

CHAPTER TWENTY-FIVE

Sarita had to close her eyes to avoid dizziness. The blue, ten-inch, plastic rectangle, a buttercup yellow, four-inch, plastic circle, a green, five-inch, plastic triangle and a red, seven-inch, plastic octagon floated above her head. She tried to relax as she laid back on the table in Exam Room No. 2 of the Evergreene Medical Clinic. Controlled breathing helped to calm her stomach. Wyn stood to her side, held her hand, and gently rubbed her forehead. "You are more precious to me than all the grains of desert sand."

Nurse Nancy Pritchurt stood poised with chart in hand as Dr. Merenspinn entered the room and washed his hands. "Great to see you, Morelands! And how are things at the ranch?"

Wyn sat in the grey arm chair against the wall, removed his cowboy hat and held it in his left hand. "Calves are popping out all over the place! I've hired a couple of extra hands and sure wish I had about five other Spence Woodson's. I don't know what I'd do without him right about now."

"Speaking of Spence," said Dr. Merenspinn, "I need to have him stop by my house some Sunday afternoon when he's in town. I need help with a couple of items. I've heard he's a pretty good handyman."

"Sure thing. I'll tell him. Does he know where you live?"

"I'll give you my address before you leave. Now, to the most important part of your day. Sarita, how've you been feeling?"

She mustered her best smile as she folded her arms across her chest. "No matter how much sleep I get, I still feel exhausted most of the time. I'm struggling emotionally because I feel like I'm letting Wyn down. I can't take care of the household duties, especially when he's gone from sun up to sun down this spring."

Dr. Merenspinn smiled. "There's no need to feel that way or pile guilt upon yourself. The most important thing is to take care of yourself, so your twins will be born healthy. There's a direct correlation between a calm, stress-free pregnancy and the initial health of a baby." He continued with his exam as Nurse Nancy made some notations on Sarita's patient chart.

Wyn paid far more attention to the calves being born within the past couple of weeks than he'd done in prior years. "Say, doctor, can you explain how our babies are developing? I mean, about how much would they weigh and all that good stuff?"

Removing his latex gloves and turning as he sat on the small stool, Dr. Merenspinn explained, "Let's take another look at Sarita's chart. Looks like you're at about nineteen weeks, so this is an important time for your twins' nervous systems. Nerve fibers are beginning to connect, and they are developing their senses of smell, taste, touch, hearing and vision. Your babies will know your smell right at birth just like a baby calf knows that of its own mother. The twins are about ten inches long each from head to toe."

Wyn set his cowboy hat on his knee and held up both hands about a foot apart. "So, about this long?"

The doctor smiled broadly. "Since there are two babies inside Sarita's womb, it starts getting crowded because they've grown so much." He looked into her eyes, "You might start feeling lots of pushing and pulling inside there sort of like they're jockeying for position.

"They'll have a very thick coating to protect their skin called the vernix caseosa. That's critical as it helps to protect them from the prolonged time immersed in the amniotic fluid and can also help protect them from infections that can be passed at birth. By the time of your next visit, their eyes will be fully formed even though they don't yet have color."

Wyn glanced at Sarita. "We've wondered if one of them would have one blue eye and one brown just like their mamma does."

"Time will tell on that one. It's certainly unique."

Nurse Nancy helped Sarita sit upright on the exam table and lay the large white protective covering over her. Wyn stood to his feet. "Any ideas where we can get some help during the daytime way out at the ranch house? With calving season and spring work in full swing, none of the neighbors could help even if they wanted to.

"Mama Merna's arm's out of the cast, but it's still pretty weak. She's not really even driving much right now. Debbie Drebner's been picking up supplies for her from the Merc when she makes a run to town. We were doing just fine until Francie Fletcher bunged up her back. Sounds like she'll be out of the saddle for a while."

Suddenly Nurse Nancy stopped writing and looked up. "Have you checked at the Tottale Temp Agency in town?

Surely there's someone who could use some extra money right now. The perfect person for the job would be Evan Briarley since he's a physical therapist, but you do need a woman for the job, don't you?"

Sarita laughed for the first time all day. "I would hope to shout we need a woman for the job! I've heard Evan's a great cook, but I much prefer a female inside the house with me. Nothing personal against Evan. I hope you understand that. Great idea on the agency though."

Nurse Nancy's longing sigh at the mention of Evan's name could be heard throughout the room. She closed her eyes and slumped into the empty chair.

Dr. Merenspinn met the Morelands at the front counter of his clinic after they'd made their next appointment. He handed a small white envelope to Wyn.

SPENCE

Driving to their next stop, Wyn and Sarita talked about who could possibly render some assistance to them, especially during the busy spring season in the ranching community. Sarita's blanched complexion was no match for the woman standing in line ahead of her and Wyn at Tottale's Temp Agency in downtown Ridgemonte.

The stranger turned half way around and smiled as her auburn brown, shoulder length, curly hair accentuated her flawless, bronzed, suntanned face. Large golden hoops dangled from both ears. The redwood, micro suede, ruffle vest highlighted her red and white, embroidered bohemian blouse along with the skinny leg, dark brown, knit denim leggings.

All Sarita could see were black and white spots in front of her eyes. Wyn whispered to her, "Would you like to sit in one of those chairs over yonder while I take care of this?" She reached for his hand. Before he could extend his forearm to help Sarita, her feet flew out from under her as she collapsed onto the buckskin colored, carpeted floor. The woman whirled around and bent down over her. Turning Sarita onto her back, she tapped her gently, and asked, "Are you okay? Can you hear me?"

"Yes, I can. I just feel so weak. Who are you?"

"I'm Blythe Bennetelli, but that can wait. Let me unbutton your coat." As she fanned Sarita with her employment application, Blythe continued, "Back up, folks, and give her some breathing room."

The man standing behind the counter yelled, "Move over to this next line, please. We're temporarily closing this one."

Wyn returned with a cup of water. Sarita tried to sit up, but Blythe stated, "Not so fast, dear. You need to lie still to allow blood to flow fully to your brain. Also, we don't want you fainting again in a short while."

Wyn and Blythe joined Sarita on the floor. Extending his hand, he introduced himself. "You need a job, Blythe? What kind of work are you looking for?"

"I can do most anything. I'm escaping a murky, fairy-tale life which I knew was too good to be true before I ever started it. I know pretty much the price of everything but the value of nothing."

"Are you running from the law? 'Cause if you are, I don't know why you'd be standing in this line looking like that."

"Looking like what?"

"All suntanned like you've been on a boat on the water for a full year or longer."

Blythe's shoulders relaxed as she checked Sarita's pulse. "84 beats per minute. Just stay still for a while longer, dear, and we'll help you to your feet."

Facing Wyn and flashing a smile, she explained, "I guess you could say I have a permanent suntan, courtesy of my employment. I've never been arrested for anything if that's what you're concerned about. I just ended a relationship with a man old enough to be my father who owned a fleet of yachts on the other side of the world."

Wyn gulped. *Yachts.* "How did you get from clear over there to clear over here?"

Blythe grinned slyly. "Let's put it this way. I didn't walk that far. How about you? I sure hope you can find a steady job since your wife's got a bun in the oven."

"I've got more than a steady job. It's beyond full at the moment."

Sarita moaned as she pulled on Wyn's sleeve. "Please help me up, so we can get out of here and go home."

Blythe and Wyn stood Sarita to her feet. She swayed back and forth then steadied herself. Wyn suggested, "How about we sit in those chairs in the front row?"

Covering Sarita with his wild rag and coat, Wyn asked Blythe, "Where are you living?"

"The Cresner Apartments for now."

Sarita commented, "We know exactly where they are. I lived there until Wyn and I got married last summer. How do you like them?"

"They're a far cry from what I'm used to, but beggars can't be choosers."

Carefully scrutinizing her elaborate clothing ensemble, accessories, and makeup one more time, Sarita opined, "You don't look like a beggar to me, not dressed like that. I really appreciate your help and kindness. It seemed like you instantly knew what to do when I fainted."

Blythe reached behind her ear to secure one of the golden earrings. "I wanted to get as far away from my former life as I possibly could. When I landed on American soil, I took a bus across the county and hitched a ride as high into the mountains as I could find. There's a real lure to the wild west country. I've studied wolves for years and am fascinated by them. There's sure to be some in this kind of topography.

"I landed in Ridgemonte with one suitcase and a few dollars to my name. Previously taking care of an eighty-seven-year-old man for many years requires some experience and expertise. That's my heavily condensed story. Now, what's yours?"

Wyn hinted, "I work on a ranch outside of town. Can I see your application?" He read it and handed it to Sarita.

Studying the line of few people in the room, Blythe commented, "Most people in this area must already have jobs if there are any to be had."

"There aren't that many people around here to start with," Wyn explained. "Not compared to big cities anyway.

If you're looking for lotsa folks, you best look elsewhere. According to what you wrote here, you were a personal assistant. You don't really go into much detail as far as the who and the what is concerned."

Blythe blushed, but it was not readily apparent. "As I previously told you, I was connected with an elderly man. I did whatever he needed done on any particular day which included a variety of things. Due to his age and health conditions, I also needed to know CPR, First Aid, and basic life skills." She glanced at the clock. "The agency closes in twenty minutes, so I'd better get my application turned in."

With Blythe waiting her turn at the counter, Wyn asked Sarita, "What's your opinion of Blythe? Do we dare take a chance on her?"

Sarita needed help buttoning her coat. "I'm so exhausted now I don't have an opinion, Wyn. You'll just have to do what you think is best. I trust your judgment."

Where are Tom and Merna when I need them the most? They took a chance on me once upon a time. Maybe it's time for me to take a chance on someone else who needs a chance.

Wyn and Sarita stood in the entryway of the building as they waited for Blythe to exit the agency. "Wait up, Blythe! We were standing in line because we're looking for someone to help us at the ranch house 'til the twins are born. Interested?"

She gasped. "Twins! They'll be a handful. What would the job require, and when would I start? What would it pay? I have no mode of transportation."

Wyn explained, "We need someone to stay with Sarita during the day as she's confined to bed rest. The job would require you to cook meals, clean house, do laundry, and those general sorts of things. Nothing too demanding. It pays minimum wage, meals, and a nice, comfy guest bedroom. Not to mention quiet, country living. Since you don't have a car, maybe we could ask Mama Merna if she'd let you drive her pickup. You can start in the morning if that works for you. I can give you a lift from your apartment out to the ranch."

"Truth be known, I can't really afford that apartment much longer. I'd be willing to give it a try. My name means 'Joy & Happiness,' so maybe I can paint some of that onto your picture."

Returning home after a long afternoon, Wyn opened a can of stew to which he added a can of peas and placed it on top of the stove to warm. Sarita laid on the couch and covered herself with another one of her Grammy Mabel Siddonz's hand-sewn quilts.

She was just dozing off to sleep when Wyn exclaimed, "Well, it's about time! Sarita, I've got to get ahold of Chet right away. There's a front-page colored picture in this week's issue of *The Ridgemonte Rider*. That big furniture store in Cinder Valley burned to the ground last week. Sad to say it was arson. You'll never guess who's being rung up on the charges along with two other guys. They broke into it after dark, poured gas onto the furniture, and watched it burn. Shane nearly got away, but one of his partners in crime turned him into the police.

"When he worked at the Toppens Ranch, Shane always did have a chip on his shoulder regarding people who had more than he did. I still think he was the one who set fire to the Sabblonti Ranch using Spence's muffler that Priscilla made for him. He probably thought he was starting a fire on the Toppens Ranch just out of spite. How could he even think of doing something like that, especially to Tom and Merna who'd always been so kind to him? I guess the only satisfaction Chet will get out of the deal is knowing Shane will spend time behind bars."

After eating supper and cleaning the kitchen, Wyn placed a call to the Lower Sabblonti Ranch House to talk with Chet. Sarita listened sympathetically to Wyn's side of the conversation as he read the in-depth newspaper article to Chet.

"So, there you have it, pardner! I realize this won't help you and Stormy recoup your lost cattle, but hopefully justice will be served and Shane will learn from his mistakes."

CHAPTER TWENTY-SIX

Nelson Merrill carried the last load of the split wood into their large barn as Marita swept the hay leaves into the large dustpan. Placing his arm around her waist, they surveyed their surroundings with much satisfaction.

"Don't rightly know why I'm bothering to build a fire in the wood stove in the corner since there'll be enough hot air inside here to lift the barn from it's foundation!"

"Now, Nelson, don't be so dramatic. Surely by my having cooked twice as much Merrill beef as usual, that'll help to sooth everyone's frayed nerves. Not to mention the sheepherder coffee by the gallons to go with my famous, frosted, five-inch cinnamon rolls."

Ranchers from all six surrounding counties as well as some from the far northeastern part of the state arrived in droves. Word of the recent wolf kill had spread like a summer wildfire throughout the region.

Striking the bottom of an old kettle with a hammer, Nelson bellowed for everyone to pipe down. "Thanks for showing up today to get this wolf showdown on its way. First of all, I want to thank my beautiful bride, Marita, and her culinary crew, for makin' all the fixins for us today. It's hard to make important decisions on an empty stomach. Leastwise, that's how I tend to look at it. Hustle on through the chow line, then let's get down to business."

Dr. Shaw was the last one through the line by design. He and Nelson had put forth their best efforts to script the situation in the allotted time frame. Dr. Shaw had drawn the short straw, allowing him the privilege of presenting the main speaker for the gathering.

"I'd like to introduce Mr. Roscoe Rhineback, the Wolf Program Coordinator for the Fish and Wildlife Service of our state."

"Thanks, Dr. Shaw," Roscoe said. His curly blonde hair fell across his face afer he removed his hat. He swept it to the side. "I didn't expect quite this large of a crowd. I'm sure it's because of the delicious spread we've just consumed.

"I want to start with a bit of background if I may. After decades of hunting and trapping nearly made wolves extinct in the upper midwest along with the western part of our country, they were reintroduced into certain areas. They were a protected species in this state until 1995.

"After they were delisted, the FWS took over general management. Then things went crazy in the federal court system, sort of like a ping-pong game where part of the time the state was in control, and the rest of the time the federal government was in control which it still is as of this date.

"In addition, when an area experiences a prolonged drought such as you've had, the predators drop down to a lower elevation. If there's a scarcity of deer and elk, they'll go after whatever they can find."

Wilbur Drebner stood to his feet. "Sorry to interrupt you, Roscoe, but you're not telling us anything we don't already know. What I do want you to tell me is how to get to the point to where we don't have to worry about getting strung up if we shoot or trap the wolves killin' our cattle, horses, dogs, and whatever else they can find."

It took a few minutes to restore order after those in attendance echoed Wilbur's sentiments.

Roscoe resumed, "While I understand your frustration, it's important to keep in mind that as long as wolves are on the endangered species list, they can only be killed in defense of human life. During the years that the state was in control, our agency killed a record number of wolves which corresponded with the record number of livestock killed."

Rees Broomfield countered, "That still doesn't solve our problem. One cow, calf, horse, or stock dog is one too many. In the past, way too many wolves were allowed in areas where our cattle graze, especially in the high country. You guys seem to think that you don't need to get rid of any wolves until you see dead carcasses on the ground.

"The last time we went through this, some lawyer told us to string electric fences to protect our cattle. There's no power within a hundred miles of some of those places. What were we supposed to do? Plug the fencing into a wild currant bush out there or something?"

Volcanic laughter erupted throughout the barn and continued for several minutes.

Nelson asked, "Say, Roscoe, what about compensation for the cattle I've already lost this spring due to wolf kill? Also, if they eat the unborn fetus, can we collect double for the cow and calf?"

"That's a great question, Nelson. Ranchers are allowed compensation for livestock killed if they take pictures of their dead animals and send them to us. I can't guarantee how long it will take to get a check or how much it will be. You know the old saying, the check's in the mail . . ."

Laughter could be heard nowhere.

"Now you tell me. Like I carry a camera with me everywhere I go."

"Put it in your saddlebag or wrap it around your neck," suggested Wilbur.

Samuel Stixon, brood mare farm owner, decided to offer his two cents worth, "Keep in mind that some of these left wing nut groups of people think it's fair game for the ranchers to get compensated for their losses, but no wolves should be killed or removed just because they keep on killing. After all, they say, isn't that what wolves were born to do?"

Rees was back again, "Well, a check sure can't replace a calf or a cow, much less all the work it took to raise them and maintain our ranches. If a herd senses predators in the area, the cows start to lose weight. Even the bulls don't express as much interest in them. They're as edgy as the cows and none of 'em can settle down to graze or do what they do best. Since wolves follow deer and elk, maybe the FWS should concentrate on increasing that population in the high country."

"Speaking of elk," Roscoe resumed, "I've heard of an instance where a pack of gray wolves walked through a herd of over 100 elk, dropped to a lower elevation, and took after the cattle, most of which were heifers."

Nelson approached the front of the barn and stood next to Roscoe. "Let's wrap this up. You're welcome to stay as long as you like to talk to individual ranchers. We must join together to battle this wolf problem. We can't just shrug our shoulders, walk away, and have the attitude that it's part of life and doing business in the high country. That's not going to cut the mustard nor save our herds."

"Nelson, I want to thank you and your wife for your hospitality," Roscoe said. "Remain vigilant and make sure to substantiate your losses with pictures. Also, keep your group together to help one another, and stay on the good side of your state legislators."

Wilbur turned to Rees and said, "Didn't I tell you this would be a sheer waste of time and effort? What a joke! I think that character needs to get some of those curls trimmed from the top of his head. He might want to find a different job while he's at it."

Yatey offered up some humor to release the stifling air from the barn. "Say Wilbur, did you hear the one about the two ranchers?"

"Can't quite recollect if I have."

"Two ranchers were bragging. One says, 'It takes three days to drive across my ranch.' The other rancher says, 'I used to have a pickup like that too.'"

Wilbur slapped his thigh twice. "Good one, Yatey."

As Roscoe started placing his paperwork inside his zippered briefcase, he turned to his right and noticed someone fully smiling as her auburn brown, shoulder length, curly hair accentuated her flawless, bronzed, suntanned face. Large diamond hoops dangled from both ears. The forest green vest highlighted her light green turtleneck along with the black, boot cut, denim jeans.

Blythe spoke in a hushed tone, "I've always wanted to look a real-life wolf in his eyes. That's one of the main reasons I'm here right now. Besides that, something's got to be done to preserve all of these creatures in the wild that were here before some cowpoke decided he wanted to plunk his cattle on the same land. If I close my eyes, I can hear the animals scream if their pelts are used for coats for women.

"You just might be the guy who could help with all that. Not to mention some other things. Maybe you and I could go for a drive on the weekend when you're not working your regular shift and look for wolves."

Flinching after catching the flesh of two of his fingers inside the zipper, Roscoe replied, "So sorry. None of that is within the confines of my work description. Now if you'll please excuse me, I've got to get going to my next speaking engagement."

Nelson and Wyn spotted Blythe following Roscoe to his white, mud-splattered, 4-wheel drive FWS pickup. Wyn ran after her. Nelson rescued him in the nick of time as he confronted Blythe, "Aren't you supposed to be at my home taking care of my wife?"

"She was resting comfortably when I decided I needed to take a little break. After all, it's not every day that I get to hear about wolves which is one of my keen interests."

Wyn advised, "I think it might be wise for you to prioritize your interests."

CHAPTER TWENTY-SEVEN

Jodell's Jewelers located in downtown Cinder Valley, Ignee County, always rose to the occasion to produce the rarest of gems or the most sterling jewelry creations when needed. Dr. Shaw's assistant, Jacobe Davone, had never transported something quite this costly although he hoped to someday in the near future.

Nurse Dawn Rowann tried to shed a tinge of guilt when unlocking the front door of Macey Meadows' rental at 812 Flame Street, Ridgemonte. While there was a part of Dawn's personality which liked to assist with covert operations, she would offer a full-on apology later in the evening.

Fellow Nurse Caroline Crutchens dutifully reported for work at Mintner Medical Center feigning greater symptoms of a migraine as her daytime shift progressed.

Jacobe entered the parking lot of Mintner at precisely 2:50 p.m. to release the air from the front driver's side tire of Macey Meadows' vehicle.

Her father, Doug Meadows, had never been assigned to a decorating committee in his entire life; however, he'd inflated many a balloon when working for a theme park during his teenage years. Emmy, Macey's long-haired white cat, sporting a green-jeweled collar, was having a blast batting them throughout the house.

Charge Nurse Joyce Stone proved she could do far more than manage an entire hospital floor as she walked throughout Macey's house delegating and distributing red tote boxes loaded with everything needed to temporarily transform it.

Marita Merrill, along with her country catering crew, arrived with soup kettles filled to the brim with: Irish Hearty Beef Stew, Dublin Coddle, baskets of Brown Soda Bread and Irish-Style Scones; quart jars of pickled asparagus and garlic dill pickles; bowls of angel food cake; whipped cream; strawberry cake; and her jelly roll pans of chocolate-pecan frosted buttermilk brownies. After all, one couldn't pay some ranchers to even look at angel food cake which they described as eating stale air.

Dr. Shaw answered the anticipated telephone call at the front desk of his building.

"Shaw Vet Clinic."

"Benny, can you come help me?" wailed Macey. "I just discovered I have a flat tire. I need to drive Caroline home in her car. She's struggled through an intense migraine all day. Or maybe you could send Jacobe to help us, please."

"Jacobe's already flown the coop for the day. I guess I could close up shop a little early. I thought you just bought new tires for your car a short while ago."

"I did. I think the tire shop sold me a lemon or re-tread."

"I've got a portable air compressor on the back of my truck. I'll meet you as soon as I can at Mintner."

After inflating the tire, time was of the essence for Dr. Shaw. Distracted as he emerged from the Men's Restroom inside the hospital lobby and running to his truck, he plowed into a woman causing the papers in her hand to fly everywhere.

"Excuse, me. I'm a bit preoccupied and didn't even see you."

"Not a problem. I'm new in town and needing weekend work. Do you have any ideas where else I might look?"

Dr. Shaw tuned out the conversation. The woman seized his right arm which caused him to jump backward.

"Please don't touch me. I don't even know you."

"I've always had a thing for handsome men with a chiseled chin and inviting grin."

She removed her oversized, oval sun glasses, parted her full lips, flipped her auburn, curly hair to the back, and poured on her charm.

"Allow me to officially introduce myself. I'm Blythe Bennetelli and am employed part-time for the Morelands. That job is beyond a drag which requires way too much physical labor, especially for some backward western hicks. Gifted with attributes such as I have, one shouldn't have to work quite so hard all week long. I'm looking for a cushy desk job or something with a lighter shift."

Dr. Shaw fumed, "You don't deserve the job at the Morelands! They are some of the finest people one could ever hope to meet."

Macey's blood pressure skyrocketed when driving Caroline's car into the parking lot just in time to see a strange woman pounding on Dr. Shaw's driver's side window. Blythe blew him a kiss in the wind before walking toward her car. She turned around, crossed her arms and held them close to her chest, then extended her hands in the air as if to say, "This hug's for you."

"Can this day finally be over?" Macey screamed.

Before he could emerge from his truck cab, Macey also pounded on the driver's side window.

Pressing the side button to automatically lower it, and before Dr. Shaw could mount his defense, Macey glared at him.

"Would you mind explaining what's going on here? Who's she? And why are you all dressed up in those nice clothes? I've never known you to look like that before evening. Here I thought I could trust you."

Racing to get back into Caroline's car, Macey drove straight to The Shadowy Merc. She grabbed a small, plastic shopping cart just inside the front door and headed for the frozen food's aisle. Filling the basket with a family-sized supreme pizza, three quarts of Cherry Chocolate Sundae ice cream, salted peanuts, and Carmel sauce, she headed straight for the counter.

Checker Cannaleah inquired, "Are you having a party tonight, Macey?"

"Not on your life! This is for me, and I'll probably end up eating all of it over the weekend."

Cannaleah handed the sales receipt to Macey, and asked, "Rough day at Mintner?"

"Outside, not inside."

"Outside? What's going on outside?"

Macey fought back her tears. "I wish I knew."

"Hope you find out."

"Who needs men anyway?"

"Well, I'd sure like one!" Cannaleah exclaimed. "I've been looking for a very long time."

Five blocks from her house, Macey remembered her car

was still back at Mintner Medical Center. She turned around, drove there, parked Caroline's car on the east side of the building in a secured area, then headed for home.

Crying more than she thought possible, she lowered the visor and looked in the mirror. Her tri-colored, brown eye makeup mixed with her green eye-liner and tousled hair made for quite the sight.

I knew I should not have let my guard down and trusted some country veterinarian. No wonder Sarita Sabblonti Moreland never gave him the time of day. All that song and dance he tried to sell me about never dating anyone in college and waiting for the right woman to come along.

How could I have been so naïve and stupid? It's a good thing my parents have never met him. How could a college-educated nurse be so desperate? Something isn't always better than nothing. Wait until I tell Caroline all about this fiasco! Thank God it's Friday night, and I don't have to face humanity until 7:00 Monday morning.

Macey fumbled the key inside the lock of her front door as she jostled the melting ice cream inside the grocery bag. A blast of an unfamiliar pleasant aroma and a chorus of "Surprise!" greeted her as she entered. Startled, she ran straight into her daddy's arms. "What are you doing here? Where's Mom?"

Sherry emerged from the living room where she'd been mothering Sarita. Tears saturated both parents' shoulders as Macey couldn't control hers.

Dawn had given Caroline a ride to Macey's house. Both nurses quickly offered to help Macey. "Let's get you looking presentable, and we can explain everything."

Emerging from her bedroom in a lovely, buttercup

yellow and blue, ankle-length dress and a fresh makeover courtesy of Dawn, Macey mustered courage to face her guests.

Dr. Shaw was the last to arrive. He felt the temperature drop thirty degrees when he entered the house. He tried to make eye contact with Macey and followed her around for a few minutes, but she was doing her level best to ignore him in every way possible.

He whispered to her, "Can I talk to you privately in your guest bedroom for a couple of minutes, please?"

"There's no way I'm going back there with you. If you want to talk to me, you can wait until everybody leaves tonight. Then I might give you ten minutes max inside the kitchen. Nothing beyond that."

"I can explain everything, and I really need to talk with you BEFORE everyone leaves tonight. Trust me when I tell you this."

"I'm finished with trying to trust you."

Dr. Shaw located Doug Meadows in the back yard. They lighted the propane fireplace accented with colored stones. Shades of aquamarine and emerald green danced in the spring mountain air. Macey glanced out her kitchen window. Both men were laughing and acting like they'd known each other for years. Doug had his arm draped around Dr. Shaw's back as both of them were nodding their heads up and down.

It was sitting and standing room only inside Macey's house and in the back yard. There were enough parked cars and pickup trucks lining three and four streets from her house to fill a used car lot.

The recent showers left the air refreshingly clean and the

evening dew sparkled on the perennial foliage and bushes. Robins had arrived earlier than usual to start making their nests. When the sun set, everyone moved their chairs closer to the firepit. Venus could be observed just above the horizon if one took the time to look.

There was no more of a consummate hostess than Marita Merrill. Whether she had ten cents or ten million dollars, she had the unique ability to make everyone feel welcome, loved, and valued. Ridgemonte residents had been the recipients of her culinary heritage for decades.

Macey's manners shone brightly throughout the evening despite her set-to with Dr. Shaw in the Mintner parking lot. Late in the evening, as everyone visited around the fire and with Emmy in both arms, Macey made the rounds to profusely thank her parents, Doug and Sherry Meadows, the Merrills, Morelands, Drebners, Broomfields, Stixons, Dawsons, Merna Toppens, Dr. Merenspinn, Nancy Pritchurt, Spence Woodson, Fenn Bridgemore, Priscilla Fletcher, Francie Fletcher, Preacher Len and Lizzelle Longbowe, Jacobe Davone, Chet Castins, Evan Briarley, her fellow co-workers, and finally Dr. Shaw.

Just as she approached him, Emmy jumped from her arms into his. He stroked her fur along with her jeweled collar. She licked his face and purred contently. Macey was sore displeased with Emmy at the moment. *Perhaps she can tell that he's been around other animals.*

There had already been enough dessert served, but Joyce Stone had all who were present, on que, sing the traditional birthday song as Evan marched in with a sheet cake he'd baked for the occasion, complete with firecracker candles spitting in the air.

He'd placed some of the unlit firecrackers in his hair. A classic Evan maneuver! Nancy memorized his every move. *When should I make my next one?*

Macey opened her gifts with "oohs and aah's" from the females in attendance as Lizzelle and Priscilla served freshly brewed cowboy coffee on serving trays.

Not wanting to be rude, but due to sheer exhaustion, Macey secretly hoped her surprise party would wind down soon. Wyn and Sarita distracted her with legitimate questions concerning the birth of twins. Part of her wanted to say, "Your doctor's right over there. Go ask him!"

Dr. Merenspinn was heavily engrossed in a hushed conversation with Spence Woodson.

With her back to him, Dr. Shaw crept behind Macey and tapped her shoulder. When she didn't stand up or turn around, he walked in front of her.

The Morelands excused themselves as he bent down on his knee. Extending his hand, he waited for her acceptance.

Macey bit her lower lip as a large, pear-shaped tear dropped onto the front of her dress.

Doug and Sherry Meadows suddenly stood behind their daughter and placed their hands on her shoulders.

Nancy Pritchurt envisioned she was in a movie scene. She nearly lost her balance and toppled forward into the crowd.

Macey locked eyes with Dr. Shaw. Her heart overruled her vocal cords momentarily.

"Macey, will you do me the distinct honor of becoming my wife?"

Squealing and jumping to her feet, she knocked Dr. Shaw off balance. Jacobe and Evan helped him stand up.

Before she could utter a word, he gently grasped her left hand.

"Yes, Benny, I will!"

An immediate, questionable *Benny* echo could be heard throughout the back yard. Emerging from the shadows, which was part of the ongoing plan for the evening, Sable Shaw queried her husband, Rayford, "Did she just call him *Benny*? Since when did that begin? Good golly, he must be in love!"

"Love has a way of doing strange things, even tagging people with their unique terms of endearment," Rayford assured his bride. "Let's officially join the party, shall we, now that the surprise has been flawlessly executed?"

Dr. Shaw slid the stunning, white gold engagement ring, showcasing a dark green emerald surrounded by six clear cut diamonds, onto Macey's ring finger.

"It's beautiful! And you know how much I wanted a real emerald." She jumped into his arms, nearly knocking him to the ground a second time.

The gathering didn't officially wind down until after midnight. Some folks, such as the Morelands, headed home early. The party hearty crew made the most of it. The Shaws and Meadows couldn't be happier as Sherry and Sable sat in a secluded corner of the living room and shifted into full-on wedding planning mode.

Francie's back spasms got the best of her after several hours, so she asked if she could join them. When she couldn't stand their giddiness and joy any longer, she demanded, "You've never met before this evening. How can you be so elated over an upcoming marriage when you don't even know each other that well? What if your son or daughter isn't good enough for each other?"

Sable snapped back, "Do you presume to know what we're thinking? I've spent more hours on the phone long distance with my son since he met Macey than I have in years. I've made every effort to be a sounding board and support him."

Sherry confirmed, "I couldn't agree more. As parents, we always rise to the occasion for our children, especially when it's one of the most important days of their lives. Are your children unmarried? Is that why your teeth are set on edge?"

Francie retreated to the kitchen. Dr. Merenspinn soon joined her. They chatted briefly as he rinsed their drinking glasses in the sink.

Chet and Evan closed the front door behind them. Walking a few steps past the house, Chet caught a glimpse from the living room window of Dr. Shaw tenderly kissing Macey.

"Check that out Evan! Just think, that could be you and Nancy if you'd give her a chance. Did you see the way she was scoping you out during the evening? Looked to me like Macey wasn't the only one who'd gotten a makeover before the party started. Just sayin'."

"Wasn't looking, Chet. I had to keep the birthday cake and fire crackers corralled."

Chet's driving restriction had been recently lifted by Dr. Merenspinn the middle of March, so he'd been chauffeuring Evan around for a few weeks until his ribs fully healed. He fell asleep and snored all the way home to the Lower Sabblonti Ranch House.

Several scenes from earlier in the evening replayed in

Chet's mind as he fought sleep while trying to drive. His auto accident flashed in front of him. His yellow pickup was virtually crawling by the time he entered the driveway.

The house was pitch black when Evan walked in first and flipped the light switch on. Still groggy from sleeping all the way home, he headed straight for his guest bedroom and closed the door.

Chet decided to make a cup of strong, early morning coffee. Sometimes a person just needed to sit and think for a spell when it was quiet enough to do so. He removed his boots using the boot jack, slumped onto the couch, and placed his stocking feet on the coffee table. He couldn't hear the floor creaking above Evan's snoring.

Suddenly, he felt fingers gently gripping his shoulders. Spooked, he jumped up, and whirled around, half-way expecting to see a silhouette of The Black Raven with her black and white streaked hair.

Stormy held her index finger over his mouth signaling silence.

Chet whispered, "How'd you get in here? What are you doing? Don't you know what time it is?"

"I do have a key, remember? I lived here with you for over nine years. For the record, it's no longer night. It's early morning. What was the big shindig in town tonight?" asked Stormy.

"How'd you know we were in town?"

"I followed you into Ridgemonte earlier this afternoon and sat for a very long time in Mother's old pickup parked down the street from Macey's house. When I saw you and Evan leave, then headed I headed back down to the Lower Sabblonti Ranch house. I'm surprised you didn't see my taillights in front of you."

Chet returned to the couch. "My mind was drifting all over the place when I drove back here tonight. I tried to tune out Evan's snoring which sounds like a goose honking. You asked about Macey Meadows' birthday and engagement party. It was a lot of fun."

She walked in front of him and knelt down. "Speaking of fun, I'd sure like to have some."

Stormy freed the clasp on the front of her knee-length beaver coat and let it fall to the floor.

"Where are Beebe 'n Blue?" Chet asked.

"I put them down in the barn for the night. They weren't real happy with me, but I'm here to make you happy."

Chet kept things in check. "Stormy, a lot has happened over the past year and a half. We need to transition slowly into where we were before my bad accident."

"I know, but we've got to get back on track sometime, so why not tonight?"

Water could be heard running down the hallway. Evan thought he heard hushed voices. He peeked into the living room as Chet secured the snap on Stormy's coat.

"Good night, darlin'. Safe travels. Sleep tight."

CHAPTER TWENTY-EIGHT

Tom Toppens' absence loomed large as spring tasks mounted on the surrounding cattle ranges. Wyn and Spence met themselves coming and going with the additional layers of fatherhood and husbandry.

With Merna's arm finally being out of the cast and the most recent x-rays revealing total healing, she walked inside and outside her quiet abode in search of extra comfort for her aching heart.

Dr. Shaw found her bent over her dark brown, wooden barrels in her back yard speaking tenderly to her plants. "Oh, little Sky-Pilots with your delicate purple leaves and yellow anthems, I welcome you to my flower garden along with newcomers Pink Chainpod and cute Yellow Butter and Eggs."

He couldn't help himself, "Butter and eggs? Well, of course butter and eggs are yellow!"

Merna laughed out loud for the first time in weeks. "I'd know that voice anywhere! You're just in time for dinner. Please come inside. Did Wyn or one of the ranch hands call for an appointment? I hope everything's alright with the herd."

"I didn't intentionally plan on arriving at high noon, but

my timing couldn't be better. As far as I know, all is well with your herd. Please forgive me for not checking on you after Tom passed away.

"I'd love some dinner. Jacobe's been heating up canned chili on the stove and burritos in the microwave in the back of my clinic for days now, so I could sure use a change of pace. We've completely run out of salsa in the fridge."

Merna foraged around in her freezer for some palatable leftovers. "With one arm being in a cast for weeks and no one to cook for except myself, I don't have my normal offerings to serve you. I'll heat up this leftover barbeque beef brisket and fix some mashed potatoes to go with it. My beloved Tom would never stand for these instant ones that take five minutes to prepare on the stovetop. He always preferred the real McCoy."

Instinctively wanting to jump up and help her, Dr. Shaw refrained. "I notice you're still using your left arm to do most things such as close the oven door. Now that your arm is out of the cast, make sure to start using it again since it's your dominant one."

He listened as she reminisced about the early days of her marriage to Tom and them getting the Toppens Ranch developed. Dr. Shaw glanced at the clock, not realizing so much time had elapsed. "I have a confession to make."

Waving her right hand back and forth, Merna said, "If this is something to do with your engagement to Macey, you should be talking to someone else. I can help with all sorts of things, but that would definitely be out of bounds for me."

"I guess that did sound a bit ominous, didn't it? Truthfully speaking, I'm paying you a visit regarding Blythe Bennetelli, Moreland's daytime employee. I had a strange, unfortunate incident with her."

Setting her fork down, folding her arms at the elbows, and lacing her fingers together, Merna spoke carefully, "Is this what you mean by a confession?"

"Poor choice of words on my part. What I meant by confession is there was an ulterior motive to my stopping by to see you today. The afternoon of Macey's surprise birthday party and our engagement party, Blythe apparently stopped by the hospital to get an application for part-time employment for the weekends. She jumped me in the parking lot and was way too friendly for my liking. It would be an outright duel to see who's more brazen ~~~ her or Salina Bevvins."

A cup of piping hot coffee accompanied with a warm slice of apple pie garnished with a slab of sharp cheddar cheese appeared in front of Dr. Shaw.

"What's with this Salina Bevvins anyway?" asked Merna. "Anytime I've ever purchased groceries at The Shadowy Merc in Ridgemonte, she's been very courteous and cordial. She does seem to ask a lot of questions, however. I just thought it was because she expressed an interest in wanting a part-time job on the weekends learning how to ride the range."

"Salina? Weekends? Riding the range? You're kidding, right?

"No, I'm not. She asked if we had any job openings, and I told her to check with Wyn as he was running our outfit now."

"Speaking of job openings, I deem Blythe should get onto her next one. The day she tried to force herself on me in the hospital parking lot, she complained about the job at the Morelands as requiring too much labor, especially for backward, western hicks. I wasted no time in telling her she didn't deserve the job."

Having been born and raised in cattle country, Merna asked, "Well, what did she think the job was going to entail? Sitting on a couch, watching soap operas, eating hand-dipped chocolates, and painting her nails? What on earth did she do for a job before she arrived in Ridgemonte?"

Dr. Shaw carefully slid his bottom teeth across his upper lip. "Uh, let's just say, she was a caretaker."

"Caretaker? Well, that's exactly what the Morelands need temporarily, isn't it? So, what's the big deal?"

Chuckling, he replied, "Blythe was a caretaker for an eighty-seven-year-old man who owned a fleet of yachts on the other side of the world."

Resting her arms on her lavender-checkered apron, Merna pursed her lips, "I'd imagine taking care of one yacht would be exhausting much less a whole fleet of them. Well, what shall we do now?" Holding her chin in both hands, Merna exclaimed, "Now I get it! When shall I report for work?"

"I'll round up Wyn and have him stop by later this afternoon if he can. I guess you could say I needed to find the solution before presenting the problem to him. What might be best is if you could plan to stay with them during the weekdays to help out. I'm sure they'd love that, Grandma."

Merna erupted, "Grandma! Oh my, that word brings such joy and healing to my heart." She stepped onto the porch to grab a small cardboard box. Following Dr. Shaw to his truck, she handed it to him.

He peered into the container. "Oh, you do know how to spoil and mother all of us, don't you? What do we have here?"

Merna smiled with such satisfaction. "You said you needed salsa. I put extra onions, cilantro, and jalapenos in this batch, so have Jacobe buy more chips."

"One last thing, Merna. Check the jockey box to make sure everything's there when Blythe returns your pickup and the set of keys. She's a sly one, so we've got to keep an eye on her until she moves elsewhere. Salina Bevvins might pose a larger problem, especially since she has relatives who live in the area.

"I've been giving a lot of thought to this geographic region. It seems like it's a haven for seductive, seducing spirits whether they be in human or animal form. That's why all of us must band together to protect our community from the effects. We've got to keep the predators at bay. Better yet, run them off!"

"You've got good insight, Dr. Shaw. You won't get any disagreement from me on what you've just proposed."

S

Blitz, Chet's aged gelding, took his own sweet time getting to the high country. Yatey, Ruston, and a few other cowhands were driving what was left of the Sabblonti herd to the meadows in the top northwestern part of the vast ranch.

Yatey glassed the fence line just below the jagged mountain range. "Say, boss, looks like we better get a crew up yonder right away. There're some big gaps where the cattle could escape or predators could enter. Got to preserve what we got left. That rancher meeting at Merrill's was a waste of my time. Don't quite know how you felt about it. If I owned a herd, I'd be pretty discouraged right 'bout now."

"Couldn't agree more. I know you've been goin' seven days a week from dawn 'til dusk. Are those new ranch hands pullin' their weight?"

Yatey dismounted to cinch up his saddle on Nickers and adjust the stirrups. He offered his mount the uncored half of his apple. "Yeah, for the most part. A couple of them are still tryin' to get the hang of weanin' the calves from their mamas and movin' them from meadow to meadow. Sure enough, there's one they missed."

Chet pulled his cowboy hat down on his forehead as he squinted in the afternoon sun. "Did Ruston get a new horse? What happened to his old one? Surely he didn't get conned into buying a mare or did he? Leastwise, that horse he's on sure walks like one."

"You're seeing things, Chet. Ruston's had the same horse for over eight years. He can't even afford a new pair of boots much less a new horse. After more than enough lessons, he's finally learned how to shoe his the right way. I thought I'd never get him to figure that out.

"I won't let him near Nickers. He always wanted to hammer the nails in the wrong angle and didn't wait long enough for the horseshoes to heat up before trying to shape them. Nice kid. Just a little concrete between his ears, that's all."

Blitz whinnied to greet the newcomer. Nickers even got into the act while Yatey led him to the reservoir to get a long drink.

Chet whistled loudly. *Wheeee – Whewww!* "I can't quite believe my eyes! You really weren't joking, were you?"

Blitz butted Chet's backside repeatedly as he leaned into Diamante, Jantzi Belle's old mare. As of late, they'd been stablemates at the Lower Sabblonti Ranch house.

Stormy loosened her stampede strings, lifted her hat, and let her long, dark hair fall to her shoulders. She waited for Chet's blast regarding her mother's old ranch clothing, but none came forth. Slowly shifting her weight to her left side, she swung her right leg over Diamante's back, jumped to the ground, and opened one of her leather saddle bags.

"I'm impressed," said Chet. "Pretty long ride all in one stretch. How'd you manage that?"

"I've been practicing a lot. Now that Evan's moved on and is working for the Hearts & Hands 2 Help Home Care, and you leave the lower ranch house early every morning, Diamante and I've taken short rides most days to get my body in shape. I told you I was serious about helping you on the range. Is this proof enough?"

She handed him a foot-long sandwich wrapped in tin foil and a piece of beef jerky.

Chet smiled slowly. "I'd say you're getting closer."

"Closer to what?"

"To where we left off before your mother fell to her demise and most everything came off the rails."

Stormy pulled Diamante's reigns over her head and held them tightly as she sat cross-legged on the ground. "Shall we sit for a bit?"

Chet shook his head back and forth. "Still can't sit that low on the ground. My leg starts talkin' to me then."

She leaned backwards on both elbows, stretched her legs out, and crossed them as she flipped the ends of the reigns back and forth on her knees. "Sorry, I totally forgot about that. I could help you with some leg stretches if you'd like to stop by the Main house sometime or I could always head your direction after the sun goes down."

"I don't think we're quite there yet, but keep up the good work. I've just got to make sure in my heart and mind that the leopard has changed its spots."

Stormy looked around. "I don't see any leopards. I thought all you had to contend with up here were bobcats, cougars, coyotes, and wolves."

Shaking his head, Chet stated, "Rethink what I said, Stormy. If a leopard changed its spots, would it still be a leopard? Of course not! When you prove to me that you can consistently be the same woman you were before your mother died, then a whole lot of things will start happenin' around here, and fast!" He held his inviting smile just a little longer than usual this time.

She envisioned duct tape over her mouth which she'd also been practicing in the mirror, mirror on the wall, but it just didn't stick. "I watched a calf nursing from its mother as I rode up here this afternoon. I've hinted several times now that I'd like to try having some more kids since we've suffered three miscarriages during our marriage."

Chet helped her stand to her feet. "I know what you want, and there's a way for you to get what you want."

CHAPTER TWENTY-NINE

Almost the first half of 2001 was in the ranching record books. Evergreene Medical Clinic in Ridgemonte was busting at the seams with third and fourth generation ranching families having young ones of their own. Some of the regulars such as Evan didn't quite cotton to having to wait quite so long for an appointment. Monday mornings seemed to be some of the worst. It was standing room only at 10:45 a.m. on June 18th.

An elderly patient struggled to stand at the counter longer than necessary disputing the amount of his charges. The vacationing clerk added nothing to the solution. Francie Fletcher, the fill-in clerk, attempted her explanation one more time, "We've billed your insurance company twice, but they seem to be awfully slow. Perhaps you should contact them."

"You're the only one that's slow. I watched you try to add a column of figures on that adding machine over there. I could do a better job of it myself even if I was blindfolded! Of course, you know what they say about left-handed folks, especially women. Their brains operate backwards. Maybe you should make your own appointment with Merenspinn or find a different job. Don't expect payment anytime soon."

Francie slumped into her office chair over the whispers of her fellow front office workers, one of whom didn't bother to hide her opinion, "Can our beloved doctor continue to practice medicine? Let's just hope he exercises better judgment when treating his patients than he does with hiring his office help. What could he have been thinking when he announced Francie would be joining us? We're the ones who need help now!"

Nurse Nancy opened the door to Exam Room No. 7 and patted the paper-covered table. "Up here so Dr. Merenspinn can take a look at you. I'll get your vitals. My, you do have a fever! Odd time of the year for the normal bugs which can cause that." Before leaving the room, she said," Just so you know, we're running way behind this morning."

Evan perused the two-year-old magazines in the rack, none of which struck his fancy. *I should have brought my paperback novel with me.*

Dr. Merenspinn didn't bother to tap on the door before entering. "Evan, your ribs should be pretty much healed by now. Any other ailments? I see you've got a fever. I'll order some current labs for you just to make sure."

"I've had a spike in diarrhea of late. Also, I'm having some pain when I breathe deeply, but I think that may be related to my rib injury earlier this year. I have some shaking and chills along with a lot of gas. Of course, the Briarley clan is known for its horrendous belching and gas attacks, every last one of us." Nurse Nancy couldn't muffle her giggles.

Shining a small, black flashlight into Evan's pupils, Dr. Merenspinn commented, "I don't really see any sign of jaundice in your eyes or your skin. The diarrhea could be a sign that there's excess fats in the digestive tract that aren't being broken down properly. I've heard you're a great chef."

Dr. Merenspinn reached inside the top wooden drawer and selected some brochures. "Here's some very helpful information on healthy meal planning. If there are concerns following your lab results, then I'll order a scan for you at Mintner, so we can get to the bottom of this.

"You're still plenty young enough to take control of your health before you need to have any major surgeries or other related problems. Stop in the back of the clinic and the med tech will draw your blood. Oh, by the way, how are things at your new job?"

"Fine, but dull."

"Dull?"

"Yes. Everything's boring compared to the continuing Sabblonti saga."

Clicking his pen and inserting it inside the pocket of his lab coat, Dr. Merenspinn said, "Believe it or not, there are times when dull isn't so bad after all."

S

It was a rare instance in which Evan didn't feel like firing up his grill on the small eastern balcony or have something scrumptious baking in his oven. His visitors hesitated before gently knocking on the partially opened

232

front door of Cresner Apartment No. 519. Hearing nothing, yet quite concerned, they tiptoed inside, setting their offering on the counter. The makings of a platter of thick, bacon-wrapped, whole water chestnuts, and mild jalapeno, parmesan cheese, artichoke dip was in plain view. The illustrated *Healthy Food Choices* pamphlets, courtesy of Dr. Merenspinn, were nowhere to be seen.

In the middle of a dream, Evan began wiping his face, wrinkling his nose, and squirming. *Who's that tickling me? I thought I heard the faintest tinkle of a bell.*

Evan hunched over when trying to rise from the couch. Nurse Nancy scooped her Siamese cat, Sir Shelton, into her arms.

"I just found out we're neighbors. How convenient! Did you know your front door was unlocked and open? That can be kind of dangerous in these parts, or so I'm told, with all of the seasonal ranch workers and ever-present drifters. The saloon's not far from us either. I had to call the apartment manager and ask him to install a dead-bolt lock on my front door. I'm of the opinion that there's danger everywhere, and the landscape is draped in desert camouflage. You just never know who or what is lurking out there."

Keeping his head down until he could think properly, Evan replied, "I'm not the least bit concerned about somebody breaking and entering even though I do like my privacy. A LOT."

"Sir Shelton and I made dinner for you tonight since you're a tad under the weather. I split the large Cob salad I made, half for you, and half for me. Since I no longer eat salad dressing, I didn't bring any for you. In days gone by, I used to have a little salad with my chunky Bleu Cheese dressing."

"Thanks. Sorry, I'm just not up to having company right now. Probably not for quite a while actually."

Not easily deterred after having just read the most recent issue of *Exceptional Romance Advice* from cover to cover, Nurse Nancy wistfully commented, "When your health improves, Sir Shelton and I currently reside in Apt. No. 419, literally one floor below you. It would be a very short elevator ride or just a hop, skip, and a few jumps down the fire escape on the side of the building."

S

July 4th dawned in the triple digits without a leaf on a tree moving in the slightest. Stormy had spent the past few days pouring over her mother's and grandmother's recipes in an attempt to put together a surprise for Chet at the Lower Sabblonti Ranch house when he returned late in the evening.

Calculating cooking times and temperatures for her culinary attempts, she opted to drive to Ridgemonte for the necessary supplies as opposed to the time required to travel to Cinder Valley. The mercantile in Horsewood County couldn't guarantee to carry what she needed since she'd not yet graduated to improvising and substituting when it came to cooking.

With lengthy list in hand, Stormy entered The Shadowy Merc. She glided up and down the aisles with a happy heart. Doing the right thing just made one feel good most of the time. Her homemade potato salad recipe called for bottled pimentos which were stacked on the end of Aisle No. 6. Clearing her throat, Stormy said, "Excuse me, please. I need to get something on the bottom."

Whirling around, store clerk Salina Bevvins sneered, "Well, if it isn't *Miss* Stormy. Heavy on the **Miss, not Mrs**. No surprise to see you. Snakes normally appear in the high country in hot weather to sun themselves and shed their skins.

"Speaking of skin, looks like you could use an exfoliating scrub treatment or two. Also, it appears you've really piled on the pounds over the winter. Is Chet happy about that? I'm dying to let him know I've lost 20 pounds since I last saw him. I'm sure he'll be elated. Not much seems to get past those double robin egg blue eyes of his."

Stormy pushed her shopping cart to the right to round the corner. Salina stopped it abruptly with both feet. "What's the matter, can't you take a little inside heat in the midst of the searing outside heat? My trustworthy country connections tell me you still have NOT fully connected with the man of my dreams. I'll have him lassoed by the end of this year. You can take that to the bank!"

"Last time I checked, the name Salina was not on the same checking account as Chet's. Mine is. Don't you ever forget that!"

Boiling over, Salina lunged toward Stormy and slapped her violently across the face.

Not flinching or backing down, Stormy slapped Salina

across her face, mounting strength she didn't know she had. This continued unabated for the next three minutes.

Sheriff Jeff Jensen appeared not a moment too early, shoving both bottles of iced tea in his hip pockets. "Alright, alright, ladies. Break this up, right now. Stormy, is that you? Who started this anyway, and why?"

Stormy, with finger and thumb in the figure of a pistol, pointed at Salina. "I've got something she's desperately wanted for a very long time, but cannot have, nor is she ever going to have."

Sheriff Jensen looked at both women and then spoke carefully, "Is the something a someone, perhaps?"

Nodding affirmatively, Stormy answered, "Yes, Sheriff, you're on the right trail now."

"Speaking of trail, Stormy, I've gotten some recent news. Would you mind swinging by my office? I might even be able to scare up some ice."

"What about me?" Salina hollered. "You just wait. I'll mount a door-to-door campaign against you when you run for re-election. I don't mind wearing out several pairs of shoes getting rid of you!"

He'd received far worse threats.

Having just witnessed the incident at the opposite end of the aisle and needing some relationship advice himself, Evan exited The Shadowy Merc and headed for the Sabblonti range. Not that his worn-out, brown van could make it to the tallest peak. Surely Chet was out there somewhere, maybe near a watering hole taking a siesta.

CHAPTER THIRTY

Sheriff Jeff Jensen thinned out the stack of mounting paperwork on his desk and cranked up the air conditioning unit full blast. He'd informed his dispatcher to wave Stormy right on in when she blew in and to fetch some ice packs from the cooler in the far back cell of the county jail.

Stormy sat across from the sheriff, leaning on her elbow with a fresh ice pack wrapped in a towel resting on the side of her face.

"Sorry about what happened to you in The Merc. It looked like you were holding your own though. I'll have to make this brief right now since I've just gotten two disturbing the peace calls from downtown. These national holidays are notoriously busier even in the remote high desert regions.

"Some of the ranch hands have the day off in between cuttings of hay and still need to grow up a bit. Seems like certain ones of them never mentally left their high school rodeo arenas. Five of them started drinking beer at 8:00 this morning."

He scribbled some notes on a lined sheet of paper. "You'd visited us earlier in the year about the funds being stolen by the Alottos from your Sabblonti bank accounts

237

inside the Bank of Blunte. They sure made off with a lot of the family's hard-earned money.

"We started out working with the Blunte County authorities. That led to the state authorities and ultimately to the feds since it continued east across several state lines and dealt with money being stolen from a federally insured banking institution.

"Blake Benson, the Southwest District Brand Inspector, failed his polygraph test a couple of months back. We still don't know how much he knew with respect to all that was going on."

Stormy asked, "Does Blake still have his job as the brand inspector for our state?"

Sheriff Jensen continued to scan the information inside the manila file folder on his desk. "As it pertains to Blake, I'm not sure. I would sincerely doubt it. He always struck me as a shifty sort of character from the first time I met him. Always more impressed with his own importance than necessary.

"The one gold nugget in Blake's polygraph and related sworn statements is that we were able to get the license plates to the pickup and trailer Alottos had before they drove into the sunrise."

The air conditioner unit emitted three loud groans and stopped. Sheriff Jensen removed his sweaty cowboy hat revealing his sandy colored hair parted right down the middle. Perhaps he settled on this style to match the scar in the middle of his forehead which sorta made for one long continuous line.

"We've just gotten a letter from the federal agent we've been working with. Let's see, it's postmarked June 26th. I even saved the envelope. Course it takes a while to get from New Jersey clear out here."

Stormy shifted the ice pack from one side of her face to the other. "New Jersey? Alottos drove all the way there?"

"It would appear as though they did. Apparently, it didn't take them long to wade through the money in the Atlantic City casinos. They sold their old beater pickup and some odds and ends to a marginal pawn shop and headed for Mississippi to do some river-boat gambling. That's where the trail went stone cold."

She gasped, "Mississippi? You've got to be kidding me!"

"Casinos and live poker games primarily. No lotteries, horse racing, or pinball machines in that state."

Sighing several times, Stormy surmised, "Well, I can see how it would be hard for horses to race on top of river boats. Unless they were Shetland ponies. Speaking of horse racing, did you know Chet worked for a race track before he moved here and we tied our knot?"

With his nerves already somewhat fried early in the day, Sheriff Jensen slicked down both sides of his hair before donning his cowboy hat. "When you see Chet, can you please let him know what we've been able to piece together thus far? If I find out any future developments on the Alottos, I'll let you know."

Stormy shook hands with the sheriff. "Thanks for all of your valiant efforts. Chet and I really appreciate it. I'm making him a special holiday meal tonight to celebrate. I'll bring him up to speed then."

"What are you celebrating? Other than the 4th?"

"Progress."

S

Blitz split his left front hoof on the trail, so Chet had spent most of the day resting him off and on until he could get down to the horse trailer. With his right leg still not 100%, especially to bear the partial weight of a horse, he needed to get home and get Dr. Shaw dialed up. A welcoming sight met him in his driveway.

"I've sorely missed you, ol' buddy! Please tell me you brought me one of your fine, home-cooked meals. Too bad you don't know how to shoe a horse. On second thought, maybe you could lift Blitz's leg while I play farrier."

Despite the stabbing stomach pain, Evan belly laughed. "No cooked meals on board. Sorry, I have no clue how to shoe a horse. Where's Yatey, Ruston, or one of your hired cowhands?"

"I didn't make it far enough up the mountain meadows to find them today. Gotta call the doc."

Evan walked inside the Lower Sabblonti Ranch house and couldn't help himself. He slowly started organizing the living room, washing the dishes in the sink, and clearing the clutter from the kitchen table. "How about I make us a pot of coffee?"

"You're hired! Wanna cook me a steak while you're at it? There're some spuds in the lower bin of the fridge. Ah, no need to tell you where anything is. Have at it!"

Chet called The Shaw Vet clinic at straight up 6:00. Dr.

Shaw let it go to the voicemail recording as he was closing up for the night. When he heard the caller's voice, he knew he couldn't let it slide.

Sensing he had just about enough energy to drink a cup of coffee and drive home, Evan didn't mince words. "I'll have to give you a rain check on cooking a meal for you, Chet. I've got something going on which is giving me a lot of belly pain. I went to see Merenspinn. We're still waiting on some lab results. Hope it's not my gall bladder."

"I sure hope it isn't either. That would be a real revolting development. How are you gettin' along with your new job? Just thought it would be easier all the way around if you lived in town now that you're workin' there. Your ol' gas guzzlin' van would really burn up your monthly budget if you continued to drive back and forth from here each day."

Evan added lots more cream to his coffee and stirred it slowly. "New job's okay. At least it pays the bills. It's just so boring."

Chet laughed. "Trust me when I tell you boring isn't always a bad thing. Beats drama any day of the week."

Evan hesitated. "That's probably about as good of a lead in as I could ask for, Chet. You'll never guess who lives one floor below me in those dilapidated apartments."

"I don't even know what that word means. Cresner apartments? Where Sarita lived before she and Wyn got hitched?"

"Yes, same place. Run down. Not the best in other words."

Grabbing a handful of salted mixed nuts from the can inside the pantry, Chet ate like there wasn't any supper forthcoming. "I have no idea who lives in that apartment building these days. Just don't tell me it's The Black Raven."

The pupils of Evan's eyes grew quite large. "Had not even thought of her. Good grief, I sure hope not. Well, Nurse Nancy Pritchurt and her Siamese cat, Sir Shelton, complete with a tinky, little, silver bell around his neck, are my neighbors. They paid me a visit today complete with a Welcome Wagon gift of a Cob Salad, minus the dressing, which chapped me royally."

Chet laughed even louder as he slapped the kitchen counter several times. "Nurse Nancy. And a cat to boot? With a tinky, silver bell? That's hilarious, Evan! Didn't you check to see who lived in the apartment building before you rented one of the units?"

"It's against housing authority regs to reveal who lives in any of the units. I couldn't have found out even if I wanted to. And, it's not hilarious, Chet. I fail to find any humor in this."

Pinching both of his cheeks with his hands to form a sober face, Chet said, "Okay, let's get serious here. Is this why you drove all the way out here to see me? I will say this much. You can't judge a horse by its coat or face markings. Same with a good-hearted woman.

"You'd have to be blind not to see Nurse Nancy's been pining over you long after the pine needles fell to the ground in these here mountains. You, of ALL people, should know that I'm pretty much the dead dog last one to be giving any advice to anyone when it comes to women."

Evan shook his head back and forth. "How so? You've had two of them hot on your trail for quite some time now. Well, maybe not two of them at the same time, but boy howdy, they're red hot after you now. You best be lookin' over both shoulders.

"You should have seen the smack down inside The Shadowy Merc earlier today. Based on her actions, I'd advise you to consider giving Stormy a second chance. I'd say she's dead serious right about now."

Dr. Shaw didn't bother to knock using the black, horse shoe-shaped knocker on the front door. Oblivious to what he was wading into but being pretty good at reading faces, he said, "Something tells me Blitz can wait another fifteen minutes or so. I'll take my coffee with cream and sugar, Evan."

"Comin' right up, Doc. Pull up a chair. I'll give you the blow-by-blow account," offered Evan. He lost track of who laughed louder, whether it was Chet or Dr. Shaw.

Two hours later, Stormy could have sworn she heard a bull pen in full bellow as she walked into the Lower Sabblonti Ranch house to deliver her husband's surprise dinner. The first casserole pan with large handles held Chet's favorite pot roast with extra vegetables, brown gravy, and biscuits. She laid it in the center of the table. All three gentlemen jumped up to offer assistance to carry in the remainder of the spread.

Dr. Shaw and Evan looked at each other, nodded, then headed for the front door.

Stormy sincerely offered, "You're more than welcome to stay for supper. I cooked all of this by my lonesome."

Evan turned to Chet, "Wisdom always brings success. Think long and hard about it. Silly me! I guess I should listen to myself before trying to dispense advice to you."

His mercy nearly got the best of him. He thought about giving her a hug, but reconsidered. No amount of pancake makeup could cover up Stormy's bruised face. He'd let Chet apply the healing while he concentrated on his own.

CHAPTER THIRTY-ONE

"That was one mighty fine meal, Stormy. You really pulled out all the stops on that one, especially making it all from scratch. Your wifey rating increased quite a bit."

She took her own sweet time clearing the table and washing the mounds of dishes. Long, hot, summer nights held the possibility of all sorts of things if one played her cards just right. Chet's snoring provided the perfect, short term buffer Stormy needed. Gathering the stack of paperwork and retreating to the back bedroom, she quickly scanned the most important set.

Returning to the kitchen and savoring the notion of a night under a 98% full moon, she jumped when Chet wrapped both arms tightly around her waist. She turned and tried not to cringe from pain when he held both sides of her face in his palms. Forgetting about the Salina slaps, he apologized profusely. Standing on her tiptoes since he was almost a foot taller, she ached for a long, passionate kiss.

Drops of water from their kitchen clean up dampened the most recent statement from Cattlemen's Central. "Oh, that reminds me," Chet said. "I've been meaning to call that Vaughn McJune who bought those bulls from me. Looks like he shortchanged me. I knew I should've gotten the money from him at that dive Feather Nest Diner. When he met you at the ranch that day, did he say when he was going to deliver the rest of the payment?"

Stormy stared intently at the top sheet of the statement. "How much does he still owe you?"

"Ten grand. And I aim to get it sooner than later."

Her recent visit to the public library was sure to yield quick dividends. She'd been putting some early morning insomnia hours to good use studying *Short Lessons for The Fine Art of Diplomacy.*

"With you spending so much time on the range and working to get our herd and ranch built up again, would you mind if I started helping with some of the bookwork? Mother always helped Daddy quite a bit in that regard. Since we're both working toward the same goal now, I would be happy to check on the ten thousand dollars."

Chet yawned loudly and shook his shoulders. "How'd it get to be past midnight so fast? I feel like I'm runnin' to catch up these days. After my accident, Evan took care of most everything. Good thing since you went, uh, well, I'll stop there while I'm ahead."

"Let's just call a truce regarding the past year and a half, shall we? The important thing is what we decide from now on and how we act on our decisions. So, do I have your permission to handle the banking and pay the bills?"

The clock struck one. "I'll put you on a temporary basis to see how you do. You've got to stay in touch with me. You can't be runnin' hither and yon 'cause I sure don't plan on chasin' after you. Understood?"

"Yes, I understand completely. It's bed time. Shall we?"

Chet lifted his right arm and pointed down the hallway, "I can't guarantee what kind of shape the guest bedroom's in. Evan normally kept things done up. You're welcome to spend the night there if you want."

Stormy flipped the kitchen light switch off to hide her flamed face. "I was hoping for my side of our bed in our master bedroom."

"Sorry to let you down. We dare not put the cart before the horse 'til we get everything completely ironed out."

Back at the Main Sabblonti Ranch, Stormy wound down by knitting together the beginner's baby blankets.

S

Braezee, Chet's beloved mare, was no match for his gelding, Blitz, when it came to riding the range in the high country. She was much slower following her foot surgery in 1999 and required far more dry-lotting. His discouragement increased as he dropped to a lower elevation and tied her to a large Juniper tree in a small grove near the creek.

"You've got enough slack in your rope and some tender shoots to tide you over 'til Beebee and I get back." She drew in a deep breath, then let it out slowly and audibly through her enlarged nostrils. Braezee repeatedly put her head forward and down, then exhaled, emitting deep fluttering breaths.

"Now don't you go and try layin' guilt trips on me too. I've got enough of that goin' on with Stormy. What's with you girls, anywho?"

Chet strained to hear a familiar sound near Alder Creek Reservoir. *Kwaaw, Kwaaw, Kwaaw* could be heard in short, clipped repetitions followed quickly by *Chirp, Chirp, Chirp.*

The shiny, black plumes on the heads of the mountain quail bobbed up and down as the males scratched on the ground looking for seeds. "I need to head to a different range. Even the females are signaling, 'I'm lonely!'"

A large Cooper's hawk sent them scurrying for cover under a small rock outcropping.

Beebee left his calling cards on the freshly blooming, scarlet, Skunk Flowers adorning the meadow.

Yatey, Ruston, and crew split off earlier in the day to move part of the herd further east. Stark white thunderheads billowed in the late afternoon sky. The wind whistled through the pine trees just as Chet reached the base of the mountain. "Blasted weather! Just when I finally make it up here to scope out how much fencing material we need, nature gets riled up."

A glint of metal flickered back and forth as the sun peeked in and out of the storm clouds. Chet was limping more than normal by the time he reached the old pickup about a mile away. He wasn't used to climbing over rocks and through dense sagebrush to get to where he wanted to go and was totally ticked after realizing he could have driven that far.

Well-worn boot soles were all he saw. Perceiving she was injured as she lay face-down on the bench seat, Chet grabbed both ankles and shook her legs. "Wake up! Wake up! What are you doing out here?"

Before she could answer, a young man stood up outside

the passenger side of the pickup. He removed one of Chet's old cowboy hats to brush his long, wavy, dark-brown hair away from his wide forehead. A layer of fine dirt mixed with the rosy tip of his bulb nose, left cheek, and chin could double for a jig-saw puzzle. When he smiled, it looked like he was sporting sixty-four teeth. His long sleeved, blue shirt was half-buttoned. "Gosh, you scared us! You could have at least announced your arrival."

"Stormy Suzanne Sabblonti Castins, you'd better start talking fast," fumed Chet. "I'm no longer playing the fool!"

"Allow me to explain before things get completely out of hand here. I'm Professor Ashton Walton from our state's land grand university. Stormy contacted me a couple of months ago requesting I accompany her to the igneous rock formations on the Sabblonti Ranch to take some core samples. We scheduled our appointment for today since I'm also teaching summer school. We've trekked over quite a bit of these hills for most of the day, so Stormy's probably pretty tired."

With his hands on both hips, Chet continued, "That doesn't explain you wearing one of my cowboy hats or your half-buttoned shirt."

Professor Walton grinned broadly. "Sure it does. Stormy was kind enough to loan me a hat since I absent mindedly left mine at home. I dressed in layers and was buttoning my top shirt after removing my undershirt. All the while she was napping face down in her pickup."

"You can stop there. I don't need any further details."

Stormy interrupted, "Chet, don't go off half-cocked. I told you that I wanted to help with our finances, so I contacted the university, and they put me in touch with

Ashton. Let's get out of the wind and head for that cleft in the rock over there. Would you please be a gentleman and help Professor Walton carry that black and silver trunk?"

Ashton opened the trunk and produced a cylindrical section of rock. He'd taken several other samples from the rock formations within the ranch and state boundary lines. "I'll use the equipment in the laboratory to inspect and analyze the data in the core samples which will reveal the naturally occurring substances within.

"I plan to do this myself since I want to preserve the arrangements of the contents. The university just purchased a special high-powered microscope, so I can examine the materials inside the formation. Those can highlight features like a thin layer of a different material sandwiched between larger layers.

"Commensurate with what we find, we can also inspect and analyze using different techniques depending upon the type of data we need and/or want. A new addition to our department is a storage facility which has excellent climate control to make sure the samples stay in good condition. Stormy was of great assistance today since it's vitally important to keep the whole chunks or specimens as intact as possible. What's especially nice is that this area seems to be undisturbed for over a century."

Stormy was pleased to announce, "Yes, this land has been in MY family for generations. Since the 1800's." Her long held grin was primarily for Chet's benefit.

"Just what's all this goin' cost us, Prof, or is it Ash?"

"The initial core sampling is free of charge since it's on my time on a Saturday. It's also on my dime initially as I have some flexibility when using the school's equipment for, shall we say, 'research and development purposes.'"

Raindrops fell on their heads as they carried the trunk to Janzti Belle's old pickup.

"Can we keep this under our hats until we see what's in our rocks?" asked Chet.

Returning his old cowboy hat to him, he replied, "That was my plan all along. Stop by the university sometime. I'd be glad to give you a tour. Both you and your lovely wife.

"One other thing, before I completely forget to mention it. I suggested to Stormy that we should also collect some of the volcanic clay and ash. One of my female colleagues has been told by the manufacturer of beauty products that these mineral rich ingredients sourced from volcanic areas are highly sought after for their purifying benefits for women's skin. She says they're all the rage now for facial cleansers and masks to deep-clean.

"Volcanic sand is used to make scrubs to exfoliate and whatever else women do with their skin. With the cosmetic industry selling billions every year, I'd say we're both in the wrong line of work. I'll hop in the back and hold the trunk next to me."

Chet looked in the rear-view mirror to backup. "That clown definitely belongs in a classroom. He's as lost as a goat in a snowstorm out here on the range," muttered Chet.

Stormy carefully framed her response as they descended the mountain road. "Forgive me, please, Chet. I really wanted to surprise you with this after we got the results back from the university. I'm determined to show you that I can fulfill my role as a good wife, mother, and mountain business woman.

"Just think, after the beauty products are manufactured,

women could purchase them in The Ridgemonte Rx as well as The Shadowy Merc. This is a bonus in addition to other minerals Professor Ashton might find in those core samples.

"From now on, I'll lay all my cards on the table all the time. No more surprises."

The heaviest storm cloud suddenly appeared overhead as Chet switched the windshield wipers to the maximum. "I never was one much for playing cards. Such a sheer waste of time. No games. No surprises. You'd best stay out of this beauty products stampede. Don't believe that malarkey about the volcanic ash. The only reason for the college character using that word is because his first name is Ash.

"I've got a ranch to run. You in or you out?"

"I'm ALL in."

CHAPTER THIRTY-TWO

Neighboring ranching wives, Debbie Drebner, Marita Merrill, and Barbie Broomfield hadn't had this much fun in years. They'd been trying to round up the other ranchers' wives, Sarita's former co-workers, her neighbors and friends for quite some time. With a little more than three weeks to go until the twins were due to arrive, everything was thrown into over-drive. Sunday evening, July 8th, the Drebner Ranch was buzzing like a hive of honey bees.

A more creative cake had probably never been baked than Marita's triple tiered. Blue icing for the bottom layer, yellow icing for the middle, and pink for the top. Just to cover both possibilities. Miniature, dark brown, rocking horses circled the bottom layer, horse shoes the middle one, and white cowboy hats for the top. Beige colored lariat shapes encircled the bottom of each layer.

Debbie had stuffed the party favors inside the plastic baby bottles. She'd borrowed and laundered several of Wilbur's colored bandanas for the table coverings. Two little sets of matching cowboy boots graced the center surrounded by two old cow bells.

Barbie was in charge of the games which some guests were already dreading, the first of which was to guess the items in the diaper bag. Anne-Marie Diller, wife of Sarita's former employer in Ridgemonte, easily won that one. Small wonder since she'd raised five children. The real stumper for the evening was the game using the letters in the words *cowboy* and *cowgirl* to suggest names for the twins.

Macey Meadows scored the highest on this one. With the winners' gifts also bearing the theme of a baby shower, she received no shortage of ribbing when opening her gift of two receiving blankets. Fellow nurse, Dawn, really poured it on, "Make sure to show those to the good doctor." Everyone laughed.

Mama Merna helped Sarita place her feet on the hassock to help her be more comfortable as she opened her gifts. The first set was numbered in chronological order which Priscilla carried in from the porch. #1 was two high chairs; #2 was two cribs; #3 was two infant car seats; and #4 was an extra-long, little red wagon with high, wooden sideboards.

Overcome with joy, Sarita asked, "Priscilla, how did you and Spence . . . ?"

Priscilla spoke softly, "He brought those over earlier this afternoon and said, 'Let's just call it a combined effort.'"

Mama Merna's double set of hand-sewn diapers were admired by all in attendance as were Nurse Nancy's hand-sewn bibs and burping cloths, both short and long.

The three hostesses had pooled their resources and purchased matching sets of fitted crib sheets, bath towels and washcloths, bath toys, and teething rings.

Lizzelle Longbowe, gentle as the pastel petals printed on her dress, presented Sarita with two record books titled *Baby's First Five Years* along with matching stuffed animals in the shape of little ponies and cow dog baby rattles.

Sarita was just about to open her gift from Molly Stixon

who was expecting her eighth child. Seems like Stixon's were keeping with their theme of a growing brood mare farm. The front door opened widely when Stormy dropped her purse as she juggled her large gift in both hands.

Molly blurted out, "Of course, leave it to you to try to upstage your sister. Seems like you're never really where you're supposed to be when you're supposed to be there. I'm surprised you got invited here this evening. After all, this isn't a lingerie party, so you can make another scene like you did at Tom Toppens' Memorial Dinner."

The house didn't move nor did anyone inside it. When no one made any effort, Lizzelle walked toward Stormy. "Good evening, and welcome. It's nice to have you. Please come in and join us. May I present your gift to your sister?"

"Thank you, Lizzelle. Yes, please do."

Sarita's heart wanted to jump up and hug Stormy, but her swollen feet and ankles were not cooperating. She continued to open Molly's gift of a white plastic bath tub chock full of infant toiletries.

Stormy stayed back from the other women who formed a horse-shoe shape in the large living room. As Marita cut her cake placing pieces on baby themed paper plates, Barbie began to serve those in attendance. Francie and Priscilla followed with a choice of lemon iced tea or tropical fruit punch. It was much too hot for coffee.

Lizzelle handed the last gift to Sarita. "Oops, looks like we forgot one."

Sarita struggled to untie the thin, curly ribbon with curls on both ends. Mama Merna came to the rescue with the kitchen shears. As the contents were revealed, simultaneous tears formed in both sisters' eyes.

"Stormy, these matching baby blankets are beautiful! Did you drive all the way into Cinder Valley to get these?"

"No, they're not from Cinder Valley. I made those for you, Wyn, and your twins."

"Seriously? You must have been at it for a while."

Stormy nodded affirmatively. "I guess you could say that. I learned a lot in the process."

The smell of sour grapes lingered in the air as Molly retorted, "You've still got a lot to learn. How could one sister have turned out so well and the other one such a failure? That will never happen to any of my children."

Priscilla made the rounds with the iced tea pitcher. "Mrs. Stixon, need a refill? I brought extra sugar, just for you. No lemons."

Lizzelle sat close to Sarita and launched into suggestions for keeping up with the baby books, especially year number one. "When they get their first haircuts, make sure to save a few locks, and put them in here."

Neither refreshments nor conversation were extended to Stormy who closed the door gently behind her. *I guess people forgive according to their own timetable. It's not my fault Mother left the Sabblonti fortune to me. Too bad I don't still have all of it!*

Wilbur Drebner loaded all of the Moreland's baby gifts into the back of Merna's pickup. Arriving home after dark, Wyn's childhood excitement was on full display as he carried them into their home. His very pregnant wife was too tired to even notice the hand-tooled, wooden bassinettes on the north side of the living room bearing the Toppens' cattle brand across the front of each one. Preacher Len had been very busy in his woodshop for months on end.

Wyn tucked Sarita into bed. Walking into the living

room, he hugged one of the fuzzy little stuffed ponies before placing it in the bassinet, gently rocking it from side to side. He went outside, sat on his favorite, oversized log, and looked up at the sky. Locating the constellation, Bootes the Herdsman, he knew it was a continued sign for him.

"Oh, Bootes, I know you can't understand me. You've got your celestial crew of two bears, two lions, a lynx, a giraffe and a dragon. I've got my own crew now. The one thing we do have in common is two dogs.

"What I wouldn't give to know my real mother and father! Ace and Jantzi Belle Sabblonti are both dead. Tom and Merna Toppens lost their only son, Toby, when he was two years old. Tom was gone long before I needed or wanted him to be. There're no living natural grandparents to love our children. The world can be a cruel, cold place, if I choose to camp there in my mind. Best be ridin' forward."

CHAPTER THIRTY-THREE

Coyote yelps awakened Wyn from a sound sleep around 4:00 a.m. He'd slept soundly throughout most of Sarita's tossing and turning during the night. Not feeling her arm when extending his across the mattress, he quickly turned the light on. She emerged from the bathroom with both hands resting on her very large abdomen. "I knew I shouldn't have had any cake and punch last night. I feel so lightheaded this morning."

Glancing at the clock while mentally calculating what all needed to be done on a Maintenance Monday, Wyn asked, "Do you want me to stay with you until Mama Merna gets here? She normally shows up about 8:00 to start her week."

"No, I'll be alright until she arrives. You've been saying how much you need to get done before our babies get here, so you best start your day as early as you can. I love you. Wish I could help you."

Wyn turned the air conditioner up and gently stroked her forehead. "Don't fret about not helping me. Motherhood is a full load for you right now. My real comfort is knowing you're not going to take our youngins' and dump 'em off at an orphanage."

Merna struggled to open the front door of Moreland's home at ten minutes past eight to the sounds of moaning and whimpering. She ran to the back bedroom to find Sarita curled up in somewhat of a fetal position. Her pale face said it all.

She labored to get the words out, "I'm having a lot of cramping. Please call the doctor."

"I know his office doesn't open until 9:30. I'm taking you straight to Mintner."

Trying to dress Sarita into something other than her summer nightgown was just about more than Merna could handle with her arm still not 100%. "When did Wyn leave? Did he say where he was going this morning?"

She spoke in barely audible tones, "He said something about the meadow in the far corner of the ranch."

Merna hurriedly assisted Sarita inside her pickup and drove to the main highway. There was no time to call the bunkhouse for Spence or one of the other hired hands. Their day started before the break of day.

Never having driven this fast in her entire life, Merna didn't notice the flashing lights behind her, but she ultimately heard the siren. Sheriff Jeff Jensen approached her driver's side window and tapped on it. Flustered, she had trouble opening it.

"Good morning. Driving quite fast, especially for someone your age."

"Something's wrong with Sarita. I'm taking her to Mintner. Write me a ticket if you need to, but we can't dally here. Is there any way you could drive to the ranch and try to find Wyn?"

"I'll let you off with a warning this time. Since I prefer to round up ranchers rather than their kids, I'll do my best to find him. Any idea where he might be working?"

"Sarita thinks it's probably the meadow in the far corner of the ranch. That would be east."

Continuing to smile, Sheriff Jensen said, "There aren't roads to a lot of those meadows."

Exasperated, Merna said, "Why on earth do you think the county supplies you with a 4-wheel drive rig. Get gone, so I can!" She rolled up the window and drove to the hospital, parking right in front of the main entrance.

Nurse Macey Meadows was in the process of confirming a patient discharge for later in the day when Merna spotted her. "Can you help? Quickly now. Sarita's in the cab of my pickup. She's complaining of not feeling well. I brought her here because Dr. Merenspinn's office doesn't open for another hour or so."

Macey looked at the wall calendar. "This might also be the week he's on vacation. I can't recall for sure last night at the baby shower just when Nurse Nancy said that was going to be."

Merna wrung her hands together. "Oh, I hope not! Who can help us? Is Dr. Linke here this morning?"

Turning a complete circle, Macey whispered, "He's making his rounds, but you don't want Sarita anywhere near him. Worst case scenario, I can help out. I completed my midwife course since I considered moving to Australia."

"Australia? Does Dr. Shaw know about this?"

"That was BEFORE our engagement party of which I knew nothing about."

"Back to Linke," Merna said. "He's one of our ranching community surgeons as well as general hospital doctor. Surely he can handle emergencies."

Macey's sixth sense kicked in as she could feel the small

under hairs on the back of her neck standing up.

"Meadows, you're not getting paid to stand around and gab with the general public this morning. If you don't have enough work to do, I can most certainly assign you some additional patients. You're highly overpaid as it is."

He clicked his pen back and forth several times. "Hear that familiar sound? It's the instrument which can sign your termination at Mintner Medical Center."

From her peripheral vision, Merna could see both of Dr. Linke's hands shaking excessively as he gripped his clipboard tightly. He was much thinner than the last time she'd seen him although his face was quite swollen with hives on both cheeks. She walked straight to the front counter and requested a wheelchair for Sarita and the clerk to call Evergreene.

Francie and Dr. Merenspinn arrived at the clinic after having met for breakfast at The Sage Hen Café. Lack of familiarity of a new working routine caused her to answer the phone earlier than normal office hours.

"Francie, this is Merna. Can you ask Dr. Merenspinn to get to Mintner as soon as he can? It's Sarita. She's cramping and not feeling a bit good."

She located him in the back of his clinic donning his blue monogrammed, short-sleeved, white overcoat. "Doctor, it's Sarita Moreland. Merna Toppens took her to the hospital. She's requesting you head over right away. It definitely sounds like something might be going wrong."

He hurriedly handed her his overcoat as he brushed ever so closely to her right side. "It's Den from now on? Remember? None of this 'doctor' business. Can you please hang this up and lock the front door to our clinic right

261

behind me? I'll be back as soon as I can. You and the other gals can adjust the morning appointments if necessary. Nurse Nancy will be here shortly, and she's fantastic help if you encounter any problems."

Francie replayed that fresh conversation more than once in her mind. *Den? Wonder if that's short for Dennis? Or is it Denzel? Our clinic? He seemed a bit rattled, but, then again, he's very close to the Morelands and their outfit.*

How can someone so intelligent read so much into a casual country breakfast totaling $19.97? But, then again, can't say as I've minded the weekly bouquet of flowers being delivered to my front door or him sending a handyman to fix my broken washing machine.

Sarita was wheeled into Birthing Room No. 2 on the 4th Floor of Mintner Medical Center. Nurses Macey and Dawn were getting her connected to all of the necessary equipment to monitor her vitals as Mama Merna paced the hallway. Sarita's blood pressure plummeted despite having her connected to oxygen. Charge Nurse Joyce Stone scrambled to get a C-section team assembled immediately. The last one to arrive was the nurse anesthetist.

After connecting Sarita to a fetal heart monitor, Dawn informed the doctor, "We have a deceleration."

Without speaking, he signaled to his team that there might be an umbilical cord wrapped around one of the baby's necks. "Great teamwork on getting that IV and epidural going. Now Sarita, you shouldn't be feeling any pain, but you may feel some pressure or tugging as the operation is being performed."

Making eye contact with the nurse anesthetist who nodded affirmatively, Dr. Merenspinn continued.

"Let's help her blood pressure just a bit more, Macey. Tilt her, so she's leaning a little more to her left side."

He skillfully made a horizontal incision across Sarita's midsection, pushed her bladder down, made an incision into her uterus, and released the amniotic fluid. He smiled inwardly when observing it wasn't brown. Carefully reaching inside, he drew out Sarita's first born son, followed by her beautiful daughter. After severing the umbilical cords, both babies were gently laid upon Sarita's chest.

Dr. Merenspinn directed Macey to give the injection to release the placenta. Just as he was closing Sarita's uterus using dissolvable stitches along with each layer of her stomach muscles and sewing up the initial incision, Wyn entered the birthing room. Tears had already drenched his mask and the front of his hospital gown. It took every ounce of strength Sarita could muster to smile at him.

Macey gently lifted the baby boy from Sarita's chest followed by Dawn doing the same with the baby girl. They dried the babies off and wrapped them tightly in heated blankets.

Merna met Dr. Merenspinn in the hallway. "Whew, what a relief! Your twin grandbabies are finally here, safe and sound. They are just shy of 33 weeks, so we'll need to keep all three of them here for a few days. Mintner just got a new prenatal breathing machine to help newborns. Both of them were breathing fine right after I delivered them, but we'll probably have to give them some treatments on the machine to help them along. Would you like to go in and meet them?"

"Wild horses couldn't keep me out of there!"

Sarita opened her eyes to see Wyn and Merna with

their arms around each other's waists. Mama Merna may be short and sweet, but was she ever strong when she needed to be!

Macey pulled the boy ever so close to her chest as Wyn arched his eyebrow and held out both hands.

"Okay, alright!" she giggled. "Now don't be alarmed. Both of them are bald as a billiard ball. No hair yet. Your son weighs 3.9 pounds, and your daughter 3.7 pounds. Both of them are 16 inches long."

Dawn handed the newborn twin girl to Merna. The nurse anesthetist continued to monitor Sarita as she slept.

Suddenly Merna giggled. "We went completely through that baby shower and not one person thought to ask about names for these two."

"You're right!" exclaimed Dawn.

Wyn grinned. "We were trying to keep it under our hats. Our son will be named Tennyson Thomas Moreland in honor of Tom Toppens. That was a bit fancy for my likin', but Sarita dreamed it up. Our daughter will be named Madeline Merna Moreland in honor of Mama Merna Toppens. We'll call them Tenny and Maddy. I figured out their nicknames."

Merna squeezed little Maddy tighter than she should have done which caused her to let her voice be known to the world.

Macey rubbed her tender little cheek. "She just might be known as Mighty Maddy some day with a voice like that one! Oh, you're beyond adorable."

Before leaving the birthing room, Nurse Dawn Rowann announced, "I'm driving straight to The Shaw Vet Clinic. Anybody else want to accompany me to get a fire lit under our county vet? There's no way his fiancée wants to wait three more years to get married and five more years to have her first kid. I'm going to ditch his annual planner. Time to get Shaw & Shaw launched once and for all!"

Merna and Wyn arrived at the Moreland's home just before the sun set. With much skepticism after spotting the coolers on the front porch, Wyn opened the red one. The note taped to the inside of the lid read,

"Congratulations, Wyn & Sarita! Meat loaf with brown, mushroom gravy, mashed spuds with butter, and candied carrots. Frosted raisin bars for dessert.

Enjoy, Aunty Stormy"

Setting the table for dinner, Merna asked Wyn, "Did I hear you mumbling something about a Black Raven? We haven't seen any of those in these parts for a while now."

"Just making sure of our food source, Mama Merna."

CHAPTER THIRTY-FOUR

Little preemies were quite rare at Mintner Medical Center necessitating extra shifts for some of the nurses who didn't seem to bother one bit. It helped considerably that it was the dog days of summer and not the dead of winter when the mountain roads and streets could be more than challenging.

Tenny seemed to be adding body weight more quickly than his twin sister, Maddy. She not only fought breast feeding, but also supplemental bottle feeding. Nurse Nancy Pritchurt had worked with La Leche League International in her previous employment. She faithfully stopped by Mintner each afternoon after leaving work to render assistance and encouragement to Sarita.

The same people present for Dr. Shaw and Macey's engagement party, minus both sets of their parents, put their collective efforts on display for a surprise first anniversary party on Sunday evening, July 29th, at the Moreland's. Their timing was impeccable as it was Tenny's first day in his new home. Maddy's lungs weren't developing as quickly as Tenny's which was an added element for her additional hospital stay.

Tenny was completely worn out by the end of the long summer evening. Macey, Nurse Nancy, and Priscilla vied for who could hold him the longest. Even the most casual observer noticed that Dr. Shaw, Evan, and Spence seemed to be watching little Tenny a little more closely than one might expect.

Marita Merrill satisfied everyone's stomachs and palate's along with circulating a clipboard asking for volunteers to help deliver meals, drive Sarita to the hospital, and whatever else needed to be done for the Morelands. This was one well-run ranching community when it needed to be. It always seemed to deliver just what was needed and more. Sometimes just in the nick of time.

Chet lowered his head to a 45-degree angle and managed a half smile when walking to his pickup which was parked next to Evan's van. He'd not paid much attention to Nurse Nancy leaving the house, making two trips to carry her serving dishes to the trunk of her car. Nor did he chide very often, but this time he didn't let it ride. "Evan, ever thought of giving her a lift every now and then, especially when you're both headed the same direction?"

"Just not quite there, yet."

"Where's there?"

"The matrimony of my mind."

"Sounds like a reality TV show or a title of one of those paperbacks on that circular metal rack at the Ridgemonte Rx."

Evan roared, "And just how would you know about that metal rack?"

"Maybe a little birdie told me."

"Birds don't talk that kind of intimate language. Neither do bees."

For some unexplainable reason, Macey never liked the

month of August. She wanted it to be over before it began. One thing she was certain of – she was never getting married during any one of those thirty-one days. Ever.

Maddy Moreland was gradually gaining weight despite experiencing daily bouts of colic. Nurse Nancy seemed to have the magic touch to quiet her during each visit. She tried rubbing the unusual little fold in Maddy's delicate skin just above her right eye wanting it to disappear. The very next day when she would report just like clockwork, the strange fold was still there.

Dr. Merenspinn wanted Maddy to be weighing at least six pounds before discharging her from Mintner. Also, he monitored her daily breathing reports which revealed her oxygen level was still a bit below normal. He'd been at the hospital virtually every day for three weeks delivering babies for his patients. This cycle was nothing new to him. When winter arrived in the high country, a new crop of young ones was sure to follow just about nine months later. He planned his annual vacation some other time. Next year's would hopefully be a lengthy, river cruise with a special lady friend.

In the middle of all this, Macey's Grandpa Meadows passed away unexpectedly. She took a week off work to attend his funeral and visit family. In some respects, sad as it was, this proved to be a welcome respite from the increasing, unnecessary scrutiny at the hospital. Her mother, Sherry, treated her to lunch at one of the dining shops inside the airport.

Macey picked at her Summer Chef's Salad with her fork, leaving most of it inside the bowl. One of her longtime faves, Fresh Raspberry Cheesecake, couldn't entice her today.

Sherry expended more effort than normal to engage her daughter in meaningful conversation. She surmised that it should have been her father, Doug, who took her to the airport. When they talked, it was as if the water faucet was never turned off.

"We're all sad Grandpa M is no longer with us. Is everything okay? You've seemed unusually preoccupied during this entire visit."

Macey scooted her bowl in front of her, placed her elbow on the table, and fingered her engagement ring on her left finger. "To tell you the absolute truth, if Benny hadn't proposed to me when he did, I'd have already left the hospital, even if I didn't have another job."

"You do love your fiancé, don't you? If you're not sure, you should break your engagement right now. Don't lead him on. That's grossly unfair. Do you remember Deena that attended high school with you? She decided AFTER the rehearsal dinner that she didn't want to go through with the marriage. I felt so badly for her parents who met everyone at the church the next day to try to explain to them. What a hassle! Can you imagine having to take back all of those bridal shower and wedding gifts?"

Macey reached for both of her mother's hands and held them. Looking at her intently, she explained, "I love Benny with my whole heart. He's not the issue. It's that Hospital Administrator and General Surgeon, Dr. Linke, who's the problem."

Sherry looked at the time and gasped, "To be continued. Grab your boarding pass. You might need to run to your gate or you'll miss your flight!"

"That might not be all bad."

"Macey, consider Dr. Shaw, or shall I call him Benny?"

Laughing, Sherry laid cash on the table, and hugged her daughter good-bye.

CHAPTER THIRTY-FIVE

The twins were nearly a month old before Maddy could be released from the hospital. To the casual observer, it might seem like there was a used car and truck auction scheduled for late in the evening of August 8th in the driveway of the Moreland residence.

Wyn arrived home all dusty and dry from having finished stacking some hay in the large, upper meadow of the Toppens' Ranch. When he walked through the mud room in the back of their home, he could have sworn a full-on hen party was in full squawk.

Nurse Nancy had been patiently pacing the kitchen floor as she waited her turn to hold the bundle of joy. Earlier in the evening, Debbie Drebner thought it would be fun to dress the baby in a matching yellow and white, gingham summer dress and bonnet. Barbie Broomfield was quite adept at her Jack-in-the-box routine as she jumped back and forth across the couch and chairs taking pictures. After all, this was a red-letter day!

Perhaps overstimulation led to baby's crying jag which continued for about twenty-five minutes. Finally, Marita suggested, "Nurse Nancy, it's your turn now. You've got the special infant touch to quiet her down."

She chose the rocking chair and placed a burping cloth

over her shoulder. "When's the last time she ate?"

Marita replied, "I'm not sure. I'll find out."

"Let's get that bonnet off you, shall we? Maybe that's part of the problem." Nurse Nancy cuddled her in her arms as she began to hum a lullaby. She walked back into the kitchen where the evening light was much brighter.

Wyn emerged from the wash room as Nurse Nancy was closely examining the baby under the lights above the kitchen sink. In hushed tones, she voiced her concern to him. "I know babies can change in appearance somewhat the first few weeks after they're born, but are you sure this is your daughter? Every day I held Maddy in the hospital, she had this strange fold of skin above her right eye. Now it's gone. This baby girl weighs more than 6 lbs. I can surely tell you that!"

"How am I supposed to know? Should we take her back to the hospital? Sarita's just now getting to where she can sleep a little bit at night. I don't dare mention anything to her at this late hour. What if we can't find Maddy?"

Nurse Nancy calmed herself as she rocked the baby in her arms. "Dr. Merenspinn and I'll meet you, Sarita, and the infants at the hospital tomorrow. He doesn't know that yet, but he'll be there. Let's say around 12:30 ish. That's when he normally takes a short lunch. I'll have no peace in my spirit until we get to the bottom of this."

S

Evan stayed up late reading his paperback novel. He

heard the front door in the apartment directly below him open and close several times early in the morning. Covering his head with his down pillow didn't muffle the noise. *Help, help, get me out of here!*

Francie Fletcher didn't much care for Molly Stixon the first time she met her, much less the middle of the morning on Thursday, August 9th when she arrived with no appointment on Evergreene's overflowing schedule. Brash would be a compliment when describing her. With babe in arms and two of her younger brood hanging onto her elongated, summer, knit top, she roared, "I'm here to see Dr. Merenspinn. Now. And don't tell me he doesn't have time to see me."

Not knowing the protocol for checking patients into a waiting room but deeming it couldn't be that difficult, Francie opened the door, ushered the Stixons into the first empty one, and said, "The doctor will be in shortly." At least that's what Francie had always been told for her own appointments.

She located Dr. Merenspinn in his office and closed the door behind her. He looked up from his desk. "Does this mean you are finally saying *yes* to my summer evening, outdoor theatre, dinner invitation?"

Waving both hands in front of her, she cautioned, "You know I would never come into your office uninvited. That's not what this is about. Molly Stixon's demanding to see you immediately. She seems very upset. I put her in one of the exam rooms. I was so shook up, I can't remember which one it is. Something else is out of sorts. Nurse Nancy never misses a day of work. She hasn't called in yet either."

He smiled. "I'll handle it. We doctors are good at

calming people down. Now, you relax. Since Nancy's not here yet, time for you to help out."

Entering Exam Room No. 5, Dr. Merenspinn couldn't get the first word in edgewise. Molly Stixon started a five-minute, non-stop rant. "Look at this baby! What did you do to her during delivery? She didn't look like this in the hospital! Not to mention that she doesn't look anything like my other kids looked when they were born. You should know. You've delivered every single one of them.

"Samuel and I have one mold for our kids. Line them all up, side by each, and every one of them looks like a dead ringer for the other one. Their baby pictures all look alike. Even Samuel said this baby didn't look like one of his. I sure as the world am NOT that kind of woman!"

Francie held onto the supply cabinet in the corner of the room to steady herself.

Nurse Nancy opened the exam room door. "Doctor, sorry I'm late. I left my car door open last night which ran the battery down, so I couldn't get it started until about half an hour ago. Someone in the parking lot used their set of jumper cables to help me out."

She didn't escape Molly's wrath either. "That's your lousy excuse. I'm still waiting for his."

Dr. Merenspinn calmly requested, "Mrs. Stixon, please lay the baby on the exam table, so we can weigh her." Merely by instinct, Nurse Nancy bent down to look closely at her, then exclaimed, "Yes, this is Maddy Moreland! I just knew that little skin fold would still be on her face."

"Ah, ha! I knew this was your mistake, doctor! You better admit it," shrieked Molly.

"Mrs. Stixon, I didn't make any mistake at all. I'm not

the one who actually hands the baby to the parent or parents when it's time for him or her to leave the hospital. If you'd like, my staff and I can meet you at Mintner and get things properly taken care of." With that explanation, she stormed out of Evergreene Medical Clinic with two of her brood wailing and running after her.

Francie was deeply lost in reflection. *Doesn't she realize what other people may think of her when she acts like that?*

Nurse Nancy reminded Francie a second time, "You can ride with me to Mintner if you would like. Dr. Merenspinn wants both of us there in the event we need to sign an affidavit."

Wyn, Sarita, and Tenny Moreland along with the baby girl were waiting in the private room on the 4th floor of Mintner Medical Center when Dr. Merenspinn, Francie Fletcher, and Nurse Nancy with babe in arms arrived. Macey Meadows arrived three minutes later. Charge Nurse Joyce Stone, Dr. Linke, and Molly Stixon along with her two young ones arrived simultaneously. The room needed some fresh, cool air.

Dr. Linke rocked back and forth on his heels as he loudly barked orders. "Stone, produce copies of both birth certificates. Morelands and Stixon, carefully examine these baby girls. Apparently, someone is implying they were sent to the incorrect homes when discharged from the hospital. That's never happened under my watch. If there's been a mistake, Meadows, you better own it. Right here, right now. In front of all of these witnesses since I'll be preparing my report for the hospital board."

"Try again, Linke. I haven't even been here for the last week."

Sure as the world, Nurse Nancy gently handed Maddy to her loving mother, Sarita. Molly Stixon approached Wyn, "Let me see if that's my baby." After carefully scrutinizing her, she declared, "Yep, sure is. Looks just like the other seven did when they were born." She slammed the door behind her. Francie looked to see if there were fang marks in either of Wyn's suntanned hands.

CHAPTER THIRTY-SIX

Mintner Medical Center ordered several mandatory classes for all employees following the baby girl mix-up. They were scheduled for the remaining Saturdays during the month of August. There were a lot of interactive activities and lessons to reinforce proper protocol and to help prevent lawsuits from being filed against the hospital.

In addition, the hospital immediately instituted a policy allowing only certain personnel be permitted inside the ICU unit to care for newborns.

Charge Nurse Joyce Stone eagerly paged Nurse Macey Meadows. Upon her arrival at the nurse's station, Joyce explained. "It looks like we may have figured out what happened with the baby girls. Sarita Moreland and Molly Sitxon gave birth to daughters one day apart, both of whom ended up in the ICU for several days for different reasons. During some of this period of time, you were out of town attending your Grandpa's funeral.

"Baby Stixon was profoundly jaundiced and Maddy Moreland had to be placed upon a specialized breathing machine. With both newborns being within close proximity simultaneously, one of the hospital employees carelessly removed the wrist bands when bathing both babies, neither of whom had any hair or distinctive markings. After bathing

277

and cleaning the infants, the employee obviously switched the identifying wrist bands."

"Thankfully, it was caught right away and remedied," Macey said.

Breathing a huge sigh of relief, Joyce agreed. "You better know it!"

Much to Macey's delight, Dr. Shaw donned his creative, entertainment cap to prepare delicious suppers at 812 Flame Street, Ridgemonte, to romance his favorite nurse during her six-day work weeks. He even provided foot massages along with fresh strawberry smoothies as Emmy, Macey's cat, laid on the couch next to him.

Some evenings were spent helping her redecorate her living room, complete with a brass wall sculpture featuring a herd of running horses; rich, earth-toned Native American arrow design rug; topped off with a wooden armoire with patina accents, wrought iron hardware, and hammered metal inserts. Opening the large, cardboard box containing the tan, turquoise, gold, and red *Sky and Earth* bedding collection, Dr. Shaw opted to let her carry that down the hallway to her bedroom.

Despite all this, Macey still seemed to be on edge. She wasn't irritated with her favorite veterinarian and fiancé. There were times when specific administrative agencies didn't move real fast despite the heat.

Rees Broomfield was kind enough to deliver one of his older, gentle geldings to the Shaw Ranchette early Sunday morning, September 2nd. Macey's spirits soared when Dr. Shaw removed the blindfold from her eyes while sitting inside his pickup. Her *thank you* kiss lasted longer than Rees' blush. No tellin' when their lip-lock would end, so he might as well head on down the highway.

Macey napped as Dr. Shaw drove to the high country with Beau, his gelding, and Rees' horse in the trailer. Jetter, Dr. Shaw's dog, laid his head on Macey's right leg for a little siesta of his own.

Dr. Shaw parked in the exact same spot that he and Macey visited last year. They rode the horses for a short while, returning before the afternoon heat.

"I'm really enjoying the beautiful saddle you gifted me last Christmas. How'd you know the perfect size?" Macey asked as she dismounted from the horse.

"As previously stated, we vets have more gifts than meet the casual eye."

"I still maintain it was just a lucky guess."

"Call it what you may. You look mighty fine with or without your saddle."

She followed him to a large rock. He motioned for her to sit as close to him as possible as their cowboy boots dangled precariously over the edge.

"When I first started riding Beau up here, I didn't have the appreciation for these mountain ranges as I do now. My perception was they were cold, distant, dynamic domains painted with varying shades of gray, charcoal, black, white, and red. Pine, Mahogany, and Juniper trees didn't appear where I thought they'd be.

"A person could spend some of the spring, summer, and fall months photographing the wondrous wildflowers. Close your eyes, inhale, and see if you can discern between any of these: Orange Sneezeweed, Sticky Geranium, and the King's Crown. My love for the desert has blossomed over time, just like it has for you."

Macey's eyelids were slowly closing with each of Dr. Shaw's descriptive sentences. She nearly jumped off the rock when she heard a sonic boom directly overhead. It was a good thing they'd secured Rees' gelding to a tree. Otherwise, they might have to look for him in Fantone or Horsewood counties.

"What on earth just happened?" she asked.

"The Air Force Base uses part of this area for fighter jet training, but only in the late summer and early fall. That's one of the things I've not yet become accustomed to in this area. The first time I heard it, I nearly jumped out of my skin!"

Macey exclaimed, "Look, way over there, Benny! Those blasted jets scared that precious little fawn. It's so cute with its little spots. I wonder where its mommy is? Oh, there's two of them! The first one already ran over the side of that hill."

"Must be the season for twins, even in the high desert mountains."

"Do they run in your family?" asked Macey.

"The deer or twins?"

She playfully pinched his ribcage. "Stop that. You know what I mean. Twins."

"I have no idea. I'll have to ask my madre. Does your family have a history of twins?"

"With everything I have going on now, I don't even want to find out."

He'd prepared another tasty picnic lunch which they leisurely enjoyed on the patchwork quilt. Due to sheer exhaustion, both of them fell into a deep sleep. Jetter's barking at the squirrels in the tree awakened Dr. Shaw first.

He rolled over and drew Macey close to him. He whispered into her ear, "Want to set a wedding date?"

She rubbed her eyes and sat cross-legged on the blanket. "Yes, I'm ready to officially launch Shaw & Shaw, so how about next June?"

"Is there something special about that month?"

"It's the traditional bridal month; however, September is giving it a real run for its money."

He couldn't hide his frown. "September is a whole year away. How about May or June?"

Touching his top lip, she teased, "Is this the same Dr. Shaw who had his feet in concrete and said we would get married in four years and start our family in seven? What made you change your mind? Are you that same guy? Would the real Dr. Shaw please stand up?"

Playfully, he quickly jumped to his feet. "Let's just chalk it up to the power of persuasion."

"Persuasion? Such as from a certain Mintner employee named Nurse Dawn Rowann?"

Disappointed in himself, he thought he could pull this off without letting the cat out of the bag. "Yes, Dawn, along with several others."

He headed for the horses to untie them and lead them to the stream for a drink before loading them into the trailer. She ran after him and tugged on his shirt. "Who are the several others."

"I'm sworn to secrecy."

She firmly stopped him. "Not one secret, ever, Benny. Understood?"

"Yes. Never any secrets between us. Those can be very dangerous. I've told you everything about myself. There are no skeletons in any closets; no locked doors; no black holes; no previous girlfriends or engagements; no fake identities from the witness protection program; no nothing. What you see is what you get."

"Sorry, I overreacted. Please forgive me. I've heard too many stories from my fellow colleagues about their rocky romances or failures to reveal before saying *I do*."

Dr. Shaw burst out laughing. "Is that because you're standing on a rock right now?"

"Oh, stop it. You know what I mean. Not one more step until you identify who the others are in this plot with you."

"I wouldn't call it a plot. Only novelists use those. My mother who talks at least twice a week to your mother. Also, my marriage counselors."

She turned from the overhead sunlight to look straight into his eyes. "You're seeing a marriage counselor already? Is it one of those counselors at that clinic in Fantone in Tranquility Falls County? I've been told they're a strange group."

This time he doubled over in laughter. "Well, I guess Chet and Evan would sort of qualify as counselors."

Macey's hollers of "Chet and Evan!" could be heard in the next canyon from where they were standing.

"I just said that in jest. I'm not seeing an official marriage counselor and don't plan on it. I'm settled enough to know what I want in life."

"You really had me going on that one! I guess it's good to yuck it up here in the beautiful mountains and release some of my stress. But, seriously, Chet and Evan? Surely you don't talk to them about us, or do you?"

Dr. Shaw swung the back door of the horse trailer open.

"Rest assured, I talk to them very little about us. They desperately try to give me advice, however."

"Well, why don't both of them concentrate on their marriages and leave us alone?"

Realizing he better quit while he was ahead, Dr. Shaw loaded the geldings into his trailer and headed on down the trail. The high mountain country always seemed to hold the answers to most everything if one could drive around in it long enough to find them.

CHAPTER THIRTY-SEVEN

Three-day weekends and every national holiday were never long enough for Macey's work-a-day world. Now that it had cooled off some in the evenings, she'd started running again to help relieve some of her stress. Dawn Rowann joined her Wednesday evening, September 5th.

Macey had placed the yellow buds inside her ears to listen to music for the first half-mile. Dawn gently removed them. "Ready to hear my Labor Day Weekend story? While it didn't have anything to do with hush puppies, there was a pair of blue suede shoes."

Squeals of delight followed both runners all the way down Flame Street, around the corner, and onto the newly-surfaced, asphalt greenbelt. "Just get on with it, Dawn! The suspense is taking the wind out of me."

Dawn had to stop momentarily to catch her breath. "Promise me you're not going to laugh at me, make snarky comments, glare at me with those intense emerald eyes, or prejudge me, okay?"

"I promise," reassured Macey.

"The reason I even hesitate bringing it up is because it might inadvertently pertain to your fiancé."

Macey's running shoes abruptly hit the asphalt. "Dr. Shaw? He told me this past weekend during our mountain trek that he had no secrets, bottomless pits, or anything to hide."

Dawn gently gripped both of Macey's shoulders. "Calm down. Look at me. Take a deep breath. Just listen."

"I'm walking to hear the rest of this. Forget running for the time being."

The faster Dawn talked, the faster they both walked.

"Believe it or not, our fellow nurse, Caroline Crutchens, decided to have an impromptu masquerade party at her apartment the same evening you and Dr. Shaw were returning from riding the horses.

"Knowing Caroline like we do, it seemed way out of character for her. The stress level from working five days a week coupled with those required Saturday classes drove her to it.

"She and I went to The Shadowy Merc and just started loading food into a grocery cart along with some beverages. We were throwing stuff in there like it was our last meal. This is only part of the introduction."

Macey downed a full bottle of water. "Don't hold back on my account."

Dawn continued, "I'm beginning to wonder if there's ever anything done in this town without a motive. As we continued in super party planning mode, I dressed in an appropriate costume, so I could clown around as I played *Mountain Hostess with the Mostess* in the kitchen. I nearly drove my mother nuts on the phone as she tried to walk me through how to make some appetizers, finger foods, and what have you."

"Who'd you round up for this shindig anyway?"

"That's where the story quickly expands. I'd never

looked twice at Jacobe Davone. The guy's just an assistant in a vet clinic, right? Unbeknownst to me, he'd been meeting Caroline off and on for months to have coffee with her seeking her advice of how and when to ask me to go on a date. She advised him, 'Just do it.' He's an extrovert when it comes to work, but shifts into an introvert most other times."

Signaling she needed to stop and stretch her hamstrings; Macey formed the *time out* sign with both hands. "I'm still waiting for the blue suede shoes punch line."

"Quiet, demure, sweet Caroline has another side to her. She took Jacobe to our local thrift shop, *The Second Time Around,* and Verntoola, the owner, went hog-wild as she dug into her deepest inventory."

Dawn motioned for them to move off the greenbelt and sit on the grass for a few minutes. "When Jacobe blew into the kitchen carrying six packs of pop for the party, he instantly had my full-on attention. He was all decked out in two-tone, orange plaid trousers rolled up to mid-ankle, white polo, a blue suede over jacket, and matching shoes. Two sizes too big, but who was looking at his feet?

"The real stinger was the oval-shaped, high-crown, round-pinched Fedora, complete with blue suede ribbon & adorned with a male pheasant feather. As I took the drinks from his hands to place inside the fridge, I zeroed in on his black beard and perfectly groomed mustache. His boyish shyness was magnetic."

Unable to control her laughing, Macey peppered Dawn with questions faster than she could answer them. "Did you ask him who took care of his grooming for him? Were you painted to the nines with that thick, gloppy paint used for clowns? How about the red wig and matching press-on fingernails? And you expected Jacobe to look twice?"

They stood up, and Dawn ran after Macey farther down the greenbelt. Ultimately, they stopped to sit on a wooden bench under a cottonwood tree.

"Jacobe and I spent most of the evening sitting outside Caroline's small deck overlooking the town. He kicked off those clodhopper shoes and put his feet on the ice chest. We couldn't hear ourselves think inside the small apartment. The music was blaring, and some people were hollering as they played board games. They'd put money into a plastic purple bowl for team winners. That's when the roaring really began.

"By this time, I'd consumed three plates of food, removed my red, yarn wig, and plastic nose. If the poor guy could sit there through all of that and still look at me, perhaps he really is interested. It took some digging to unearth his major hang-up."

Macey removed the ear bud set that was loose around her neck. "We all have them," she readily admitted.

Dawn explained, "Apparently, Jacobe's is that he's just a clerk. He wants to open his own woodworking shop, but there's not enough demand for that in these parts. I greatly encouraged him that he's not a failure just because of his present station in life. All of us need to exercise our gifts and talents."

"What else could he add to woodworking?"

Gesturing as if to place a cap on her head, Dawn said, "I've been wracking my brain trying to come up with ideas. Vast mountain horizons promise bold opportunities."

The evening breeze accompanied them on the remainder of their walk as they rounded the corner to head up Flame

Street. Dawn's allergies spiked as the cotton floated through the air. She sneezed several times. Her nose turned red even without the red plastic, clown bulb.

"Do you deem there's a chance for those blue suede shoes to start walkin' your direction?" asked Macey.

Dawn beamed. "Sure do. All the while I'm talkin.' "

Macey *high-fived* Dawn before she got into her car to head home. "Only two more quiet days at Mintner and then the weekend. Hallelujah! Can't wait."

CHAPTER THIRTY-EIGHT

Most Friday mornings dawned with anticipation for the majority of Shadow Butte County residents who worked in Ridgemonte. The weekenders were the exception.

One of Mintner Medical Center's Charge Nurses, Joyce Stone, had already packed all but one of her suitcases. The other three had been ready since early July. The switched baby debacle had delayed her sandy beach, clear turquoise water, island getaway. Nothing had better stand in the way now.

The county employee, dressed in his incognito best, didn't bother to remove his cowboy hat when leaning over her desk. Joyce offered him a toothpick to hasten his efforts to remove a chunk of whatever it was between his two front teeth. Maybe the cat did have his tongue. He moistened his lips. She placed her hand over the phone receiver, and whispered, "Do you need some help?"

He showed her the front of the number ten, white business envelope. She placed the caller on hold, hung the receiver up, and replied in a hushed tone, "Your best bet is to wait in the hallway on the surgery recovery floor."

"And that would be which number?"

She held up the middle three fingers of her right hand.

Hurriedly ending her telephone call, Joyce announced to her assistant that she needed to pick up a prescription at the hospital pharmacy and would return thereafter. Ignorance truly can be blissful.

Dr. Linke spewed orders to Nurse Caroline Crutchens who needed a pair of track shoes. He stomped down the hallway heading for Room #302.

Sheriff Jeff Jensen stepped right in front of him. Dr. Linke ran straight into him and kept walking. Just before entering the patient's room, the sheriff bent down and slipped the envelope under the doctor's black and white tennis shoe. He announced with authority, "You've been served."

Whirling around to lambast the server, Sheriff Jensen was quicker on the draw. He tipped the brim of his hat downward, nodded, and walked off.

His hands shaking like a dry leaf in the wind, Dr. Linke tore the envelope on its side and removed the contents. His steely eyes darted back and forth.

I have to appear before the State Board of Medicine at 9:00 a.m., September 28th to answer the charges that I have stolen controlled narcotics from Mintner Medical Center and have been using controlled substances.

*It will be an evidentiary hearing. An attorney for the Board of Medicine will be presenting witnesses and evidence to the Board. I can testify, present witnesses, and offer any evidence I have to refute the allegations. I can hire an attorney to represent me if I wish. The board could revoke, suspend, or restrict my license to practice medicine. **REVOKE, SUSPEND, OR RESTRICT** . . .*

Unable to make it to the public bathroom in the hallway, Dr. Linke's gangly body bent forward like a leaning tower,

290

and regurgitated into the sink inside the patient bathroom in Room #304. His repetitive vomiting continued for the next few minutes.

Nurse Crutchens stood stark still in the hallway. The x-ray technician wheeled the patient into the room and helped her into bed. Caroline crept into the room, leaned over the bed, and said, "The doctor is making his rounds. He'll be with you soon."

Meanwhile back at The Shadow Butte County Sheriff's office, Jeff Jensen, with his legs crossed resting on top of his cluttered desk, asked to speak to the clerk at the State Board of Medicine.

"Sheriff Jensen reporting. I did get the notice served just a few minutes ago. No real fireworks, but, then again, it's way past the 4th. Much friendlier atmosphere when serving the pharmacist at the Ridgemonte Rx, however. I'll have my secretary send the process server bill."

Dr. Linke slowly retreated to the doctor's lounge. With his hands on the table, he massaged his throbbing head. Words swam like Black Betta Fish in an aquarium before his eyes. He walked to the calendar on the wall, and stated, "I've got three weeks. I'll bet that two-bit sheriff sat on this notice for a month."

Scouring around for a phone book, he opened the yellow pages. He clenched the corners of pages 135-136, his anger crumpling the ads.

The hissing sounds could be heard in the distance as the front-office receptionist answered the call, "Dunne & Dunne, Chartered, can I help you?"

"Get me your best attorney on the line. I don't have all day."

She yawned, and hung up.

Infuriated, he dialed the same number again.

"Dunne & Dunne, Chartered, can I help you?"

"Yes, good morning. This is Dr. Linke in Ridgemonte. I need to make an appointment as soon as possible to see your best attorney. I've got a hearing coming up."

The receptionist cradled the thickly padded, beige phone under the left side of her chin as she peered into her hand mirror to apply her fresh, apricot-colored lipstick. She held her hands up to her face to make sure the shades of orange matched on her lips and fingernails.

Rubbing her lips together, she replied, "Well, now, that's quite a bit better. "Doctor, what's your last name again?"

"Linke. That's Linke with an 'e'. "

"So, do you say that Link or Linkee? Like rhyming with stinky or plinky?"

"Link. The *e* is silent. Like you'd really know what that means."

Peering at the laminated piece of cardboard on the right-hand side of her desk which listed *Doctors/Medical Personnel/ Lawyers* at the very top, which fees were also at the top of the senior partners' billings, she icily replied, "11:00 a.m. next Monday."

"Yes, satisfactory. Thank you."

Dr. Linke hadn't driven to work for months. He'd walked there most of the time under the auspices of keeping one's coronary health in great shape or in rare instances had his mother chauffer him. On tomorrow's to-do list would be the hard sell for her to shop for some furniture in Cinder Valley while he spoke with Duncan Dunne.

News of the upcoming hearing blew through every

square inch of Mintner Medical Center with hurricane force on Monday. While the unpopular doctor was in the midst of a fray, the nurses didn't let any time slip away. With subpoena in hand, Charge Nurse Joyce Stone spoke with the other summoned witnesses in the employee lounge during the lunch hour.

"I know that some of you have been maintaining careful documentation for months. There's nothing to be concerned about. All of you are excellent employees and extremely competent. Just answer every question you're asked to the best of your ability. Always tell the truth. Are there any concerns?"

Caroline Crutchens suggested they car pool which was wholeheartedly agreed upon. "I'll offer my car, but can someone else plan to drive?"

Turning her attention to her fellow nurse, Macey, she commented, "I really admire you, Macey. I don't know how you've borne the brunt of Linke's hostility all this time. I've hardly slept a minute since last Friday."

With game plan in hand, the hospital employees quietly retreated to their work. Being on the right side of the law supplies one with strength, wisdom, and peace, even in the midst of a storm.

Returning to the doctor's lounge close to 4:00 p.m., Dr. Linke desperately looked for anyone who'd give him the time of day. Even the janitorial staff played hard of hearing.

Sitting in the basement of his mother's home, it dawned on him just before dawn. *Any witnesses for sale anywhere?*

CHAPTER THIRTY-NINE

Maddy and Tenny Moreland were a little more than two months old when the autumn winds could be heard through the pine boughs. Wyn had taken his little family for a horse and buggy ride for a change of scenery as the Quakies dotted the landscape with their bold reds and golds. They spotted a regal, six-point, Whitetail deer feeding at the edge of the meadow. One of its antlers was broken at the mid-point, possibly having lost it to one of the territorial rivals.

Chukars emerged from the nearby bushes at the sound of the horses' hooves. Sarita glanced at her beloved. Her cheeks were finally rosy again. Two of her most precious possessions were sleeping soundly underneath four of the fourteen baby blankets they'd received at their baby shower.

Tenny was a quiet, calm baby whose days and nights flowed seamlessly. Surprising as the genetic world can sometimes be, he's the one who'd ended up with one brown eye and one blue eye stemming from his mother's family tree.

Maddy's breathing and colic were improving quickly. Her little face filled out as she put on weight, erasing the fold above her eye. Aunty Stormy had even started stopping

294

by occasionally to give Mama Merna a helping hand at the Moreland residence.

Wyn paid Mama Merna a visit early Sunday morning in her home. She sat quietly in her rocking chair hemming Tenny's miniature cowboy suit. Maddy's little western dress sat on the end table next to her. He sensed something was not quite right, but he couldn't put his finger on it.

While fitting Wyn for his vest, she reminded him, "You best tell that groom to stop by and get fitted for his wedding. Fenn also. My fingers don't work as fast as they used to, so I've got to allow more time. Not to mention that Priscilla chose crushed velour fabric for some of her accessories which slows me down somewhat. Speaking of Spence, any idea where they're going to live after they get married?"

"None, but I know he's itching to get out of that bunkhouse. Now, please don't get me wrong. He's really appreciated being able to live there. Fenn just lets stuff pile up to the ceiling. Laundry, trash, dishes, catalogs, bills, you name it."

"Nothing a good woman can't fix in short order," Merna offered. "Oh, before I completely forget to mention it, Chet happened to stop by late last evening looking for you. Did he make it on down to your place before dark?"

"No, I haven't seen him for the past couple of weeks. We're starting to round the cattle up from the far corners of the ranch, so we're not only wearing our horses out but ourselves to boot."

Merna reached into her apron pocket to grab her floral hankie to dry the onslaught of tears. "Some terrible news. It seems that Evan Briarley had to leave Ridgemonte two days ago. His brother and sister-in-law perished in a terrible auto accident somewhere in the Midwest. Missourah, I think. Evan was named the guardian of the minor children in the handwritten will. All I can think about is those kids without a mother."

Overcome with grief himself, Wyn comforted Merna. He pulled Tom's old, overstuffed chair closer to hers. "That pierces my heart like sharp arrows released from a quiver. Those poor youngins'. Who will be their mama now? Do you know any more details?"

Merna regained her composure. "The only thing Chet said was the parents had left the children with another Briarley family who already have seven kiddos of their own. Evan's brother had received a nice promotion at work. They'd planned to be gone a few days to celebrate their anniversary, so they had two things to be happy about.

"A semi, or I guess they call them a *triple*, was high-balling it down the freeway. A black tarp blew off the second trailer landing on the windshield of Evan's brother's SUV. He lost control at the wheel and they ran into a cement barrier. Both he and his wife were pronounced dead at the scene."

Wyn glanced at the living room wall. His eyes rested upon Tom and Merna's 50th wedding anniversary picture. His eyes moved to the right and saw two-year old Toby on his little, wooden rocking horse. He walked to the window sill and held on firmly with both hands.

Merna continued, "I asked Chet why on earth Evan's brother would have named him the guardian knowing full well he's not married yet. Chet said that Evan was the children's favorite uncle, hands down. In fact, the kiddos called him, 'Unkie Van.'

"Apparently at the annual family reunion last year, Evan told his brother that he planned to start dating a sales clerk at a country western store in Cinder Valley clear down there in Ignee County. I believe her name is Shasta. When I heard it, I thought of the brand of pop sold at The Shadowy Merc in Ridgemonte.

"Evan had one of those falling meteors in his eyes though. Turns out Shasta moved to Texas to hitch her star to another wagon. According to Chet, he couldn't very well pursue her there because he was living down at the Lower Sabblonti Ranch house. Evan was still taking care of Chet while Stormy was away trying to reinvent herself or whatever in the Sam Hill she was doing."

The kitchen timer sounded. Wyn offered to remove the contents from the oven. Waiting another twenty minutes for one of the loaves of cinnamon raisin bread to cool, he wrapped it in tin foil. At Mama Merna's request, he gave her a big hug.

"You best take care now, Wyn. Somehow, all this is gonna work out. Just don't ask me how."

Chet had given Sabblonti Ranch cowhands, Yatey and Ruston, their range and cattle duties for at least the next week. He knocked on the only door of Cresner Apartment No. 419. Waiting for a few minutes but hearing nothing, he turned to walk down the metal staircase on the side of the building, realizing too late that the elevator would have been best for his right leg. With her towel in hand and dressed in her housecoat, Nurse Nancy called Chet's name.

She invited him inside, politely excusing herself for a few minutes while she did the final rinse on her experimental *Borne Blonde* hair color, the one featured in last week's

Ridgemonte Rx flyer. It was buy one, get the second at 50% off. Even nurses had to live on a budget if they were not yet married to a wealthy baron in high dollah, cattle country.

"What a pleasant, Sunday surprise, Chet! Why, I didn't think you even knew where I lived. Would you like some coffee? How about a fancy dessert to go with it? My freezer is chock full of those."

Before he could answer, Nancy opened her refrigerator freezer, selected an assortment, placed them on a silver tray, and entered the living room. "Your choice. I'll zap it in the microwave while I make your coffee. Black, with or without sugar?"

"Lotsa cream if you happen to have any, please."

Chet's heart was stirred with kindness as Nancy stirred the heavy whipping cream into his coffee, spilling some of it on the kitchen counter. While she cleaned the mess, his eyes landed on the opened page of the current issue of *Western Romances Revisited* resting on her inverted, antique white, cast iron, slipper clawfoot bathtub. *Would something like this ever be used to decorate the living rooms of either one of the Sabblonti Ranch houses?*

To the right of this was a handwritten response to an ad. All he could take in were a few words from the bottom line:

SINGLE BLONDE WITH LOTS OF ATTRIBUTES JUST WAITING TO UNLOAD THEM ON A HANDSOME MAN WHO WILL APPRECIATE THEM. CONTACT N. PRIT . . .

"Homey apartment you have here, Nancy. Looks like you might have a crush on copper with the gourd, pumpkin, bowls, and candle holders or whatever you call those things."

Blushing without having applied her daily blush, Nancy zinged, "I have only one major crush in life right now. These apartment accessories really warm the room, don't you think?"

"That kinda stuff is far from my long suit. You'd best be asking somebody else. I'm sorry to burst in on you unannounced on a weekend since that's your only time off. I really appreciate your hospitality."

Suddenly, Sir Shelton, Nurse Nancy's seal-point Siamese cat, darted across the living room. Hunching its shoulders, it walked sideways in front of Chet. Sir Shelton's tinky, silver bell made a sound each time he put his paw on the floor. *That cat would drive me bonkers. The only thing a cat is good for is a mouser inside a barn. I sure hope Evan doesn't mind the ding-a-ling.*

Patting his stomach after inhaling a fancy dessert plate filled with one half-dozen, frosted Brown Sugar Pecan Squares and Lemon Bars, he continued, "Better top it off with some more coffee and call it good for this morning. Evan mentioned you probably liked to cook a lot. Those pecan jobs really hit the spot!"

After Chet uttered Evan, her current favorite name, Nancy asked, "Is this a social visit or does your family need some medical help? I can offer general nursing advice, but anything more than that would require you to make an appointment at the clinic. Of course, you could always solicit advice from Evan."

"No way to sugar coat this one, Nurse Nancy."

She quickly closed the magazine and set her coffee cup on top to secure it.

Chet extended both of his arms full length, laced his fingers together, and flexed them. "Evan's in some pretty deep water right about now. Matter of fact, I'd say he's just about ready to drown."

"Can't he swim? Come to think of it, I've been listening for his door to open and close. I haven't seen his van leave the parking lot for a few days. Maybe he's been walking to the local gym. I heard they just reopened the pool there. There was a water contamination issue in the deep end."

Stroking his black mustache, Chet slowly floated out the few details he knew regarding Evan's family's terrible loss.

"I thought you might like to know what's going on since you're Evan's closest neighbor and all. Plus, you like to whip up the groceries, so maybe you can help feed those kids when they first arrive.

"I've had a few days to think long and hard about what I'd do if I had to try to corral all five at once. My first thought was to ride off into the sunset and not return for a while. That wouldn't accomplish anything, would it? It just might drive me straight back to the race horse track where I used to work."

Nancy jumped up from the couch and walked into the kitchen. Chet noticed the swath of hair she'd missed with her morning dye job. He'd let Evan fill that in if it got that far.

She emerged from the kitchen with a cat-themed note pad and pen. Sir Shelton walked around and between her feet, purring loudly. "Here's the phone number for my apartment or you might suggest to Evan that he can always find me at Evergreene Medical Clinic. I'd love to help him get a new swimming suit. Maybe we could even get matching ones."

CHAPTER FORTY

Brunch had been promised to all of the medical staff who'd been required to testify at Dr. Linke's rescheduled hearing in front of the State Board of Medicine on October 11th in Cinder Valley.

Jacobe Davone had spent Friday procuring the supplies at The Shadowy Merc. Store clerk, Cannaleah, worked in tandem with him to let him know exactly what hours Salina Bevvins would be there so as to avoid the supreme snoop factor. He worked late into the evening helping Dr. Shaw spruce up his ranchette three miles outside Ridgemonte. Jacobe even ironed the table cloths and napkins.

The nursing staff was ushered inside on this glorious fall Saturday morning to the sounds of peaceful, melodic music and seated at card tables arrayed with hand-crafted truffles placed inside miniature blue and white flowered music boxes, courtesy of Sable Shaw. Macey smiled inwardly when recalling that her candy-making lesson during calendar year 2000 was truly taken to heart by her fiancé.

Charge Nurse Joyce Stone sampled one of the raspberry ones, savoring every ounce. "Chocolates are a woman's best friend."

Dawn Rowann quipped, "I thought diamonds trumped chocolates any ol' day of the week."

Nurse Nancy Pritchurt sighed as she devoured three of the coconut variety all at once.

Dr. Shaw plated the morning offering as Jacobe, with a free-flowing, green linen napkin draped over his forearm, served Bountiful Breakfast Quinoa Bowls.

Nurse Caroline Crutchens was quickest, "This is too pretty to eat! Three avocado slices, seven chunks of smoked breakfast sausage, two lime wedges, some black beans, two roasted garlic cloves, sautéed red bell peppers, one sunny-side up egg, all garnished with fresh parsley and chives. Macey, do you realize you're marrying the guy who fixed this?"

The "'yums' . . . Can you believe how tasty this is? Best breakfast I've had in years", and repeated, raving reviews could be heard in the kitchen while Jacobe made a fourth pot of coffee.

When Dr. Shaw entered the room, Macey collared him and gave him a big, thank-you kiss. He laughed, "Guess it's a good thing we both like garlic!"

Joyce tapped her juice glass with her fork. "Shall we toast the good veterinarian and his assistant? I'm especially impressed with the avocadoes this late in the season."

Dr. Shaw replied, "I'm sure we're looking at the last of them for now."

The women took turns around the table thanking and praising Dr. Shaw and Jacobe.

Dawn scooted her chair closer to Caroline, so a folding chair could be placed next to her for Jacobe.

"I just hope I don't put on all the weight I lost during this whole Linke lash-up."

Caroline said, "That makes two of us."

Dr. Shaw surmised the reason none of the other women spoke or mentioned Dr. Linke was because either they'd already hashed it out among themselves or had no words left. Macey hadn't wasted a minute calling him when she returned after the hearing. He'd not seen her this happy since he'd met her.

He decided to place a gentle capstone on the matter. "The important thing for all of you, Dr. Linke, his patients, and the hospital in general is the State Board of Medicine suspended his license to practice until he successfully completes treatment. After that, he can petition the board to have it reinstated."

Caroline's final comment wasn't lost on Nurse Nancy or any of the other single nurses in attendance. "Hope is on the horizon. Just think of the endless possibilities of the doctor who will be replacing Linke." All but Macey and Dawn clinked their glasses together to a hearty, "Amen!"

Nurse Nancy quickly regained her senses. Not everyone in attendance had heard of Evan's recent plight of his brother and sister-in-law perishing in an auto accident, leaving five children who survived. She gave them the condensed version thereof. Nancy offered, "I'd like to host a welcome party for the children, but my apartment is so small. I invite your ideas and teamwork."

Joyce readily replied, "I would be more than happy to host. That's a splendid idea, Nancy. Your merciful heart really shines through which is one of the things I appreciate the most about you."

Nancy continued, "I sincerely apologize for throwing such a damper on our celebratory morning. I just found out about this."

Macey didn't miss a beat. "Who will take care of all those kids? Five all at once? I plan on having one kid maybe every five years." Dr. Shaw looked straight ahead, didn't take the bait, then all eyes were on Nancy.

"Don't look at me!" she shrieked. "A *Quint Welcome* is my contribution. I can't get Evan Briarley to look twice at me despite repeated attempts. I'm gleaning elsewhere at the moment."

"Where's elsewhere?" asked Caroline.

"I'll meet you Monday for lunch at the Sage Hen Café in Ridgemonte. Let me know what time is best for you. I wish I would have thought of this a long time ago," Nancy said.

Early that evening just as Nancy prepared to watch one of her favorite chick flicks, she heard a loud rental truck engine in the parking lot of Cresner Apartments. Children bailed out of it and started chasing each other on the asphalt, all but the youngest who had his little blue blankie wrapped around his arm and wrist as he sucked his left thumb. She melted into her recliner and wept.

Retaining her composure, she turned the TV off, rinsed her face in cold water, and stared out the window. The sheer shock and fatigue had already taken its toll on Evan.

He'd not recalled seeing a stark blonde-headed woman in the vicinity before he'd left to collect the children. She approached from a distance and gathered the youngest in her arms, drawing him very close.

Evan lumbered toward her frantically waving both arms and demanding, "Put him down!"

"Calm down, Evan. That's no way to talk to me. You're going to frighten the poor child. It's not like he hasn't been through enough already."

He leaned uncomfortably close to her. "Nancy, is that you? What on earth did you do to your hair? It's dark brown in the back and blonde in the front and on the sides."

"You're just saying that because you don't like me. You'd best be nice to these kids or they won't like you either."

He'd started to retreat then walked back toward her. "These kids adore me. Why do you think I'm the one who ended up with them?"

She tried to gently hand the youngest one to Evan, but he grabbed her around her neck with his little blanket covering Nancy's face.

When Evan reached both arms for him, he pouted, and declared, "No."

"Would you like some help this evening?" Nancy asked.

"Not unless you want to keep the little one who seems to have already glommed onto you."

She thought carefully before replying, "I doubt it's in the best interest to split the children up. They've already been through tremendous trauma."

"Since when did you become such an expert on children and traumatic situations?"

As he gently removed the whimpering little boy from Nancy's arms, she answered, "I've never claimed to be an expert on anything, Evan."

Before unloading the truck, he looked at his watch. "Hop in, kids. We're going for a fun ride." Securing the youngest in the car seat, he headed out of town, drove to the S curve on the highway, and turned left heading into the sunset.

Back at Cresner Apartment No. 419, Nancy was putting

the finishing touches on the dye job in the back of her hair after taking her hand mirror and looking in the front mirror. She stuffed the current issue of *Western Romances Revisited* inside her backpack. Monday's lunch appointment would apply the soothing salve the nurses needed when they launched their brilliant strategy.

CHAPTER FORTY-ONE

Evan banked on Chet being as highly predictable as he'd been during the entirety of 2000. Driving slowly past the Main Sabblonti Ranch house, the oldest of the Briarley children, a nine-year-old girl, exclaimed, "Unkie Van, that's a huge house! What's it doing way out here?"

His shoulders, arms and wrists screamed with pain as did his behind. "That old house has been there for a really long time. There's an even longer story that goes with it."

"I like long stories. Can you tell it to me?"

"Sure. There was this old woman named Jantzi Belle Sabblonti. She lived there for many years, and then she fell out of the upper window and d . . .

"Uh, look, kids! Did you see that badger over there?"

One of the younger boys busted him, "That's not a badger. Before Mommy died, she took us to the library. We got to look through a picture book about animals."

Then all of the children started crying. Evan was never so happy to see Chet's pickup parked inside the driveway of the Lower Sabblonti Ranch house. *True friends are the familiar instruments who play soothing melodies during the unexpected tragedies of life.*

Stormy gasped when opening the front door. Chet stood closely behind her with his hands wrapped tightly around her slim waist. Evan raised his eyebrows above his bulging eyes.

"Come on in!" boomed Chet. "Looks like you brought the whole herd, Evan. Want to join us for supper? It's a good thing Stormy fixed extras."

She got on her knees and extended both arms to the little boy. He walked behind Evan's legs with his tattered blankie dragging the floor. The little four-year old boy ran to Stormy and leaned into her shoulder. He hung onto the back of her apron and followed her around as she sat extra plates on the table. When handing him the forks and spoons, he stood on his tiptoes and set them beside each plate. He even sat on her lap while they ate.

Evan and Chet spoke in hushed tones as Stormy cleaned the kitchen. As the oldest girl helped her, she asked, "Where does your mama live?"

Stormy dried her hands and sat at the table. Patting a chair, she said, "Come and sit with me, please. My mother isn't here anymore. She passed away."

"Were you sad like me when she died?"

"I still am." Stormy hugged her gently.

"Did people like your mama?"

"I loved my mama. My daddy loved my mama. My husband loved my mama. I don't really know about anyone else. Let's finish the dishes, shall we? I'll bet we can find some ice cream in the freezer. Chet does like his ice cream."

Stormy listened to the intense activity as she calmly wiped spaghetti sauce from the table, floor, counters, and front of the refrigerator.

All five kiddos stood in front of the fireplace mantle in the living room as Evan lined them up from oldest to youngest. "It's the perfect time for you to meet my family. Nine-year-old Emma, seven-year-old Vannessa, five-year-old Andy, four-year-old Monty, and two-year-old Jedidiah."

Emma proudly announced, "We call him Jeddie for short. Mama said that would be easiest." She wiped her eyes with the bottom of her striped top.

"Stormy, would you mind taking the kids outside for a little bit?" Evan asked. "They could expend some energy before we head home. Being cooped up inside the truck for hours hasn't been a ton of fun."

She'd already thought of the idea herself. "Come on children, let's walk down the lane, shall we?"

Evan headed into the kitchen and dug around the bottom of the pantry. "Chet, you got anything to make a coffee royal or some such?"

"Not so as you would notice. Besides, you're driving precious cargo tonight. Best wait until another time."

He sunk deep into the living room couch. "Chet, what am I going to do? That makes an instant half dozen of us now. My brother hadn't been able to afford life insurance. He'd just recently applied for a policy, but it wasn't approved at the time of his death. They had no home. Just rented. Wonderful family. No material wealth to speak of." Laying his head on the back of the couch, he stared at the ceiling. "I've never felt so lost in my entire life."

Chet started pacing in front of the fireplace. "Can any of your other brothers and sisters or family members help out?"

"They all live paycheck to paycheck. Salt of the earth people, but none of them have any vast holdings or extras to speak of. I just can't do this alone."

Curling his thumbs inside his front jean pockets, Chet looked squarely at Evan. "Seems to me like you've got a decision to make. Maybe you'd better swallow your pride and take a good, long look at Nurse Nancy Pritchurt or get your scope out and start scopin' out somebody else.

"You'll go plum batty in less than a month tryin' to do this by yourself. Sure, there's enough ranchin' folks around to help out short term, but you best be thinkin' long haul here, buddy."

"Speaking of Nancy, how'd she know about these kids anyway?"

Chet sat across from Evan and looked him square in his eyes. "I stopped by her apartment to tell her. I thought that'd be best since she lives so close to you. She could sorta help out for a few days. The other reason you'd best be decidin' on which way your romantic notion is spinnin' is something I saw on her tub."

"Tub?" Evan choked. "Did you use her can when you visited?"

"Negatorie, good buddy. I don't make a habit of using women's bathrooms."

They both laughed. "I guess that didn't quite come out like I planned. You know what I mean. First of all, I don't visit women I don't know unless it's an absolute emergency. I definitely don't use their cans. I'd stop at a stop and rob store and use one before doing that!"

Evan heard childrens' voices in the distance. "Explain the tub deal quickly."

"Nancy's coffee table is an inverted tub sitting in her living room."

"And you're pushing me to marry her?"

"Maybe yes, maybe no." Chet said. "She was in the process of filling out one of those dealie bobs in the back of a magazine. Searchin' for Mr. Right or whatever you wanna call him. Marry that up with a half blonde dye job and a tub turned upside down. You figure it out. I'm still tryin' to figure Stormy out after all these years."

Evan grinned for one of the few times in several weeks. "Looked to me like you're starting to figure it out. You were draped around her like a lamp shade when she answered the front door tonight."

Chet hummed and hawed, "You could say we're getting' the horses saddled for a long winter's ride. Gotta coupla extra saddles I could loan you. Interested?"

CHAPTER FORTY-TWO

Priscilla Fletcher sat across the Longbowe's kitchen table not having touched the chicken salad sandwich, tomato basil soup, and condiments so lovingly prepared by Lizzelle. This was her third and final solo, pre-marital appointment with Preacher Len and his wife. She and her fiancé, Spence Woodson, had completed their combination appointments. Somehow, Spence had managed to complete his individual ones in addition to keeping up with his duties as Assistant Ranch Foreman on the Toppens Cattle Ranch.

Fall responsibilities seemed no less daunting than any other season: thoroughly cleaning, servicing, and storing hay equipment; sorting cattle for shipping; weaning replacement heifers; and vaccinating and sorting cows. Those were the main jobs.

Spence told Priscilla there were many minor ones. She'd tried to keep her heart attitude in check and not let bitter resentment build toward Fenn Bridgemore and the other cowhands besides Spence who worked on the Toppens Ranch. *And just exactly what did those other guys do all day long? Watch black and white, western re-runs on TV?*

Lizzelle drilled deep on Saturday afternoon, November 17th. "Priscilla, you're only about six weeks from walking down the aisle at this point. If you have any reservations whatsoever, you need to voice them now. You're not very talkative today."

Preacher Len excused himself to go outside for a few minutes. When he returned, Priscilla's tongue still wasn't moving.

She asked Preacher Len, "You're a man whose been married a long time. I think you'd be the best one to answer my questions. Nothing personal, Lizzelle."

Through several crying episodes, Priscilla eked out her questions. "Spence doesn't seem like he's had time for me the past few months. He appears to be able to make time for everyone and everything else except me. I don't want to head into our marriage with him acting like that. I need and want to be first place in his heart. Since you're a man, I'd like some input from you."

Preacher Len talked as slowly as he moved on any given day. "A rancher's life is beyond busy. I was under the impression you knew this. It's vital you decide in your heart if you can live the life of a rancher's wife day in and day out.

"Marriage is teamwork. A tremendous amount of it. Just think for a moment of your job at the Shadow Butte County Recorder's Office. Not all of you have the same jobs to do every day, but you work together to get the job done. I would imagine some days there are some of you who have much more to do than others. Do you agree?"

Priscilla scowled. "I don't see how the recorder's office has anything to do with our marriage. Indirectly, I guess it would since I work there."

"I was only trying to think of an example. I can tell you from our sessions with Spence that he absolutely loves you with his whole heart, can't wait to get married, and will make a fine husband. He's a very principled man. You just need to decide if you want to give him that opportunity. Men like Spence don't remain bachelors for any length of time."

The Longbowes had learned a long time ago these type of premarital sessions couldn't be rushed. Lizzelle reheated Priscilla's soup in the microwave.

In between spoonfuls, she warmed up. "I think Spence has not been spending much time around me because of my mother. He probably thinks that after we're married things will be much easier. Have you ever performed wedding ceremonies for couples who did not have the blessing of their parents?"

Lizzelle laughed first. "More than once."

Preacher Len confirmed, "I can't tell you how many. In fact, I'd like to have a dollar for every one of them. I could probably buy a good horse and top-dollar tack with the total amount."

Priscilla took the last bite of her sandwich and bread and butter pickle. "Maybe the problem is me. I need to move my mother out of first place and put Spence there. I thought I'd already done that. I'm not marrying her for heaven's sake. I'm marrying Spence, the man of my dreams!"

Lizzelle asked, "I just have one very important question before you leave?"

"And that would be?"

"Are you going to provide lots of space heaters at your ceremony?"

"Oh, my gosh! I'd not even thought of that. Thank you. I'll put that on Spence's list. Never mind, I'll put that on my *teamwork* list."

Lizzelle's hug lingered just long enough for Priscilla. She departed from the Longbowe's residence with peace in heart, but without spotting the brown van parked at the bottom of the hill.

Preacher Len welcomed Evan, Andy, Monty, and Jeddie Briarley. Emma and Vannessa had started attending school in Ridgemonte, the first few weeks of which had been quite turbulent.

Lizzelle coaxed little Jeddie who finally agreed to sit on her lap. She'd decorated little brown sacks and filled them with goodies and small toys before the children arrived.

Evan and Preacher Len retreated to the back of their house. A pot of hot coffee and freshly baked orange rolls graced the table in the study. Evan, never one to stand on formalities, helped himself in short order.

Four-year-old Monty's tears hit Evan's ears. "I'd like to bat the breeze for a while, Preacher, but sounds like we better cut to the chase. Speaking of chase, that's basically what I'm here for. Thanks for putting me on your schedule on such short notice."

The corners of Preacher Len's mouth turned upward. "I don't have a schedule of my own. The Good Shepherd plans mine. I just try to get up every day and listen for His marching orders." He picked up his frayed, black leather Bible and read Psalm 23 aloud.

Evan stopped chewing, wiped his hands on a napkin, and listened intently. "Those words are so comforting to me right about now. Do you and your wife have any kids?"

Preacher Len carefully closed his Bible and laid it on the bookshelf. "Unfortunately not. There's not a subject that's taxed my mind more in all the time of our ministry than that. I've pleaded with the Lord for an answer, but He's never given one. His grace is sufficient for Lizzelle and me."

Evan was completely stumped. "Uh, I'm not following you at all on that one."

"I guess another way I could phrase it is I fought the Lord way too long on the subject of children. I went through guilt trips, feeling inadequate, depression, anger, the whole gamut. When I get to Heaven, perhaps He'll explain it to me.

"So, rather than wasting my whole life, I decided to just put my hand in His hand and walk with Him every day. There's no One and nothing more powerful than He is. If he wanted us to have kids, well, He sure enough knew how to create them or get them to us."

Evan stared at the half empty, aluminum pan of rolls. Preacher Len hadn't taken a bite of them. "Are you saying these five kids I just inherited might be part of His plan? Is that how He operates?"

Preacher Len declared emphatically, "He does whatever He pleases in Heaven and on Earth. Far be it from me to try to ask Him why He does what He does. Matter of fact, here's an extra Bible. Take this home and read the book of Job."

Not hearing a peep from the kiddos at the moment, Evan didn't dare leave without having his next question answered. "The real reason I'm here is to talk to you about marriage. Seems like you and your bride figured it out decades ago."

Preacher Len truly enjoyed these types of sessions and certainly not at the expense of those in attendance. He patted the new Bible, and said, "Again, everything you need to know about marriage is printed within these two covers."

"Even how to select your wife in the first place?"

"Yes, for the most part. God will guide you in the final selection if you follow Him. Does there happen to be someone you're considering at the moment? She sure as heaven's sake needs to want and love kids!"

Evan shook his head back and forth in frustration. "This is what's driving me nuts, Preacher Len: I thought the man was supposed to pursue the woman, not the other way around."

Preacher Len's oversized stomach jiggled when he laughed. "I would say that's primarily true; however, don't discount a situation or opportunity where a good woman shows some interest ahead of the natural course of things." He hoped his broad grin would help Evan with the non-verbals.

"Say, I've got a simple, practical exercise for you that I sometimes suggest to those we're counseling for their upcoming marriages. Take a piece of paper and draw a line down the center of it. In the left-hand column write the cons and in the right-hand column, enter the pros of the woman you're considering.

"If you have several women on the horizon, then just make a separate sheet for each one of them. Then pray and listen. God will show you the perfect one. Let peace be your governor and guide you."

Evan eyed the wall of built-in shelves inside the hickory-paneled den chock-full of books. "It will be a miracle if I can get any guidance or have any peace trying to take care of this flock."

"That's why you'd better plan on carving out at least a few minutes every day to listen to The Good Shepherd and read your Bible. You need a wife sooner rather than later. Even the Good Book says a prudent one is from the Lord."

Preacher Len shook Evan's hand enthusiastically.

The children hugged Evan's pant legs as he stood in the living room for a few more minutes. "Thanks so much for your time, Longbowes. Come on kiddos, I've got to round up some paper and a pencil."

CHAPTER FORTY-THREE

It had been Stormy's normal routine to visit Chet primarily on the weekends the past couple of months. The Wednesday after Thanksgiving, he was surprised to see Jantzi Belle's old pickup parked in the driveway of the Lower Sabblonti Ranch house when he returned from meeting Yatey. She hummed softly as she applied the wall paper strip above the dresser in one of the guest bedrooms.

Chet's whistle startled her. "Nice decoratin' job, Stormy. You gettin' this fixed up for Evan's youngest, so you can take care of them down here every once and a while? Say, isn't that new furniture, too? How'd you get that in here all by your lonesome?"

She placed her right forefinger around one of his belt loops. "I'm glad you approve. I just thought a little boy would like a room with accents of ponies, lariats, cowboy hats and boots."

"Well, I'm a big boy, and it looks mighty fine to me. You'll be able to rock Jeddie in that chair when he shows up."

Chet generally paid close attention to things in plain sight. Thankfully, he didn't ask what was under the queen-size blanket resting on the far side of the wall.

She suggested Chet rest for a bit in the living room while

she fixed supper. Blue and Beebee were the first to sense someone outside on the porch. Blue growled as he lowered his head near the threshold.

"I think someone's at the door, Chet. Can you please check? I'm washing spuds and veggies in the sink right now."

Chet opened the door just as Sheriff Jeff Jensen raised his hand to use the horseshoe shaped door knocker.

"Come in. Hope you're not the bearer of bad news. Have a seat in the living room. How about a cup of cowboy coffee? I'm sure it's better than that stuff you drink in town!"

Sheriff Jensen removed his cowboy hat and requested an audience with both Chet and Stormy. It looked to her like he'd used just a titch more bear grease in his hair to make a perfectly straight line down the center of it.

He drank a bit of his coffee before launching into his explanation. "Well folks, I sure do wish I had a better report for you. I just returned from a nationwide law enforcement conference on the east coast. I was there for five days. On the evening of the third day, I wasn't feeling too shiny, so I headed back to my hotel room a little early.

When I turned on the cable news station, you'll never believe whose pictures, or I should say mug shots, I saw."

Stormy gasped. "It wasn't Less and Meg Alotto was it?"

Sheriff Jensen replied, "It most certainly was."

Chet slapped his right knee. "Those lousy crooks! Tell us more."

The sheriff continued, "There isn't a whole lot else I can tell you, unfortunately. I called the authorities the next day and explained who I was and that we'd been looking for them for several months.

"I was told there was an outstanding warrant for embezzlement for Meg from a large utility company. It sounds like she used one of her fake ID's to get hired in the first place. Then she proceeded to rip them off the same way she did the Sabblonti Ranch when she set up the fake account at the Bank of Blunte.

"One of the investigators told me that the Alottos had blown all the cash they stole from you at the casinos. In Meg's statement to the authorities, she also mentioned something about stealing a large amount of cash which was stored inside the Main Sabblonti Ranch house. There was something about some money that smelled like smoke or had been through a house fire. Does this sound at all familiar to you?"

Chet chimed in, "If there was any money inside the ranch house, it was probably there before Jantzi Belle died."

Stormy scowled, "It sounds like Meg went through every square inch of our home. I feel so violated! I hope the Alottos get locked up for a very long time. They deserve it!"

"They're basically beyond destitute now," explained Sheriff Jensen. "It sounds like Meg was a professional embezzler and Less was her partner in crime when he drove her across various state lines with the stolen money. It's a pretty sad tale when it's all said and done."

The sheriff finished his coffee and headed for the door. "I'd love to stay and bat the breeze for a while longer, but I just met a new lady friend in town, so I've got a hot date tonight."

Chet and Stormy thanked him and watched him leave the driveway.

"No use cryin' over spilled milk, Stormy. What'd you

whip up for supper? Or I guess I should ask how long you're stayin' this evenin'?"

Her mind raced. "Um, I wasn't sure when you'd be getting back home. Seems like it's earlier than normal."

"That's because all the cattle are down from the hills now. Good thing 'cause Yatey, Ruston, and all of us are plum wore out."

Stormy's calculations were yielding slow dividends. Hoping to buy some additional time on the end of supper, she opened two cans of chili, prepared some package dough, and dropped it by spoonfuls on top of the mixture. A heated can of corn and a bowl of sliced peaches seemed to quell Chet's hunger.

He retrieved some small Juniper branches from the bed of his pickup to start an aromatic fire. Sitting as close as she could next to him on the couch as they ate, she reflected, "Thanksgiving Day at the Morelands was so enjoyable. I could hardly hear myself think when the Briarley kids were inside the house. I surely don't mind having them around. A lot of noise is a challenge for me though."

Chet got up to turn the light switches off. "I thought all these years you didn't like too many lights. Never thought of the noise."

"That's because you could sleep through a tornado or an earthquake. Speaking of sleep, I brought an outfit I think you'd especially enjoy tonight."

After supper, and staying true to his own self, Chet led Stormy to the front door and helped her with her coat. "I'm just not quite there yet. But I can totally promise you this: I've kept myself on the straight and narrow this whole time. Don't plan on doin' anything else. How about you collect a few more of those *outfits* as you call 'em, and I'll let you know what I think of 'em. One of these days here right quick like."

No wrath, outbursts, tears, or scalding rhetoric ensued.

All was quiet on the western porch of the Lower Sabblonti Ranch house.

S

Evan didn't get to sleep before 2:00 a.m. three nights in a row. The fees at the local daycare were devouring his grocery budget. Monty and Jeddie cried themselves to sleep every night.

Emma needed help with her spelling words for ten minutes each evening after supper. She washed the dishes inside the kitchen sink as Evan dried them. One particular word on tonight's list hit him right between the runnin' lights. Her teacher had instructed the students to say the word aloud first, then spell it.

"*S t u b b o r n. Stubborn.* Unkie Van, what's that word mean? I never heard Daddy or Mamma say it."

The glass he was drying slipped from his hand and crashed onto the floor. "Sheesh! Hand me that broom over there."

Emma slid her trembling hands deeper into the kitchen

sink to hide them when hearing the glass break. After wiping down the counters, she dutifully collected her list of spelling words and placed it inside her school bag.

Vannessa helped Andy and Monty into their pajamas. Emma applied toothpaste to the little toothbrushes. She hugged each of her siblings good night as she tucked them into their sleeping bags on the floor. Her imaginary bedtime story was just a little bit shorter this evening.

At the stroke of midnight and feeling like he might have a stroke, Evan took a quick shower, shaved, applied some five-year old aftershave, and donned virtually the only dress clothing he owned. His socks didn't match, but that was sure to be the least of his concerns at the moment. He double checked to make sure the front door was securely locked.

An orange-gold, harvest moon provided extra light for his quiet footsteps down the metal staircase on the side of the Cresner Apartment building. "Be bold, be strong, be courageous." He'd just read a combination of those words in the book Preacher Len had gifted him.

He rapped on the door several times to no avail. His fist pounding finally produced results. With her turquoise and black sleeping mask resting on top of her head and matching buds dangling from both ears, Nurse Nancy jerked the door wide open.

"You don't have to beat the door down for crying out loud! Jimminey Crickets, get inside."

Laugh or cry, Evan, what's it gonna be? "Do you have a few minutes you could talk to me?"

She stood at the far end of the living room with her arms crossed. "Your timing has never been good. At least not as far as my life has been concerned."

His eyes swiftly swept the room, landing upon the cover of the *Western Romances Revisited*. A handwritten, addressed, stamped envelope rested on top of it.

"Do you realize it's after midnight? I have to get up at 6:00 and go to work in the morning. Make that this morning." Nurse Nancy still hadn't cracked a smile of any sort.

Evan raised his voice and threw both arms into the air. "Well, do you realize that I have five kids to take care of plus work full time? When do you think I have any time to sleep, much less any time for myself?"

"I have no idea. That's not my problem. I've offered to help you. Every invitation I've ever extended to you has been ignored or blown off. I'm not just some last resort case or someone to help you through a rough spot.

"I have a lot to offer a man, but you've never bothered to even look once, much less twice." He WAS looking now. Nancy's hurriedly tied, short, silky bathrobe had come untied. He motioned for her to cinch it up.

A scene Evan had watched in an old movie flashed through his mind. He calmly suggested, "This sounds sorta silly. Could I go outside, gently knock on the door again, and would you please let me in? Let's just call it 'Take Two.'"

"My better judgment tells me no. You've got one chance left."

"I'll take it," Evan stated emphatically.

"Don't knock for five minutes, please."

Before Evan stepped outside, he looked at his watch. Pacing the balcony in front of the apartments, his mind revisited his Senior High School Prom night. He'd not remembered that his date on that occasion could well have been Nurse Nancy's twin standing inside her apartment.

She was waiting for his knock. It's amazing what a woman could do in five short minutes.

All decked out in a long, lavender, lounge dress with freshly combed hair, tropical breeze perfume, and matching lavender accessories, she hurriedly closed the door behind him.

"Don't look at the clock," Nancy directed. "It's only going to contribute to our fatigue."

"Is it okay if I remove my house slippers?" Evan asked. "I generally go barefoot when I'm inside."

She dimmed the lights in the living room. "Yes, only your slippers," laughing uproariously when she saw his socks. One cat design and the other one a dog.

He slid the magazine to his left and laid the crumpled sheet of notebook paper on the coffee table. "This is what I wanted to talk to you about."

Nancy tried to read the paper, but needed more light. Evan relaxed as serenity settled over the room. He looked straight ahead, but saw the trickle of a tear mixed with pink rouge running down her left cheek as she silently reviewed both columns.

She knelt down before him as he sat on the couch. "Did you write this or did you have some help?"

"I wrote it myself, and I mean every single word of it. Cataclysmic events have a way of properly reordering a man's priorities. I came to the realization almost too late that my mind was still parked back in my college frat-rat days. I would like to start courting you, but I have no idea on God's green earth how that's going to happen since I've inherited

327

an instant family. It's surreal how life has a way of changing in a moment's time."

As the clock neared two, the moment she'd yearned for was finally upon her. Nurse Nancy lovingly stated, "Rest assured, we're not the first couple to start a romance with five kids in tow. This isn't how I'd imagined it would be either. We're at the intersection of dreaming or reality. What choose you?"

No one could top a sly Briarley grin. He took both of her hands to help her stand. "Marriage isn't about the past. It's about the future. I choose you." Pulling her as close to him as he could, he hadn't realized how good it could feel.

"Nancy Briarley has a nice ring to it," he quipped.

"That's supposed to me my line!"

She sank into his arms for a blazing kiss.

There was no way Evan wanted to blight his future. Neither did Nancy. He never imagined he'd ever want to be this close to her. Reality ruled as he bid her 'Good night' or rather 'Good morning' three minutes later.

As soon as the front door closed, Nancy hurriedly scooped up the magazine and stamped envelope. Neither would see the light of day. She returned to her bedroom, opened her dresser drawer, and produced a small, lined theme book where she'd practiced signing her name for almost a year.

Nancy Anne Briarley

Examining her bare left ring finger under the bedroom lamp, she sighed. "Alas, the man is far more important than the ring."

Four short hours later, Evan heard Jeddie crying out, "Mommy, mommy."

They'd tried to establish some sort of morning routine, especially for school days. Emma mixed the orange juice and filled the short glasses.

Andy looked all around the table. "Unkie Van, I don't see no grape juice, but you gots purple round your mouth. Can I have grape stead of orange?"

His voice trailed down the hallway toward the small bathroom. "Time to head to school and daycare, kiddos." Surely no one ages nine and under recognized lavender shades of lipstick.

CHAPTER FORTY-FOUR

Betty Lou Bradford, Shadow Butte County Recorder, inverted the rose-shaped, candy molds onto white doilies. She ran the bridal shower committee the same way she did her office, with precision and efficiency. Snagging some of her dishwater blonde hair drawn tightly into a bun on top of her head inside her jeweled, cat-eye shaped, reading glasses, she quickly sought the assistance of her husband. He was sorely vexed trying to unwind it, so she handed him the foot long, black-handled, all-purpose scissors. "Just whack where you need to, Elmer! I can't see the back of my hair anyway."

With Ace and Jantzi Belle Sabblonti both deceased, Betty'd spent an inordinate amount of time, energy, and resources the past several months to correct the boundary lines of the Merrill and Sabblonti Ranches as it pertained to the vital Alder Creek.

The creek and reservoir belonged to the Merrill Ranch until late 1995 when one of Sabblonti's hired hands cut the five-strand, barbed wire fence of Merrill's Ranch in order to allow the Sabblontis' cattle to drink from Alder Creek.

After crafting her cauldron of deceit, Jantzi Belle Sabblonti had managed to obtain a copy of the title deed to the land and forge the seller's signature. With only one month remaining in 2001, Betty Lou could really relax and enjoy this day.   Not to mention the fact that it was much easier to face Marita Merrill who was due to arrive in less than thirty minutes with all of the food for the festivities. Betty Lou had the corrected deed listing the Merrills as the rightful owner of the creek and reservoir. The vital piece of paper was resting safely inside a large brown envelope inside her home office. She planned to give it to Marita in a few short hours.

Babies, brides, and bouquets were the theme of the moment. Bradford's living room was all atwitter as Maddy and Tenny Moreland were passed around from woman to woman.

Marita had prepared four different types of brunch quiches complete with her Cloverdale buns and coconut fruit salad. She'd had to keep a close eye on Nelson, her husband, who'd scarfed down one-quarter of one pan of freshly baked rolls and several bites of the salad before she could get them loaded into her rig to head to town. She'd opted for a four-tier, heart shaped, lemon flavored cake slathered with butter cream icing to serve to the ladies.

Learning a long time ago how to keep most everyone happy, Betty had prepared pretty much everything in 50% pink, Priscilla's favorite color, and 50% purple which was Nancy's.

Elmer had stayed up until after ten o'clock last evening filling the clear glasses with pinto beans and placing a fresh succulent on top of each one. Far be it from him to question what would pass for a centerpiece at a luncheon. He sure as the world wasn't going to count out every bean just to make sure there was an equal amount in each glass.

Before the women arrived, Elmer had dialed up dinner

with Delbert Dawson and some of his other buddies at The Sage Hen Café. He could already taste the hot, open-faced beef sandwich, drowning in thick, brown country gravy. He hadn't quite decided on what kind of pie it would be today.

There's always a reward at the end as far as Elmer was concerned. Everyone in attendance at the café would be waiting with baited breath for yet another one of Delbert's thick yarns which he liked to spin by the country mile.

To everyone's sheer amazement, Stormy had offered to hand craft the shower favors. Pink-and-white striped and purple-and-white striped, petite, cardboard boxes were alternated at each of the place settings on the portable tables. No telling how long it took her to cut out each of the heart shapes and sprinkle the silver glitter on top. Little flag banners streamed from the sides, with Priscilla & Spence on the pink ones, and Nancy & Evan on the purple ones.

Nancy kept eyeing Betty Lou's large patio door covering graced with floor length, white, see-through linen strips. Swags of greenery ensconced with pink roses and purple carnations, courtesy of Daisy's Floral Shop, accentuated the area. For a fleeting moment, she envisioned her and Evan exchanging their vows right then and there. *What a perfect backdrop! Maybe Evan could just wrap one of those transparent, linen drapes around me and hold me tight forever.*

Betty Lou's strong bent as a business woman vetoed any bridal shower games. She'd also set the boundary lines that this was a *Miscellaneous Shower.* The younger crowd, if they felt inspired, could host the personal one, perhaps on some other occasion. Speaking of other occasions, Molly Stixon was not in attendance. Betty Lou and her collective committee had vetoed that invitation straight out of the chute. Since Stormy seemed to be making more of a positive effort on many fronts, the committee members decided they'd give her the benefit of the doubt and invite her. They were amazed she offered to make the hand-crafted favors.

Molly seemed to pack the matches or lighter fluid to ignite most any situation at any given time. After taking a long time to iron out the Alder Creek forged property deed fiasco, Betty Lou didn't want any hassles, issues, arguments, or anything of the sort.

Catherine Harrison, free-lance artist, graphic designer, and photographer, was beyond elated that almost every lady in attendance had purchased one of her hand-crafted cards to accompany their gifts for the brides to be. Barbie Broomfield inquired of her, "Where do you get your inspiration for these? I sure wish I had that kind of talent!"

"Even though I've loved flowers, nature, and the desert since I was a young girl, my artistic talent didn't fully bloom until later in life," Catherine explained. "I like to spend time hiking, taking pictures, and visiting old mining towns. The solitude fires up my paint brushes. I'm developing a whole new line now showcasing each of the fifty states. You'd love ours!"

"I'll have to check it out the next time I stop in to see Daisy at her shop."

No one could have been more surprised than Nancy when it was time to open the gifts. Priscilla had graciously suggested that her special day could be shared with Nancy whose head was still in the clouds after Evan had proposed to her in probably not the most storybook fashion. Nancy had settled in her heart that it was more than generous to be able to share in just the food and festivities.

Evan's few possessions coupled with Nancy's aged ones were adequately upgraded during the shower. Assuming Spence and Priscilla would be living in her rental for the next year, her gifts trended toward the basics of linens and kitchen ware.

Priscilla hooped and hollered when opening her last gift which was the perfect accompaniment for the centerpiece at her table.

Betty Lou and her staff at the recorder's office presented Priscilla with a short-sleeved, pink, knit top with black lettering which read,

FORGET THE

Cinderella Slippers

This Princess Wears

Spurs with her Boots

Precisely on que, Macey looked at Betty Lou who nodded her head once. With great fanfare, Dawn and Caroline carried a large box procured from Daisy's floral shop which had previously housed fresh flowers during their shipment. Just for grins, they'd used about one-half roll of shipping tape to test Nurse Nancy's patience when opening it.

She squealed with sheer delight when opening the matching monogrammed, yellow and green, country kitchen aprons complete with oven mitts, pot holders, and linens.

Spunky Dawn Rowann voiced the actual gift selection which had been vetoed by the hostess ~~ matching Charmeuse satin robes. They were silky, shiny, and floated luxuriously like water against the skin. She'd make sure to request those for her bridal shower when she and Jacobe Davone got hitched. He may not know they were getting married, but he'd come to his senses soon.

Caroline Crutchens completed the opening of the gifts with, "We know the kitchen won't be the only hot place in the Briarley house!" Betty Lou's laugh escaped before she could put the lid on it.

Priscilla's co-workers presented her with a paper plate sporting all of the bows from her shower gifts which she'd traditionally use at her rehearsal dinner as the mock bridal bouquet.

Merna Toppens looked all around the room for Francie Fletcher and just about voiced what some in attendance had wondered the entire time.

Betty Lou answered the knock on the front door. "Come on in, Francie," Betty Lou said. "I saved you a plate of food and a piece of cake."

Sighing inwardly, Priscilla cautiously approached her mother. "We've missed you. Glad you could finally make it."

Francie smiled at her daughter. "I'd hoped to be here much earlier. It took me longer than I thought it would to remove the paint from my hands."

"Today, of all days, you decided to paint?" asked Priscilla. "You've known about my shower for six weeks now." She anticipated a wrapped gift from her mother, but there was none in the offing.

Nurse Nancy relieved the tension. "With everything unfolding so quickly, I want to make sure that all of you know you're invited to our wedding two weeks from today, December 15th, at 2:00 in the afternoon at the Main Sabblonti Ranch house. No gifts please. Your presence will be our presents."

Stormy basked in the serenity.

CHAPTER FORTY-FIVE

Over the highways and through the western states, the Briarley clan caravan traversed to the high desert mountains. Their collective, mid-west communities had taken up collections of money, traveling supplies, and a few wedding gifts prior to their departure. Evan, overcome with emotion and relief, greeted his elderly parents, siblings, cousins, and shirt-tail relatives.

The Pritchurts, much smaller in numbers, arrived in en masse the day before the wedding. Nancy's mother cradled her wedding gown on her lap the entire trip. They'd opted to lodge at The Silver Jack Motel in Cinder Valley, so Evan's family members could stay with local ranchers in Shadow Butte County.

December 15th dawned with the sunlight melting the frost throughout the countryside. Evan was confident Preacher Len helped make that happen when he offered a prayer the night before at the rehearsal in front of the fireplace in the living room.

Children of all sizes scampered throughout the Main Sabblonti Ranch house and in the front yard. Nelson Merrill and his recruits arrived with two covered trailers loaded to the rafters with the wedding feast. They'd butchered more than one fatted calf for the occasion.

Grandma Briarley had corralled the youngest of the grandchildren shortly before the ceremony as Evan's brother helped him into his borrowed blue suit. There was definitely a generational blessing to the Briarleys having a similar body build.

Evan's brother strummed the traditional wedding march on his Mahogany wood guitar as Nancy walked from the hallway into the living room escorted by her stately father. Her mother gasped when she saw her daughter wearing her bridal gown from 1960. She reached for the hand of her other daughter, and gripped it tightly.

With every step Nancy deliberately took, it was like an ethereal cloud of white lace floating through the jam-packed room. The enhanced v-neckline, tea-length, white gown with interior tulle petticoat and taffeta lining were attached to an outside layer of cascading, antique white lace. The full length, lace-covered sleeves, and iridescent sequins in a cascading arrangement, mirrored those on the cuffs.

Her shoulder-length veil was held in place with white, teardrop-shaped pearls affixed to a headband. The white, satin, two-inch heels matched her dress.

Evan wasn't even looking at the dress, veil, or shoes. Or the amethyst necklace Nancy's parents had gifted her on her special day. Or the return to her original, velvety, chocolate brown hair color. The majority of menfolk of Evan's clan knew him all too well and were not surprised he wasn't fixated on the bride's attire.

Stormy ponied up the money to purchase two, thin wedding bands from Jodell's Jewelers in Cinder Valley. She held Chet's right hand the entire time they drove down and back to get them. When Evan and Nancy recited their vows, Chet stood in amazement as the ring size Evan had plucked out of thin air for his bride was spot on.

Their short ceremony allowed for more reception time. Evan's sister and her family, who were staying with the Broomfields, offered to take the five children, so Evan and Nancy could have at least one weekend alone.

Women pitched in to put the house in order after the wedding ceremony. The Briarley bunch, every one of them so easy to entreat, made fast friends with the Pritchurts.

Some of the ranchers sat in the barn swapping their twenty-year old tales. They tried not to allow the declining cattle prices to throw a damper on the gathering. Their repeated attempts to gain some ground on the rapidly growing wolf population had fallen on deaf ears.

Wilbur Drebner maintained his original stance on the matter, "I still say we just need to take matters into our own hands. That's the only way we're ever gonna get rid of 'em permanently." Dr. Shaw slipped out the side door of the main barn and walked toward the house in search of Macey. She was sitting next to Mrs. Pritchurt heavily engrossed in a wedding lace conversation.

Stormy reminded herself that her primary wedding gift to the Briarleys was allowing them to have the Main Sabblonti Ranch house all to themselves for the weekend and beyond. She'd stayed behind at the house to make sure they had everything they needed before congratulating them one more time and bidding them good evening.

It was the dark of the moon when Stormy finally arrived a the Lower Sabblonti Ranch house. Thankfully, Chet had left the front door unlocked. Her huge hopes were definitely dashed when she turned the knob to the master bedroom where he was fast asleep only to discover it was locked. Pressing her ear against the door, she could hear Blue and Beebee stirring inside the room. *What else must I do to make Chet open his heart to me again?*

Nancy's wedded bliss wasn't so blissful at three o'clock the next morning. Not having had the opportunity to spend much time at all around Evan before their wedding and most definitely not used to his sleeping habits, she had to shake him hard.

"Evan, Evan, do you hear that?"

He rolled over to the sounds of windows opening and closing on the third floor of the Main Sabblonti Ranch house. Whispering, he asked, "Did my sister dump the kids off in the middle of the night? The door isn't closed! What if . . .?"

They heard footsteps running up and down the hallway. Then the windows slammed shut.

Arm in arm, they tiptoed out of the bedroom and hesitated before turning the light switches on. Walking throughout the house, they determined there were definitely no children anywhere.

Thankfully, Sir Shelton, Nancy's Siamese cat, emerged safely from underneath one of the beds in the third-floor guest rooms. Nancy nestled him in her arms. "Your little silver bell has never sounded so sweet in my ears!"

They beat feet to Preacher Len's house early thirty.

Lizzelle Longbowe was just getting inside their car to drive to church when the Briarley's blew in. "Problems already?"

Nancy blushed heavily as Evan stammered, "Not with us. There's someone in that Sabblonti house. Both of us heard it a few hours ago. We need you and Preacher Len to help us."

"He's already at the church. He goes in early every Sunday morning to pray. I'll make sure to mention it to him. I'd invite you to church, but we've never had anyone attend in their bathrobes. We'll plan on another time."

Evan grinned, "Uh, we're still honeymooning." Nancy jabbed him in his ribs forgetting they were still tender all these months later.

As they drove back to the Main Sabblonti Ranch house, Nancy said, "I'm so in love with you. If you had a big zipper in front, I'd crawl inside and live there."

"I'm more in love with you than you'll ever know. I could kick myself in the rear for having wasted so much time."

They counted their many blessings less than twenty-four hours after becoming husband and wife. Evan commented, "Stormy really came through in the clutch by offering the Main Ranch house."

Craning her neck to the extreme left Nancy queried, "Stormy did that?"

"She most certainly did. It's hers to offer. She owns both houses, buildings, all the land, cattle, cattle brands, horses, dogs, rigs, equipment, everything."

Nancy looked for a blanket inside the van, but didn't see one. "What about Chet?" she asked. "What does he have?"

"He doesn't own a pot or a window. All he's got is what Ace and Jantzi Belle Sabblonti gave him which is a couple of horses and a pickup. He wrecked one pickup and recently bought another used one."

She frowned. "Isn't this a community property state?"

"That it 'tis," Evan explained as switched hands on the steering wheel. "Everything I mentioned a couple of minutes ago is Stormy's sole and separate property that she inherited when Jantzi Belle died."

"Well, what about her sister?"

"Sarita got zero, zip, zilch, nada, nuttin'."

Evan and Nancy even laughed the same way.

He continued, "Although Wyn and Sarita will most probably inherit the Toppens Ranch when it's all said and done."

Striking a serious note, Nancy had the presence of mind to ask, "If there's something wrong with the house, maybe that's why Stormy offered to let us live there."

Caressing her left knee as he entered the driveway, Evan assured her, "That's Preacher Len's department. We've got a few more hours to play house until the Longbowes show up."

Later that afternoon, Nancy heated some leftover beef and trimmings from their wedding feast in the oven as Preacher Len and Evan walked around the outside of the main house.

Preacher Len looked to the roof of the house and back down to the foundation. "The Lord has blessed you and Nancy with a Children's Home."

"Nancy says she wants at least a dozen," Evan retorted.

"You're just about half way there already!"

Evan was highly intrigued as Preacher Len dipped his finger in the vial of oil and touched each of the doors and windows all the while commanding the evil spirits to flee. He uttered some words which Evan surmised must have stemmed from his ancestors, probably way back in those family orchards. The preacher did the same thing inside the house. Nancy was still in the honeymoon clouds and nearly burned the evening's offering.

Evan pressed Preacher Len, "How'd those evil spirits or ghosts or whatever they are get inside here in the first place?"

Securing his container of anointing oil inside the little pouch and tying it to his belt loop, Preacher Len explained, "It usually happens when someone or something opens a spiritual door. There are good spiritual doors and bad ones. Keep reading the Good Book I gifted you, and it will become much more evident to you.

"A quick example of a good door is to open it and invite Jesus into your life. He stands at the door of your heart and knocks. A bad door would be if you start flirting with or carrying on with someone other than your beautiful bride."

"No chance of that happening, Preacher. It does beg the serious question of what transpired on this big spread over the centuries, however."

Preacher Len shook Evan's hand. "You'll have plenty to keep you busy without laboring to find the answer to that question anytime soon."

Evan looked intently at Preacher Len. "What do we do if those unwanted visitors come back?"

"The same thing you saw me do right here today."

"I don't speak that strange language," Evan said.

"English will work."

CHAPTER FORTY-SIX

Priscilla Fletcher had spent the past eleven and a-half months planning her wedding. Her lists spawned additional ones. At least Macey was planning on getting married next year. It was Nancy Pritchurt, now Nancy Briarley, who'd stolen Priscilla's thunder, booming claps of which sounded above her apartment.

She'd been trying to nail down her landlord to get the lease signed for another year. The thought of spending another minute visiting Spence in the Toppens' bunkhouse was enough to drive her to the bug house.

Sinking deeper into despair than she'd realized, Spence's mother, Judith Woodson, along with her sister, Maviss Living, arrived just in the nick of time. They'd bonded like super glue with Priscilla ever since they'd met her on Christmas day. Francie Fletcher was still AWOL.

Due to the sheer volume of work required for year's end at the Shadow Butte County Recorder's office, none of Priscilla's co-workers could get additional time off. Of particular interest to Betty Lou Bradford had been the increase of recording documents pertaining to financing statements under the uniform commercial code which covered timber to be cut, minerals or the like, including gas and oil, pursuant to a specified section of the state code, or

344

fixtures.

There'd also been a legal flare up of sorts wherein Betty Lou refused to record some documents which were not authorized by law to be recorded. The county prosecutor was holding her hand and walking through the legal lash up with her.

Marita Merrill, severely underpaid and overworked, took sheer delight in major productions. She had forbidden Nelson, her husband, to go anywhere near their huge barn since Christmas eve except to haul things in and out of there.

Nelson didn't lack in recruiting skills. He'd rounded up Wilbur Drebner, Rees Broomfield, Wyn Moreland, Chet Castins, Fenn Bridgemore, Evan Briarley, Preacher Len, Dr. Shaw, Jacobe Davone, Delbert and Brent Dawson, Dr. Den Merenspinn, Elmer Bradford, Yatey and Ruston, and even Sheriff Jeff Jensen when he wasn't working in his official capacity along with his deputy, Leo Jeelon.

Quite merrily reminding everyone that the first sparks between Spence Woodson and Priscilla Fletcher began two years ago in this exact place inside their barn while sitting on some hay bales, Marita declared that a definite upgrade was needed. Cider was sure to be served by the gallons. When she uttered the words *major transformation*, Nelson grunted and groaned. His male companions roared.

Marita bathed her words in honey before serving them to her captive audience, "Cattlemen and dear friends, I'll paint the big picture first. That might be easiest. I have several clipboards here with what needs to be done. If you want to draw straws or use cards to see who does what, have at it. I'll even furnish the decks.

"EVERYTHING needs to be removed from the barn

temporarily. Nelson can show you where to the stack the hay and straw bales outside. We need to be able to eat off the floors. Well, maybe not literally, but you get my drift. Eight-foot tables and folding chairs will be delivered by Ridgemonte Rental Agency along with linen tablecloths, so make sure to wash your hands in the utility sink in the corner before spreading them on the tables.

"The bags of pink helium balloons and the helium tanks will also be delivered by the rental agency. We want them filled and released, so they'll stick to the ceiling and rafters. For those of you who don't mind standing on ladders, the large, pink bolts of organza fabric need to be secured to the sides and center beams of the barn to produce a canopy effect.

"Some of your wives will be here shortly to help with the table settings. Oh, before I forget. Wilbur, did you bring your chainsaw to cut the petite wooden rounds for the centerpieces?"

Wilbur boomed, "Sure did!"

Marita continued, We're going to place a votive candle inside quart jars and light those when we sit down to eat. Dr. Shaw, I hope you remembered the used horseshoes to place against each jar." He nodded affirmatively.

"We'll need lots of additional wood cut for the stove. Extra space heaters will be delivered at the same time as the tables and chairs."

Her eyes twinkled before delivering the next instruction and holding up a strand of small white lights, "For those, shall we say, finish carpenters among you, the real fun job is going to be stringing these between the support beams and wrapping them in light pole fashion!

"Let's plan to keep the panel doors on the west side free and clear, so people can go in and out during the evening. To that end, please set the rectangular tables for the bridal party facing north.

"Coye's Stringers will be providing the music, and everybody enjoys their tunes. Nelson's already filled my dance card. We'll leave the east end of the barn free and clear for that and set up the buffet tables on the south side.

"The theme for all this is *Denim and Lace.*"

Spence Woodson, the groom to be, looked at Fenn Bridgemore and said, "Well, at least I can take care of the denim."

Fenn zinged, "Before it's all said and done, you'll be taking care of the lace, too. Better wake up, pardner."

Yatey leaned into Chet, "Who's pickin' up the tab for this high dollah weddin'?"

He reached inside his rear jean pocket, and opened his empty wallet. "Not this cattleman."

CHAPTER FORTY-SEVEN

Spence Woodson's mother, Judith, had determined to remain in the background as much as she could until Priscilla reluctantly pulled her front and center. Maviss Living shadowed both of them, mostly for much needed moral support.

Merna couldn't be pried loose from Tenny and Maddy Moreland, so Barbie Broomfield picked up the slack placing the final stitches in the wedding garments.

Even though Priscilla didn't know Sarita Moreland all that well, she wanted to extend the courtesy of asking her to be her matron of honor since Wyn was Spence's best man. Fenn Bridgemore and Tiffany, Priscilla's co-worker, rounded out the attendants. The Moreland twins were much too young to be the bride and groom's flower girl and ring bearer. Nancy Briarley's suggestion of Vannessa and Monty was just perfect.

Seven was the magic New Year's Eve hour. Some guests, doubling as the wedding preparation crew, arrived hours earlier. Parked beneath the full moon's canopy, vehicles lined the road beyond a country mile leading into the Merrill Ranch. Guests followed the festive music with every step. The aroma of Merrill's barbequed beef propelled them inside the barn door.

Love, the Tie that Binds

The Merrill's large ranch house served as the bridal headquarters. Daisy Freemille and her assistant, Catherine Harrison, arrived in ample time with the bridal bouquet, flower sprays, wrist corsages, and boutonnieres. They'd done a splendid job implementing Priscilla's accent colors of burgundy, silver, sage green, and white.

Catherine offered her services to be the official wedding photographer using her expensive camera she'd won in the statewide photo festival earlier in the year. Her entry featuring an old abandoned homestead covered with heavy winter frost near a ghost mining town was unanimously voted number one.

It 'twas a good thing it wasn't very far from the Merrill Ranch house to their barn since it was a titch chilly after sundown. Coye's Stringers launched their celebratory tunes setting the perfect tone just after all guests had been seated inside. Nelson Merrill's recently installed grey mechanical door opener was a real winner.

Barbie Broomfield had to hurriedly add a ten-inch insert in the back of Spence's burgundy, brocade vest. No guest was the wiser.

Preacher Lenn and Spence entered through the side door. Lizzelle had even trimmed her ever lovin's locks for his role in the evening. She insisted he leave his hat at home.

Maviss and Judith were escorted in first and seated temporarily at one of the round tables close to the main door. A few minutes earlier, Maviss had a firm discussion with Priscilla regarding extending grace to her mother on her most important day, so she wouldn't live to regret it.

Andy Briarley, led Miggy, Spence and Priscilla's Bernese Mountain Dog, toward Preacher Len, Spence, and Fenn. She quietly laid at Spence's feet nibbling the large, pink bow tied around her neck.

Monty was telling his own little story to the plastic rings tied to the silver, satin pillow as his sister walked behind him. She decided she didn't want to drop the flower petals because someone might accidently step on them. Then they would be crushed, and that would hurt.

Tenny wailed when spotting his mother, Sarita, gliding gracefully toward her husband, Wyn. Her burgundy velvet, A-line, princess, floor-length dress with ruffle-split front and silver-lace-sash captured all of Wyn's attention, despite her not yet having shed her extra maternity pounds. Maddy's little button nose wrinkled when Merna brushed it with the edge of an extra thick blanket.

Fenn's fantasy grew when eyeing Tiffany in her light, sage green dress matching the description of Sarita's. It might have taken an extra hand or two to get Tiffany's long, plastic zipper secured from behind.

A few guests surmised Coye or members of his country western band omitted some notes ahead of the wedding march, but they hadn't missed a beat.

Francie Fletcher, her hair drawn up on the sides and in the back to form an elaborate French roll, slid both of her hands down her hips to smooth the elegant, silver colored, crushed velvet, floor-length dress, complete with burgundy lace sash. She reached inside her daughter's bent arm to help steady her. Dr. Merenspinn extended his assistance on the opposite side.

Priscilla's bold, pink, bouffant bridal gown presented a challenge when getting down the aisle. After a couple of steps, Francie and Dr. Merenspinn opted to just walk as closely to her as possible. Multiple layers of pastel pink lace mushroomed from the original bodice and ankle-length skirt. The strapless, fuchsia, satin bodice portrayed a gown more appropriate for a summer wedding.

Following a very short wedding ceremony, Preacher Lenn announced, "It's my distinct pleasure to introduce Mr. and Mrs. Spence Woodson." The crowd erupted in applause. Spence held Priscilla in his arms as they leaned back for an elaborate kiss. Barbie Broomfield came from behind to drape the white, crushed velvet, bolero over Priscilla's shoulders.

Spence whispered to his bride, "Now I get it! Your ONE surprise for our day. You always look fantastic in pink."

The buffet line formed quickly as it does in cattle country following any kind of celebration. The bridal party was served at their special table. Cider flowed by the gallons.

Perhaps some noticed an intimate huddle at the end of the bridle table following the meal. Francie held hands with Spence and Priscilla. "I want to ask you to please forgive me for the despicable way I've treated both of you. There's no excuse for my behavior or words. Please know how much I love both of you and plan to fully support you."

All three of them were crying. Spence hugged Francie and said, "No problem, Mom. I completely forgive you. Welcome to the Woodson herd!" Priscilla laughed and hugged her mother repeatedly.

Marita had baked seven strawberry flavored sheet cakes. Nelson hadn't even asked to sample the pink icing as she slathered it on top of each one.

Spence and Priscilla decided to dispense with a lot of the traditional *first dances* other than their own since their family structures were non-traditional at the moment. As the children frolicked on the dance floor, some observed and hoped their sadness fled away.

Dawn Rowann, glued to Jacobe Davone's side for most of the evening, tried to encourage Caroline Crutchens. "Any prospects here tonight?"

"Cowboys really aren't my type. I'm holding out for the new surgeon arriving in two weeks. I've salivated every time I look at his profile picture. Intense slate eyes, a mysterious smile, and what appears to be a soft beard. In some respects, he minds me quite a bit of Dr. Shaw who's finally engaged. I thought we'd never get him on his way to the altar!"

Tripping over her floor-length, midnight blue, jacquard gown which she'd not purchased at *The Second Time Around*, Dawn wrapped her arms around Jacobe's neck as they danced the night away. He looked quite dapper himself all decked out in a matching, long-sleeved, western shirt complete with light blue pearl snaps. The blue suede shoes were home buried in his closet underneath mounds of laundry.

Several guests may have thought it a bit strange the bride and groom left quite early in the evening. Priscilla relived the magical moments of their wedding as Spence drove to their honeymoon destination located at the far eastern end of Horsewood County.

Spence dimmed the headlights, but kept the pickup motor running. Priscilla asked, "We're staying here tonight? Whose house is this anyway?"

"Come inside with me, my beloved."

She squirmed and giggled as he carried her across the

threshold.

He gave her the guided tour through each room of the house, ending in the master bedroom heavily decorated with pink, forest green, and burgundy furnishings. The sheets had been turned down with heart shaped, chocolate mints placed on each pillow.

Priscilla stated, "I simply can't sleep here tonight until I know the whole story."

Raising both eyebrows, he smiled. "Okay, but just the shortened version for the next few minutes. I've waited two years for tonight.

"Mrs. Spence Woodson, you and I are the proud owners of not only this beautiful ranch house, but the 220 acres all the way around it!"

"No way!"

"Yes way!"

She jumped for joy.

"All you need to know right now is that all of this is a wedding gift from Dr. Merenspinn and your mother."

Priscilla placed her hands on her hips and protested loudly, "But she doesn't have any money."

Spence explained, "Maybe not at this very moment. She's the one who did all the cleaning, painting, furnishing the house, cleaning up the yard, and umpteen other things. Your mother virtually lived here the past few months, but she never slept in the house."

Priscilla burst into tears. "How could I have been so awful to my mother?"

"You're not in the least. The last time I checked, crying was not on our honeymoon agenda."

S

Definitely memorably enough back at the Merrill's barn, Dr. Merenspinn located Francie sitting next to Judith and Maviss. He skillfully requested a sentimental slow song after one of Coye's Stringers' half hour breaks.

While Dr. Merenspinn and Francie had combined their efforts toward getting the new home ready for Spence and Priscilla the past several months, this had served its purpose in thawing Francie out considerably. It hadn't left time for much else except an occasional meal at a restaurant or a cup of coffee at The Sage Hen Café.

Dr. Merenspinn led her onto the dance floor after he'd unplugged a few of the strands of lights here and there in the barn. It didn't surprise her at all that he was such a good dancer. *Was there nothing this man couldn't do or achieve?*

His steps came to a standstill. She was so caught up in the moment, she leaned fully into him. Holding her long, slender, left ring finger, he slid the elegant, three carat, marquise-shaped diamond to the bottom. She drew in both shoulders as he spoke softly in her left ear, "Will you marry me?"

Francie cupped his cheeks inside her palms. "You know I will!" Both of them were oblivious to the ruckus outside. As they walked off the dance floor, Dr. Merenspinn saw something flying through the air. "Stay right here. I'll be back in a jiffy." She sauntered to where Merna and Stormy were seated, each of them rocking a twin.

Sheriff Jensen wrapped a lariat around his left hand and elbow as he stood in front of Salina Bevvins. "Try that again, and I'll have you arrested for assault and disturbing the peace."

Chet brushed the dirt and hay leaves off his jeans, shirt, and western vest.

Dr. Merenspinn tugged on Deputy Jeelon's black coat sleeve. "What did I miss?"

He chuckled. "Seems Salina, or The Black Raven as Chet calls her, tried to lasso him here tonight while he was standing next to those hay bales over there talking to Evan. She bragged that she'd spent five months practicing roping one of those steer heads shoved into a hay bale. Actually, she's pretty good at it."

Framing one of those authoritarian, fatherly sorts of frowns, Dr. Merenspinn asked, "Just whose side of the law are you on anyway?"

Deputy Jeelon offered no response.

Chet thanked the sheriff and his deputy. He motioned for Evan to follow him around the side of the barn. "I need a witness, so stay beside me." He walked toward June Slader's old pickup and called, "Salina!"

She whirled around and glared at him. Chet announced, "I'm telling you this once and only once. I have no interest in you whatsoever. I'm a happily married man and plan to stay that way. Quit stalking me or I'll have Sheriff Jensen arrest you."

Salina jumped inside her aunt's pickup and revved the engine as her spinning tires spewed dirt and hay leaves into the air.

Evan watched as she drove down the lane.

Grinning from ear to ear, Chet said, "You had something important to talk to me about. So, what is it, Evan?"

"Nancy and I don't know how to thank you for letting us move into the Main Sabblonti Ranch house. We've talked about it at great length, and decided it would be best for her to stay home with the three youngest kiddos. I'll have to drive into Ridgemonte for work every day, but I don't plan to add any additional stress on top of what we've already got going on. Nancy stopped at the library the other day and checked out a book with baby names."

"You're not wastin' any time, are you?"

"She's the one who's got a fire lit under me."

Chet handed an extra set of house keys to Evan. "Things are lookin' up."

Evan chortled. "They are?"

"Yep. That geologist character Stormy rounded up has some dynamite news. I'll be down tomorrow afternoon, so we can get the new year started off with a blast."

Stormy exited the wedding reception and located her husband. "Ready?"

"Totally, darlin'."

In her mind, it had never taken so long to travel to the Lower Sabblonti Ranch house. She reflected, "I've been looking over our cattle herd the past few months. We're not completely down and out. It's already a new year, so let's plan to start rebuilding what's been entrusted to us."

Once inside, she took her husband's hand and led him to the back of the house. Turning the light on and removing the covering, she revealed their newly transformed guest bedroom which she'd converted into a country-western decorated nursery, complete with matching mahogany baby furniture.

She leaned into Chet's side, "What do you think? Using some of the proceeds from the sale of our breeding bulls, I redesigned this part of the house. I told you that I would account for the money, so here's what I bought. I hope it's okay with you. Please forgive me for not immediately telling you the truth regarding the $10,000 from the sale of the bulls to Vaughn McJune. I just really wanted to surprise you."

"And you did! Looks mighty fine to me. I love you and forgive you, Stormy. You've really made a solid effort over the past few months to show that you love me and want to work hard on the Sabblonti Ranch."

"Chet, love will be the tie that binds us together forever."

She removed her cowboy boots and danced around the living room until her head was spinning like a top. Winding down, she sat cross legged in front of Chet.

Leaning her head back, Stormy released a melodious love song that echoed throughout every room of the Lower Sabblonti Ranch house.

Chet proclaimed,

"SABBLONTI RANCH, YOU'RE STILL OURS!

STORMY, GET READY!"

CAST OF CHARACTERS

A

Ace Sabblonti, Stormy's and Sarita's deceased father
Al Gibson, member, Ignee County Rodeo Board, in charge of rodeo grounds and maintenance
Andy Briarley, Evan Briarley's nephew
Anne-Marie Diller – Dr. Diller's wife
Aprilily – young homeless mother with two children; clerk, Jodell's Jeweler's, Cinder Valley
Aunt Jonsey Kiddle – Stormy and Sarita Sabblonti's maternal aunt

B

Barbie Broomfield – Rancher Rees Broomfield's wife
Beau Cheval, Dr. Ben Shaw's Appaloosa gelding
Betty Lou Bradford, elected Clerk and Recorder, Shadow Butte County
Bolo & Browny – Tom Toppens' matched pair of draft horses
Blake Benson, Southwest District Brand Inspector
Blythe Bennetelli, Temp. Agency worker assisting Wyn & Sarita Moreland
Brent Dawson, employee, Dawson's Dealership, Ridgemonte; Delbert Dawson's son

C

Cannaleah – grocery store clerk, The Shadowy Merc, Ridgemonte
Caper Sadler – rodeo clown

358

Carl's Car Corral – auto dealership, Cinder Valley
Caroline Crutchens – Mintner Medical Center Nurse
Carson Tayer – Chairman, Ignee County Rodeo Board
Catherine Harrison – free lance artist, greeting card designer, flower shop supplier, and Daisy's childhood friend
Cecilia Linke, Dr. Linke's mother
Chara Tankton, bank teller, Cattlemen's Central
Chet Castins, Stormy Sabblonti's husband
Cinder Valley Scoop – Cinder Valley newspaper
Clark, salesman, Carl's Car Corral, Cinder Valley
Cord Calhoun – Rodeo Announcer
Country Cate's Western Wear – western clothing store in Cinder Valley
Coye's Stringers – Country Western Band

D
Daisy Freemille – owner, Daisy's Floral Shop, Ridgemonte
Dawn Rowann – Mintner Medical Center Nurse
Dean Kendall – member, Ignee County Rodeo Board, in charge of rodeo announcer, clown, and musical group
Debbie Drebner – Rancher Wilbur Drebner's wife
Delbert Dawson, owner, Dawson's Dealership, Ridgemonte
Duncan Dunne, attorney in the firm Dunne, Dunne, & Dunne, Chtd., Cinder Valley
Doug Meadows, Macey Meadows' father
Dr. Ben Shaw – Veterinarian, Ridgemonte
Dr. Den Merenspinn, medical doctor, owner of Evergreene Medical Clinic, Ridgemonte
Dr. Diller – Dentist, Ridgemonte
Dr. Linke – Mintner Medical Center Physician
Dr. Martin Markeeth, Psychotherapist, Fantone

E
Earl's Saddle Shop – Cinder Valley
Ed Tilmore – manager, Bank of Blunte
Elmer Bradford, husband of Shadow Butte County Recorder, Betty Lou Bradford
Emma Briarley, Evan Briarley's niece
Evan Briarley, Chet Castins' Physical Therapist
Evergreene Medical Clinic, Ridgemonte

F
Feather Nest Diner – restaurant, Fantone
Fenn Bridgemore – ranch hand, Toppens' Ranch
Francie Fletcher, Priscilla Fletcher's mother

G
Gib's Gas – gas station in Ridgemonte
Gwen Hybrenth – retiree, Ignee County Rodeo Board

I
Ignee Grange Hall, Cinder Valley
It's Sew Time – fabric store, Ridgemonte

J
Jacobe Davone – employee, Shaw Veterinarian Clinic, Ridgemonte
James Harrison, Catherine Harrison's husband
Jantzi Belle Siddonz Sabblonti, Stormy's and Sarita's

deceased mother
Jed Brennon – owner, Jed's Appliance Center, Ridgemonte
Jeddidiah Briarley, Evan Briarley's nephew
Jodell's Jewelers – jewelry store, Cinder Valley
Joyce Stone – Mintner Medical Center Charge Nurse
Judith Woodson – Spence Woodson's mother

L
Lambent's Funeral Home - Ridgemonte
Lane – cowboy drifter, Ridgemonte
Leo Jeelon – Shadow Butte Deputy County Sheriff
Less Alotto – Sabblonti Ranch Foreman
Lilac Novis – Aunt Jonsey Kiddle's great-granddaughter
Lindi – bank teller, Bank of Blunte, Blademere
Lizzelle Longbowe, Preacher Longbowe's wife
Logan Novis – Aunt Jonsey Kiddle's great-grandson
Lonnie Browne, Assistant Manager, Cattlemen's Central, Ridgemonte
Lorena, head clerk, DMV, Shadow Butte County Courthouse
Luger – ranch hand, Toppens Ranch
Luetta Londers – Parade Chairwoman, 75th Annual Ignee County Rodeo & Roundup, Cinder Valley

M
Macey Meadows – Mintner Medical Center Nurse
Madeline Merna Toppens – Wyn & Sarita's twin daughter
Marita Merrill – Nelson Merrill's wife, Shadow Butte County
Meat & Greet Drive Inn, restaurant, Ridgemonte
Meg Alotto, bookkeeper, Sabblonti Ranch

Merna Toppens – Tom Toppens' wife, Toppens' Ranch
Mintner Medical Center – Ridgemonte hospital
Mitch Bentz – member, Ignee County Rodeo Board, in charge of rodeo stock
Molly Stixon – wife of brood mare farm owner, Samuel Stixon
Monty Briarley, Evan Briarley's nephew

N
Neil Rolan, member, Ignee County Rodeo Board, in charge of rodeo grounds and maintenance
Nelson Weston Merrill – rancher, Shadow Butte County
Nurse Nancy Pritchurt - Dr. Merenspinn's nurse, Evergreene Medical Clinic, Ridgemonte

P
Preacher Len Longbowe, county preacher
Priscilla Pauline Fletcher – employee, Shadow Butte County Recorder's Office
Professor Ashton Walton – Geology professor at the state's land grant university

R
Rayford Shaw – Dr. Shaw's father
Res Broomfield – cattle rancher, Shadow Butte County
Ridgemonte Rider – Ridgemonte newspaper
Ridgemonte Rx – Ridgemonte drug store
Rory, motel clerk, Silver Jack Motel, Cinder Valley
Roscoe Rhineback – Wolf Program Coordinator for the state's Fish and Wildlife Service
Ruston – younger cowhand who works for Sabblonti Ranch

S
Sable Shaw - Dr. Shaw's mother
Sagebrush Sorority Sisters – in charge of annual parade for Ignee County Rodeo & Roundup, Cinder Valley
Sage Hen Café – restaurant, Ridgemonte
Salina Bevvins - a/k/a The Black Raven– store clerk, The Shadowy Merc, Ridgemonte
Samuel Stixon – owner, broodmare farm, Ridgemonte
Sarita Sabblonti Moreland– Stormy Castins' sister; Wyn Mooreland's wife
Shade Stock Company – rodeo stock supplier
Shane – cowboy, ranch hand employed by Toppens' Ranch
Shasta – sales clerk, County Cate's Western Wear, Cinder Valley
Sheriff Jeff Jensen – Shadow Butte County Sheriff
Sherry Meadows – Macey Meadows' mother
Silver Jack Motel – Cinder Valley
Slim Shade – owner, Shade Stock Company
Spence Woodson – Assistant Ranch Foreman, Toppens' Ranch
Stanley Elson, Treasurer, Ignee County Rodeo Board
Stewart Sanders, manager, Cattlemen's Central, Ridgemonte
Stormy Sabblonti Castins, heiress to the Sabblonti cattle ranch and family fortune; Sarita Sabblonti Moreland's sister

T
Tennyson Thomas Moreland – Wyn & Sarita's twin son
The Mane Place, hair styling salon, Cinder Valley
The Second Time Around – thrift shop, Ridgemonte
The Shadowy Merc – grocery store and mercantile, Ridgemonte
The Tall Blues – country western singing group

Tom Toppens – owner, Toppens' Ranch
Tonette – Sarita Sabblonti's co-worker, Dr. Diller's office, Ridgemonte
Tottale Temp. Agency – temporary employment agency in Ridgemonte
Travis Fisen – employee, Lambent's Funeral Home
Trent Davies – Assistant Chairman, Ignee County Rodeo Board

U
Uncle Kent Kiddle – Stormy and Sarita Sabblonti's maternal uncle

V
Vannessa Briarley, Evan Briarley's niece
Vaughn McJune – Tranquility Falls cattle rancher
Verntoola – thrift shop owner, The Second Time Around, Ridgemonte
Vonnetta, hairstylist, The Mane Place, Cinder Valley

W
Wilbur Drebner – cattle rancher, Shadow Butte County
Wyn Moreland -Toppens Ranch Foreman, Sarita Sabblonti's husband

Y
Yatey – older cowhand that works for Sabblonti Ranch

Z
Zib's Towing – Ridgemonte Tow Truck Business

ABOUT THE AUTHOR

Sheila Eismann, author and publisher of twelve books, is third in her lineage of five female writers and poets. She endeavors to enhance the lives of others through education and encouragement via penning her inspirational and fictional books. Eismann, co-founder of Idaho Creative Authors' Network (ICAN), speaks at Womens' and Writers' Conferences.

Please peruse Sheila's website www.sheilaeismann.com and sign up to receive her blog posts and newsletters. Send her an email at sheila@sheilaeismann.com to let her know which character was your most favorite in this novel along with the best part of the story. Happy Reading!

Where to find Sheila Eismann online:

Email: sheila@sheilaeismann.com

Website: www.sheilaeismann.com

Facebook: www.facebook.com/sheila.eismann

Blog: www.sheilaeismann.com

LinkedIn: Sheila Eismann

Etsy Store: www.etsy.com/shop/BooksbySheilaEismann

OTHER BOOKS AVAILABLE FROM AUTHOR SHEILA EISMANN & DESERT SAGE PRESS which can be purchased from: www.sheilaeismann.com or www.amazon.com.

Western Fiction Book One of The Sabblonti Series, *Jantzi's Jokers*, features Jantzi Belle, matriarch of the Sabblonti family, who has worked for decades to keep her cattle empire intact. Life takes a drastic turn when she receives a late-night visitor. The brief disappearance of her Last Will and Testament could complicate matters between her daughters, Stormy and Sarita. Stormy and her husband, Chet Castins, are struggling to work through the loss of their three children. Against all odds, drifter Wyn Moreland makes a bold move when he decides that Sarita is his beauty to rescue. The county veterinarian, Dr. Ben Shaw, is also vying for her affections. Will Wyn emerge as the winner? Just prior to the dawn of the New Year, revelations come forth regarding forgery, cattle rustling, and land exploitation. Will the Sabblonti Empire survive, and more importantly, who will control its reins?

The Sabblonti Saga accelerates in Book Two of the Series, **A Stormy Year**. Riding her high horse after inheriting the family fortune, Stormy Castins is determined to reinvent herself following her husband's accident. Blinded by jealousy, ambition, and naivety, she hires Less and Meg Alotto to oversee her vast high desert mountain domain. While Stormy is away, the cattle herd ends up in disarray.

Amidst the hot dry season, romance is blooming on several fronts despite a major showdown during a mid-summer celebration. The pesky Black Raven continues to wreak havoc at the most inopportune times.

Unable to overcome the vengeance which strikes by way of a mysterious range fire combined with the dire deeds of a cagey couple, the Sabblonti Ranch is in shambles just as Stormy starts to regain her senses. Humility is the prescription needed to open her eyes in order to realize what's truly important in life. The sparks from a belated holiday rendevous set Chet and Stormy on their path to recovery.

Sheila Eismann

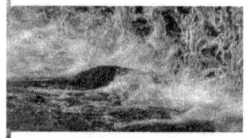

Sheila F Eismann

In this collection of true stories titled ***Stirrings of The Spirit***, author Sheila F. Eismann invites you to walk with her family through several valleys en route to some mountain tops as they learned to rely on God in the most harrowing of circumstances.

RECOGNIZE
YOUR
CIRCLES

A Humorous Look
Into Life's
Relationships

Have you ever wondered why you were the last one to hear of THE big social event of the year? Well, wonder no longer after reading this e-book titled ***Recognize Your Circles***! When volunteering for an organization years ago, author Sheila F. Eismann was introduced to the concept of "the circles of your life." Since the idea was so beneficial to her, she decided to share it with all of you.

Straight From the Horse's Trough
Gardening Help for
the Suburbanite and Urbanite

Sheila F. Eismann

Straight from the Horse's Trough is a humorous read to render assistance to the suburbanite or urbanite who desires to live a healthier lifestyle by growing his or her own food, but is faced with the challenge of a small space in which to do so. This e-book is chock full of how-to steps and includes pictures to remove guesswork from the project.

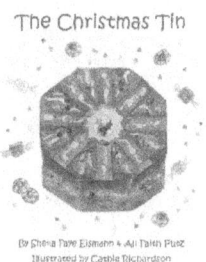

The Christmas Tin

By Sheila Faye Eismann & Ali Faith Pultz
Illustrated by Cathie Richardson

The Christmas Tin is a most delightful read for the young at heart anytime during the year. This endearing book is based upon a true story featuring the older of the two authors when she was a young girl and conveys the timeless message that "love truly is the best gift of all." Children will especially enjoy all of the colorful illustrations contained within this treasure.

Everyone can use a little encouragement ~~ a dose of what is beneficial, ethical, and honorable. ***Heart to Heart From God's Word*** provides this for you. Penned with humor and wisdom, the daily tidbits are paired with Bible verses that convey life-changing principles which are designed for readers of all ages transcending cultures and continents. This devotional will challenge you to grow and fulfill your God-given destiny. It can also double as a prayer journal.

A Woman of Substance is a practical, interactive, and entertaining 12 week Bible study penned to help equip you to fulfill your God-given destiny and impact the culture for Jesus Christ at the same time. It can be used as a stand-alone study or devotional and works well in a group setting, too. It is designed for women ages junior high through adult.

FREEDOM IS
YOUR DESTINY!

Daniel T. Eismann

Freedom is Your Destiny! Vietnam Veteran, Dan Eismann, using combat experiences to illustrate spiritual truths, invites you to take a journey with him as he presents a rock-solid strategy for not only fighting your spiritual battles, but winning the all-important war. In the midst thereof, the most vital aspect is that you realize you can experience freedom and become all that God has destined you to be!

Settle into your special reading spot; grab a cup of tea or your favorite meal. Be stirred as you read and ponder **Poetry Time, Volume One**; allow Sheila's words to encourage and heal.

Sheila Eismann